THE PRINCESS AND THE PLAYER

BY
KAT CANTRELL

Kat Cantrell read her first Mills & Boon novel in third grade and has been scribbling in notebooks since she learned to spell. What else would she write but romance? She majored in literature, officially with the intent to teach, but somehow ended up buried in middle management in corporate America, until she became a stay-at-home mum and full-time writer.

Kat, her husband and their two boys live in north Texas. When she's not writing about characters on the journey to happily-ever-after, she can be found at a soccer game, watching the TV show *Friends* or listening to '80s music.

Kat was the 2011 Mills & Boon So You Think You Can Write winner and a 2012 RWA Golden Heart Award finalist for best unpublished series contemporary manuscript.

One

Auwck. Auwck.

Bella Montoro's eyelids flew open at the raucous and unwelcome alarm clock. One of the pair of feral blue-and-gold macaws who lived in the tree outside the window of her Coral Gables mansion had chosen today, of all days, to wake her early.

Miami was full of wild macaws and normally, she loved them. Today, not so much.

Groaning, she smooshed a pillow over her head but the pressure didn't ease her champagne headache and the barrier didn't muffle the happy squawks of her feathered friend. Fine. It was time to drag herself out of bed anyway.

She sat up. A glance through the bay window confirmed which bird it was.

"Good morning, Buttercup," she muttered sarcastically, but with the window closed, the macaw couldn't hear her.

She didn't dare open the window for fear she'd frighten her away. Both Buttercup and her mate, Wesley, were as wild as the day was long, and Bella enjoyed it when they deigned to hang out with her. She watched them groom themselves for as long as she dared since she wouldn't get to see them for a while once she left Miami for the small country of Alma—today's destination.

Bella had always known she was descended from royalty, but a dictator had been ruling her ancestor's country for ages. She'd never expected the political climate to shift. Or for the Montoros to reclaim the throne. But it had happened and though her father was first in line to become king, his divorce rendered him ineligible for the crown due to Alma's strict laws. Then her oldest brother, Rafe, had abdicated his place so he could focus on the new baby he and his fiancée, Emily, were expecting.

Her other brother, Gabriel, had stepped up, adopting his new role with an ease Bella admired. And while she liked the tiny island country of Alma well enough to go back for her brother's coronation as the new king, the promise of bigger and better parties didn't fully make up for having to leave behind the things she loved in Miami.

She was also leaving behind her great-aunt Isabella, who might draw her last breath any day now. Rafe would check in on her of course, and Bella could call. But still. It wasn't the same as having daily access to the woman who always had a kind word and gentle piece of advice, no matter what the occasion. Bella had been named for her father's aunt, and they shared a kinship that transcended age.

Her father owed her for agreeing to this move to Alma. Big time.

Bella watched Buttercup groom her feathers for a moment, and then turned away from the beautiful view of the grounds. She might not see this house again either, and she'd taken for granted how much she loved living here. Now that the day of her departure had arrived, everything had gotten real, really fast. She'd been an American her whole life and while she'd always enjoyed the privileges of being a Montoro, becoming a member of Alma's royal family carried heavy responsibilities with few tangible rewards.

Not that anyone had asked her opinion.

With far too much racket for Bella's taste, her maid, Celia, bustled into the bedroom and frowned at the crumpled, glittery dress on the floor as she stepped over it. "They have plenty more hangers at the store if you've run out, Miss Bella."

Bella grinned at the woman who'd been her friend, confidant and occasional strong shoulder for years, blessing her for sticking to their tried-and-true teasing instead of becoming maudlin over the irreversible changes that had ripped through the Montoro family recently.

"Got hangers," Bella informed her around an involuntary yawn. "Just not the will to use one at three a.m."

Celia sniffed as if displeased, but an indulgent smile tugged at her mouth nonetheless. "Seems like a gal about to get on a plane in a few hours might come home at a decent hour."

"Oh, but it was my last night in Miami!" Bella protested without any real heat and stretched with a moan. "I had lots of people to see. Lots of parties to attend."

"Hmpf. Lots of money to talk your friends out of, you mean."

Celia was one of the few people who recognized that Bella's involvement in wildlife conservation wasn't just a rich girl's cute hobby. It was Bella's passion and she used her connections. Shamelessly. And it wasn't an accident that she'd been named the top fund-raiser in Florida by two different conservation groups.

"You say that like it's a bad thing." Bella shook her head as Celia selected an outfit from the overflowing closet and held it out with a raised eyebrow. "Not that one. The blue pantsuit for the plane. With the cropped jacket."

Like a well-rehearsed ballet, Bella and Celia danced around each other as they navigated a bedroom that closely resembled a post-hurricane department store. Everyone joked that you could always tell when Bella had whirled through a scene because nothing was in one piece afterward. It was a reference to Bella's birth during the harrowing hours of Hurricane Andrew, before FEMA had started cracking down on evacuations.

Both mother and baby had emerged from the storm without incident, but Bella held the private belief that the experience had branded her soul with hurricane-like qualities she couldn't shake. Not the least of which was a particular talent for causing chaos.

Celia began packing Bella's suitcases while her mistress dressed and they laughed over Bella's account of the previous night's parties, as they'd done many a morning over the years. But this would be the last time for a long time. Maybe forever, depending on what happened in Alma.

Bella kept up the light banter, but she was pretty sure the shadows in Celia's eyes were reflected in her own. As the hour grew near for Bella to leave for the sun-drenched islands of Alma, she couldn't stand it any longer. "I wish you could go with me to Alma!"

And then to her mortification, Bella burst into tears.

Celia folded Bella into her arms and they clung to each other. When Adela, Bella's mom, had finally ditched her cold, unsatisfying marriage the day after Bella's eighteenth birthday, Celia had been the one who stuck around to make sure Bella didn't get into too much trouble. Best of both worlds—she had someone who cared, but who also couldn't tell her what to do. Bella did not like being told what to do.

"There, now. Your brother will look out for you and besides, you'll be having so much fun as the new princess, you won't even notice I'm not there."

"That's not true," Bella sniffed and hugged Celia tighter. "Gabriel will be busy with king stuff and spend all his free time with Serafia now that they're getting married. What if I'm banished to some out of the way place—*alone*?"

She wouldn't put it past her father to lock her up in the palace dungeon or do something else equally archaic since he seemed bent on rediscovering his old-fashioned side. That last photo of her to hit the tabloids? Totally not her fault. How was she supposed to know the paparazzi had hidden in the foliage surrounding Nicole's pool? Everyone else had shed their swimsuits, too, but Bella was the only one they'd targeted, of course.

Rafael Montoro the Third was not amused. Apparently it was problematic that her father's business associates and soon-to-be-king Gabriel's future subjects in Alma could easily access naked photos of Bella.

No one seemed to remember that she was the victim in that scandal.

Celia snorted. "With Gabriel about to take the throne, your father will want the whole family in the public eye, gaining support for your brother. You're the only princess Alma's got, sweetie. They'll love you and so will your fiancé. Your father can't lock you away *and* expect you to marry the man he's picked out."

"Yeah, I've been trying not to think about that." Her head started pounding again and that fourth glass of champagne last night started to feel like a bad idea. But her friends had been determined to send her off in style to her new life as the sister of the king of Alma, so how could she refuse?

Besides, anything that helped her forget the arranged marriage her father was trying to force down her throat was a plus in her book. Fine time for her father to remember he had a daughter—when it was important for the Montoro family to strengthen ties with Alma through marriage. How come Gabriel and Rafe didn't have to marry someone advantageous? Her brothers had chosen their own brides. It wasn't fair. But her father had made it clear she was to get on a plane and meet this man Will Rowling, who was the son of one of Alma's most powerful businessmen.

Maybe she should be thankful no one had thought to match her with Will's father. Seemed as if that might be more advantageous than marrying the son. She shuddered. *No* marriage sounded like fun, no matter who the guy was.

If Alma turned out to be horrible, she'd just come home. Rafe and Emily were going to make her an aunt soon, and she'd love to hang out in Key West with the baby. Nobody dictated Bella's life but her.

"Mr. Rafael isn't completely unreasonable. After all, he did agree to let you meet Will and see how things go. Just remember why you're doing this," Celia advised.

Bella's guilty conscience reared its ugly head and she eased out of Celia's embrace before the older woman sensed it. "It's my royal obligation to help Gabriel ascend to the throne," she mimicked in her father's deep voice. "The whole family needs to be in Alma to prepare for the coronation."

But that wasn't really why she'd agreed to go. Miami had grown too small to hold both Bella and Drew Honeycutt. Honestly, when you told a guy that you just wanted to have fun and not take a relationship seriously, he was supposed to breathe a sigh of relief.

He was not supposed to fall to one knee and propose after two months of casual dating. And then plaster his second proposal on twenty billboards around the city, along with Bella's picture and a cartoon heart around her face. The third proposal spread across the sky in the form of a "Will you marry me, Bella Montoro?" banner behind a small plane, which flew up and down South Beach for six hours while Bella was at a private cookout on the penthouse terrace of Ramone, the new guy she'd been seeing. A fan of drama Ramone was not. Thanks to Drew, he'd bowed out.

And Bella had really liked Ramone, dang it; the more

he drank, the more money he handed over for her wild-life charities.

Drew followed her around, popping up at parties and museum openings like a bad penny, espousing his love for Bella with horrific poetry and calf eyes galore. It would be great if she could tell him off, but Honeycutt Logistics did a lot of business with Montoro Enterprises and she couldn't afford to irritate her father further. Plus, she was 97 percent sure Drew was harmless and worse, he seemed genuinely baffled and brokenhearted over her continual rejection of his proposals.

Each Drew sighting was another kick to the stomach. Another reminder that she was the hurricane baby, destined to whirl through people's lives and leave havoc in her wake. If only she could find a way to *not* break everything into little pieces—even though it was always an accident—she'd feel a lot better. She hated hurting people.

It was probably not a bad plan to disappear from the Miami scene for a while.

Celia managed to get Bella into the car on time and with all her luggage. The gates parted and Bella waved goodbye to Buttercup, Wesley and the house she'd grown up in as the driver picked up speed and they exited the grounds. Sun sparkled across Biscayne Bay and her spirits rose with each mile marker along the highway to the private airstrip where the Montoro Enterprises jet waited to fly her to Alma.

This was an adventure no matter what and she was going to enjoy every second of the sun, sand and royal parties ahead. By the time she'd boarded the plane, buckled her seatbelt and accepted a mimosa from Jan—the same flight attendant who'd given her crayons and coloring books once upon a time—Bella's mood had turned downright cheerful. Cheerful enough to sneak a glance at the picture of Will Rowling her father had sent her.

He was classically handsome, with nice hair and a

pleasant smile. The serious glint in his eye might be a trick of the light. Serious she could do without and besides, this was the guy her *father* had picked. Chances were Will and Bella would get on like oil and water.

But she'd reserve judgment until she met him because first and foremost, Alma was about starting fresh and Will deserved a chance to prove they were meant for each other. If he came out strong with a fun-loving nature and swept her off her feet, she'd be okay with a fabulous love affair and passion to spare.

Though she couldn't deny that one of the big question marks was what kind of guy would agree to an arranged marriage in the twenty-first century. There was probably something really wrong with Will Rowling if he couldn't meet women on his own. She probably had a better chance of her plane flying into an alternate universe than finding her soul mate in Will Rowling.

For the fourth time, someone kicked sand in James Rowling's face and for the fourth time, he ignored it. If he let loose with a string of curses—the way he wanted to—he'd only alert someone to his presence here, and James was trying to be invisible.

Or at least as invisible as one of Alma's most notorious failures could be. Maybe in fifty years he could fade into the woodwork, but every single citizen of Alma—and probably most of the free world—had watched him miss that goal in the World Cup. Anonymity was scarce.

So far, no one had recognized him with Oakleys covering his eyes and a backward ball cap over his hair. The longer he kept it that way, the better. The last thing he wanted was a bunch of questions about why Real Madrid had dropped his contract. It wasn't hard to look that one up…along with pictures of James leaving a bar in Rio with a prostitute…not that she'd mentioned money to *him*. Or worse, questions about whether he planned to stick around his adopted homeland and play for Alma's reserve football team—*soccer* team if the questioner was American.

No comment.

A reserve team was for beginners. He would get a new professional league contract, period. If not around here, then maybe back in England, where he'd been born. There was no other alternative. Football was his life.

Peeling his shirt away from his sticky chest, he leaned back into his short-legged beach chair, stuck his legs straight out and closed his eyes, somehow sure the elusive measure of peace he sought would be within reach this time. He almost snorted. When had he turned into an optimist?

There was no peace to be had and if there was, it sure as hell wouldn't be found in Alma, the capital of boring. Not to mention his father's presence permeated the entire island, as if Patrick Rowling's soul lived in the bedrock, sending out vibrations of disapproval on a regularly scheduled basis.

That's why James was at the beach at Playa Del Onda, soaking up the sun instead of doing whatever it was his father thought he should be doing, which would never happen because James lacked the capacity to do what his father said. It was like a mutated gene: his father spoke and James's brain refused to obey. He automatically did the opposite.

"Ooof!" Air whooshed from his lungs as something heavy landed square on his chest.

Then his beach chair flipped, tossing him into the sand on top of something. It squealed.

Some*one*. When his vision cleared, the tangle of supple-bodied woman and blond hair underneath him captured his complete attention.

He gazed down into the bluest set of eyes he'd seen in a while. Something shifted inside as the woman blinked back, her beautiful heart-shaped face reflecting not an iota of remorse over their risqué position. Her body had somehow slid into the grooves of his effortlessly and the slightest incline of his head would fuse his lips to hers.

She'd fully gobsmacked him.

Their breath intermingled. She seemed in no hurry to unstick her skin from his and in about two and a half seconds, his own body would start getting into the moment in a huge and inappropriate way.

Sexy strangers signaled big-time problems and he had enough of those.

Reluctantly, he rolled off her and helped her sit up. "Sorry about that. You okay?"

"Totally." Her husky voice skittered across his skin and he was hooked on the sound of it instantly. American. His favorite. "My fault. I was focused on this thing instead of where I was going."

She kicked at a Frisbee he hadn't noticed lying in the sand two feet away. But who'd pay attention to a piece of plastic when a fit blonde in a tiny bikini landed in your lap? Not him.

"I like a girl who goes for the memorable introduction."

It was certainly a new one. And he'd experienced his share of inventive ploys for getting his attention. Knickers with cell phone numbers scrawled in marker across the crotch, which he discovered had been shoved into his pocket. Room keys slipped into drinks sent over by a knot of football groupies at a corner table. Once, he'd gone back to his hotel room after a press junket to find two naked women spread out across his bed. How they'd gotten in, he still didn't know.

The logistics question had sort of slipped his mind after ten minutes in their company.

"Oh, I wasn't angling for an introduction." She actually blushed a bit, which was oddly endearing. "I really didn't see you there. You kind of blend into the sand."

"Is that a crack about my British complexion?" he teased. "You're pretty pale yourself, darling."

She laughed and rearranged her hair, pulling it behind her back so it didn't conceal her cleavage. A move he thoroughly appreciated. This gorgeous klutz might be the best thing that had happened to him all week. Longer than that. The best thing since arriving in Alma for sure.

Maybe it wasn't so bad to be stuck here cooling his heels until a football club whose jersey he could stomach wearing knocked on his door.

"No, not at all. I wouldn't be so rude as to point out your flaws on our first meeting." She leaned forward, her vibe full of come-hither as she teased him back.

Intrigued, he angled his head toward her. "But on our second date, all bets are off?"

Glancing down coquettishly, she let loose a small smile. "I'm more of a third-date kind of girl."

His gut contracted as the full force of that promise hit him crossways. She was a unique breed of woman, the most fascinating one he'd met thus far on this stupid rock he was being forced to call home for the time being. The memory of her hot flesh against his was still fresh—it was enough to drive him mad. And he suspected she knew exactly what she was doing to him.

"I have a feeling you'd be worth the wait."

She picked that moment to stand and for some reason, the new angle cast her in a different light. It tickled his mind and he recognized her all at once. Pictures of the new princess had graced every news channel for the past couple of weeks, but she'd been clothed. Regardless, he should have recognized her sooner and maybe not disgraced himself by flirting with a woman who probably really had no clue she'd stumbled over a former football player for Real Madrid.

A princess—especially one as fit as Bella Montoro—wasn't running around the beach at Playa Del Onda looking to meet guys, whether they were semifamous or not. Which was a dirty shame.

He shoved his hat back onto his head and repositioned his sunglasses, both of which had flown off during the sand tango.

Ms. Montoro... Princess Bella... Your Royal Highness... What did you even call her when her brother hadn't been crowned yet? Whatever the form of address, she was way out of his league.

But that didn't mean she thought so. She hadn't bothered to hide the frank attraction in her gaze when she'd been in his arms earlier. If there was anything he knew, it was women, and she might be royalty but that didn't necessarily make her off-limits.

He quickly scrambled to his feet in case there was some protocol for standing when princesses stood...even if she was wearing a postage stamp–sized white bikini that somehow covered everything while leaving nothing to the imagination.

No point in beating around the bush. "Am I permitted to call you Bella or is there some other title you'd prefer?"

"What, like *Princess*?" She wrinkled her nose. "I'm not really used to all that yet. And besides, I think we're a little past that stage, don't you?"

The feel of her soft curves flush against his body flooded his mind and his board shorts probably wouldn't conceal his excitement much longer if he didn't cool his jets. "Yeah. Formality isn't my specialty anyway. Bella it is."

Strangely, calling her Bella ratcheted up the intimacy quotient by a thousand. He liked it. And he wanted to say it a bunch more times while she lay stretched out under him again. Without the bikini.

She smiled and glanced down, as if the heat roiling between them was affecting her, too, and she didn't know quite what to do with it. "This is all so awkward. I wasn't sure you knew who I was."

Shrugging, he stuck his hands behind his back because he had no clue what to do with them. It was the first time he'd been unsure around a woman since the age of fourteen. "I recognized you from your pictures."

She nodded and waved off her friend who'd most likely come to investigate the disappearance of her Frisbee partner. "Me, too. I wasn't expecting to run into you on the beach or I would have dressed for the occasion."

Ah, so she *did* know who he was—and dare he hope there was a hint of approval there? She'd gotten rid of the friend, a clear sign she planned to stick around for a while at least. Maybe he wasn't so far out of her league after all. "I'm a fan of your wardrobe choice."

Laughing, she glanced down. "I guess it is appropriate for the beach, isn't it? It's just not how I thought meeting you would go. The picture my father sent painted you as someone very serious."

"Um…you don't say?" He'd just completely lost the thread of the conversation. Why would her father be sending her pictures, unless… Of course. Had to make sure the precious princess didn't taint herself with the common riffraff. *Stay away from that Rowling boy. He's a boatload of trouble.*

His temper kicked up, but he smoothed it over with a wink and a wicked smile. "I'm every bit as bad as your father warned you. Probably worse. If your goal is to seriously irritate him, I'm on board with that."

He had no problem being her Rebel Against Daddy go-to guy, though he'd probably encourage her to be *really* bad and enjoy it far too much. Instantly, a few choice scenarios that would get them both into a lot of trouble filled his mind.

Her eyes widened. "He, uh, didn't warn me about you… Actually, I'm pretty sure he'd be happy if we went out. Isn't that the whole point of this? So we can see if we're suited?"

This conversation was going in circles. Her father wanted them to date? "He's a football fan, then?"

She shook her head, confusion clouding her gaze. "I don't think so. Does that matter to you, Will?"

"Will?" He groaned. This was so much worse than he'd anticipated. "You think I'm Will?"

More importantly, her father had sent her a picture of Will for some yet-to-be-determined reason, but it wasn't so she could flirt with Will's twin brother on the beach. And this little case of mistaken identity was about to come to an abrupt halt.

Two

Bella laced her fingers together as she got the impression all at once that she wasn't talking to the man she thought she was. "Aren't you Will Rowling?"

He had to be. She'd studied his picture enough on the plane and then again last night while she tried to go to sleep but couldn't, because she'd been wondering what in the world her father was thinking with this arranged marriage nonsense. And then she'd come to the beach with the daughter of one of the servants who was close to her age, only to trip over said man her father had selected.

Except he was staring at her strangely and the niggle of doubt wormed its way to the surface again. How could she have made such a mistake?

"Not Will. Not even close," he confirmed.

He grinned, and she let herself revel in his gorgeous aqua-colored eyes for a moment because she didn't have to fight an attraction to him if he wasn't the man her father picked out for her.

The sun shone a little brighter and the sea sparkled a bit

bluer. Digging her toes into the warm sand that suddenly felt heavenly against her bare feet, she breathed a sigh of relief and grinned back.

This was turning out better than she'd hoped. Geez, she'd been one heartbeat away from believing in love at first sight and trying for all she was worth to shut it down. Because she'd thought he was Will Rowling. Imagine *that*. Her father would be insufferable about it and demand they get married right away if she'd become smitten so fast. It would have been a disaster.

But if this extremely sexy man wasn't Will—*perfect*. She slid her gaze down his well-cut body, which a T-shirt and long shorts couldn't hide. Of course she'd felt every single one of his valleys and hard peaks. Intimately.

No. This was *not* perfect. She was supposed to be meeting Will and seeing if they got along, not flirting with some look-alike stranger who made her itch to accept the wicked invitation in his gaze, which promised if he got her naked, he'd rock her world.

With no small amount of regret, she reeled back her less-than-innocent interest.

"Well, sorry about that, then," she said and held out her hand. Might as well start over since this whole thing had blown up in her face. "Bella Montoro. I guess you already knew that, but I'm at a disadvantage."

His rich laugh hit her a moment before he clasped her hand in his and the combination heated her more than the bright sun or her embarrassment. "I'm the one at a disadvantage, if you were hoping I was Will. I'm James. The other Rowling. Will is my brother."

"Brother? Oh," she drawled as it hit her. "You and Will are twins."

"Guilty." His eyes twinkled, sucking her under his spell for a moment.

"Then I'm doubly sorry." Mortified, she racked her brain, but if her father had told her Will had a twin brother, she surely would have remembered that. "I've made a complete mess out of this, haven't I?"

"Not at all. People confuse us all the time. It's fine, really."

It was not fine. It was so the opposite of fine, she couldn't even wrap her head around how *not fine* it was. Because she'd just realized this sensually intriguing man she'd accidentally tripped over was the *brother* of the intended target of her father's archaic arranged marriage plan.

If that didn't complicate her life a million times over, she didn't know what would.

Her hand was still gripped tight in his and he didn't seem in any hurry to let her go. But he should. She pulled free and crossed her arms, wishing for a cover-up. Why did that glint in James's eye cause her to feel so exposed all at once?

"I'm curious," James said casually as if the vibe between them had just cooled, which it most definitely had not. "Why did your father send you a picture of Will?"

"Oh, so I would know what he looks like." Actually, she'd demanded he do so. There was no way she was getting on a plane to meet someone blind.

"I'm sensing there's more to the story." His raised eyebrows encouraged her to elaborate.

"Wouldn't you wonder about the appearance of a person your father wanted you to marry? I sure did."

Surprise flew across James's face. "Your father wants you to marry Will? Does Will know about this?"

"Of course he does. Your father was the instigator, actually. You didn't know our fathers cooked up this idea of an arranged marriage?"

His laugh was far more derisive this time. "The elder Rowling doesn't share much of what goes on his head. But somehow it doesn't shock me to discover dear old Dad wants his son married to a member of the royal family. Did you agree?"

"No! Well, not yet anyway. I only agreed to meet Will and see what happened. I'm not really in the market for a steady relationship, let alone one as permanent as marriage."

Groaning, she bit her lip. Too late to take that back, though it had been the God-honest truth. Regardless, spilling her guts to the brother of her potential fiancé wasn't the best plan. James would probably run off and tell Will his future bride had felt up his brother on the beach—totally not her fault!—flirted with him—maybe partially her fault—and then declared marriage to be worse than the plague.

Instead of falling to his knees in shock, James winked and dang, even that was sexy.

"Woman after my own heart. If you don't want to get married, why even agree to meet Will?"

Why was she still standing here talking to the wrong brother? She should go. There was nothing for her here. But she couldn't make herself walk away from the spark still kicking between them.

"It's complicated," she hedged.

She sighed and glanced over her shoulder, but there was no one in earshot. She didn't want to draw the attention of a camera lens, but surely it couldn't hurt to spend a few minutes chatting with the man who might become her brother-in-law…so she could keep reminding herself that's who he was to her. If nothing else, she could set the record straight in case he intended to repeat this conversation verbatim to his brother.

"I'm the king of uncomplicating things," James said with another laugh that curled her toes deeper into the sand. "Try me."

It wasn't as if anyone was expecting her back at the gargantuan house perched on the cliff behind them. Gabriel was never home and her father… Well, she wasn't dying to run into him again.

She shrugged. "We're all new at this royalty thing. I don't want to be the one to mess it up. What if I don't try with Will and it has horrible repercussions for my brother Gabriel? I can't be responsible for that."

"But if you meet Will and you don't like him, how is that different than not meeting him in the first place? Either way, you don't end up with him and the repercussions will be the same."

How come she'd never thought of that? "That's a good point."

"Told you. I can uncomplicate anything. It's a skill." James's smile widened as he swept her with an impossible to misinterpret look. "I just figure out what I want to do and justify it. Like…if I wanted to kiss you, I'd find a way."

As his gaze rested on her lips, heat flooded her cheeks. And other places. She could practically feel the weight of his kiss against her mouth and he hadn't even moved. A pang of lust zinged through her abdomen and she nearly gasped at the strength of it. What was it about him that lit her up so fiercely?

"You shouldn't be talking about kissing." She inwardly cursed. That should have come out much more sternly, instead of breathy with anticipation. "Flirting as a whole is completely off-limits."

A hint of challenge crept into his expression and then he leaned in, stopping just short of touching her earlobe with his mouth. "Says who?"

"Me," she murmured as the scent of male and heat coiled up low in her belly, nearly making her weep with want. "I'm weak and liable to give in. You have to be the strong one and stop presenting me with so much temptation."

He laughed softly. "I'm afraid you're in a lot of trouble, then."

"Why?"

"Because I have absolutely no reservations about giving in to temptation."

The wicked smile spreading across his face sealed it—she *was* in a lot of trouble. She was supposed to marry his brother. And the last thing she needed was to set herself up for a repeat of the Drew Debacle, where she accidentally broke James's heart because she ended up with Will. Better all around to stay away from James.

Why did the wrong Rowling have to be so alluring and so delicious?

Maybe she could find Will similarly attractive if she just gave him a chance.

"I'll keep that in mind." All right, then. She was going to have to be the one to step away. Noted.

So step away. Right now.

Through a supreme act of will, she somehow did. James's gorgeous aqua eyes tracked her movement as she put one foot, then two between them. He nodded once, apparently in understanding but definitely not in agreement.

"See you around, Princess."

He stood there, one hip cocked in a casual stance that screamed Bad Boy, and she half waved before she turned and fled.

As she climbed the stairs to the house, she resisted looking over her shoulder to see if she could pick out James's yellow T-shirt amidst the other sun worshippers lounging on the white sand. He wasn't for her and there was no getting around the fact that she wished otherwise.

James Rowling was forbidden. And that might be his most attractive quality.

Bella entered the Playa Del Onda house through the kitchen, and snagged a glass-bottled cola from the refrigerator and a piece of crusty bread from the pantry. Both the colas and the bread tasted different in Europe but she didn't mind. All part of the adventure.

Thoughts still on the sexy man she'd abandoned on the beach, Bella munched on the bread as she climbed the stairs to her bedroom. She almost made it before a dark shadow alerted her to the fact that her least favorite person in the house had found her.

"Isabella." Her father's sharp voice stopped her dead, four steps from the landing on the second floor.

"Yeah, Dad?" She didn't turn around. If you didn't stare him in the eye, he couldn't turn you to stone, right?

"Is that how you dress to go out?"

"Only when I go to the beach," she retorted. "Is there something new you'd like to discuss or shall we rehash the same subject from last night? You didn't like that outfit either, if I recall."

Ever since Adela, Bella's mother, had left, this is how it went. Her father only spoke to her when he wanted to tell her how to run her life. And she pretended to listen. Occasionally, when it suited her, she went along, but only if she got something out of it.

"We'll rehash it as many times as it takes to get it through your scattered brain. Gabriel is going to be *king*." Rafael stressed the word as if she might be confused about what was happening around her. "The least you can do is help smooth his ascension with a little common sense about how you dress. The Montoros have no credibility yet, especially not with that stunt your brother pulled."

"Rafe fell in love," she shot back and bit her tongue.

Old news. Her father cared nothing for love, only propriety. And horror of all horrors—his eldest son had gotten a bartender pregnant and then abdicated the throne so he could focus on his new family. In Daddy's mind, it fell squarely into the category of impropriety. Unforgivable.

It was a reminder that her father also cared little for his daughter's happiness either. Only royal protocol.

"Rafe is a disappointment. I'll not have another child

of mine follow his example." He cleared his throat. "Face me when we're speaking, please."

She complied, but only because the front view of her bikini was likely to give him apoplexy and she kind of wanted to see it.

He pursed his lips but, to her father's credit, that was his only reaction. "When have you arranged to meet Will Rowling?"

Ah, of course. Complaining about her bikini was a smoke screen—this was actually an ambush about her arranged marriage. With the scent of forbidden fruit lingering in her senses coupled with her father's bad attitude, she'd developed a sudden fierce desire to spend time with someone who had clearly never met a good time he didn't like.

And his name wasn't Will. "I haven't yet."

"What are you waiting for, an invitation? This is your match to make, Isabella. I'm giving you some latitude in the timing but I expect results. Soon." The severe lines around his mouth softened. "This alliance is very important. To the entire Montoro family and to the royal legacy of Alma. I'm not asking this for myself, but for Gabriel. Remember that."

She sighed. "I know. That's why I'm here. I do want to be a credit to the royal family."

Hurricane Bella couldn't whirl through Alma and disrupt the entire country. She knew that. Somehow, she had to be better than she'd been in Miami. The thought of Miami reminded her of Buttercup and Wesley, her feathered friends she'd left behind. Some said the wild macaws that nested in southern Florida were people's pets set free during Hurricane Andrew. She'd always felt an affinity with the birds because they'd all survived the storm. Buttercup and Wesley could continue to be her source of strength even from afar.

"Good. Then arrange to meet Will Rowling and do it soon. Patrick Rowling is one of the most influential men in Alma and the Montoros need his support. We cannot afford another misstep at this point."

It wasn't anything she hadn't heard before, but on the heels of meeting James, the warning weighed heavily on her shoulders. Gabriel hadn't wanted to be thrust suddenly into a starring role in the restoration of the monarchy to Alma's political landscape. But he'd stepped up nonetheless. She could do the same.

But why did it matter which Rowling she married anyway? Surely one was as good as the other. Perhaps she could turn this to her advantage by seeing where things went with James.

"I'll do my best not to mess this up," Bella promised.

If it didn't matter which Rowling she picked, that meant she didn't need to call Will anytime soon. The reprieve let her breathe a little easier.

Her father raised his eyebrows. "That would be a refreshing change. On that note, don't assume that you left all the tabloids behind in Miami. The paparazzi know no national boundaries. Stay out of scandalous situations, don't drink too much and for God's sake, keep your clothes on."

She saluted saucily to cover the sharp spike of hurt that she never could seem to stop no matter how many times she told herself this was just how he was. "Yes, Father."

Escaping to her room, Bella took a long shower but it didn't ease the ache from the showdown with Rafael.

Why did she still care that her father never hugged her or told her he was proud of her? Not for the first time, she wondered if the frosty temperature in her father's demeanor had caused her mother to leave. If so, Bella hardly blamed her. She hoped Adela had found happiness.

Happiness should be the most important factor in whom you married. The thought solidified Bella's resolve. If her father wanted a match between the Montoros and the Rowlings, great. Bella would comply—as long as the Rowling was James.

She'd rather see where that led than try to force a match with the right brother.

Why shouldn't she be allowed to be as happy as Rafe and Gabriel?

The loud, scornful whispering at the next table over started to annoy James about two bites into his paella. Couldn't a bloke get something to eat without someone publicly crucifying him? This time, the subject of choice was his lack of a decision on whether to take a spot on Alma's reserve team.

The two middle-aged men were in complete agreement: James should be happy to have *any* position, even though Alma wasn't a UEFA team. He should take his lumps and serve his penance, and then it would be acceptable to play for a premiere club again, once he'd redeemed himself. Or so the men opined, and not very quietly.

The paella turned to sawdust in his mouth. He was glad someone knew what he needed to do next in his stalled career.

Playing for Alma was a fine choice. For a beginner. But James had been playing football since he was seven, the same year his father had uprooted his two sons from their Guildford home and moved them to the tiny, nowhere island of Alma. Football had filled a void in his life after the death of his mother. James loved the game. Being dropped from Real Madrid had stung, worse than he'd let on to anyone.

Of course, whom would he tell? He and Will rarely talked about anything of note, usually by James's choice. Will was the perfect son who never messed up, while James spent as much effort as he possibly could on irritating his father. James and Will might be twins but the similarities ended there—and Will was a Manchester United fan from way back, so they couldn't even talk football without almost coming to blows.

And Will had first dibs on the woman James hadn't been able to forget. All without lifting a finger. Life just reeked sometimes.

Unable to eat even one more bite of the dish he'd found so tasty just minutes ago, James threw a few bills on the table and stalked out of the restaurant into the bright afternoon sun on the boardwalk at Playa Del Onda.

So much for hanging out at the beach where fewer people might recognize him. He might as well go back to Del Sol and let his father tell him again how much of a disappointment he was. Or he could swallow his bitterness and get started on finding another football club since none had come looking for him.

A flash of blond hair ahead of him caught his eye. Since Bella had been on his mind in one way or another since he'd met her the day before, it was no wonder he was imagining her around every corner.

He shouldn't, though. She'd been reserved for the "right" Rowling, the one who could do no wrong. James's black sheep status hadn't improved much. Frankly, she deserved a shot at the successful brother, though he had no clue if Will was even on board with the match their father had apparently orchestrated. When Bella mentioned it yesterday, that was the first he'd heard of it. Which didn't mean it wasn't legit.

The woman in front of him glanced into a shop window and her profile confirmed it. It *was* Bella.

Something expanded in his chest and he forgot why he wasn't supposed to think about her. Unable to help himself all of a sudden, James picked up his pace until he drew up alongside her. "Fancy meeting you here."

Tilting her head down, she looked at him over the top of her sunglasses and murmured something reassuring to the burly security detail trailing her. They backed off immediately.

"James Rowling, I presume?" she said to him.

He laughed. "The one and only. Getting in some shopping?"

"Nope. Waiting around for you to stroll by. It's about time. I was starting to think you'd ordered everything on El Gatito's menu." She nodded in the direction of the restaurant he'd just exited and leaned in to murmur, "I hope you skipped the cat."

She'd been waiting for him? The notion tripped him up even more than her wholly American, wholly sexy perfume, for some odd reason.

"I, uh, did. Skip the cat," he clarified as he caught her joke in reference to the restaurant's name. "They were fresh out."

Her smile set off a round of sparks he'd rather not have over his brother's intended match.

"Maybe next time."

"Maybe next time you'll just come inside and eat with me instead of skulking around outside like a stalker," he suggested and curled his lip. What was he *doing*—asking her out? Bad idea.

One of her eyebrows quirked up above the frame of her sunglasses. "I can say with absolute authority that me noticing you heading into a restaurant and accidentally-on-purpose hanging around hoping to run into you does not qualify as stalking. Trust me, I'm a bit of an expert. I have the police report to prove it."

He had a hard time keeping his own eyebrows from shooting up. "You're a convicted stalker?"

Her laugh was quite a bit more amused this time. "Not yet. Don't go and ruin my perfect record now either, okay?" She shrugged and slipped off her sunglasses. "I picked up a stalker in Miami a couple of years ago. So I'm pretty familiar with American law. I would hope it's reasonably similar in Alma."

Sobering immediately, he tamped down the sudden and violent urge to punch whomever had threatened Bella's peace of mind. She'd mentioned it so casually, as if it wasn't a big deal, but it bloody well *was*. "What do you mean, you picked up a stalker? Like you went to the market to get milk and you just couldn't resist selecting a nutter to shadow you all the way home? No more jokes. Is he in jail?"

That may have come out a little more fiercely than he'd intended, but oh, well. He didn't take it back.

Wide-eyed, she shook her head. "He was practically harmless. A little zealous with his affections, maybe. I was out for the evening and he broke into my bedroom, where he waited for me to come home, bouquet of flowers in hand, like we were a couple. Or at least that was his sworn testimony. When my father found out, he immediately called the police, the mayor of Miami and the CEO of the company who'd sold him the security system installed on the grounds. I'm afraid they were rather harsh with the intruder."

Harmless? Anyone who could bypass a security system was far from harmless.

"As well they should have been." James developed an instant liking for Bella's obviously very level-headed father. "Was that the extent of it? Do I need to worry about the nutter following you across the pond?"

James had had his share of negative attention, invasions of privacy and downright hostile encounters with truly disturbed people. But he had fifty pounds and eight inches on Bella, plus he knew how to take care of himself. Bella was delicate and gorgeous and worthy of being treated like the princess she was. The thought of a creepy mouth-breather following her through the streets of Alma in hopes of doing depraved things made him furious.

"I doubt it. I haven't heard a peep from him in two years." She contemplated James with a small smile and crossed her arms over the angular sundress she wore. "You seem rather fierce all of a sudden. Worried about me?"

"Yes," he growled and shook his head. She was not any

of his concern—or at least she shouldn't be. "No. I'm sure your security is perfectly adequate."

He waved at the pair of ex-military types who waited a discreet distance away.

"Oh, yeah. My father insisted." Her nose wrinkled up delicately. "I'm pretty sure they're half security and half babysitters."

"Why do you need a babysitter?"

He couldn't leave it alone, could he? He should be bidding her good afternoon and running very fast in the other direction. But she constantly provoked his interest, and it was oh-so-deliberate. She wasn't walking away either and he'd bet it was because she felt the attraction sizzling between them just as much as he did.

Hell, everything he'd learned about her thus far indicated she liked the hint of naughtiness to their encounters… because they weren't supposed to be attracted to each other.

"I have a tendency to get into trouble." She waggled her brows. "These guys are here to keep me honest. Remind me that I have royal blood in my veins and a responsibility to the crown."

That was too good of a segue to pass up. "Really? What kind of trouble?"

"Oh, the worst kind," she stressed and reached out to stroke his arm in deliberate provocation. "If you've got a reputation to uphold, you'd best steer clear."

The contact of her nails on his bare arm sang through him. This was the most fun he'd had all day. "Sweetheart, I hate to disillusion you, but I've managed to ruin my reputation quite nicely all by my own self. Hanging out with you might actually improve it."

"Huh." She gave him a wholly inappropriate once-over that raised the temperature a few thousand degrees. "I'm dying to know. What did you do?"

"You really don't know?" That would be a first.

When she shook her head, he thought about glossing

over it for a half second, but she'd find out soon enough anyway. "Mishap in Rio. Some unfortunate photographs starring me and a prostitute. I swear, money never came up, but there you go. The world didn't see it as an innocent mistake."

Gaze locked on his, she squeezed his arm. "Man after my own heart. Of all the things I thought we might have in common, that was not it. I'm recovering from my own photographer-in-the-bushes fiasco. Cretins."

"Oh, that's too bad. Sorry."

A moment of pure commiseration passed between them. And it spread into something dangerously affecting. They shared a complete lack of reverence for rules, their chemistry was off the charts and they were both in Alma trying to find their footing. It was practically criminal that he couldn't explore her gorgeous body and even more attractive mind to his heart's content.

But he couldn't. While he might have competed with Will over women in the past, this one was different. James wasn't in a good place to start anything with a woman anyway, especially not one who would live in the public eye for the foreseeable future. She needed to be with Will, who would take care of her and not sully her with failure.

Not to mention that his father seemed to have struck some kind of bargain with the Montoro family. Until James knew exactly what that entailed, he couldn't cross the line he so badly wanted to.

She'd flat out told him he'd have to be the strong one, that he should stop tempting her. So that was the way it had to be.

James smiled and slipped his own sunglasses over his eyes so she couldn't read how difficult this was going to be for him. "Nice to see you again, Bella. I've got an appointment I'm late for so I've got to dash."

Casual. No commitment to calling her later. Exactly the right tone to brush her off.

She frowned and opened her mouth, but before she could say something they'd both likely regret, he added, "You should ring Will. Cheers," and whirled to take off down the boardwalk as fast he could.

Being noble tasted more bitter than he would have ever anticipated.

Three

James's rebuff stayed with Bella into the evening.

Apparently he wasn't of the same mind that a match between the Rowlings and Montoros could work just as easily between James and Bella as it could with his brother.

Being forced into a stiff, formal dinner with her father didn't improve her mood. Gabriel and Serafia were supposed to be there, too, which was the only reason Bella agreed, but the couple had yet to show.

Five bucks said they'd lost track of time while indulging in a much more pleasurable activity than dinner with Little Sister and Frosty Father. Lucky dogs.

Bella spooned up another bite of Marta's gazpacho, one of the best things the chef had prepared so far, and murmured her appreciation in case her father was actually paying attention to her today. But her mind was back on the boardwalk outside El Gatito. She'd have sworn the encounter with James would end with at least a kiss in the shadows of a storefront. Just to take the edge off until they got behind closed doors and let the simmering heat between them explode.

"Isabella." Her father's voice startled her out of an X-rated fantasy that she shouldn't have envisioned at all, let alone at the dinner table.

Not because of the X factor, but because it had starred James, who had cast her off with the lovely parting gift of his brother. *Call Will.* As if James had already grown tired of her and wanted to be clear about what her next steps should be.

"Yeah, Dad?" He must have realized that they were actually sitting at the same table. For once. She couldn't remember the last time they'd eaten together.

"You should know your great-aunt Isabella has decided to spend her last days in Alma. She arrived this morning and is asking after you."

Sudden happy tears burned Bella's eyelids. "Oh, that's the best news ever. Isn't she going to stay here with us?"

"The restoration of the monarchy is topmost on your aunt's mind." Rafael's gaze bored into her; he was no doubt trying to instill the gravity of royal protocol. "Therefore, she is staying in Del Sol. She wished to be close to El Castillo del Arena, so that she may be involved in Gabriel's coronation to the extent she is able."

Bella swore. Del Sol was, what? An hour away? Fine time to realize she should have taken her father up on the offer of a car...except she hadn't wanted to learn all the new traffic laws and Spanish road signs. Too late now—she'd have to take the chauffeured town car in order to visit Tía Isabella.

"Playa Del Onda is practically like Miami." Bella grumbled, mostly to herself. "You'd think she'd prefer the coast."

Her father put his spoon by his plate even though his bowl of gazpacho was still almost full. It hadn't been long enough since the last time they'd dined together for her to forget that meant a subject of grave importance was afoot and it wasn't her aunt's preference of locale.

"I have another matter to discuss. How was your first meeting with Will Rowling?"

Biting back a groan, she kept eating in a small show of defiance. Then she swallowed and said, "I haven't scheduled it yet."

Her father frowned. "I have it on good authority that you spoke to him today. On the boardwalk."

Spies? Her father had stooped to a new low. "I wasn't talking to Will. That was James."

Oh, duh. Her brand new security-guards-slash-babysitters had spilled the beans. Too bad they were the wrong beans.

Rafael's brows snapped together. "I cannot make myself more clear. Will Rowling is the man you should be pursuing."

Bella abandoned her spoon and plunked her elbows on the table to lean forward, so her father didn't miss her game face. "What if I like James better?"

Never mind that James had washed his hands of her. Regardless, it was the principle of the thing. Her father liked to try and run her life but failed to recall that Bella's typical response was to tell him to go to hell.

"James Rowling is bad news wrapped with trouble," Rafael shot back with a scowl. "He is not good enough for my daughter."

It seemed as if James had quoted this exact conversation to her yesterday on the beach. What was he, psychic? James's comment about the photographs that had gotten him into trouble crossed her mind and she realized there must be more to the story. She actually knew very little about the man other than the way he made her feel when he looked at her.

She eyed her father. What if Rafael had *told* James to brush her off? Would James have listened? She wouldn't put it past her father to interfere and now she wished she'd chased James down so she could ask. Shoot. She'd have to arrange another accidental meeting in order to find out.

"Maybe I'd like to make that decision on my own."

"Perhaps you need a few more facts if you're determined to undo the work I've already done on your behalf." Her father rubbed his graying temple. "Will Rowling is the next CEO of Rowling Energy, and he will be of paramount importance to your brother's relationship with the entire European oil market. How do you suppose the Montoros will lead a country rich with oil if we do not have the appropriate alliances in place?"

"Gabriel's smart. He'll figure it out," she said, but it came out sounding a little sullen. As smart and capable as Gabriel may be, he'd never been king before and besides, Alma hadn't had a king in a long time, so her brother would be a bit of a trailblazer.

She owed it to Gabriel to give him a leg up.

"Have you given any thought to Will Rowling's feelings, Isabella? You haven't reached out to him in the three days since you've arrived. You could not have insulted him more if you tried."

No, she hadn't thought of that. She swore. Her father had a very small point. Miniscule. But a point nonetheless. How would she feel if Will had come to Miami to meet her and then didn't call her, choosing instead to flirt outrageously with her best friend, Nicole, for example?

She'd hunt Will down and tell him to his face what a dog he was. So why should she get a pass to do whatever pleased her? It didn't matter if her father had scared off James—this was about doing what she said she'd do.

"I'll meet Will. Tomorrow, if he's free," Bella promised and turned her attention to eating. The faster the gazpacho disappeared, the faster she could as well.

It didn't go down as well this time. Righteousness wasn't as fun as it looked in the brochure.

* * *

Will Rowling took Bella's call immediately, cleared his schedule for the next morning and agreed to take her on a tour of Alma. He'd been very pleasant on the phone, though his British accent sounded a bit too much like James's for her liking.

When Will picked her up at 10:30 a.m. on the dot, she flung the door open and actually had a bad Captain Obvious moment when she realized Will *looked* like James, too. *Duh.* As common as fraternal twins were among the moneyed set of Miami, she'd never actually met a set of identical twins.

She studied him for a long second, taking in the remarkable resemblance, until he cleared his throat and she found a dose of manners somewhere in her consciousness. "I'm so sorry! Hello. You must be Will."

"I don't know if I must be, but I am Will," he agreed.

Was that a joke? Trying not to be too obtrusive, she evaluated his expression but it was blank. With James, she never had to wonder. "I'm Bella, by the way."

"I assumed so. I have your picture."

Of course he did. And this was her house. Wasn't this fun? "Are you ready to go?"

"Yes, if you are." With a smile that didn't reach his eyes, he held out a hand toward his car, and waited until she left the house to follow her so he could help her into the passenger seat.

Will climbed into the driver's seat and buckled his seat belt carefully before starting the car, which guilted Bella into fastening hers as well. Seat belts. In an itty-bitty place like Alma, where nothing happened.

She sighed and pasted on a bright smile. "Safety first."

Usually she trotted that line out during a condom discussion. She almost cracked a joke along those lines, but something told her Will might not appreciate the parallel. Sinking down in her seat, she scouted for a topic of discussion. They were supposed to be seeing how they meshed, right?

Will must have had a similar thought process because he spoke first. "Thanks for arranging this, Bella. I'm chuffed to show you around Alma, but I'd like to know what you might be interested in seeing. Anything jump out at you? I'm at your command."

Did he mean that in the double-entendre way? A provocative rejoinder sprang to her lips that she'd have let fly if she'd been in the car with James. Should she flirt with Will, the way she normally did on a date, or would that just lead to him taking her up on it, when she wasn't even sure she wanted him to? Maybe she should just be herself, but what if Will hated her immediately? Would her father lay another guilt trip on her?

All of this second-guessing was making her nuts. She wasn't with James, and *everyone*—including James— wanted her to make nice with the proper Rowling. Yeah, she'd looked up James last night, finding far more information about him than she'd expected, and little of it would fit the definition of the word *proper*.

No one, not even James, had thought it relevant to mention the man was a professional soccer—*football* in Europe, apparently—player. Since he appeared to have quite a bit of fame, maybe he'd assumed she already knew. Regardless, bad press followed James around like it did her. No wonder her father had nearly had a heart attack when she mentioned James's name. He was the very opposite of the proper brother.

Proper pretty much covered Will's personality. Five minutes in, and judging by the stiff set of Will's shoulders, he wasn't as much of a fun time as his brother. Hopefully, she'd judged wrong and would soon discover otherwise.

"Thanks," she responded. "I've only seen the coast and a bit of Del Sol. Why don't you pick, since this is your home?"

"No problem." He shot her a small but pained smile, cluing her in that this whole set up might be as difficult for him as it was for her.

She should give him a break. "So, Will. How long have you lived in Alma?"

An innocuous enough subject, hopefully, and given the brothers' accents, it was a safe bet they hadn't been born here.

"Since I was seven. My father moved us here from England."

"Oh, that must have been quite an adventure."

She'd lived in Miami her whole life and living someplace new did have appeal for that reason alone. If only this arranged marriage business hadn't soured the experience of coming to Alma, she'd be having a blast. And that was why she still didn't think of it as her home... She still reserved the right to go back to Miami and play aunt instead of princess if the royal pressure grew too great.

Though with Tía Isabella's arrival in Alma, going home held much less appeal.

Will's face remained expressionless, but he tapped his pinky on the steering wheel in a staccato rhythm as he drove north out of Playa Del Onda along the coastal road that circled the main island.

"The move was difficult," he said shortly and paused so long, she wasn't sure he planned to continue. But then he said, "My mother had just died."

"I'm sorry," Bella murmured. "That *would* be difficult on young boys."

All at once, she realized this was James's history as well as Will's. And now she was absurdly interested in learning more. The gorgeous deep blues of the bay unfurled as far as the eye could see on her right but she ignored the spectacular view in favor of watching Will.

"Thanks." He glanced in the rearview mirror and double-checked the side mirrors before changing lanes. Will Rowling might very well be the most careful driver she'd ever met. "Look, let's just get all of it out on the table, shall we?"

"Depends on what you mean by *all* and *table*," she countered, a little puzzled by his abrupt change of subject.

Was this the part of the date where he expected her to air all her dirty laundry? She'd never had a long-term relationship, never wanted one, never thought about what went into establishing a foundation for one. Maybe they were supposed to spill deep, dark secrets right off the bat. She was *so* not on board with that.

"About the arranged marriage," he clarified. "We should clear the air."

"I'm not a lesbian looking for a fake husband and I don't have a crazy uncle chained up in the closet, if that's what you're fishing for."

He flashed a brief smile, the most genuine one yet, giving her a glimpse of what he might be like if he loosened up a little. "I wasn't fishing. I meant, I wanted to tell you that marriage wasn't my idea. I'm not after your title or your fortune."

"Oh. Then what are you after?"

The smile vanished as his expression smoothed out into the careful nothingness he'd worn since the first moment. "Aligning myself with the Montoros through marriage is advantageous for Rowling Energy. It would be fitting if we suited each other. That's the only reason I agreed to meet you."

Ouch. That was kind of painful. Was she actually disappointed his motives for this pseudo-date nearly matched hers word for word? Well, not really, but no woman liked to find out a man was only interested in her connections. At least he'd admitted it up front.

All on the table, indeed.

"Yeah. I get that. My father pretty much insisted that I get on a plane and fall in love. Not necessarily in that order." Her lips twisted into a grimace automatically.

"Since we're on the subject, would you really go through with it?"

"Marriage, you mean?" A shadow darkened his gaze though his eyes never left the road. "Rowling Energy is on the brink of gaining a starring role on the world's oil stage. Our alliance makes very good sense. My assumption is that you thought so as well."

"Wow." Bella blinked. Had he memorized that careful statement in one sitting or had he repeated it to himself in the shower for the past week so he could get it out without stumbling? "I bet you say that to all the girls."

If she'd ever had any shred of doubt about her ability to tolerate an arranged marriage, it had just been crushed under the heel of Will's ambition. There was no way she'd marry *anyone* unless the words *deliriously happy*, *scorching passion* and *eternal love* entered into the conversation about a hundred times first, and even then, vows would be far, far in the future.

His eyebrows rose slightly. "Meaning?"

She rolled her eyes. "I just hadn't pegged you for a romantic. That's all."

"It wasn't intended to be romantic," he explained, and she had the distinct impression he really thought she'd needed the clarification.

As nightmare dates went, this one hit the scale at about eleven point five. So much for being herself. *Check, please.*

"Will, I have a confession to make. Instead of seeing the sights, I'd really like a ride to Del Sol to visit my great-aunt Isabella." She blazed ahead before he could say no. "She's very sick and I'd like to see her. The timing is terrible, I realize, but my mind is just not where it should be for this outing."

Hitching a ride hadn't been her intent when she'd called him, but a savvy woman knew when to cut her losses and she might offend Will if she screamed bloody murder in his ear…which she might very well do if forced to spend five more minutes in his company.

This was not going to work out. Period. The last thing she wanted was to be stuck in a horrible marriage to a cold-hearted man, as her mother had been. If it didn't make you happy, why do it? Why do *anything* that didn't have fun written all over it?

"No problem." Will checked forty-seven points of the car's position and did a U-turn to head to the interior of the island. "I sensed that you were distracted. Glad to know the reason why."

Yet another reason they would never work—obviously Will read her about as well as she could read Spanish. She'd been the opposite of distracted, but only because she'd been hoping for a scrap of information about James, God knew why.

"Yeah, I'm a mess. My aunt has Parkinson's and her prognosis is…not good." Bella left it at that and choked back the wave of emotion for a situation she couldn't change and hated with all her heart.

Good thing Will wasn't her type. Now she had the morning free to visit Tía Isabella and she didn't even have to feel guilty about it because she'd gone out with Will, as ordered.

"I'm sorry," Will said earnestly. "You should definitely visit her. We can go out another time when you're feeling more in the mood for company and conversation."

Oh, so *she* was the problem in this equation? She scowled but didn't comment because then she might say something she couldn't take back about the stick up Will's butt. "Sure. That would be nice."

"Well, this may be an ill-timed invitation, then, but Rowling Energy is throwing a party tonight at my father's house for some of our elite associates. Would you care to attend as my date? Might be less pressure and more fun than being one-on-one like this, trapped in a small car."

How…reasonable. Oh, sure it was strictly an opportunity for Will to trot her out around his snobby business partners who only cared about whom he knew. She wasn't stupid. But a party was right up her ally and the magic word *fun* only sweetened the pot. With enough champagne, she might even forget the whole setup reeked of royal responsibility and actually have a good time. Less pressure, as advertised.

Maybe she'd misjudged Will Rowling. "I have the perfect dress."

"It's settled, then."

In no time and with only one internet map miscalculation, they found Tía Isabella's narrow cobblestone street in the heart of Del Sol. Like a true gentleman, Will helped Bella from the car at the door of her great aunt's rental house, and had a word with Tía Isabella's housekeeper to ensure Bella would have a return ride home. The housekeeper promised to have a car sent from Playa Del Onda, so Will took his leave.

All in all, Will seemed like a nice, upstanding guy. He was certainly handsome enough and had gorgeous aqua-colored eyes. Too bad she couldn't get the sexier, more exciting version she'd tripped over at the beach off her mind.

"Patrick James Rowling!"

James groaned and thought about ducking out the door of the sunroom and escaping Casa Rowling through the back gate. When his father three-named him, the outcome was never fun nor in his favor.

Actually, any time his father spoke to him it was unpleasant. Even being in the same room with Patrick Rowling reminded James that his mother was dead and it was his father's fault. Time healed all wounds—except the ones that never should have happened in the first place. If his father hadn't yelled at his mum, she wouldn't have left in tears that night back in Guildford. Then his mum's single-car accident would never have happened. He and

Will wouldn't have become motherless seven-year-old boys. The fractured Rowling family wouldn't have subsequently moved to Alma, where James didn't know anyone but Will, who was too shell-shocked to do anything other than mumble for nearly a year.

But all of that had happened and James would never forgive *or* forget.

As a result, James and Patrick gave each other a wide berth by mutual unspoken agreement, but it was harder to do when under the same roof. James should really get his own place, but he still wasn't sure if he planned to stay in Alma, so here he was.

Patrick Rowling, the man who'd named his first born after himself in a moment of pure narcissism, stormed into the sunroom and shoved a newspaper at James's chest with a great deal more force than necessary. "Explain this."

"This is commonly known as a newspaper." James drew out the syllables, ladening them with as much sarcasm as possible. "Many civilized nations employ this archaic method of communicating information and events to subscribers. Shall I delve into the finer points of journalism, or are we square on the purpose of this news vehicle?"

His father's face had grown a deeper, more satisfying shade of purple the longer James baited him. A thing of beauty. James moved his half-empty teacup out of the line of fire, in case of imminent explosion. It was Darjeeling and brewed perfectly.

"You can dispense with the smartass attitude. I've had more than enough of it from you to last a lifetime."

What he really meant was that he'd had enough of James doing the opposite of what Patrick commanded. But if James toed the line, how could he make his father pay for his sins? Of course, his father could never truly pay in a lifetime. The sad part was that James might have settled for an apology from his father for all the horrible things he'd caused. Or at least a confession. Instead, his father heaped praises on Will the Perfect Son and generally pretended James didn't exist.

Until James managed to get his attention by doing something beyond the pale. Like whatever had gotten the elder Rowling's dander up this time.

His father poked the paper again. "There's a rather risqué photo of you on the front page. Normally, I would brush it off as further proof you care nothing for propriety and only your own self-destruction. But as it's a photo of you with your brother's fiancée, I find it impossible to ignore."

"What?" His brother had a *fiancée*? "What are you talking about?"

James shoved his father's hand away and shifted the paper so he could see the front page. There it was, in full color. He whistled. What a gorgeous shot of Bella in his arms. Her hair all mussed and legs tangled in his. He might have to cut it out and frame it.

Wait... *Bella* was Will's fiancée? This was news to James. Last he'd heard, Bella planned to see how things went before committing to marriage. Had Will even *met* Bella yet?

"Your timing is impeccable, as always. Now that we're all caught up, please explain how you managed to create a scandal so quickly." Dear old Dad crossed his arms over the paunch he liked to pretend gave him a stately demeanor, but in reality, only made him look dumpy.

Obviously they were nowhere near caught up.

"Maybe that's Will—did you ever think of that?" James challenged mildly and went back to sipping his tea because he had a feeling he'd need the fortification.

"Your brother is with the Montoro princess as we speak and it's their first meeting."

Montoro princess. Really? James rolled his eyes. His father couldn't be more pretentious if he tried. "If they hadn't even met until today, how are they already engaged?"

Waving his hand with a snort, Patrick gave him a withering look. "Merely a formality. They will be engaged, mark my words. So as far as you're concerned, she's your brother's fiancée. Will is quite determined to woo her and I've never seen him fail at anything he set his mind to."

Despite what should be good news—his father had deliberately thrown the word *fiancée* in James's face even though it wasn't true—James's gut twisted at the thought of Will and Bella together. Why, he couldn't explain, when he'd been the one to suggest Bella should ring Will. Obviously, she'd taken his advice and rather quickly, too. He'd just run into her in town yesterday.

"Smashing. I hope they're having a fantastic time and fall madly in love so they can give you lots of royal babies, since that's the most important accomplishment a Rowling could hope to achieve." The sentiment had started out sincerely but halfway through, disappointment had tilted his mood. James lived his life with few regrets but stepping aside so Will had a fair shot with Bella ranked as a decision he'd questioned more than once.

"Don't change the subject. If you deliberately staged that picture with the princess to ruin your brother's chances, the consequences will be dire," his father warned.

James couldn't quite bite back the laugh that burst out. "Oh, please, no. Perhaps you'll disown me?"

What else could his father possibly do to him besides constantly express his displeasure in everything James did? Being signed with Real Madrid hadn't rated a mention. Being named captain of the Alma World Cup team wasn't worthy enough of a feat to get a comment.

Oh, but miss a goal—that had earned James an earful.

Patrick leaned forward, shoving his nose into James's space and into his business all at the same time. "If you don't stay away from the Montoro princess, I will personally ensure you never play football again."

James scoffed. "You're off your trolley. You have no power in my world."

And neither did James, not now. It pricked at his temper that his father would choose that method to strike at him. Patrick clearly failed to comprehend his son's life crisis if he didn't already know that James had managed to thoroughly subvert his own career with no help from anyone.

The threat gave him a perverse desire to prove he could come back from the twin failures of a missed goal and a dropped contract. He needed to play, if for no other reason than to show everyone James Rowling couldn't be kept down.

"Perhaps. Do you want to wager on that?"

James waved nonchalantly with one hand and clenched the other into a tight fist. What colossal nerve. A supreme act of will kept the fist in his lap, though letting it fly against the nearby wall might have ended the conversation quite effectively.

"Seems like pretty good odds to me, so don't be surprised if I roll the dice with Bella." He waggled his brows. "I think that picture is enough of an indicator that she fancies me, don't you think?"

Which might have been true when the picture was snapped, but probably wasn't now that he'd stepped aside. Will would be his charming self and Bella would realize that she could have the best of both worlds—the "right" Rowling and her father's blessing. Probably better for everyone, all the way around.

Deep down, James didn't believe that in the slightest. He and Bella had a spark between them, which wouldn't vanish with a hundred warnings from the old geezer.

"The monarchy is in its fledgling stages." Patrick hesitated for the first time since barging into the sunroom and James got the impression he was choosing his words carefully. "Rowling Energy has a unique opportunity to solidify our allegiance and favor through the tie of marriage. There is only one Montoro princess."

"And only one heir to the company," James said sourly. "I get it. Will's the only one good enough for her."

His father sighed. The weariness that carved lines into his face around his mouth had aged him quickly and added a vulnerability to his expression that James hadn't been prepared for. Patrick had never been anything other than formidable for as long as James could remember.

"I would welcome you at Rowling Energy if you expressed but a smidgen of determination and interest." Then his father hardened back into the corporate stooge he'd become since entering into the high stakes oil market. Dad had too many zeroes in his bank account balance to truly be in touch with his humanity. "Will has done both, with remarkable success. If you would think of someone other than yourself, you'd realize that Will has much to gain from this alliance. I will not be at the helm of Rowling forever. Will needs every advantage."

Guilt. The best weapon. And it might have worked if James truly believed all that drivel. Marrying into the royal family was about his father's ambition, not Will's.

"Maybe we should let Bella sort it on her own, eh?" James suggested mildly. He didn't mind losing to Will, as long as the contest was fair.

"There's nothing to sort," his father thundered, growing purple again. "Stay away from her. Period. No more risqué pictures. No more contact. Do not ruin this for your brother."

To put the cap on his mandate, Patrick Rowling stormed from the sun-room in much the same manner as he entered it. Except now Bella Montoro had been transformed into the ripest forbidden fruit.

James had never met a scandal he didn't want to dive headlong into, especially when it involved a gorgeous woman who clearly had the hots for him. Pissing his father off at the same time James introduced himself to the pleasures of Princess Bella was just a sweet bonus.

Four

Bella spent two wonderful hours catching up with her great aunt Isabella, but the sickly woman grew tired so easily. Coupled with the fact that Isabella's advanced Parkinson's disease meant she was bedridden, it was difficult for Bella to witness her once-vibrant aunt in this condition. Regardless, she kept a bright smile pasted on throughout their visit.

But even Bella could see it was time for her to leave lest she overtire Isabella.

Before she asked her aunt's nurse to call a cab, Bella took Isabella's hand and brought it to her cheek. "I'm glad you decided to come to Alma."

"This is where I choose to die," Isabella said simply with a half smile, the only facial expression she could still muster. "I will see Gabriel become king and my life will be complete."

"I wish you wouldn't say things like that."

It was depressing and wretched to think of the world spinning on without Isabella, whom Bella loved unconditionally and vice versa. Her throat burned with grief and unreconciled anger over a circumstance she couldn't change.

Geez, she'd been less upset when her mother had left. That had at least made sense. Parkinson's disease did not.

"It is but truth. All of us must make our lives what we can in the time allotted to us." Isabella paused, her voice catching. "Tell me. Have you visited the farmhouse yet?"

"What farmhouse?" Had her father mentioned something about a farmhouse and she'd been too busy ignoring him to remember? Shoot. She'd have done anything Isabella asked, even if the request came via her father.

"Oh, dear." Her aunt closed her eyes for a moment. "No, I don't believe I imagined it. It's white. In the country. Aldeia Dormer. Very important. My mother told me and Rafael of it. My brother is gone, God rest his soul, so I'm telling you. You must find it and…"

Trailing off with a blank expression, Isabella sat silent for a moment, her hand shaking uncontrollably inside Bella's as it often had even before her aunt's disease had progressed to include forgetfulness and the inability to walk.

"I'll find the farmhouse," Bella promised. "What should I do when I find it?"

"The countryside is lovely in the spring," her aunt said with bright cheer. "You take your young man with you and enjoy the ride."

"Yes, ma'am." Bella smiled. Wouldn't it be nice to actually have a "young man" in the sweet, old-fashioned sense that Isabella had meant? Bella had only mentioned Will because her father had apparently told Isabella all about the stupid arranged marriage. It was the first thing her aunt had asked after.

"Wear a red dress to the party tonight and take photographs." Isabella closed her eyes and just when Bella thought she'd fallen asleep, she murmured, "Remember we all have a responsibility to our blood. And to Alma. I wish Rafael could be here to see his grandson take the throne."

"Red dress it is," Bella said, skipping over the royal responsibility part because she'd had enough of that for a lifetime.

Wasn't it enough that she was going to the party as Will's date when she'd rather be meeting James there? And if James happened to show, would it be so much of a crime if she danced with him once or twice? She'd still be Will's date, just the way everyone wanted, but would also give herself the opportunity to find out if James had pawned her off on his brother because he didn't like her or because of some other reason.

Guilt cramped her stomach as her aunt remained silent. Yeah, so maybe Bella considered it a possible bonus that she might run into James at the party. Was that so bad?

"Isabella, I—" Bella bit her lip before she spilled all her angst and doubt over what her father had asked her to do by giving Will a chance. Her aunt was tired and didn't need to be burdened with Bella's problems.

"The farmhouse. It's part of the Montoro legacy, passed down from the original Rafael Montoro I, to his son Rafael II. And then to his son Rafael III. Remember the farmhouse, child," her aunt wheezed out in the pause.

"I will." Before she could change her mind again, Bella went for broke. "But I might take a different young man with me than the one my father wants me to marry. Would that be a bad thing?"

"You must make your own choices," her aunt advised softly. "But beware. All choices have consequences. Be sure you are prepared to face them."

Isabella's shaking hand went slack as she slipped off into sleep for real this time. Bella took her leave reluctantly and slid into the waiting car her father had sent for her, wishing her aunt wasn't so sick that they could only have half of a conversation.

What had Isabella meant by her warning? During the hour-long ride back to Playa Del Onda, Bella grappled with it. Unfortunately, she had a sinking feeling she knew precisely what her aunt had been attempting to tell her. Being born during a hurricane hadn't infused Bella with a curse that meant she'd always leave broken hearts in her wake. It was her own decisions that had consequences, and if she wanted to be a better person than she'd been in Miami, she had to make different, more conscious choices.

Hurricane Bella couldn't cut a swath through Alma, leaving broken pieces of her brother's reign in her wake. Or broken pieces of her father's agreement with Will's father. Mentioning all of Bella's ancestors hadn't been an accident—Isabella wanted her to remember her roots.

Either she had try for real with Will and then tell him firmly it wasn't going to work, or she had to skip the party. It wasn't fair to anyone to go with the intention of running into James for any reason.

By the time the party rolled around, Bella was second-guessing the red dress. She'd never worn it before but distinctly remembered loving it when she'd tried it on at the boutique in Bal Harbour. Now that she had it on… the plunging neckline and high slit in the skirt revealed a shocking amount of flesh. But she'd promised Isabella she'd wear red, and it was too late to find another dress.

And honestly, she looked divine in it, so… Sexy red dress got the thumbs up. If she and Will were going to get along, he'd have to accept that she liked to feel beautiful in what she wore. This dress filled the bill. And then some. If a neckline that plunged all the way to the dress's waistband caused a problem with Rowling's business associates, better she and Will both find out now they weren't a good match.

The chauffeur helped her into the back of the Montoro car. Thankfully, Will hadn't offered to pick her up so she had an easy escape if need be. *Please God, don't let me need an escape.*

Within ten minutes, the car had joined the line of Bentleys, Jaguars and limousines inching their way to the front steps of the Rowling mansion. Like the Montoros' house, the Rowlings' Playa Del Onda residence overlooked the bay. She smiled at the lovely sight of the darkened water dotted with lighted boats.

When Bella entered the double front doors, Will approached her immediately, as if he'd been waiting for her. His pleasant but slightly blank expression from earlier was still firmly in place and she bit back a groan. How long were they going to act like polite strangers?

Jaw set firmly, Will never glanced below her shoulders. Which sort of defeated the purpose of such a racy dress. What was the point of showing half her torso if a man wasn't even going to look at it?

"Bella, so nice to see you again," Will murmured and handed her a champagne flute. "That dress is stunning."

Okay, he'd just earned back all the points that he'd lost. "Thanks. Nice to see you, too."

His tuxedo, clearly custom-cut and very European, gave him a sophisticated look that set him slightly apart from the other male guests, most of whom were older and more portly. Will was easy on the eyes and commanded himself with confidence. She could do worse.

Will cleared his throat. "Did you have a nice afternoon?"

"Yes. You?"

"Dandy."

She sipped her champagne as the conversation ground to a halt. Painfully. Gah, normally she thrived on conversation and loved exchanging observations, jokes, witty repartee. Something.

The hushed crowd murmured around them and the tinkle of chamber music floated between the snippets of dialogue, some in English, some in Spanish. Or Portuguese.

Bella still couldn't tell the difference between the two despite hearing Spanish spoken by Miami residents of Cuban descent for most of her life.

She spotted her cousin Juan Carlos Salazar across the room and nearly groaned. While they'd grown up together after his parents died, he'd always been too serious. Why wasn't he in Del Sol managing something?

Of course, he looked up at that moment and their gazes met. He wove through the crowd to clasp Will's hand and murmur his appreciation for the party to his hosts. Juan Carlos was the kind of guy who always did the right thing and at the same time, made everyone else look as if they were doing the wrong thing. It was a skill.

"Bella, are you enjoying the party?" he asked politely.

"Very much," she lied, just as politely because she had skills, too, just not any that Juan Carlos would appreciate. "I saw Tía Isabella. I'm so glad she decided to come to Alma."

"I am as well. Though she probably shouldn't be traveling." Juan Carlos frowned over his grandmother's stubbornness, which Bella had always thought was one of her best traits. "Uncle Rafael tried to talk her out of it but she insisted."

The Montoros all had a stubborn streak but Bella's father took the cake. Time for a new subject. "How are things in the finance business?"

"Very well, thank you." He shot Will a cryptic glance. "Better now that you're in Alma working toward important alliances."

She kept her eyes from rolling. Barely. "Yes, let's hear it for alliances."

Juan Carlos and Will launched into a conversation with too many five-syllable words for normal humans to understand, so Bella amused herself by scrutinizing Will as he talked, hoping to gather more clues about his real personality.

As he spoke to Juan Carlos, his attention wandered, and Bella watched him watch a diminutive dark-haired woman in serviceable gray exit by a side door well away from the partygoers. An unfamiliar snap in Will's gaze had her wondering who the woman was. Or rather, who she was to Will. The woman's dress clearly marked her as the help.

Will didn't even seem to notice when Juan Carlos excused himself.

"Do you need to attend to a problem with the servants?" Bella inquired politely.

She'd gone to enough of her parents' parties to know that a good host kept one eye on the buffet and the other on the bar. Which was why she liked attending parties, not throwing them.

"No. No problem," Will said grimly and forced his gaze back to Bella's face. But his mind was clearly elsewhere.

Which told her quite a bit more about the situation than Will probably intended. Perhaps the dark-haired woman represented at least a partial answer for why Will seemed both pained by Bella's presence and alternatively agreeable to a marriage of convenience.

Bella had come to the party as requested by God and everyone and she deserved a chance with Will. He owed it to her, regardless of whether he had something going on with the diminutive maid.

"Look, Will—"

"Let's dance." He grabbed her hand and led her to the dance floor without waiting for an answer, off-loading their champagne glasses onto a waiter's tray as they passed by.

Okay, then. Dancing happened to be one of her favorite things about parties, along with dressing up and laughing in a private corner with someone she planned to let strip her naked afterward.

For some reason, the thought of getting naked with Will made her skin crawl. Two out of three wasn't bad, though, was it?

The quartet seated in the corner had switched from chamber music to a slightly less boring bossa nova–inspired piece. Not great, but she had half a chance of finding a groove at least.

Was this how the people of Alma partied? Or had the glitzy Miami social scene spoiled her? Surely not. Alma was one of the wealthiest countries in the European Union. What was she missing?

Halfway into the song, Will had yet to say a word and his impersonal hand at her waist might as well have belonged to an eighty-year-old grandfather. This might go down in history as the first time a man under thirty had danced with her and not used it as an excuse to pull her into his strong embrace. It was as if Will had actually wanted to *dance* or something.

None of this screamed, "I'm into you."

Perhaps the problem with this party lay with the host, not the country. Will might need a little encouragement to loosen up.

When the interminably long dance finally ended, Bella smiled and fanned herself as if she'd grown overheated. "My, it's a little warm in here."

Will nodded. "I'll get you another glass of champagne."

Before he could disappear, she stopped him with a hand on his arm, deliberately leaning into it to make the point. "That's okay. Let's go out on the terrace and talk."

The whole point was to get to know each other. The car trip hadn't worked. Dancing hadn't worked. They needed to try something else.

"Maybe in a few minutes," Will said with a glance around the room at large. "After I've played the proper host."

Disappointment pulled at her mouth but she refused to let a frown ruin her lipstick. "I hope you won't mind if I escape the heat for a bit by myself."

For a moment, she wondered if he'd really let her go.

He'd invited her, after all, and hadn't introduced her to one person yet. This was supposed to be a date, wasn't it?

"Certainly." Will inclined his head toward the double glass doors off the great room. "I'll find you later."

Fuming, Bella wound through the guests to the terrace—by herself!—and wondered when she'd lost her edge. Clearly a secluded terrace with a blonde American in half a dress didn't appeal to Will Rowling. What did—dark-haired housekeepers?

Great, she thought sourly. Bella had come to the party with the genuine intent of seeing where things might go with Will, because she said she would. Because she'd bought into the hoopla of being a princess, which came with responsibilities she'd never asked for nor wanted any part of.

But she'd done it, only to be hit over the head with the brutal truth yet again. The man her father wanted her to marry had less than zero interest in her as a person. She wouldn't be surprised to learn Will was perfectly okay with a hard-core marriage of convenience, complete with separate bedrooms and a paramour on the side.

Sounded an awful lot like her parents' marriage, and *that* she wanted no part of.

She shuddered, despondent all at once. Was it asking too much for someone to care what she would actually have to sacrifice with this mess her father had created?

The night was breathtaking, studded with stars and a crescent moon. Still, half the stone terrace lay in shadow, which went perfectly with her mood. Leaning on the railing, she glanced down into the crash of ocean against the cliff below.

"Thinking of jumping?"

The male voice emanating from behind her skittered down her spine, washing her in a myriad of emotions as her heart rolled and her pulse quickened. But she didn't turn to face him because she was afraid if she actually glimpsed

James for even a fraction of a second, all of her steely resolve to work things out with his brother would melt like
gelato in the sun. And the leftover hot sticky mess would
be difficult to clean up indeed.

"Would you stop me?" she murmured.

"No. I'd hold your hand all the way down, though."

Her eyelids fluttered closed. How had he managed to
make that sound so daringly romantic?

The atmosphere shifted as he moved closer. She could
feel him behind her, hear the intake of his breath. A sense
of anticipation grew in the silence, peppering her skin with
goose pimples and awareness.

Before it grew too intense, she blurted out, "I called
Will."

James wasn't for her. She needed to keep reminding
herself that.

"I gathered that." He sounded amused and reckless simultaneously. "I plan to personally drive him to the eye
doctor tomorrow."

"Oh? Is he having problems with his eyes?"

"Obviously. Only a blind man would let you out of his
sight, especially if he knew you planned to be alone on a
moonlit terrace. Any plonker could be out here, waiting
to ravish you."

She'd been so wrong. Other than a similar accent,
James's voice was nothing like Will's. Will had yet to lose
the ice while James breathed pure fire when he spoke.

"Good thing his moral, upstanding brother is the only
one out here. He wouldn't dare lay a finger on me."

Maybe James needed a reminder that Bella and Will
were supposed to get married, too. After all James had
been the one to cool things off between the two of them,
which had absolutely been the right thing to do.

"Yeah? While Will's having his eyes examined, maybe
I'll get my IQ checked, then," James said silkily.

"Feeling a little brainless this evening?"

"I definitely feel like my brain has turned to mush. I think it's that dress. Your bare back framed by that little bit of fabric…it makes me imagine all sorts of things that probably aren't very smart." The frank appreciation in his voice floated through the still night, wrapping around her deliciously. "Let me see the front."

"No." Feeling exposed all at once, she crossed her arms. "I didn't wear this dress for you."

"Shame. I'm the only one here who fully appreciates what's underneath it."

In a flash, her core heated with the memory of being in James's arms on the beach, his hard body flush with hers.

"You shouldn't speak to me like that," she said primly, and nearly gasped as he drew achingly close to her back. She could sense his heat and it called to her.

"Because you don't like it?" he murmured, his mouth not two inches from her ear in a deliberate tease that shot sensation down the back of her throat.

Her breath caught and she gripped the railing lest her weak knees give out. "Because I do."

He laughed and it spiked through her with fingers of warmth.

"That's right," he said smoothly, as if recalling something critically important. "You're weak and liable to give in to temptation. Everything I've always wanted in a woman."

"That's so funny. I'd swear you brushed me off at our last meeting," she couldn't help but reply. It still stung, despite all the reasons why she suspected he'd done so.

"I did," he admitted in an unprecedented moment of honesty. Most men she'd ever met would have tried to pass it off, as if she'd been mistaken. "You know why."

"Because you're not interested."

The colorful curse he muttered made her smile for some reason. "You need *your* IQ checked if you believe that."

"Because my father scared you off?"

"Not even close."

"Because I'm supposed to be with Will," she said definitively and wished it hadn't come out sounding so bitter.

"Yes." James paused as if to let that sink in. "Trust me. It was not easy. But he's my brother."

"So you're okay with it if I marry Will?"

She imagined Christmas. That would be fun, to sit next to her boring husband who was screwing another woman on the side while the man she'd been dreaming about sat across the room. As Mr. Rowling carved the turkey, she could bask in the warm knowledge that she'd furthered a bunch of male ambition with her sacrifice to the royal cause.

"Is that what you want?" he asked quietly, his voice floating out on the still night air.

The question startled her. She had a choice. Of course she did. And now she needed to make it, once and for all.

The night seemed to hold its breath as it waited for her to speak. This was it, the moment of truth. She could end this dangerous attraction to the wrong brother forever by simply saying yes. James would walk away.

Something shifted inside, warring with all the sermons on responsibility and family obligations. And she couldn't stand it any longer.

She didn't want Will.

Whirling, she faced James, greedily drinking him, cataloguing the subtle differences in his features. He and Will weren't identical, not to her. The variances were in the way James looked at her, the way her body reacted. The heat in this man's gaze couldn't be mistaken. He was all James and 100 percent the object of her desire.

She let her gaze travel over his gorgeous body, clad in a tuxedo that fit like an extension of his skin, fluid and beautiful. And she wanted nothing more than to see the secrets it hid so carefully beneath the fabric.

He raked her with a once-over in kind that quickened her

core with delicious tightness. *That* was how a man should look at you in such a dress. As if he'd been presented with every last fantasy in one package.

"The back was good," he rasped, his voice clogged with undisguised desire. "But the front…"

Delighted that she'd complied with Isabella's fortuitous request to wear red, she smiled. "I do like a man at a loss for words."

Moonlight played over his features and glinted off the obscenely expensive watch on his wrist as he swept up her hand and drew her closer. So close, she could almost hear his heart beating.

"Actions speak louder and all that." His arm slid around her waist, pulling her to within a hairsbreadth of his body and she ached for him to close the distance. "Plus, I didn't want to miss your answer."

"Answer to what?"

He lowered his head to murmur in her ear, "What it is that you want."

If she wanted Will, Bella had about two seconds to say so, or James would be presenting the woman in his arms with some hot and heavy temptation. He preferred to get on the same page before that happened because he had a bad feeling *he* might be the weak one on this terrace.

With so much forbidden fruit decked out in a mouthwatering dress that screamed sin and sex, he'd rather not put his ability to resist Bella to the test. But he would resist if she said no, regardless of whether he'd been baiting her in hopes of getting her to break first. Because then he'd be in the clear if she came on to him, right?

The sharp intake of her breath and a sensuous lift of her lips gave him all the nonverbal communication he needed. Then she put the icing on it with a succinct, "Will who?"

The gap between their bodies slowly vanished until their torsos brushed, but he couldn't have said if he closed it or she did. This was not what he'd planned when Bella had inadvertently joined him on the terrace, but it was certainly what he'd fantasized might happen if she'd given him the slightest encouragement.

With her lithe little body teasing his, her curves scarcely contained by that outrageous dress, he could hardly get his mind in gear long enough to form complete sentences. "You could have just said that from the outset."

"You could have said *call me instead of Will* on the boardwalk."

Not if he'd hoped to sleep at night he couldn't have. Of course, he'd done little of that anyway, tossing and turning as he imagined this gorgeous, vibrant woman with his brother.

He nodded in concession, hardly breathing for fear of alerting her to how very turned on he was. "It was my one noble gesture for the decade. Don't expect another one."

She laughed and he felt it vibrate against his rock-hard lower half, which did not improve matters down below. Dangerous and forbidden did it for him in the worst way and when both came in a package like Bella, he might as well surrender to the moment right now. They were both aware of where this was headed, weren't they?

"You know, you spend a lot of time blabbing about how wicked you are, but I've yet to see evidence of it." Her brow arched saucily, turning silvery in the moonlight. "What happened to my man of action?"

"You wanna play?" he growled and slid his hand to the small of her back, pushing her deep into the crevices of his body. "Here's round one of How Bad Can James Be?"

Tipping up her head, he captured her smart mouth with his lips, molding them shut while tasting her simultaneously. What started as a shut-up kiss instantly transformed, becoming slow and sensuous and exploratory as he delved into her sweetness. She met him stroke for stroke, angle for angle, silently begging him to take her deeper.

He *finally* had Bella in his arms. Exactly as he'd ached to have her since releasing her from their first embrace.

Still in the throes of an amazing kiss he never wanted to end, he pinned her against the stone railing, wedging their bodies tight and leaving his hands free to roam where they pleased.

And that creamy expanse of flesh from neck to waist had been calling his name for an eternity. Almost groaning with the pleasure of her mouth under his, he slid a palm north to let his fingertips familiarize themselves with her bare back. Heated, smooth flesh greeted his touch. Greedily, he caressed it all and she moaned throatily, flattening her back against his palm, pleading for more.

He gave it to her.

Nearly mindless with the scent of Bella filling his head, he held her closer in his arms, sliding a knee between her legs to rub at her sweet spot. Heavenly. He wanted to touch every part of her, to taste what he'd touched. To take them both to nirvana again and again as the blistering, forbidden attraction between them was allowed free reign once and for all.

Suddenly, she tore her mouth free and moved out of reach, breathing heavily. "That was...um—"

"Yeah." Earthshaking. Unprecedented. Hotter than Brazil in the summer. "Come back so I can do it again."

He reached for her and for a second, he thought she was going to do it. Her body swayed toward him and his mouth tingled in anticipation of locking on to those lips of hers again.

But then she shook her head, backing up another step. "I can't be with you like this. It's not fair to Will. We have to straighten everything out first."

Bloody hell. Will hadn't crossed his mind once while James kissed his brother's date. Any of dear Father's business cronies could have come upon them on the terrace and there were few people in Alma who confused the twins.

Everyone knew James had inherited Grandfather Rowling's priceless antique watch—much to Patrick's chagrin. It was the first thing people looked for when in need of a handy way to identify the brothers.

"Yes, of course you're right." Though his body ached to yank her back into his arms, he gave her a pained smile instead. "This isn't over."

"Oh, no." She shot him an indecipherable look. "Not by half. The next time you and I are together, I will be naked and screaming your name."

His eyelids flew shut and he groaned. "Why can't that happen tonight?"

"Because as far as the rest of the world is concerned, Will is the Rowling I'm supposed to be with. I've had too many scandals mess up my life to knowingly create a preventable one. That's why it must be perfectly clear to everyone that Will and I are not getting married before you and I get naked."

Grimly, he nodded, the photo of the two of them on the front page fresh in his mind. They should probably address that, too, at some point, but he'd topped out on issues he could reasonably deal with.

"You should go. And go fast before I change my mind." Or lose it. "I'm fresh out of nobility *and* the capacity to resist you."

She whirled and fled. He watched her beautiful back as she disappeared inside the house, and then went in search of a bottle of Jameson to get him through what promised to be a long night indeed.

Five

James cornered Will in his Rowling Energy office at 9:05 a.m. This was the earliest James could recall being awake, dressed and out of the house in quite some time. But this cat-and-mouse game had grown tiresome, and the man who shared his last name, his blood and once upon a time, had even shared a womb, had the power to end it.

"Will."

James didn't cross the threshold out of respect for the fact that he was on his brother's turf. Instead, he waited for him to glance up from his report. Will's expression remained composed, though James caught a flash of surprise in the depths of his gaze, which the Master of Calm quickly banked.

"Yes?"

And now they'd officially exchanged two words this week. Actually, James couldn't remember the last time they *had* talked. They'd never been close. Hell, they were rarely on the same continent, but that wasn't really the reason. The divide had started the night their mum died and grown exponentially over the years.

"We have to talk. Can I come in?"

"Since you're here already, I suppose." Will's long-suffering sigh said he deserved a medal for seeing James on such short notice.

James bit back the sarcasm strictly because he was the one with the mission, though his brother's condescension pricked at his temper. The brothers would never see eye to eye, though why James cared was beyond him.

They'd taken different paths in dealing with the single most defining year of their lives, Will choosing to compensate for the loss of everything familiar by becoming whatever their father said, as long as the remaining parent paid attention to him.

James compensated for his mother's death by lashing out at his father, refusing to forgive the ultimate crime—though James could never run far enough or get into enough trouble to drown out the sound of his own conscience. While he'd never forgive his father for driving his mum out into the rainy night, back in the deepest reaches of his soul, he blamed himself more.

Because he'd heard them arguing and hadn't done anything. What if he'd run out of his hiding place to grab on to his mum and beg her not to leave? She wouldn't have. He knew she wouldn't have. But she'd probably assumed both her boys were asleep. One of them had been.

James took a deep, not at all calming breath as he settled into one of the wingback chairs flanking Will's desk. "It's about Bella."

"Ms. Montoro? What about her?"

James rolled his eyes. "Well, I was going to ask how serious you are about her, but that pretty much told me."

"How serious I…" Will's gaze narrowed. "You've got the hots for her."

That didn't begin to describe what had happened on the terrace last night. Or every moment since the princess had blinked up at him with those big eyes after upending his world. "If you're determined to see this arranged marriage through, I won't stand in your way."

Steepling his hands, Will sat back in his chair, contemplating James carefully. "Really? That's a first."

"What's that supposed to mean?"

"When was the last time you considered anyone above yourself? Especially when a woman is involved."

James was halfway out of his seat before he checked himself. Fisting his hand in his lap as he sat back down, he forced a smile. "I won't apologize for looking out for myself. No one else does. But I will concede the point. This woman is different."

He nearly choked on the words he hadn't consciously planned to say. But it was true. Bella wasn't like anyone else he'd ever met.

Smirking, Will nodded once. "Because she's earmarked for me."

Is that what he thought this was about? That James had come to Will in a fit of jealousy?

"Earmarked? Is that how you talk about her? Bella's a person, not a pile of money."

The nerve. Will had spent too much time in budget meetings if he equated a flesh-and-blood woman with reserve funds.

"Yes. But surely you realize we're talking about an arranged marriage. It's a form of currency, dating back to the dawn of time. No one is under a different impression."

James had a sick sort of realization that what Will described was probably quite right. Two fathers had struck a deal, bargaining away their children's future with no thought to what could or should go into a marriage decision. Namely, the desires of the bride and groom in question.

If he didn't miss his guess, Will accepted that. Embraced it. Thought it was a brilliant idea.

If James had known this was the case, he'd have taken

Bella straight to his room last night and skipped the formality of giving his brother a heads-up that things had changed. "Bella has a different impression. She's not interested in being bought *or* sold."

Will eyed him thoughtfully. "Why hasn't she come to me herself?"

"Because this is between you and me, brother. She didn't want to get into the middle of it." Which he fully appreciated, whether Will did or not. James had to look at himself in the mirror for the rest of his life and he'd prefer not to see his own guilty conscience staring back at him. "And she won't. Neither will I allow her to. If you say you're planning to pursue this ridiculous idea of aligning Rowling Energy to the Montoros through marriage, so be it. Just be sure you treat her like a princess."

Maybe James wasn't done being noble after all. He'd fully expected to walk in here and demand that Will release Bella from their fathers' agreement. But somehow he'd wound up caring more about Bella and how she was being marginalized than whether he'd cleared the way to sleep with her.

"I see." Comprehension dawned in Will's gaze. "You're the reason she left the party so quickly last night. Last I knew, she'd gone out on the terrace for some air, and the next, she'd begged off with a headache."

"I'm sorry," James said earnestly. "I didn't plan for any of this to happen. But Bella deserves better than to be thought of as currency. She's funny and incredible and—"

He broke off before he said something he couldn't take back, like *she's the hottest kisser I've ever met.* Somehow, he didn't think that would go over well.

"You've got it bad." Will didn't bother to hide his smirk. "Never would have thought I'd see the day. She's really got you wrapped, doesn't she?"

As if Bella called the shots or something? James tried to do the right thing one time and all he got was grief.

"She's important," James growled. "That's all."

Will grinned mischievously, looking more like Mum than he usually did. "Ha. I wouldn't be surprised if you proposed to her before her brother's coronation."

"Propose? You mean ask her to marry me?" Ice slid down James's spine and he threw up a hand to stave off the rest of Will's outpouring of madness. "That's not what's going on here. We're just… I'm not… It's that I didn't want to poach on your territory. It's not sporting."

"Gabriella. Paulinha. Abril." Ticking them off on his fingers, Will cocked his head. "I think there was another one, but her name escapes me."

Revisionist history of the worst kind. "If I recall, Abril went home with you. Despite the fact that I saw her first."

"But that's my point. We've competed over women in the past. But you have never come to me first." Will's phone rang, but he ignored the shrill buzz. "We've always subscribed to the may-the-best-man-win philosophy. So obviously Bella is the one."

Yeah, the one James wanted in his bed. That was it. Once they burned off the blinding attraction, they'd part amicably. "No way. You're reading into this."

An even worse thought occurred to him then. Did *Bella* think there was more going on here? Like maybe James wanted to take Will's place in the diabolical bridal bargain their fathers had struck? Surely not. There'd been plenty of flirting, and lots of use of the word *naked*. But no one had said anything about being serious.

Will shook his head, a smile still tugging at his lips. "I don't think so. Put your money where your mouth is."

"A bet? Seriously?" All the long hours in the service of Patrick Rowling's ego had obviously pickled his brother's brain.

"As a heart attack." Nodding at James's wrist, he pursed his lips for a beat. "Grandfather's watch. That's how bad I think you've got it. If you propose to Bella before Gabriel Montoro takes the throne, you give it to me, free and clear."

James laughed. "You are so on."

What a stupid thing to ask for. Will knew how much James loved his grandfather's watch. It was one of the few mementos from England that James had left, and Grandfather had given it to him on his eighteenth birthday. Losing it was not happening. Proposing to Bella was not happening, before the coronation or after.

Sucker's bet. James rubbed his hands together gleefully. "If I don't propose, then what? Make this worth my while."

"I'll come up with something."

James and Will shook on it.

"So this means the arranged marriage is totally off, right?" No point in going through all of this just to find out Will was toying with him.

"Totally off."

A glint in his brother's eye caught his crossways. "You were never interested in her."

"Never," Will confirmed solemnly. "Bella's got all the right parts and everything, and she would have opened up some interesting possibilities for Rowling. But she's not my type. I'm fine with cancelling the whole agreement."

Not his type. That was insane. How could Bella not be every red-blooded man's type? "You'll talk to Father?"

"Sure. It's better coming from me anyway. Now get out so I can run this company."

James got out. He had a naked princess in his future after all.

Bella's eyes started to ache after thirty minutes of trying to read the tiny map print.

"I give up," she muttered and switched off the lamp adorning her bedside table.

All of the words were in Spanish anyway. How was she

supposed to use this map Alex Ramon's assistant had given her to find the farmhouse Tía Isabella had mentioned?

When Bella had asked Rafael about it, he sent her to speak with Alex Ramon, Alma's deputy prime minister of commerce. His assistant helped her scour the royal archives until they found one solitary mention of the abandoned farmhouse in a long list of Montoro holdings. But there was little to go on location-wise other than *Aldeia Dormer*, the name of a tiny village.

At least Mr. Ramon's assistant had managed to find the key to the property tucked away in a filing cabinet, a real plus. Assuming the key still worked, that was.

Now she just had to find the farmhouse. Tía Isabella's urgency had taken root, not to mention a healthy dose of curiosity about how an old farmhouse counted as part of a legacy. There was no way Bella would actually give up.

Plus, finding the farmhouse was a project, her gift to Isabella. Bella needed a local with plenty of time on his hands and access to a vehicle to help her scour the countryside for this farmhouse. And who didn't mind ditching her babysitters-slash-security guys.

Her phone rang. She glanced at it and frowned at the unfamiliar number. That was the second time today and the first caller had been Will. Dare she hope this might be the brother she'd rather talk to? "Hello?"

"You haven't been to the beach all day." James's smooth voice slid through her like silk.

"Was I supposed to be at the beach?" With a wide grin, she flipped over on her back to stare at the ceiling above her bed, completely uninterested in cryptic maps now that she had a much better distraction.

"How else am I supposed to run into you?" he pointed out. "You never gave me your phone number."

Because he'd never asked. "Yet it appears I'm speaking to you on the phone at this very minute."

"A bloke has to be resourceful around this island if he wants to ask a princess out on a date. Apparently."

A little thrill burst through her midsection. After walking away from James at the party, she'd mentally prepared for any eventuality. A woman didn't get between brothers, and James, for all his squawking about being a bad boy, wouldn't have pursued her if Will had called dibs.

And then there was always the possibility James would grow weary of all the obstacles between them. She didn't have any guarantees she'd even hear from him again.

"This is your idea of resourceful? What did you do, hit up Will for my phone number?"

James cleared his throat. "I talked to him. About us."

That was pretty much an admission of how he'd gotten her number. "Yeah. He told me."

"Well, half my battle is won. My day will be complete if you would kindly get your gorgeous rear down to the beach."

Scrambling from the bed, Bella tore off her shorts as she dashed for the dresser and wedged the phone under her chin to pull out a bikini. "What if I'm busy?"

"Cancel. In fact, cancel everything for the rest of the day."

The rest of the day with James? She was so on board with that plan, she could hardly keep the giddiness in check. But she couldn't let *him* know how much she was into him. That was rule number one.

"You'll have to give me more than that in order for me to clear my schedule." She whipped her shirt off one-handed, knocking the phone to the floor. She cursed and dove for it. "I'm American. We invented high-maintenance dating. Make it worth my while."

Head tight to her shoulder so the phone didn't try another escape attempt, she wiggled out of her underwear.

"Trust me, sweetheart," he said with a chuckle. "I've been all over the world. I'm more than capable of handling one tiny American. If you want to find out how worth it I am, walk out the door."

"I'm not dressed," she informed him saucily. Even someone as fashion savvy as Bella couldn't tie a bikini with one hand. And for some reason, now that he knew she was naked, it was an oddly effective turn-on.

"Perfect," he purred. "I like a woman who can read my mind. What am I thinking right now?"

If it was anything close to what she was thinking, a public beach was not the best place for them to be together. "You're thinking that you'd better hang up so I can, you know, leave the house."

His laugh rolled through her and then cut off abruptly as the call ended. She hummed as she threw on her bikini and covered it with a short dress made of fishnet weave.

She hit the foyer in under three minutes and almost escaped without her security detail noticing her stealthy exit, when she heard the voice of doom call out behind her.

"Isabella."

Groaning, she turned to face her father since the cover up was just as see-through from the front as the back. The faster she withdrew from his clutches, the better. "Yeah, Dad."

"I understand you told Will Rowling you weren't interested in him. I'm very disappointed."

Of course he was. He'd have to smooth things over with Patrick Rowling and figure out another way to make everyone miserable.

"That's me. The disappointing daughter," she admitted lightly, hoping if she kept her cool, the extraction might go faster. She had a man waiting patiently for her on the beach.

"You cannot continue behaving this way. Marriage to Rowling will settle you and nothing else seems to work to that end. You must repair your relationship with him."

His hand flew up to staunch the protest she'd been about to voice.

"No, Isabella. This is a serious matter, among other serious matters I must discuss with you. However, I'm expected to accompany Gabriel to a royal function. Be here when I get back," her father commanded.

"Sure, Dad." She fled before he could tell her when he'd be back because then she could claim ignorance when she wasn't here.

Her stomach tightened as she walked down the narrow cliffside stairs to the beach. Why couldn't she have timed that better? The encounter put a damper on the joy she'd had since the moment she'd heard James's voice.

When her toes sank into the sand, she scoured the sun-worshippers for a glimpse of the whipcord physique she couldn't erase from her mind. James was easy to spot in a turquoise shirt that shielded his British complexion from the rays. Sunglasses covered his beautiful eyes and as always, he wore the expensive watch he never seemed to leave home without. He lay stretched out on a towel off to the side of the crowd, lounging in his own little cleared area.

"Thought you'd never get here," he commented when she flopped down next to him. He paused and whipped off his glasses to focus on her intently. "What's wrong?"

How bad was it that he made her so mushy just by noticing that she was a little upset? "Nothing. My father."

"Say no more." James shook his head and sat up to clasp her hand in his, squeezing it once. "I've been avoiding mine since the pictures hit."

"What pictures?"

"You don't know?" When she shook her head, he rubbed his face with his free hand. "Someone snapped us with me on top of you when you tripped over my chair the other day. We were on the front page of the Playa Del Sol newspaper. And probably all the other ones, too. I'm sorry, I figured you'd seen them. Or had a confrontation with your father about them."

Oh, that explained a lot, especially Rafael's use of his boardroom voice. "I learned the hard way to never search my name on the internet, so no, I haven't seen the pictures. And I think I just narrowly missed that confrontation. The one I had was bad enough, but fortunately, he was too busy to give me a proper talking to. I'm supposed to be home when he gets back so I can obediently listen to his lecture. Oops."

James flashed a quick grin. "You're my kind of woman."

"We seem to have a flagrant disregard for authority in common, don't we?"

"When it makes sense," James corrected. "You're not sixteen. You're a grown woman who can make her own choices. If you want to be with me, you should get that opportunity, authority figures aside."

As much as she liked his point, she was still a member of the royal family and the idea of smarmy pictures floating around upset her, especially when the actual event had been so innocuous.

"So we're both rebels, but only when presented with pigheaded fathers?"

"Exactly." His thumb smoothed over hers and he had yet to return his sunglasses to their perch over his eyes. The way he was looking at her, as if he understood her so perfectly, they didn't even need words—it took a massive amount of willpower to not throw herself into his arms.

Why were they outside in plain sight again? Her babysitters could lumber down the stairs from the house at any moment, squelching what promised to be an adventurous day.

"This wasn't exactly what I had in mind for our first date," she remarked with an exaggerated glance around. "Too many people and I'm pretty sure I remember something about getting naked. I readily admit to bucking authority when called for, but I am not a fan of sand in certain places. What shall we do about that?"

James's blue eyes went sultry and he gripped her hand tighter. "A little bird told me you were high maintenance, so I was going to take you to dinner later at Casa Branca in Del Sol. But I see the huge gaping flaw in that plan since you would indeed have to be dressed for that."

"It's also pretty public. I'd love to escape prying eyes, security details and cameras for at least one night." She frowned. Was nowhere sacred enough to spend time with a man she was just getting to know without fear of creating a whole brand-new scandal? "Can we go back to your place?"

They certainly couldn't go to hers, not with the royal lecture pending.

"Ha." James rolled his eyes, turning them a myriad of blues in the sunlight. "I can only imagine dear old Dad's aneurism when I walk through the front door with you."

No, neither of them were sixteen but it felt that way when they couldn't even find a place to be alone without overbearing parents around. So it was time for an adult solution.

"New plan," Bella chirped. "I've heard a rumor of an abandoned farmhouse that's part of our family's royal property. But I don't know where it is. I need someone with a car and a good knowledge of the roads in Alma to help me find it. Know anyone like that who's also free to drive around with me?"

"James's Abandoned Farmhouse Locators, at your service." He bowed over her hand with mock ceremony. "Let's plan on making a night of it. We'll get some takeout. Do you want to run back upstairs to grab a few things?"

"Give me five minutes." She mentally packed an overnight bag. Had she brought that smoking hot lingerie set she hadn't worn yet?

"Four." He raised her hand to his lips and kissed it. "That bikini is killing me. I want to untie it with my teeth and take a good hard look at what's underneath. Then my mouth will be busy getting acquainted with every inch of your naked body."

She shuddered as his words lanced through her core with a long tug. "I'll be back in three."

Six

The small cockpit of James's car filled with the scent of Bella instantly. It was exotic, erotic and engaging, flipping switches in his body he'd have sworn were already wide open from the visual of Bella at the beach in that little bikini.

How was it possible to be even more turned on when you were already blind from lack of release?

She'd changed into a little white sundress that hugged her curves. The tiny straps begged for a man's hands to slip them off her shoulders, kiss the smooth flesh and then keep going into the deep V of her cleavage.

It was going to be a long, long drive through the interior of Alma as they looked for an abandoned farmhouse Bella insisted they could find. Problem was, he wanted her now, not in two hours after they crisscrossed the island in his green Lamborghini, which was hardly invisible.

As they clicked their seatbelts, his phone buzzed and he glanced at it out of habit, already planning to ignore whatever it was. Nothing could be more important than Bella.

Except it was a text message from Will. Who never texted him. Frowning, James tapped the screen of his phone and read the message.

I had nothing to do with this, but thought you should know.

Nothing good was going to come of clicking the link Will had sent, but forewarned was forearmed, so James did it anyway.

Montoro Princess to Wed the Heir to Rowling Energy.

The headline was enough. He didn't need to read the rest.

With a curse, he tilted his phone toward Bella. "Now taking bets on which of our fathers is behind this."

She glanced at it and repeated his curse, but substituted the vilest word with a more ladylike version, which put a smile on his face despite the ill-timed, fabricated announcement.

"Mine," she announced with a snort. "Control and dictate is exactly his style."

"Sure you're not describing my father?" James returned. "Because that's his MO all day long."

"No, it's my father. Definitely. But it doesn't matter." She grabbed his phone, switched it off and stuffed it in the bag at her feet. "You can't have that back. No more scandals, interfering fathers and marriage alliances. Just drive." She glanced over her shoulder. "And now. Before my babysitters figure out I'm not in the house."

Since that sounded fine to him, he backed out of his beachside parking place and floored the gas pedal, heading west out of Playa Del Onda.

"This is a gorgeous car," she commented with apparent appreciation as she caressed the dashboard lovingly in a way that immediately made him want her hand in his lap instead of on his car. "I dated a guy in Miami with an

Aventador, but it's so flashy without any real substance. The Gallardo is more refined and I love the color."

God, she *was* going to kill him before the day was over. "You know cars? I can't begin to tell you how hot that is."

She shrugged with a musical laugh, knocking one of the straps of her dress askew and drawing his attention away from the road. Dangerously.

"It's hard to live in a place like Miami without gaining at least some passing knowledge. I'll let you in on a secret, though. We girls always judge a man by his car. Mercedes-Benz? Too serious. Porsche? Works too hard. Corvette? Too worried about his hair."

James laughed in spite of the discomfort going on down below that likely wouldn't ease for an eternity. "So my Lamborghini is the only reason you wanted to go out with me?"

"The car test only works if you haven't met the guy yet. We're strictly talking about taking someone's measure in the parking lot."

He shifted to take a hairpin curve as they wound away from the beach into the more sparsely populated inland roads of Alma. Since he had no idea what they were looking for, he'd drive and let her do the surveying.

"Then I'll go with my second guess. You wanted to go out with me because I'm a witty conversationalist." He waggled his brows and shot her a sly smile. "Or door number three—I know a trick or two between the sheets."

He'd meant to be flirtatious, but now that it was out there, he realized the conversation with Will still bothered him a bit. Bella had said on numerous occasions that marriage wasn't her thing. Regardless, establishing the ground rules of what they were doing here couldn't hurt.

"Both." Blond hair swinging, she leaned on the emergency brake between them, so close he imagined he could hear her heart beating. "We have all night long and I do love a good conversation, especially in the dark. But if you forced me to choose, I'd go with door number three."

Brilliant. So they were both on the same page. They were hot for each other and wanted to burn it off with a wild night together. "Just so you know, with me, sheets are optional."

Awareness tightened the atmosphere as she let her gaze travel down his chest and rest on the bulge in his pants. He could hardly keep his attention on the road. Who wanted to watch the scraggly countryside of Alma when a goddess sat in the adjacent seat?

"By the way," she said. "I think we just passed the road we were supposed to take."

With a groan, he did a quick U-turn and drove down the street barely noticeable in the overgrowth of trees and groundcover. "I didn't know we had directions. Maybe you could speak up earlier next time?"

"Sorry, I'm a little distracted. Maybe you could stop being so sexy for a couple of minutes." Fanning herself as if he'd heated her up, she trailed a finger down his bicep muscle and toyed with the crook of his elbow.

"Me?" he growled. "You're the one in that knockout dress. All I can hear in my head is your voice on repeat, when you said the next time we were together, you'd be naked."

"Oh, did I forget to tell you?" She kissed the tip of her finger and pressed it to his lips, but she pulled away too quickly for him to suck the finger into his mouth the way he wanted to. "I'm naked under this dress. Wanna pull over?"

He nearly whimpered. "I cannot possibly explain how much I would like to do exactly that. But we are not getting it on in the car like a couple of horny teenagers. You deserve to be treated right and that includes a bed and me taking my time enjoying you."

Besides, they might be headed into the heart of rural Alma, but the roads were not deserted. They passed cars constantly. People knew who drove the only green Lamborghini on the island and all it would take was one idiot with a camera phone for another risqué picture of James and Bella together to land in the public eye. It was a dirty shame he hadn't tinted the windows on his car.

Until they straightened out the marriage announcement, it would create so much less of a jumble if they kept a low profile.

"Then drive faster," Bella suggested, and her hand wandered over to rest on his inner thigh, where she casually stroked him. Innocently, as if she touched him all the time, except she hadn't touched him like *that* before and his vision started to blur with unrequited lust.

He stepped on the gas. Hard.

"Where are we going?" Driving around until they stumbled over a farmhouse that may or may not exist had started to sound like the worst idea he'd ever agreed to.

"This is the main road to Aldeia Dormer, right?" When he nodded, she pointed at the horizon. "The assistant I talked to thought she remembered that the farmhouse was on the outskirts, before you hit the village. If you keep going, we'll find out."

"What if I just take you to a hotel and we check in under an assumed name?"

He had plenty of practice with parking in an obscure place and passing out discrete tips to the staff so he and his lady friend could duck through the kitchen entrance. Why hadn't he insisted on that in the first place? The text from Will had muddled him up, obviously. There was a former castillo-turned-four-star-bed-and-breakfast on the south side of Playa Del Onda that he wouldn't mind trying.

She shook her head with a sad smile and it was so much the opposite of her normal sunny demeanor, he immediately wanted to say something to lighten the mood. But what had caused such an instant mood shift?

"My aunt asked me to find the farmhouse. It's important to her and maybe to Gabriel. She said it was part of the Montoro legacy. We're already so close. I promise, if we don't find it soon, I'll reconsider the hotel."

Her earnestness dug under his skin and there was no way he could refuse. "Sure. We'll keep going."

Okay, maybe she was a little different from other women he'd dated. He certainly couldn't recall catering to one so readily before, but that was probably due to the degree of difficulty he'd experienced in getting this one undressed and under him.

They drove for a couple of miles, wrapped in tension. Just when James started to curse his flamboyant taste in cars, they crested a hill, and she gasped as a white farmhouse came into view.

Wonders of wonders. "Is that it?"

"I'm not sure." Bella pursed her lips as he drove off the main road onto the winding path to the farmhouse and parked under a dangerously dilapidated carport.

Would serve him right if this ill-conceived jaunt through Alma resulted in a hundred grand worth of bodywork repairs when the carport collapsed on the Lamborghini. "I thought you said it was off this road."

"Well, it's supposed to be. But I've never been here before," she pointed out. "Maybe there are a hundred white farmhouses between here and Aldeia Dormer."

"Only one way to find out." He helped her from the car and held her hand as they picked through the overgrown property. "Don't step in the tall weed patches. There might be something living in them you'd rather not tangle with."

She squeezed his hand. "I'm glad you're here, then. I'll let you deal with the creepy crawly stuff."

"I'll be your hero any day."

Her grateful smile made his chest tight with a foreign weight because he felt like a fraud all at once. The only heroic thing he'd ever done in his life was give Bella an opportunity to be with Will if she chose. When had he last expended any appreciable effort looking out for someone else's welfare?

He could start right now, if he wanted to. No reason he couldn't keep an eye out for opportunities to throw himself in front of a bullet—figuratively speaking—for an amazing woman like Bella. If she'd smile at him like that again, the payoff wasn't too shabby.

The farmhouse's original grandeur still shone through despite the years of neglect. Once, the two-story clapboard house had likely been the home of a large family, where they gathered around an old wooden table at supper to laugh and tell stories as dogs ran underfoot.

As if he knew anything about what a family did at supper. Especially a family whose members liked each other and spent time together on purpose. Did that kind of lovely fairy tale even exist outside of movies? He swallowed the stupid lump in his throat. Who cared? He had no roots and liked it that way.

The property spread beyond the house into a small valley. Chickens had probably clucked in the wide backyard, scolding fat pigs or horses that lived in the wooden pens just barely visible from the front of the house. The fences had long fallen to the weed-choked ground, succumbing to weathering and decay.

James nearly tripped over an equally weathered rectangular wooden board hidden by the grass and weeds. He kicked at it, but it was solid enough not to move much despite the force of his well-toned football muscles. Metal loops across the top caught his attention and he leaned down to ease the board up on its side.

"It's a sign," Bella whispered as her gaze lit on the opposite side.

James spun around to view the front. In bold, blocky letters, the sign read *Escondite Real*. "In more ways than one."

Unless he missed his guess, this was indeed the property of royalty. Or someone's idea of a joke.

"No one told me to brush up on my Spanish before I came here. What does it say?" Bella asked with a mock pout.

"Royal Hideaway. Is this where your ancestors came to indulge in illicit affairs?"

Mischievously, she winked at James. "If not, it's where the current generation will."

"Illicit affairs are my favorite." Taking her hand again, he guided her toward the house.

"Look. It's beautiful."

Bella pointed at a butterfly the size of his palm. It alighted on a purple bougainvillea that had thrived despite the lack of human attention, the butterfly's wings touching and separating slowly. But the sight couldn't keep his attention, not when Bella's face had taken on a glow in the late afternoon sunlight as she smiled at the butterfly.

God, she was the most exquisite woman he'd ever seen. And that was saying something when he'd been hit on by women renowned the world over for their beauty.

"Let's check out the inside." He cleared the catch from his throat, mystified by where it had come from. Women were a dime a dozen. Why didn't Bella seem like one of the legion he could have in his bed tomorrow?

It didn't matter. Will hadn't seen what he thought he'd seen when James cleared the air with him. The watch on his wrist wasn't going anywhere anytime soon.

Bella fished a set of keys from her bag. The second one turned the tumblers in the padlock on the splintered front door. It opened easily but the interior was dark and musty. Of course. There wouldn't be any electricity at an abandoned farmhouse. Or a cleaning crew.

"I guess we should have thought this through a little better," James said. "At least we know we're in the right place since the key worked."

Any hope of stripping Bella out of that little dress and spending the night in a haze of sensual pleasure vanished

as something that sounded as if it had more feet than a
football team scrabbled across the room.

"Yeah. It's a little more rustic than I was anticipating."
She scowled at the gloom. "I'm not well versed in the art
of abandoned farmhouses. Now what?"

Bella bit her lip to staunch the flow of frustrated tears.
Which didn't exactly work.

This was all her fault. She'd envisioned a romantic ren-
dezvous with a sexy, exciting man—one she'd looked forward to getting to know *very* well—and never once had it
crossed her mind that "abandoned" didn't mean that someone had picked up and left a fully functioning house, ready
and waiting for her and James to borrow for a night or two.
The most strenuous thing she'd expected to do before letting James seduce her was kill a spider in the shower.

Graying sheets covered in cobwebs and dust obscured
what she assumed must be furnishings underneath. The
farmhouse hadn't been lived in for a long time. Decades
maybe. The property may not even have running water.
She shuddered. What had Isabella sent her into?

One tear shook loose and slid down her face.

Without speaking, James took her hand and drew her
into his embrace, which immediately calmed her. How had
he known that was what she needed? She slid her arms
around his waist and laid her head on his strong chest.

Goodness. His athlete's physique did it for her in so
many ways. He was shockingly solid and muscular for
someone so lean and her own body woke up in a hurry.
Sensation flooded her and she ached for him to kiss her
again, as he'd done on the terrace—hot, commanding and
so very sexy.

But then he drew back and tipped her chin up, his gaze
serious and a bit endearing. "Here's what we're going to
do. I'll drive into the village and pick up a few things.
I hate to leave you here, but we can't be photographed

together. While I'm gone, see if you can find a way to clean up at least one room."

His smile warmed her and she returned it, encouraged by his optimism. "You do have a gift for uncomplicating things. I'm a little jealous," she teased.

"It'll be smashing. I promise."

He left and she turned her attention to the great room of the farmhouse. Once she pulled the drapes aside, sunlight shafted into the room through the wide windows, catching on the dusty chandelier. So the house was wired for electricity. That was a plus. Maybe she could figure out how to get it activated—for next time, obviously, because there was a distinct possibility she and James might make long-term use out of this hideaway. Being a princess had to be worth something, didn't it?

Holding her breath, she pulled the sheets from the furnishings, raising a tornado of dust that made her sneeze. Once all the sheets were in a pile in the corner, she dashed from the room to give all the flurries a chance to settle. Using her phone as a flashlight, she found a broom in one of the closets of the old-fashioned kitchen.

"Cinderella, at your service," she muttered and carried the broom like a sword in front of her in case she ran into something crawly since her knight had left.

By the time he returned, the sun had started to set. She'd swept the majority of the dust from the room and whacked the cobwebs from the corners and chandelier. The throaty growl of the Lamborghini echoed through the great room as James came up the drive and parked. The car door slammed and James appeared in the open doorway, his arms weighted down with bags.

"Wow." He whistled. "This place was something back in the day, huh?"

She glanced around at the rich furnishings, which were clearly high-end, even for antiques, and still quite functional if you didn't mind the grime. "It's a property owned by royalty. I guess they didn't spare much expense, regardless of the location. I wonder why no one has been here for so long?"

And why all these lovely antiques were still here, like ghosts frozen in time until someone broke the spell.

"Tantaberra liked Del Sol." James set his bags down carefully on the coffee table and began pulling out his bounty. "My guess is this was too far out of the limelight and too pedestrian for his taste."

A variety of candles appeared from the depths of the first bag. James scouted around until he found an empty three-pronged candelabra, screwed tapers into it and then flicked a lighter with his other hand. He shut the front door, plunging the room into full darkness. The soft glow of the candles bathed his face in mellow light and she forgot all about the mystery of this farmhouse as he set the candelabra on the mantel behind the brocade couch.

"Nice. What else did you bring me?" Bella asked, intrigued at the sheer number of bags James had returned with. She'd expected dinner and that was about it.

"The most important thing." He yanked a plaid blanket from the second bag and spread it out on the floor. "Can't have you dining on these rough plank floors, now can we?"

She shook her head with a smile and knelt down on the soft blanket to watch him continue unpacking. It seemed as if he'd thought of everything, down to such necessary but unique details as a blanket and candles. It was a quality she would never have thought to admire or even notice. And in James, it was potently attractive.

"Second most important—wine." He plunked the bottle next to her and pulled out two plastic cups. "Not the finest stemware. Sorry. It was the best I could do."

His chagrin was heartbreakingly honest. Did he think she'd turn up her nose at his offering? Well, some women probably would, but not Bella.

"It's perfect," she said sincerely. "If you'll give me the

corkscrew, I'll pour while you show me what else you found in town."

He handed her a small black-cased device of some sort. It looked like a pocketknife and she eyed it curiously until he flicked out the corkscrew with a half laugh. "Never seen one of these before?"

"My wine is typically poured for me," she informed him pertly with a mock haughty sneer, lady-of-the-manor style. "Cut me some slack."

Instead of grinning back, he dropped to the blanket and took her hand. "This is a crappy first date. I wish I could have taken you to dinner in Del Sol, like I'd planned. You deserve to be waited on hand and foot and for me to make love to you on silk sheets. I'm sorry that things are so out of control for us right now. I'll make it up to you, I swear."

"Oh, James." Stricken, she stared into his gorgeous aqua eyes flickering in the candlelight. "This is exactly what I've been envisioning since I got in the car back at the beach. I don't need a three-hundred-euro dinner. I just want to be with you."

"You're a princess," he insisted fiercely. "I want to treat you like the royalty you are."

Good grief. Was all this because of the stupid joke she'd made about being high maintenance? Obviously he'd taken her at her word. Backpedaling time.

"You do that every time we're together. Encouraging me to make my own choices about who I date. Bringing me to the farmhouse simply because I asked, without telling me it was crazy. Holding me when I cry. Being my hero by making this night romantic with ingenuity and flair, despite the less than stellar accommodations. How could I possibly find fault in any of that?"

A little overcome, she stared at him, hoping to impart her sincerity by osmosis. Because he was amazing and somehow verbalizing it made it more real. Who else in her life had ever done such wonderful things for her? No one. Tender, fledgling feelings for James welled up and nearly splashed over.

He scowled. "I did those things because you needed me to. Not because you're a princess."

Silly man. He didn't get what she was saying at all. "But don't you see? I need someone to treat me like *me*. Because you *see* me and aren't wrapped up in all the royal trappings, which are essentially meaningless at the end of the day."

That was the mistake her father had made, trying to pawn her off on Will. And Will was nearly as bad. Everyone was far more impressed with her royal pedigree than she ever was. Everyone except James. And now he was being all weird about it.

Just as fiercely, she gripped his hand. "I wasn't a princess last year and if you'd met me then, wouldn't you have tried to give me what I needed instead of trying to cater to some idea you have about how a girl with royal blood should expect you to act?"

"Yeah." He blew out a breath. "I would. I just didn't want this to be so disappointing for you. Not our first time together."

Seriously? After the way he'd kissed her on the terrace? There was no freaking way he'd disappoint her, whether it was their first time or hundredth time. The location hardly mattered. She wanted the man, not some luxury vacation. If he thought dollar signs turned her on, she'd done something wrong.

"Our first time together cannot be disappointing, because you're half the equation," she chided gently. "I expect fireworks simply because you're the one setting them off. Okay?"

He searched her expression, brows drawn together. "If you're sure."

She caressed his arm soothingly, hoping to loosen him up a little. The romantic candlelit atmosphere was going to waste and that was a shame. "Yeah. Now show me what else is in your magic bag."

With a grin, he grabbed the last bag. He fished out a roll of salami, which he set by the wine, then lined up a wedge of cheese, boxed crackers and a string of grapes. "Dinner. I wish it—"

"Stop. It's food and I'm hungry. Sit down and let's eat it while you tell me stories about growing up in Alma." Patting the blanket, she concentrated on opening the wine, her one self-appointed task in the evening's preparations. It was tougher to pierce the cork than she'd anticipated.

Instead of complying with her suggestion, he took the bottle from her hands and expertly popped the cork in under fifteen seconds.

"You've done that before," she accused with a laugh as he poured two very full glasses of the chilled white wine. It was pretty good for a no-name label and she swallowed a healthy bit.

"Yep. I'm a master of all things decadent." He arched a brow and plucked a grape from the bunch to run it across her lips with slow sensuality that fanned heat across her skin instantly. "Hurry up and eat so I can show you."

Watching him with unabashed invitation, she let him ease the grape between her lips and accepted it with a swirl of her tongue across the tips of his fingers. His eyelids lowered, fluttering slightly, and he deliberately set his glass of wine on the coffee table, as if to silently announce he planned to use both hands in very short order.

She shuddered as all the newly-awakened feelings for this man twined with the already-powerful attraction. She wanted to explore his depths and let the amazing things happening between them explode. Simple desire she understood and appreciated, but this went beyond anything simple, beyond anything she'd experienced before.

"Or we can do both at the same time," she suggested,

her voice dropping huskily as he trailed his wet fingertip
down her chin and throat to trace the line of her cleavage.

"There you go again reading my mind," he murmured
and captured another grape without looking away, his gaze
hot and full of promise. "Let's see if you can guess what
I'm thinking now."

Seven

James outlined Bella's full lips with the grape and then ran it down her throat, resting it in the hollow of her collarbone. Slowly, he leaned over and drew the fruit into his mouth, sucking at her fragrant skin as he crushed the grape in his teeth simultaneously.

The combination of Bella and sweet juice sang across his taste buds. She was exquisitely, perfectly made and he wanted her with an unparalleled passion that wiped his mind of everything else.

Flinging her head back to give him better access, she gulped in a breath and exhaled on a low moan that tightened his whole body.

"Instead of reading your mind," she said, her low voice burrowing into his abdomen, spreading heat haphazardly, "why don't you surprise me with a few more strategically placed grapes?"

"You like that?"

Grapes as a seduction method—that was a first. And now he was wishing he'd bought a bushel. Gripping another one, he traced it between her breasts and circled one of her nipples. It peaked beautifully under the filmy sundress.

How had he gotten so supremely lucky as to have such a beautiful, exciting woman within arm's reach? One who didn't require him to rain expensive gifts down on her, but seemed perfectly content with simple trappings and a man paying attention to her.

All the talk of heroics made his skin crawl. She was sorely mistaken if she thought of him as a hero, but the look in her eyes—well, that made him feel ten feet tall, as if he could do anything as long as she believed in him.

The power of it emboldened him.

Urgently, he lunged for her, catching her up in his arms as he laid her back on the blanket. Her lips crashed against his in a hot, wet kiss that went on and on as their tongues explored and dipped and mated. Her body twined with his and finally, she was underneath him, his thigh flush against her core. Her hands went on a mission to discover every part of his back and he reveled in the feminine touch he'd been craving for so long.

Hooking the neckline of her dress, he dragged it from her breast. As her flesh was revealed, he followed the trail with his mouth, nibbling and kissing until his lips closed over her nipple.

She arched against his mouth, pushing herself deeper inside as he reached for a handful of grapes. With little regard for decorum, he lifted his head and crushed the fruit savagely, letting the juice drip onto her peaked nipple. The liquid wetted the tip as she watched with dark eyes; her glistening breast was so erotic, he groaned even as he leaned forward to catch an errant drop on his tongue.

Licking upward until he hit her nipple again, he sucked all the juice off to the sound of her very vocal sighs of pleasure. That nearly undid him.

"I want to see all of you," he murmured and his need was so great, he didn't even wait for her reply. Peeling off that little dress counted as one of the greatest pleasures of his life as inch by inch, he uncovered her incredible skin.

"You're so beautiful," he told her with a catch in his throat.

Something unnamable had overcome him. Something dramatic and huge. But he liked it and before whatever it was fled, he pulled a string of condoms from his pocket and rolled to the side to shed his own clothes so he could feel every gorgeous bit of her against him.

When he was naked, he rolled back, intending to gather up that bundle of heaven back into his arms, but she stopped him with a palm to his chest. "Not yet. I want to see you, too."

Her gaze roved over his body and lingered in unexpected places. His thighs. His pectorals. Her palm spread and flattened over his nipple, as if she wanted to grab hold.

When she couldn't, she purred. "Hard as stone. I like that."

"I like you touching me."

"Allow me to continue." Wicked smile spreading across her face, she ran both hands down the planes of his chest and onto his thighs, right past the area he'd hoped she was headed for. Which of course made him anticipate the return journey.

Her fingernails scraped his leg muscles lightly, and she trailed one hand over his hip to explore his butt, which tightened automatically under the onslaught. *Everything* tightened with unanswered release, including the parts he'd have sworn were already stretched to the point of bursting.

He groaned as heat exploded under her hands. His hips strained toward her, muscles begging to be set free from the iron hold he had on them. "Are you trying to make me barmy?"

"Nope. Just looking for the best places for when it's my turn with the grapes."

"Oh, it's totally your turn," he countered. "This is your dinner, too, and you must be hungry."

"At last." She knelt, grabbed a grape and eyed his splayed body. "Hmm. Where to start? I know."

She stuck the grape in her mouth and rolled it around with her tongue, her hot gaze on his erection. Somehow that was more arousing than if she'd actually tongued *him*. She caught the small globe in her front teeth and bent to run it over his torso, dipping into the valleys and peaks, her hair spreading out like a feathery torture device across his sensitive skin. When she accidentally—or maybe on purpose—dragged her hair over his erection, the light touch lit him up. Fire radiated from the juncture of his thighs outward and just as he was about to cup her head to guide her toward the prize, she leaned up on her haunches.

Plucking the grape from between her lips, she grazed his length with the wet grape, nearly causing him to spill everything in one pulse.

"Enough of that," he growled, manacling her wrist to draw it away from the line of fire. "You've obviously underestimated my appetite. Time for the main course."

She grinned. "I thought you'd never say that."

Fumbling with a condom, he somehow managed to get it secured and then rolled her underneath him. He'd been fantasizing about taking her exactly this way for an eternity. Soft and luscious, she slid right into the curves of his body as she had that day in the sand, except this time, nothing separated their skin and it was every bit as glorious as he'd imagined.

"You—" He nearly swallowed his tongue as she shifted, rolling her hips against his. The tips of her breasts ground into his torso, and it all felt so amazing, he couldn't speak.

And then he didn't have to speak as he gazed down into her blue eyes. Candlelight danced in their depths and he caught a hint of something else that hit him in the gut. As if she'd seen pieces of him that he'd never realized were there and she liked what she'd found. As if she truly saw him as a hero. Maybe she was the only one who could relate. They were both rebels—to the rest of the world—but his pain and difficulties behind the rebellion made total sense to her.

"Bella," he murmured and that was the extent of what he could push through his tight throat.

"Right here." Her low, husky voice became his favorite part of her as it hummed through him. "I was really afraid this would never happen. Make it worth the wait."

It was already so worth it. Worth the lectures from his father, worth the uncomfortable nobleness he'd somehow adopted when around her. Worth sending her away from him on the terrace when all he'd wanted to do was pull that outrageous red dress up to her waist and make her his under the moonlight.

This way was better. Much better. No fear of being caught. No loaded landmines surrounding them, no paparazzi lying in wait to cause a scandal just because they wanted to be together.

He laid his lips on hers and fell into a long sigh of a kiss that grew urgent as she opened her mouth and dove in with her tongue, heightening the pleasure.

And then with a small shift, they joined. Easily, beautifully, as if she'd been specially crafted for James Rowling. It was almost spiritual and he'd never felt such a weight to being with a woman.

He froze for a moment, just letting her essence bleed through him, and then, determined to get her to the same place of mystical pleasure, he focused on her cries, her shifts, her rhythms. He became an instant student of Bella's pleasure until he could anticipate exactly what she wanted him to do next to drive her to release.

And then she stiffened as a volatile climax engulfed her that he felt all the way to his soles. He let go and followed her into oblivion, holding her tight because he couldn't stand to lose contact with her.

As he regained cognizance, he realized she was trying to get closer, too. He settled Bella comfortably in his arms and lay with her to watch the candle flames flicker, throwing shadows of the heavy furniture on the walls of the farmhouse they'd turned into the safest of havens.

This time with Bella…it was the most romantic experience he'd ever had, which sat strangely. For a guy who loved sex and abhorred roots, romance was difficult to come by. Not only had he never had it, he'd never sought it.

Why did something as normal as sex feel so abnormally and hugely different with this woman? He couldn't make sense of it and it bothered him. As the unsettled feeling grew, he kissed Bella's forehead and separated from her.

Bustling around to gather up their abandoned wine glasses and remnants of their dinner, he threw a forced smile over his shoulder. "Ready to finish eating?"

She returned the smile, not seeming to realize that he was trying to mask his sudden confusion. "Depends. Is that code for round two? Because the answer is yes, if so."

Round two. He chugged some wine to give himself a second. Normally, he went for round two like a sailor on shore leave, but the thick, romantic atmosphere and the crushing sensation in his chest when he looked at Bella made him question everything.

What was going on here? This was supposed to be nothing but an opportunity to have fun with Bella, no expectations, no proposals before her brother took the throne.

"No code. Let's eat."

What was his *problem*? A beautiful woman who rocked his world wanted him to make love to her again. Maybe he should just do that, and everything would make sense once they were back to just two people having smashing sex. Will's bet had hashed everything.

"For now," he amended. "Got to keep up our strength."

She grinned and shoved some crackers in her mouth. "All done," she mumbled around the crackers.

Groaning around a laugh, he sat close to her on the blanket and shook off his strange mood. After all, she was Alma's only princess. What role did a disgraced football player have in the middle of all that? Especially when he didn't plan to be living in Alma permanently. In fact, a new contract would get him out from under all of this confusion quite well. He could enjoy a fling with Bella and jet off to another continent. Like always.

Obviously, there was no reason to give any more credence to the heavy weight in his chest.

There was a huge crick in Bella's neck, but she actually welcomed the pain. Because she'd gotten it sleeping in James's arms on a blanket spread over a hardwood floor.

That had been delicious. And wonderful. And a host of other things she could barely articulate. So she didn't, opting to see what the morning brought in this unconventional affair they'd begun.

Once they were dressed and had the curtains thrown open to let sunlight into the musty great room, she turned to James. "I don't know about you, but I'm heavily in favor of finding a café that'll give you a mountain of scrambled eggs, bacon and biscuits in a takeout box. I'm starving."

He flashed a quick grin. "Careful. That kind of comment now has all sorts of meaning attached. You better clarify whether you want me to feed you or strip you."

Laughing, she socked him on the arm. "You're the one who started that with the grapes. And the answer to that is both. Always."

He caught her hand and held it in his. "I'm only teasing. I'll go get breakfast. I wish you could come with me. Is it too much to ask that we go on a real date where I sit with you at an actual table?"

"We'll get there." She kissed him soundly and shoved

him toward the door. "Once I have food in me, we can strategize about the rest of our lives."

Item number one on the agenda: get this farmhouse in livable shape.

The strange look he shot her put a hitch in her stride and she realized immediately how he must have taken her comment. Okay, she hadn't meant it like that, as if she was assuming they'd become a dyed-in-the-wool couple and he needed to get down on one knee.

But what was so bad about making plans beyond breakfast? She'd had some great lovers in the past, but what she'd experienced with James went far beyond the category of casual. Hadn't he felt all the wonderful things she'd felt last night?

She rolled her eyes to make it harder for him to detect the swirl of emotion going on underneath the surface. "You can stop with the deer-in-the-headlights, hon. I just narrowly escaped one marriage. I'm not at all interested in jumping right into another one, no matter how good the prospective groom is at *feeding* me."

Which was absolutely, completely true. Saying it aloud solidified it for them both.

With a wicked smile, he yanked on her hand, pulling her into his embrace. His weird expression melted away as he nuzzled her neck.

Foot-in-mouth averted. Except now she was wondering exactly what his intentions toward her were. A few nights together and then ta-ta?

And when did she get to the point where that wasn't necessarily what *she* wanted? She didn't do all that commitment-and-feelings rigmarole. She liked to have fun and secretly felt sorry for women on husband-hunting missions. Her mother had gotten trapped in that cycle and lived a miserable existence for years and years as a result. *No, thank you.*

Nothing had changed just because of a few emotions

she had no idea what to do with. Her affair with James had begun so unconventionally and under extreme circumstances. If they'd been able to go out on a real date from the beginning, they'd probably have already moved on by now.

Good thing she'd made it clear marriage wasn't on her mind so there was no confusion, though a few other things could be better spelled out.

James sucked on her tender flesh, clearly about to move south, and she wiggled away before her body leaped on the train without her permission.

"That wasn't supposed to be a code word." She giggled at his crestfallen expression but sobered to hold his gaze. "Listen, before you go get breakfast, let's lay this out. Last night was amazing but I'm not done. Are you? Because if this thing between us was one night only, I'll be sad, but I'm a big girl. Tell me."

He was already shaking his head before she'd finished speaking. "No way. I'm nowhere near done."

Her pulse settled. *Good answer.* "So, if you want a repeat of the grapes-on-the-floor routine, I'm all for it. But I'd prefer a real bed from now on. My plan is to put some elbow grease into this place, preferably someone else's, and create a lover's retreat where we can escape whenever we feel like it."

"Are you expecting us to have to hide out that long?" Wary surprise crept into his tone, setting her teeth on edge.

"I don't know. Maybe." What, was it too much trouble to drive out here just to have a few stolen hours together? "Is what I'm suggesting so horrible?"

"No. Not at all. My hesitation was completely on the issue of hiding out. I want to be seen with you in public. I'm not ashamed of our relationship and I don't want you to think I am."

Her heart squished as she absorbed his righteous indignation and sincerity. He wanted their relationship to be aboveboard, just as he'd wanted to clear things with Will before proceeding. And that meant a lot to her. He kept trying to make her think he didn't have a noble bone in his body when everything he did hinged on his own personal sense of honor.

"I didn't think that, but way to score major points." She batted her eyelashes at him saucily. "But that aside, I don't even know if I'm staying in Alma permanently or I'd get my own place. I suspect you're in the same boat."

He'd told her he hoped to get another contract with a professional soccer—sorry, *football*—team, and that the team could be in Barcelona or the UK or Brazil or, or, or… He might end up anywhere in the world. And probably would.

"Yeah. I haven't made a secret out of the fact that I don't plan to stick around," he agreed cautiously.

"I know. So do you really think there's a scenario where either of us would be willing to parade the other across the thresholds of our fathers' houses even if we do clear up the engagement announcement?"

He sighed. "Yeah, you're right. Let's rewind this whole conversation. Smashing idea, Bella. I'd love to help you get this place into shape so I can take an actual shower in the morning."

That was the James she knew and loved. Or rather, the James she…didn't know very well, but liked a whole lot. With a sigh, she let him kiss her again and shoved him out the door for real this time because her stomach was growling and her heart was doing some funny things that she didn't especially like.

Space would be good right now.

The sound of the Lamborghini's engine faded away as she went about taking inventory on the lower floor. Apparently most, if not all, of the original furnishings remained, as evidenced by their arrangement. Bella had been in enough wealthy households to recognize when a place had been artfully decorated and this one definitely had.

The pieces had been placed just so by a feminine hand, or at least she imagined it that way. That's when it hit her that this farmhouse had probably once belonged to an ancestor of hers. Someone of her blood.

A long gone Montoro, forgotten for ages once the coup deposed the royal family. She'd never felt very connected to the monarchy, not even at the palace in Del Sol where some of the original riches of the royal estate were housed. But the quieter treasures of the farmhouse struck her differently.

She picked up a filthy urn resting on a side table. White, or at least it was under the grime. She rubbed at it ineffectually with her palm and managed to get a small bit of the white showing. The eggshell-like surface was pretty.

Maybe it wasn't priceless like the Qing Dynasty porcelain vase sitting in an art niche at the Coral Gables house. But worth something. Maybe it was actually worth more than the million-dollar piece of pottery back in Miami because it had been used by someone.

She'd never thought about worth being tied to something's usefulness. But she liked the idea of having a purpose. She'd had one in Miami—wildlife conservation. What had happened to that passion? It was as if she'd come to Alma and forgotten how great it made her feel to do something worthwhile.

With renewed fervor, she dove into cleaning what she could with the meager supplies at hand, and revised her earlier thoughts. It would be fun to put some elbow grease of her own into this house. Whom else could she trust with her family's property?

When the purr of James's car finally reverberated through the open door, she glanced at her dirty arms and her lip curled. Some princess she looked like. A Cinderella in reverse—she'd gone from the royal palace to being a slave to the dust. A shower sounded like heaven about now.

The look in James's eye when he walked in holding a

bag stenciled with the logo of the only chain restaurant in Alma had her laughing. "There is no way you're thinking what I think you're thinking. I'm filthy."

"Yes, way." He hummed in approval. "I've never seen a sexier woman than you, Bella Montoro. Layer of dirt or not."

There he went again making her insides all melty and that much more raw. She always got the distinct feeling he saw the real her, past all the outside stuff and into her core. The outside, inconsequential stuff was invisible to him. Coupled with the hard twist of pure lust she got pretty much any time she laid eyes on him, she could hardly think around it.

She shook it off. This fierce attraction was nothing more than the product of their secret love affair. Anticipation of the moment they'd finally connect, laced with a hint of the forbidden. It had colored everything and she refused to fall prey to manufactured expectations about what was happening between them.

Get a grip. "Smells like ham and biscuits," she said brightly.

He handed her the bag. "I hope you like them. I had to drive two towns over to find them."

The first bite of biscuit hit her tongue and she moaned. "I would have paid three hundred euros for this."

He laughed. "On the house. You can pay next time."

"Oh?" She arched a brow, relieved they'd settled back into the teasing, fun vibe she'd liked about them from the beginning. "Are you under some mistaken impression that I'm a liberated woman who insists on opening her own doors and paying her own way? 'Cause that is so not happening."

"My mistake," he allowed smoothly with a nod and munched on his own biscuit. "You want a manly bloke to treat you like a delicate hothouse flower. I get it. I'd be chuffed to climb all the ladders around here and wield the power tools in order to create a luxury hideaway, as ordered. You know what that means I get at the end of the day in return, right?"

"A full body massage," she guessed, already planning exactly how such a reward might play out. "And then some inventive foreplay afterward."

That was even more fun to imagine than the massage part of the evening's agenda.

"Oh, no, sweetheart." He leaned in and tipped her chin up to capture her gaze, and the wicked intent written all over his face made her shiver. "It means I get the loo first."

Eight

The farmhouse's great room looked brand-new and James couldn't take all of the credit. It was because the house had good bones and old-world charm—qualities he'd never appreciated in anything before.

Hell, maybe he'd never even *noticed* them before.

Bella finished polishing the last silver candlestick and stuck it back on the mantel of the humongous fireplace, humming a nameless tune that he'd grown a bit fond of over the past day as they'd worked side by side to get their lover's retreat set to rights.

"Did you hear that?" she asked with a cocked head.

"Uh, no." He'd been too busy soaking in the sight of a beautiful woman against the backdrop of the deep maroon walls and dark furniture. "What was it?"

"The sound of success."

She smiled and that heavy feeling in his chest expanded a tad more, which had been happening with alarming frequency all day. Unfortunately, the coping mechanism he'd used last night—grabbing Bella and sinking into her as fast as possible so his mind went blessedly blank—wasn't available to him at this moment because a workman from the municipality was on his way to restore the water connection.

It was a minor miracle the workman had come out on short notice, given the typical local bureaucracy, but once James had mentioned that he was a representative for the Montoros, everything had fallen into place.

He'd have to make himself—and his distinctive green car—scarce. Just as he'd done this morning when the bloke from the electric company had come. But it was fine. The time away had given him an opportunity to talk through strategy with his sports agent, who mentioned a possible opportunity with Liverpool. No guarantees, but some shifting had occurred in the roster and the club needed a strong foot. Brilliant news at an even better time—the sooner James could escape Alma, the better.

"Yep," he said and cleared a catch from his throat. "Only twenty-seven rooms to go."

They'd started on the downstairs, focusing on the kitchen and great room, plus the servant's quarters past the kitchen, where they intended to sleep tonight if the bed they'd ordered arrived on time, as promised. A lot had been accomplished in one day but not nearly enough.

Once they got the master bedroom upstairs cleaned up, James planned a whole silk-sheets-and-rose-petals-type seduction scene. He owed it to Bella since she'd been such a good sport about sleeping in the room designated for the help.

One thing he immensely appreciated about Bella: she joked around a lot about being high maintenance but she was the furthest thing from it. And he knew a difficult, demanding woman when he saw one, like his last semi-permanent girlfriend, Chelsea. She'd cured him of ever wanting to be around a female for more than a one-night stand, a rule which he'd stuck to for nearly two years.

Until Bella.

Since he couldn't lose his mind in her fragrant skin for... he glanced at his watch and groaned...hours, he settled for a way-too-short kiss.

She wiggled away and stuck her tongue out at him. "Yes, we have a lot of work left. But not as much as we would have if you hadn't made all those calls. You're the main reason we've gotten this far."

The hero-worship in her gaze still made him uncomfortable, so he shrugged and polished an already-sparkling crystal bowl with the hem of his shirt so he had an excuse not to look directly at her. "Yeah, that was a brilliant contribution. Hitting some numbers on my phone."

"Stop being such a goof." Hands on her hips, she stepped into his space, refusing to let his attention linger elsewhere. "You're a great person. I'm allowed to think so and don't you dare tell me I can't."

That pulled a smile from him. "Yes, Your Highness."

"Anyway," she drawled with an exaggerated American accent, which only widened his smile, as she'd probably intended. "When I was cleaning the fireplace, I realized I really need to call my father. We can't ignore the press release about my engagement to Will much longer."

Though she kept up her light tone, he could tell some stress had worked its way into her body. Her shoulders were stiff and a shadow clouded her normally clear eyes.

"Maybe we can wait," he suggested, and laced his fingers with hers to rub her knuckles. "Tomorrow's soon enough."

"I kind of want to get it over with." She bit her lip, clearly torn. "But I also really like the idea of procrastinating."

"Why?" he asked, surprising himself. He'd meant to say they should wait. Why do today what you can put off until tomorrow?

He, of all people, understood avoiding conflict, especially when it involved an overbearing father. But the distress evident in the foreign lines around her eyes had to go and he would do whatever it took to solve the problem.

Maybe it wasn't a good thing for him to encourage her to wait. Maybe she needed to get the confrontation over with. But how would he know if he didn't ask?

"My father really wants me to fall in line, like Gabriel did. When Rafe abdicated, it was kind of a big deal." She sighed. "I get that. I really don't want to cause problems because of my own selfishness."

"But you're not," he countered. "How is it a problem that you want to choose the bloke you marry?"

"Because my father says it is." Her mouth flattened into a grim line. "That's why I want to put off dealing with all of this. I'm just not ready for all of the expectations that go along with restoring the monarchy. I mean, I always knew our family had come from a royal line, but that was so long ago. Why is it so important to my father all of a sudden?"

She seemed a little fragile in that moment so he pulled her into his arms, shushing her protests over the state of her cleanliness.

"I wish I could tell you why things are important to fathers," he murmured. "Mine has yet to explain why it's so horrifying to him that I don't want a job at Rowling Energy. Becoming a world-class football player might make some dads proud."

"Not yours?" she whispered, her head deep in his shoulder.

Her arms tightened around him, which was oddly comforting. What had started as an embrace he'd thought she needed swiftly became more precious to him than oxygen.

"Nah. Will's his golden boy."

"Why don't you want to work at Rowling?"

It was the first time anyone had ever asked him that.

Most people assumed he wanted to play football and there was little room for another career at his dad's company. But even now, when he had few choices in continuing his sports career, he'd never consider Rowling an alternative.

His father wasn't the listening type; he just bulldozed through their conversations with the mindset that James would continue to defy him and never bothered to wonder why James showed no interest in the family business.

"It's because he built that company on my mother's grave," he said fiercely. "If she hadn't died, he wouldn't have moved to Alma and tapped in to the offshore drilling that was just starting up. I can't ever forget that."

"Is someone asking you to forget?" she probed quietly. "Maybe there's room to take a longer view of this. If your father hadn't moved to Alma, you wouldn't have discovered that you loved football, right?"

"That doesn't make it okay." The admission reverberated in the still house and she lifted her head to look at him, eyebrows raised in question. "I love football but only because it saved me. It got me out of Alma at an early age and gave me the opportunity to be oceans away. I can't be on the same small island as my father. Not for long."

When had this turned into confession time? He'd never said that out loud before. Bella had somehow pulled it out of him.

"I'm sorry," she said quietly and snuggled back into his arms, exactly where he wanted her.

"I'm sorry you've got the same issues with your father. But there's always gossip in a small town. We're going to be dealing with a scandal over the press release once someone catches on to us shacking up in this love nest. But I support whatever decision you make as far as the timing," he told her sincerely, though he'd be heavily in favor of waiting.

He wasn't royalty though. She had a slew of obligations he knew nothing about; he could hardly envision a worse life than one where you had to think about duty to crown and country.

"I think that's the most romantic thing you've ever said to me." Her voice cracked on the last word.

Puzzled, he tipped her chin up, and a tear tracked down her cheek. "Which part? When I called this jumble of a house a love nest or described our relationship as shacking up?"

She laughed through another couple of tears, thoroughly confounding him. Just when he thought he finally got her, she did something he couldn't fathom.

"Neither. The part where you said you support me, no matter what. It makes me warm, right here." She patted her stomach.

He almost rolled his eyes. That was laying it on a bit thick, wasn't it? "I do support you, but that's what peop— lovers…people in a rela—" God, he couldn't even get his tongue to find the right word to explain the status of what they were doing here.

Maybe because he didn't *know* what they were doing here.

"Yeah," she said happily, though what she was agreeing to, he had no idea. "That's what you do. I get that. You've always done exactly the right thing, from the very beginning. "

He scowled. "I don't do that."

He didn't. He was the guy who buckled when it mattered most. The guy whose team had been counting on him and he'd let them down. The guy who ran from conflict instead of dealing with it. Hadn't she been listening to anything he'd said about why he played football?

His character had been tarnished further with the hooker incident. James Rowling was the last person anyone should count on. Especially when it came to support. Or "being there" for someone emotionally.

"You do." Her clear blue eyes locked with his and she wouldn't let him look away. "You look in the mirror and see the mistakes your father has insisted you've made. I look at you and see an amazing man. You did hard physical labor all day in a house that means nothing to you. Because I asked you to. You're here. That means a lot to me. I need a rock in my life."

She had him all twisted up in her head as the hero of this story. She couldn't be more wrong—he was a rock, all right. A rolling stone headed for the horizon.

It suddenly sounded lonely and unappetizing. "I can't be anyone's rock. I don't know how."

That had come out wrong. He intended to be firm and resolute, but instead sounded far too harsh.

"Oh, sweetie. There's no instruction manual. You're already doing it." She shook her head and feathered a thumb over his jaw in a caress that felt more intimate than the sex they'd had last night. "You're letting someone else cloud your view of yourself. Don't let your father define who you are."

He started to protest and then her words really sank in. Had he subconsciously been doing that—letting his father have that much power over him?

Maybe he'd never realized it because he'd refused to admit the rift between him and his father might be partially his own fault. James had always been too busy running to pay attention. Even now, his thoughts were on Liverpool and the potential opportunity to play in the top league. But more importantly, Liverpool wasn't in Alma—where the woman who had him so wrongly cast in her head as the hero lived. He was thinking about leaving. Maybe he was already halfway out the door.

Which then begged the question—what if he buckled under pressure because he always took off when the going got tough?

The new bed was supremely superior to the floor.
Bella and James christened it that night and slept en-

twined until morning. It was the best night of sleep she'd ever had in her life.

But dawn brought a dose of reality. She hadn't been back to the Playa del Onda house in almost forty-eight hours. The quick text message to Gabriel to explain her absence as a "getaway with a friend" hadn't stopped her father from calling four times and leaving four terse voice mail messages. She hadn't answered. On purpose.

With the addition of running water and electricity, the farmhouse took on a warmth she enjoyed. In fact, she'd rather stay here forever than go back to the beach house. But she had to deal with her father eventually. If this matter of the engagement announcement was simply a test of her father's resolve versus her own, she wouldn't care very much about the scandal of being with James.

But it wasn't just about two Montoros squaring off against each other. It was a matter of national alliances and a fledgling monarchy. She didn't have any intention of marrying Will, but until the Montoros issued a public retraction of the engagement story, the possibility of another scandal was very real. This one might be far worse for Gabriel on the heels of the one Rafe had caused. And hiding away with James hadn't changed that. She had to take care of it. Soon.

"Good morning," James murmured and reached out to stroke hair from her face as he lay facing her on the adjacent pillow. "This is my favorite look on you."

"Bedhead?" She smiled despite the somberness of her thoughts.

"Well loved." He grinned back. "I liked it yesterday morning, too."

Speaking of which... "How long do you think we can reasonably hole up here without someone snapping a picture of us together?"

He shrugged one shoulder. "Forever." When she arched a brow, he grinned. "I can fantasize about that, can't I?

As long as I keep jetting off when people show up, what's the hurry?"

Her conscience pricked at her. James was leaving the timing of forcing the issue to her, but a scandal could be damaging to him as well. It was selfish enough to refuse to marry Will, but she wasn't really hurting him as long as they were up front about it. A scandal that broke before the retraction could very well hurt James and she couldn't stand that.

"I think I need to talk to my father today," she said firmly. "Or tomorrow at the very latest."

James deserved what he'd asked for—the right to take her out in public, to declare to the world that they'd started seeing each other. To take her to a hotel, or dinner or wherever he liked. It wasn't fair to force him to help her clean up this old farmhouse just so she could avoid a confrontation.

Except she wasn't only avoiding the confrontation. She was avoiding admitting to herself that her own desires had trumped her responsibilities. Hurricane Bella had followed her across the Atlantic after all.

"I'll drive you back to Playa Del Onda," he said immediately. "Whenever you're ready."

A different fear gripped her then. What if they got everything straightened out and she and James could be together with no fear of scandal—only for her to discover things between them were so amazing because of the extreme circumstances? The white-hot attraction between them might fizzle if their secret affair wasn't so secret any longer.

That was enough to change her mind.

"I'll probably never be ready. Let's shoot for tomorrow." That was too soon. The thought of losing her allure with James made her want to weep. "Let's get some more work on the house done today. It'll give me time to gear up. Is that okay? Do you have something else you need to be doing?"

"Nothing I would rather be doing, that's for sure. I'm completely open."

"Me, too."

And for some reason, that didn't sit well, as if she was some kind of Eurotrash princess who had nothing better to do than lie around all day getting it on with a hot athlete. That was like a tabloid story in and of itself.

The urn from the great room popped into her head. Usefulness created worth and she wanted to feel that her life had worth.

"You know what I'd like to do?" she said impulsively. "Find out if there's a wildlife conservation organization in Alma."

James, to his credit, didn't register a lick of surprise. "I'll help you find one."

Of course he'd say that, without questioning why. His unwavering support was fast becoming a lifeline. "I was involved in one back in Miami. I like taking care of poor, defenseless creatures. Especially birds. We had wild macaws on the grounds at our house and I always felt like they were there as a sign. I miss them. I miss feeling like I'm doing something to give back, you know?"

"It's a good cause," he agreed. "There are some estuaries on the east side of the main island. Lots of migratory birds and fish live there. Surely there are some organizations devoted to their preservation. If not, you're in the perfect position to start one."

Her breath caught. At last, a use for the title of princess. If her brother was running the show, he could give her backing in parliament to get some state money set aside. Fund-raisers galore could come out of that. "Thanks. I love that idea."

"If we're going to Playa Del Onda tomorrow, you want to swing by the Playa branch of the Ministry of Agriculture and Environment and see if they have any information on wildlife conservation?"

"Definitely. And then I'd like to come back and put together a serious renovation plan for the house. But I'm not suggesting you have to help," she amended in a rush.

Good grief. Everything that came out of her mouth sounded as if she was ordering him around, expecting him to play chauffer and be a general Alma guide. He might have his own life to live. Or he might realize the thrill had worn off.

"I want to help," he insisted. "My assumption is that we're still planning to lie low, even after you clear things up with your father. So that means we need a place to go. I like it here."

She let out the breath caught in her lungs. She shouldn't read into his response. But for some reason, it made her feel a little better that he wasn't already planning to ditch their relationship once it wasn't secret any longer. "I do, too."

She'd started thinking she might like to live in the farmhouse permanently. It wasn't too far from Del Sol, so she could visit Tía Isabella occasionally. If she planned to stay in Alma, she had to live *somewhere*. Why not here? No one else cared about it.

As she lay in the bed James had ordered and smiled at him in the early morning light, it occurred to her that *he* was the only reason she'd even thought about a permanent place to live. As if James and forever were intertwined.

That was enough to propel her from the bed with a quickly tossed-off excuse about taking a shower now that she could.

As the water heated up, she berated herself for dreaming about life beyond the next few days. It was one thing to question whether James would lose interest once they could go public with their affair, but it was another entirely to assign him a permanent place in her life without even consulting him.

What would his place be? Boyfriend? Official lover? She'd be living in the public eye far more in Alma than in

Miami. What if James didn't want that kind of scrutiny? She wouldn't blame him, especially given the past scandals that dogged his steps.

Of course, she didn't know his thoughts one way or another. Maybe he'd be done with their affair in a few days, regardless of the status of their relationship. Maybe the whole concept of being her long-term lover had little appeal.

What was she *thinking*?

What had happened to the girl who used to flit from one guy to the next with ease? Or for that matter, the girl who flitted from party to party? Living out here in the country would make it really difficult to stay in the scene. No jetting off to Monte Carlo or Barcelona for some fun on the Mediterranean when Alma grew too dull. But when she exited the bathroom and saw the beautiful, surprisingly romantic man still in the bed they'd shared last night, sprawled out under the covers like a wicked fantasy, all of that drained from her mind. What party—what other man, for that matter—could compare to *that*?

"Give me a few minutes and we'll get started," he promised. "Let's check out the upstairs today."

God, she was in a lot of trouble. *She* should be the one thinking about cooling things off, not worrying about whether James planned to.

But the thought of ending things with James made her nauseous.

What was she going to do?

Nine

The upstairs master suite had the most amazing four-poster bed Bella had ever seen. When she drew off the drop cloths covering it, she almost gasped at the intricate carvings in the wood. Delicate flowers in full bloom twined up the posts and exploded into bunches at the top corners.

Once she polished the wood to gleaming and whacked the dust from the counterpane and pillows, the bed took on an almost magical quality, as if it had been a gift from the fairy realm to this one.

The rest of the room was a wreck. Mice had gotten into the cushions of the chairs by the huge bay window and Bella could tell by the discoloration of the walls that some type of artwork had originally hung there, but had disappeared at some point over the years.

The floor groaned behind her and she turned to see James bouncing lightly on a spot near the bed. The planks bowed under his weight and then with a *snap*, one cracked in two. Both pieces fell into the newly created hole. It was a testament to James's superior balance and athletic reflexes that the broken plank hadn't thrown him to the floor.

"Oops," he said sheepishly as he leaped clear. "I was not expecting that to happen. Sorry."

She waved it off. "If that's the worst damage we do today, I'll consider that a plus. Why, exactly, were you jumping up and down on it in the first place?"

"When I walked over it, this section felt different, like it wasn't solid underneath. It turns out it wasn't."

Grinning at his perplexed expression, she joined him to peer into the hole. It was a shallow compartment, deliberately built into the floor. "Looks like you found the royal hiding place. Oooh, maybe there are still some priceless jewels in there."

Eagerly, she knelt and pulled the broken board from the hole. "Hand me your phone."

James placed it in her outstretched hand and when she aimed it into the gap, the lighted screen revealed a small box. Leaning forward slightly on her knees, she stuck her hand down into the space and only as her fingers closed over the box did she think about the possibility of spiders. Ick. Since it was too late, she yanked the box out and set it on the floor next to James.

"Anything else?" he asked, his body hot against her back as he peered over her shoulder, lips grazing her ear.

It shouldn't have been such a turn-on, but then, there was nothing about James that *didn't* turn her on. Warmth bloomed in her midsection and as she arched her back to increase the contact with his torso, the feel of him hummed through her.

"Maybe," she murmured. "Why don't you reach around here and see for yourself."

He must have picked up on her meaning. His arms embraced her from behind, drawing her backward into his body, and his fingers fumbled around the edge of the hole without delving more than half an inch into it.

"Nope. Nothing in there." His lips nuzzled her neck as he spoke and she could tell his attention was firmly on her. The hard length grinding into her rear said he'd lost interest in whatever else might be in the decades-old hiding place as well. "But what have we here?"

"I think you better investigate," she said, and guided his hands under her shirt, gasping as his questing fingertips ran over her sensitive breasts.

"You're not fully dressed," he accused her with a naughty laugh. "Ms. Montoro, I am shocked at your lack of undergarments. It's almost as if you expected a bloke's hands to be under your shirt."

"You say that like it's a bad thing." Her core heated as he caressed her, nudging her rear with his hard erection. "And as you're the only man around, you're welcome."

His laugh vibrated along her spine, warming her further. She loved it when he laughed, loved being the reason he was amused. Loved it when he touched her as if he'd discovered something rare and precious and he planned to become intimately familiar with every nook and cranny.

Then he got serious, palming her aching nipples, massaging and working her flesh until she could hardly breathe from wanting him. Would she *ever* get tired of that, of the gasping need and clawing desire? She hoped not.

She whipped off her shirt and tossed it on the bed, granting him full access. Arching against him, she pushed her breasts into his hands and flung her head back against his shoulder. As if reading her mind, he fastened his lips to her earlobe, sucking on it gently as one hand wandered south in a lazy pattern, pouring more fire on top of the flames he'd already ignited as her flesh heated under his fingertips.

Finally, his fingers slid into her shorts and toyed for an eternity with her panties, stroking her through the fabric, teasing her as he kissed her throat. So hot and ready, she could hardly stand waiting until he'd had his fill of exploring.

When she moaned in protest at the delay, he eased her back against his thighs and slipped off the rest of her clothing. Without a word, he picked her up and spun her around, placing her gently on the bed, his dark gaze worshipping her body.

Even that heaped more coals on the fire and she shuddered.

Through hazy vision, she watched as he knelt between her thighs and kissed each one. His tongue traced a straight line across her flesh and then he glanced up at her under his lashes as he licked her core. His tongue was hard and blistering hot and wet.

The flare of white-hot pleasure made her cry out. He dove in, tasting her in a sensuous perusal that drained her mind. *Yes*, she screamed. Or maybe that had only been in her head. Her body thrashed involuntarily as he pleasured her with his mouth, slight five o'clock shadow abrading her thighs as he moved.

Higher and higher she spun, hips bucking closer to the source of this amazing pleasure with each thrust of his tongue. The light scape of his teeth against her sensitive bud set off a rolling, thick orgasm that blasted her apart faster and harder than anything she'd ever felt before.

"Now," she murmured huskily and lay back on the counterpane in invitation. "I want your very fine body on mine."

He complied, clothes hitting the floor in a moment. He stretched out over her, his lean torso brushing her breasts deliciously. She wiggled until they were aligned the way she wanted, reveling in the dark sensation of this man covering her.

Savoring the anticipation, she touched him, letting her hands roam where they pleased. Fingertips gliding over his muscled back—gorgeously bunching as he held himself erect so he wouldn't crush her—she hummed her appreciation and nipped at his lips until he took her mouth in a scorching kiss reminiscent of the one he'd given her at her core, tongue deep inside her.

Wordlessly, she urged him on by rolling her hips, silently begging him to complete her as only he could. A brief pause as he got the condom on and then he slid into her, filling her body as gloriously as he filled her soul.

She gasped and clung with all her muscles.

James.

Absolutely the best thing that had ever happened to her. The sexiest man she'd ever been with, for sure, but also the only one who *saw* her. No pretense. No games. She couldn't tear her gaze from his face and something shifted inside, opening the floodgates of a huge and wonderful and irrevocable surge of emotion.

She let herself feel, let everything flow as he loved her. She couldn't even find the capacity to be shocked. It was dangerous—she knew that—but couldn't help it. Murmuring encouragement, his name, who knew what else, she rode out another climax made all the more intense by the tenderness blooming in her heart for the man who'd changed everything. But the wonderful moment soured as soon as her breathing slowed and the hazy glow wore off. She couldn't tell him she'd discovered all these things inside that had his name written all over them. Could she?

No. Fear over his reaction gripped her and in the end, she kept her big mouth shut. After their affair became public, maybe she could admit he'd done something irrevocable to her. But now, reeling it all back, she lay in his arms, letting him hold her tight as if he never meant to let go.

Later, when they'd finally gained the strength to dress, she noticed the box still on the floor near the broken boards. "We should open that."

She pushed at it with her bare foot and it tumbled over, lid flying open and spilling its contents all over the hardwood planks. Letters. Ten or twenty of them, old and fragile, with spidery pale blue handwriting looping across the yellowed pages.

Picking one up, she squinted at it but in the low light of the still musty bedroom, it was too hard to read. She flipped it over to see more of the same faded writing.

"What are they?" James peered over her shoulder, breath warm and inviting across her neck. "Front *and* back. Looks like someone had a lot to say."

"Oh, no." She shook her head and moved out of his reach with a laugh that came out a lot less amused than she'd intended. "You are banned from coming up behind me from now on."

She was far too raw inside to let him open her up again. Not so soon.

"What?" His wicked grin belied the innocent spread of his hands. "I was curious. I can't help it if breathing the same air as me gets you all hot and bothered."

It was a perfectly legitimate thing to say. They flirted and teased each other all the time. *All* the time, and she normally loved it.

He was just so beautiful standing there against the back-drop of the bed where he'd made her feel amazing and whole, made her feel as if she could do anything as long as he was by her side, holding her hand.

Suddenly, her throat closed and she barely caught a sob that welled up from nowhere. This was supposed to be a fun-filled, magnificently hot getaway from the world. When had everything gotten so complicated?

"I, um… Tía Isabella will want these." Bella held up the letters in one hand with false cheer. "I'm just going to go put them in my bag so I don't forget them."

She turned away from James and left the room as quickly as she could without alerting him to her distress. Apparently she'd succeeded.

And now she was completely messed up because she'd hoped he would follow her and demand to know why she was crying.

They slept in the servant's quarters again because they hadn't gotten nearly enough accomplished upstairs due to the detour Bella had sprung on James.

Not that he minded. She could detour like that all day long.

When he awoke, he missed Bella's warmth instantly. She wasn't in the bed. Sitting up, he sought a glimpse of her through the open bathroom door, but nada.

Shame. He liked waking up with her hair across his chest and her legs tangled with his. Surprisingly. This was officially the longest stretch he'd spent with a woman in... ages. Not since Chelsea. And even then, he hadn't been happy in their relationship, not for a long time. When she'd broken up with him because she'd met someone else, he'd been relieved.

Wondering where Bella had taken off to, James vaulted from the bed and dressed, whistling aimlessly as he stuck his shirt over his head. He felt a twinge in his back at the site of an old football injury. Probably because he'd spent the past few days using a different muscle group than the ones he normally engaged while strength training and keeping his footwork honed. Cleaning decades of grime from a place was hard work. But he liked the result— both in the appearance of the house and the gratitude Bella expressed.

Strolling out into the newly-scrubbed kitchen, he reached for the teapot he'd purchased, along with a slew of other absolute necessities, and saw Bella in his peripheral vision sitting outside on the back stoop. She was staring off into the distance as if something was troubling her.

He had a suspicion he knew what it was. Today they were supposed to drive into Playa Del Onda. Should he pretend he'd forgotten and not bring it up so they didn't have to go? He hated that she'd worked the whole confrontation over the engagement announcement up in her mind into something unpleasant. It really shouldn't be so complicated.

Demand a retraction. Done. Of course, getting her father to agree wouldn't necessarily be easy, but it certainly wouldn't be complicated.

In the end, he opted to join her on the stoop without comment, drawing her into his arms to watch the sun burst from behind the clouds to light up the back acreage. She snuggled into his torso and they sat companionably, soaking up the natural beauty of the wild overgrowth.

A horn blasted from the front of the house, startling them both. "Expecting someone?" he asked and she shook her head. "Stay here. I'll see what it is."

"You can't." Her mouth turned down. "I have to be the one. It's Montoro property."

Enough of this hiding and watching their step and having to do things separately so no one could take a picture of them together. They were catering to the whims of their fathers, whether she realized it or not.

"We'll go together." He rose and held out his hand.

She hesitated for so long, an uneasy prickle skittered across the back of his neck. It was way past time to dispense with all this secrecy nonsense. He wanted to do what he pleased and go wherever he wished without fear of someone creating a scandal. Today was a perfect day to stop the madness, since they already planned to confront her father.

Firmly, he took her hand and pulled her to her feet. "Yes. Together. If someone takes a picture, so be it. We're talking to your father today, so there's no reason to keep up this game of hide and seek. Not any longer."

Heaving a huge breath, she nodded. "Okay."

Together, they walked to the front, where a delivery driver stood on the front drive, waving.

"Tengo un paquete," he said, and touched his cap.

Smashing. One-day delivery, as advertised. James had been worried the gift he'd ordered for Bella wouldn't arrive in time, but obviously the exorbitant rush charge had been worth it.

"Gracias," James responded immediately. *"¿Dónde firmo?"*

Bella's eyebrows quirked. "When did you learn Spanish?"

"In like grade four," he retorted with a laugh. "I grew up in a Spanish-speaking country, remember?"

The driver held out his clipboard and once James signed, the deliveryman went to the back of the truck and pulled free a large parcel. Handing it over, the driver nodded once and climbed back into his truck, starting it up with a roar.

The package squawked over the engine sound.

"What in the world is in there?" Bella asked, clearly intrigued as James carried the box into the house through the front door, careful not to cover the air holes with his arms.

"It's a gift. For you." James pulled the tab to open the top of the box, as the Spanish instructions indicated. The box side fell open to reveal the large metal birdcage holding two green macaws. They squawked in tandem.

Bella gasped. "James! What is this?"

"Well, I must have gotten the wrong birds if it's not abundantly clear," he said wryly. "You said you missed your macaws so I brought some to you. Are they okay?"

He'd paid an additional flat fee to guarantee the birds would arrive alive. They looked pretty chipper for having been shipped from the mainland overnight.

With a loud sniff and a strange, strangled mumble, Bella whirled and fled the room, leaving James with two loud birds and a host of confusing, unanswered questions.

"I guess I muddled things up," he told the birds.

He put the cage on the coffee table and gave them some water as he'd been instructed when he ordered the birds, but his irritation rose as he poured. More water ended up on the floor than in the container.

If he could just punch something, his mood would even out. Probably.

Was he supposed to chase Bella down and apologize for spending money on her? Demand an explanation for why she'd hated the gift so much, a simple thank you was beyond her?

By the time he'd ripped open the package of bird food and poured some in the dish, she hadn't returned and his temper had spiked past the point of reasonableness. So he went in search of her and found her upstairs lying in a tight ball on the bed in the master suite. Sobbing.

Instantly, his ire drained and he crawled into the bed to cuddle her, stroking her hair until she quieted enough to allow his windpipe to unclench. "What's wrong, sweetheart?"

She didn't answer and his gut twisted.

Maybe she'd been looking for the exit and his gift had upset her. Women were funny about expensive presents, thinking a bloke had all kinds of expectations in mind if they accepted the gift.

"There aren't any strings attached to the birds, Bella. If you like them, keep them. If you don't, I'll…" *No returns*, the place had said. "…sort it."

His throat went tight again. If she was done here, the birds were the least of his problems. He wasn't ready to end things, not yet. Eventually, sure. His agent had a phone call scheduled with Liverpool today, but that was only the beginning of a long process that might not net him anything other than dashed hopes.

Had he inadvertently speeded up the timeline of their parting with his gesture?

"I like them," she whispered, her mouth buried in the bedspread.

His heart unstuck from his rib cage and began to beat again. "Then talk to me, hon. I'll uncomplicate it, whatever it is."

Without warning, she flipped to face him and the ravaged look on her face sank hooks into his stomach, yanking it toward his knees.

"Not this. You can't uncomplicate it because *you're* the complication, James."

Circles again, and they didn't do circles. Not normally. She shot straight—or at least she had thus far. Had things changed so much so quickly?

"What did I do that's so horrible?" he demanded.

The little noise of disgust she made deep in her throat dredged up some of his earlier temper, but he bit it back to give her the floor.

"You came in here," she raged, "and tore down all my ideas about how this thing between us was going to go. You understand me, pay attention to me. And worse than all of that, you made me fall for you!"

The starkness in her expression sealed his mouth shut once and for all, and he couldn't have spoken for a million euros.

"And I'm scared!" she continued. "I've never been in love. What am I supposed to do? Feel? I'm running blindfolded through the dark."

Too much. Too fast. Too...everything. He blinked rapidly but it didn't do anything to ease the burning in his eyes. He couldn't...she wasn't... *Deep breath. Hold it together.*

She was afraid. Of *him* and what was happening inside her. That was the most important thing to address first. Cautiously, he reached out and took her hand. He was so completely out of his depth, it was a wonder his brain hadn't shut down.

This was a challenge. Maybe the most important one of his life, and after all his claims of being able to uncomplicate anything, now was a good time to start. No buckling under the pressure allowed. Bella needed to feel as if she could trust him and obviously she didn't.

Heart pounding—because honestly, the freaking out wasn't just on her side—he cleared his throat. "Look me in the eye and tell me that again. But without all the extra stuff."

"Which part?" she whispered, searching his gaze, her eyes huge, their expression uneasy.

"The thing about falling for me." Her nails cut into his hand as they both tightened their grip simultaneously. This was a tipping point, and the next few minutes would decide which way it tipped. "I want to hear it straight from your heart."

His lungs seized and he honestly couldn't have said which way he wanted it to tip. What did he hope to accomplish by making this request of her? But he'd spoken the honest truth—regardless of everything, he wanted to hear it again.

"I'm falling for you," she said simply in the husky voice that automatically came out when she was deeply affected.

Something broke open inside him, washing him with warmth, huge and wonderful and irreversible. And suddenly, it wasn't very complicated at all. "Yeah. I've got something along those lines going on over here as well."

That something had been going on for a while. And he was quite disturbed that Will had realized it first. Bella was special and admitting it wasn't the big deal he'd made it out to be. Because the specialness had always been true, from the first moment her body aligned with his on the beach. It was as if he'd been waiting for that moment his whole life and when it happened, his world clicked into place.

"Really?" Hope sprang into her eyes, deepening the blue. "Like a little bit or a whole lot?"

"With no basis for comparison, I'd say it's something like being flung off a cliff and finding out exactly what maximum velocity is," he said wryly. "And it's about as scary as cliff diving with no parachute, since we're on the subject."

The smile blooming on her face reminded him of the sunrise they'd just watched together outside, before the birds had prompted this second round of confessions.

"Isn't it against the guy code to tell a woman she scares

you?" She inched toward him and smoothed a hand over his upper arm, almost as if she was comforting him—which was supposed to be his role in this scenario.

"All of this is against the guy code." He rolled his eyes and she laughed, as he'd intended. The harmonious fullness in his chest that magically appeared at the sound was an unexpected bonus. "Can you at least fill me in on why I had to pry all of this out of you with a crowbar?"

She scrubbed at her face, peering at him through her fingers. "This is not how it was supposed to go. We were going to have a couple of hot dates and maybe I would end up going back to Miami. Maybe you'd jet off to another country like you always do. No one said anything about losing my heart along the way."

A little awed at the thought of Bella's heart belonging to him, he reached out and flattened his palm against her chest, reveling in the feel of it beating against his hand. "I'll take good care of it."

He realized instantly that it was the wrong thing to say.

"For how long?" She sat up and his hand fell away. He missed the warmth immediately. "Until you get a new football contract and take off? You don't do relationships. *I* don't do relationships. Are you prepared to figure out why the hard way—with each other?"

"Yes," he said instantly. "Stop making this so difficult. *If* I get a contract, you come with me. Simple."

The alternative was unthinkable. Actually, he'd never thought about these kinds of things. Never had a reason to. Women came, women left. But this one—he had an opportunity here to grab on to her tight with both hands and no matter how much it scared him, he wasn't letting go.

Catching her lip between her teeth, she worried it almost raw. "What if we get my father to retract the engagement announcement and everything is wonderful. We can date in the open. And then we find out the only thing we had going for us was the secrecy?"

"What, you're afraid I won't be keen on all of this if we don't have to sneak around?" A laugh slipped from his mouth before he fully registered the serious set of her jaw. It finally dawned on him. "That's what you're afraid of."

She shifted uncomfortably. "It's a real possibility."

"It's a real possibility that you'll figure out the same thing," he shot back and the wracked expression on her face floored him. "You already thought of that."

Ice formed instantly in his stomach. It had never occurred to him while they were confessing unexpected feelings that he hadn't actually removed the complications. The *real* complications might only be beginning. Falling for each other didn't magically make either of them relationship material and the potential to hurt each other was that much greater as a result.

Sometimes, no matter how much you practiced, you still missed the goal. And neither of them actually had much practice. What were the odds of success?

"Why do you think I got so upset?" she countered. "You're giving me everything I've ever wanted, and then you give me things I had no idea I wanted, and my heart does all this crazy stuff when you look at me, and when you kiss me it's like my life finally makes sense, and what if I'm the one who's building up this relationship into something mythical because I really like my men with a side of forbidden?"

"Okay, breathe."

He half laughed and ran a hand through his hair. This rated as the most honest conversation he'd ever had with a woman. And that made it all the more fascinating that he was still here, determined not to buckle. Bella was worth it.

She breathed. And then dropped the second bomb. "What if I want to get married someday? Is that potentially in the cards?"

He let the idea rattle around inside for a long moment,

but it didn't completely unnerve him to consider it. He wasn't saying yes, but wasn't saying no.

"What if it is?" He captured her gaze and held it, refusing to let her look away, where she might miss the sincerity of what he was telling her. "Will that scare you as well?"

His brother had predicted that, too. Silently, he cursed himself and then his omniscient twin. Well, he hadn't proposed yet and no one was saying he would. Grandfather's watch still belonged to James. For now.

"More than I could possibly tell you," she admitted.

But she didn't have to tell him because he had a pretty good idea that the adrenaline racing around in his body closely matched what was going on with her.

"And," she continued swiftly, "I'm not saying that I will want to get married. To you or anyone. But what if I do?"

"You know what?" He tipped her chin up. "I think it's a safe bet that we have more going on here than a forbidden love angle. And I also think that no matter what, we can be honest with each other about what's going on, whether it's marriage or something else. I might be wrong, but I'm willing to take that risk. Are you?"

"Will you hold my hand?" she asked in a small voice. "When you're holding my hand, I feel like the world is a different place, like nothing bad could ever happen."

Yeah, he got that. If they could do this together, it might actually work.

Tenderly, he laced his fingers with hers and held on. "I'll never let go, not even when we hit the water. Jump with me, Bella."

Her smile pierced his heart and he started to believe they might figure this out after all. There were a lot of unknowns, sure, and they still had to sort their families—which wouldn't be as easy as he might be pretending. But it felt as if they were at the beginning of something wonderful.

It wasn't until they'd climbed into the Lamborghini

an hour later that he glanced at his phone and noted two missed calls, followed by a text message…and had the strangest sense of foreboding, as if he'd vastly underestimated the level and complexity of the complications to come.

Ten

James was quiet during the drive back to Playa Del Onda and Bella left him alone with his thoughts.

After all, she'd been the one to change the game, and while he'd admitted his feelings had grown stronger than he'd expected as well, he hadn't argued when the subject of *what ifs* came up. It was a lot to take in. A lot to reconcile.

She still didn't know how she felt about all of this either. She certainly hadn't intended to blurt out something so difficult to take back as "I'm falling for you," but he'd been so sweet, first with the birds and then the way he handled her half-coherent stream of babbling about her fears. If any man was a keeper, it was James Rowling.

So the question was, how hard was it going to be to keep him? Her father was going to freak and there was no getting around the fact that James was still the wrong brother.

No matter. She wasn't ready to let James go, not yet. Whatever happened between her and James, they had a right to pursue it. And she wasn't leaving here without her father's promise to stop interfering.

When they walked into the house—together—Gabriel and her father were waiting for her in the foyer, thanks to a text message she'd sent on the way imploring her brother to play diplomat if the situation called for it.

Judging by the frown on Rafael's face, she'd made a good call.

"What is *he* doing here?" her father demanded, making it perfectly clear that he knew Bella hadn't brought home the correct Rowling despite their similar appearances—and that Rafael's feelings on the matter hadn't changed.

Bella halted but didn't drop James's hand. He squeezed hers tight in a show of solidarity but remained silent, earning a huge number of points. "James is here because I invited him. You've caused us both problems by announcing my engagement to Will Rowling and therefore, we both have a vested interest in resolving the situation."

"The problems caused by the engagement announcement are one hundred percent at your feet, Isabella." Her father crossed his arms over his expensive suit, presumably to ensure he appeared intimidating, but he'd lost any edge he might have had by using that tone of voice with her—and the man she was pretty sure she was in love with.

"Let's not sling accusations," Gabriel interjected and she smiled at him gratefully. "Listen to Bella, Dad. She's a grown woman and this is a friendly conversation between adults."

Rafael deflated. A bit.

Gabriel's "king" lessons had paid off, in Bella's humble opinion. He'd grown a lot in the past few weeks and no one was confused about Serafia's role in that. Her future sister-in-law—also the future queen—was an inspiration and Bella was happy to call Serafia family.

"You have the floor, Isabella." Her father glowered at James but didn't speak to him again, which was fine by her. For now.

"I don't want to marry Will. I told you this already.

Why in the world would you go ahead and issue a press release saying we were engaged? Do you hate the idea of my happiness so much?" Her voice broke against her will.

Why did she still care so much that her father didn't seem to see her as anything other than a bargaining chip?

James stepped forward and addressed Rafael directly. "Sir, you don't know me and I realize I'm not your first choice for your daughter, but please understand that she makes me happy. I want nothing more than to do the same for her. I hope you can respect that."

Well, if there was any question about whether she was in love with him, that speech pretty much shot all doubt to hell. There might even be swooning in her future. She grinned at him, not even caring that she probably looked like a besotted fool.

Her father sighed and rubbed his head but before he could speak, Gabriel held out his hand to James, shaking it vigorously.

"I can respect that." Her brother nodded once at James. "I didn't get a chance to mention it when we first met, but I occasionally watched you play for Real Madrid. Bum deal that they released you. Big mistake on their part, in my opinion."

"Thanks." James smiled and bowed slightly to Gabriel, despite being told the prince didn't like formality. "And good luck to you. Alma is in brilliant hands with you at the helm."

Now that all the small talk was out of the way… "Dad, James and I are going to be a couple. You have to retract the engagement story or we're going to have a scandal on our hands. I don't want that for Gabriel or the Montoro family as a whole."

"All of which would have been avoided if you'd simply gotten with the program," Rafael insisted. "We're all making sacrifices for Gabriel—"

"Hold on a minute." The future king threw up his hands

with a frown. "Don't drag me into this. I never asked Bella to marry Will Rowling and frankly, an arranged marriage is ridiculous in this day and age. I've never understood the reasoning."

"You need the alignment with Rowling Energy," her father sputtered and might have gone on if Gabriel hadn't interrupted again.

"Yes. I do. But Bella is asking us to find another way. What kind of king would I be if I didn't at least try to take her wishes into account?" Gabriel asked rhetorically, his regal voice echoing with sincerity in the grand foyer. "Dad, I think you should consider the retraction, especially if Bella and James's relationship is what they say it is."

Gabriel shot Bella a look that said he'd taken one look at her dopey face and made all kinds of assumptions about the nature of her relationship with James. But then, bringing James with her to the showdown had probably tipped her brother off to that the moment they'd crossed the threshold. "I don't kiss and tell, so you can forget any juicy details, if that's what you're after."

Gabriel mimed putting his fingers in his ears and shook his head with a shudder.

Clearing his throat in his no-nonsense way, Rafael put on his best disappointed-father face. "It's not just the alignment with Rowling Energy that's at stake here, Isabella. You have a tendency to be flighty. Irresponsible. Marriage will be good for you, if you choose someone who settles you. Will is as steady as they come."

The unvoiced and pointed barb directed at James was: *and the man you waltzed in here with is the opposite of steady.* The sting of hearing her father's unvarnished opinion of *her* was totally eclipsed by the negativity directed toward James, who was nothing like what her father assumed.

"That's where you're wrong, Dad. Will might be good at holding a company together, but James is good at holding *me* together. He settles me in a way I've never felt before. I'd rather spend an evening with him washing windows than at a party."

The words were out of her mouth before she consciously planned to say them, but once they took root in her heart, she recognized the truth. She didn't have any desire to be the party girl she'd been in Miami. Her boredom at Will Rowling's party hadn't had anything to do with the difference in party styles across the ocean, but in the subtle changes already happening inside *her*.

"By the way," she threw in. "You haven't asked, but in case you're wondering, your irresponsible daughter has spent the past few days restoring the old farmhouse near Aldeia Dormer that's part of the Montoro holdings. It looks really amazing so far and I couldn't have done it without James's help. I've also spent almost one hundred percent of that time with him, yet I dare you to find one illicit photograph of the two of us."

"What's this about a farmhouse?" Gabriel's eyebrows drew together as he homed in on her.

"I'll fill you in later," she promised. "Can you try to be happy for me, Dad? If you can't do that, I'll settle for that retraction. I do have a strong sense of my royal obligations. I'd just like you to respect the fact that I feel differently about what they are than you do."

"I'll issue the retraction but only to avoid the potential scandal. I cannot condone this relationship. I would prefer that you do not continue seeing him." Her father's sidelong glance at James spoke volumes. There was no doubt he still considered the wrong Rowling a terrible influence.

"I can't do that, Dad. And I'm disappointed that you still can't see the value James brings to my life." Her voice cracked and she cursed herself once again for caring. Regardless, she was getting the retraction she asked for, and she'd take it.

"You're right, I can't. I fully expect that once the thrill

wears off, you'll be back to your former ways, Isabella."
With that vote of no confidence ringing in her ears, her
father motioned to James. "And if you're not, *he* will be.
This is a disaster in the making. Will it do any good for
me to warn you to keep your brother's reign at the forefront of your thoughts?"

"I always keep Gabriel in mind," she countered.

"Good, then the three of you can deal with Patrick Rowling." Her father wheeled on Gabriel with a scowl. "Since
you're taking Bella's side in this, I'll let you handle the
delicate matter of ensuring the alliance I painstakingly
put into place won't suffer."

Her father stalked off to go terrorize the staff or something.

"Sorry," Bella said to her brother with a scowl. "I didn't
mean for you to get in the middle of this. At least not that
way. Are you okay with talking to Mr. Rowling?"

Unfortunately, thanks to the hours upon hours of conversation with James at the farmhouse, Bella knew exactly
why Patrick wasn't going to be pleased with the develop-
ments.

"I'll talk to him," James volunteered, and Bella shot
him a small smile.

"That's a good idea." Gabriel's expression reflected the
gravity of the situation. "I'll speak with him as well. But
it's sticky. We have business agreements in place that could
be in jeopardy. You should lie low for a while longer until
matters are a bit more settled."

Great, more hiding. Why was it such a problem that two
people wanted to spend time together? But the mention of
things like business agreements clued her in that there was
more at stake than she might have supposed.

At least her father hadn't forbidden her to see James. He
just said he didn't want her to and made his disappointment in her clear. Fortunately, she had a lot of practice at
living with her father's disappointment. If Gabriel worked

things out with Mr. Rowling, maybe her father would come around. It could happen.

Gabriel and James talked a bit more about the logistics of their impending conversations with Patrick Rowling until James's cell phone rang.

He glanced at it and excused himself to take the call. Based on his expression, it must be shocking news indeed. Gabriel went off to do king stuff as James ended the call.

"What is it?" she whispered, almost afraid to ask. They'd barely confessed their fledgling feelings to each other, their fathers were still potential stumbling blocks in their relationship and she didn't know how many more hits they should be expected to take.

"Liverpool." His tone couldn't have been more stunned. "Management wants to meet with me. Tomorrow."

"Liverpool? Isn't that a city in England?" Then it dawned on her that he meant the football team. "They want to talk to you about a contract? That's great!"

"I have to fly to London." His enthusiasm shone from his face. Then he grew serious. "I don't know what they're going to say. But if it's an offer, it would be hard for me to turn down."

"Why would you turn it down? You can't."

"I would have to live in England for most of the year." His gorgeous eyes sought and held hers as the implications weighed down her shoulders.

This was serious, life-altering stuff, the kind of thing couples with a future considered. While she thought that was where they were headed—thought that was where she *wanted* them to go—it was another matter entirely to have Big Decisions dropped in your lap before you were ready. It was far scarier than accidentally revealing your feelings.

"We'll figure it out," she murmured, as though she knew what she was talking about. "We're jumping together. Just don't let go of my hand, remember?"

Instead of agreeing, or grabbing her hand and shooting

her a tender smile, he scrubbed at his eyes with stiff fingers. "Everything is moving too fast."

Her heart froze.

Everything? As in their relationship, too? He'd volunteered to come with her, to talk to his father and work out the issues between the Montoro family and Rowling Energy—was he having second thoughts now? "One step at a time, James. Go to England and see what they say. Then we can talk."

He nodded and swept her up in a fierce hug. She inhaled his familiar scent, soaked in his essence. That at least felt somewhat normal and it calmed her a bit.

"I'll call you the moment I know something. Guess I'll be gone a couple of days."

Watching him drive away wrenched something loose inside her and the place ached where it used to be attached. She rubbed at her chest and perversely wondered if it would get better or worse if he called with the news that Liverpool wanted to sign him. Because that's when she'd find out once and for all whether removing the temptation of the forbidden caused him to completely lose interest.

James resisted pulling at his starched collar. Barely. If he'd had more notice that Liverpool wanted a meeting, he might have scared up a more comfortable suit. Contract negotiations rarely included the player and the fact that Liverpool specifically asked for James to attend meant… what? He didn't know and it was weighing on him.

The small room got smaller the longer Liverpool's management murmured behind their cupped hands. James could tell from their less-than-impressed faces that his agent's opening pitch hadn't won anyone over.

So maybe the comfort of the suit didn't matter when your entire future was on the line.

Liverpool had expressed definite interest in picking up

James if the price was right, according to his agent, but they wanted to move fast on making a decision.

James was not leaving here without that contract. It wasn't about the money. It was about putting his mistakes behind him and gaining the opportunity to prove his loyalty to a club. He had to. To show Bella he was really the hero material she saw him as. To prove that he was worth all the trouble they'd gone through to be together.

James cleared his throat. "It's obvious you have reservations about me. What are your concerns?"

The three suits on the other side of the table all stared at him with varying degrees of surprise. Why, because he didn't subscribe to the British philosophy of keeping a stiff upper lip?

His sports agent, Spencer Stewart, shot him an annoyed glance and waved off James. "No one has reservations. We're all professionals here. So, give us your best offer and we'll consider it."

"Yes, we're all professionals," James agreed. "But these gentlemen have every right to question my capacity to act professionally. Let's call a spade a spade. I made mistakes. But I'm ready to be serious about my career and I want to play my heart out for a team willing to give me that chance."

All at once, it occurred to him that Alma's reserve team had already offered him that chance. And he'd turned his nose up at it. As if he was too good for what he considered the small time.

That didn't sit well. No club *owed* him a spot on the roster.

Liverpool's manager nodded slowly. "That's fair. As is our original salary offer. The cap is a concern, after all."

James kept his face straight, wishing he could argue. The cap was only a concern for a risky acquisition. They'd gladly pay the fines for going over the cap to gain a player with a less scandalous past. He'd have to take a pay cut if he wanted to play for Liverpool—and work twice as hard to earn it. Simple as that.

And he'd have to move to England.

A few days ago, he would have already been packed in anticipation of relocating as fast as possible. He could avoid his father for good. That conversation with dear old Dad about the agreements between Rowling Energy and the Montoros—the one he'd promised Gabriel he'd have—never had to happen.

Liverpool was the perfect solution to his relationship with Bella—if they had to lie low, what better place to do it than England?

But he couldn't get enthusiastic about it all at once. Bella deserved better than to be required to hide their relationship because of his past. She shouldn't have to move to England if she wanted to be with him, just because he couldn't get another contract.

How had things grown so complicated so fast? The king of uncomplicating things was falling down on the job.

"I need some time to weigh my options," James announced suddenly. Because he'd just realized he not only had options, he also had other people to consider outside of himself. "I appreciate the offer, and it's generous under the circumstances. Mr. Stewart will update you soon on my decision."

Liverpool wasn't the right club for him. Not yet, maybe not ever. Not until he'd proven to everyone—Bella, his father, hell, even himself—that he could stop running away from conflict and deal with the consequences of his actions. He needed to be in Alma to do that. Permanently.

Actually, this wasn't very complicated at all.

James loved football. He'd thought for so long that a professional league contract was his goal, only to find the game had completely changed on him. Bella had changed it. He wanted to be a better man for her. She was the best reason of all to find out whether he could finally stand up under extreme pressure and come out a winner.

James hurried to Heathrow, eager to get back home and tell Bella that her belief in him wasn't misplaced. That he could be the hero she saw him as. He wanted to commit to her, to have a future with her.

As he settled back in his seat and switched off his cell phone in accordance with the flight attendant's instructions, he glanced at his watch. And cursed as he realized what was happening—it looked as if Will was going to be the lucky recipient of Grandfather's watch after all.

When James got off the plane in Del Sol, he powered up his cell phone intending to call Bella immediately. *Surprise. I'm home early.*

But the first text message that popped up was from Will.

Chelsea is here. You better come talk to her. She's camped out in the lobby disrupting business.

What the hell? He swore, dove into his Lamborghini and then drove to Rowling Energy at double the speed limit. The harrowing hairpin turns should have put a smile on his face the way they normally did, but Will's text message had effectively killed any cheer he might have taken from the thrill.

If only he'd called Chelsea back yesterday, when he'd seen the missed calls on his phone, the ensuing fiasco could have been avoided. But Bella had been nervous about confronting her father and he really didn't want to talk to Chelsea in the first place. So he'd ignored her. What could they possibly have to say to each other?

Apparently that had irritated his ex-girlfriend enough for her to go to Rowling Energy and bother his brother. James had dated her for…what, four months? Not long enough for her to remember that James hated Rowling

Energy so much that he rarely set foot in the place. It had taken something as important to him as Bella to get him through the door last week.

His phone beeped. Will had texted him again. Hope you're almost here. Your ex is a piece of work.

Still fuming, James screeched into a parking spot and stomped into the elevator. Why in the hell had she taken it upon herself to disrupt an entire company in order to speak to an ex-lover she'd had no contact with for almost two years? When a bloke didn't ring you back, it meant he wasn't into you.

But when he arrived in the reception area, some of the pieces fell into place. Chelsea, looking less glamorous and far more worn than he recalled, sat on the leather couch bouncing a baby.

A baby.

Obviously she'd been busy since they'd broken up and was clearly hard up for money. What, did she think James was going to fund her for old times' sake? How dare she bring a kid in here as a sympathy ploy? His ire increased exponentially. She *was* a piece of work.

"Chelsea." She glanced up. "Can we take this outside please?"

She nodded, hoisted the baby to her hip and followed him out of the building to a shaded courtyard around the side of the building where employees sometimes ate lunch. It was thankfully deserted.

"You have a lot of nerve barging into my father's company to extort money from me," he said by way of greeting to the woman he'd had only marginal affection for once upon a time.

"That's not why I'm here and besides, you didn't call me back," she reminded him as she settled onto a bench with the baby. "How else was I supposed to find you?"

He bit back a curse. "You're barking up the wrong tree if you think I'm going to give you a dime out of the goodness of my heart because some plonker knocked you up and you're short on cash."

That would explain why she had a bargain basement fashion statement going on. When they'd dated, she spent thousands on clothes and jewelry, usually with his credit card.

"Not someone." Chelsea peered up at him, totally cool. In her element because she'd gotten his attention after all. "You. This is your daughter."

His vision blacked out for a moment as all the blood rushed from his head.

I have a baby daughter. None of those words belonged in the same sentence. Blindly, James felt for the bench so he could sink onto it before the cramp in his stomach knocked him to the grass.

"What are you talking about?" he demanded hoarsely over the street sounds floating through the privacy bushes. "I haven't even seen you in almost two years. That's a baby and they only take nine months to make."

Chelsea smirked and flipped her lanky brown hair behind her back. "She's almost a year old, Daddy. Do the math."

Daddy. His brain couldn't—*could not*—keep up, especially when she insisted on throwing inflammatory monikers onto the woodpile. And now she wanted him to do subtraction on top of it all?

"Why…wha— How…?" Deep breath. His tongue couldn't seem to formulate the right questions. "Paternity test? I want one."

Okay, now he was on top of this situation. Get to the bottom of this pack of lies and toss her out on her no-longer-attractive rear end.

She rolled her eyes. "Fine. I'll arrange one as soon as possible. But there's really no question."

The little girl picked that moment to turn her head, peering directly at James for the first time.

Aqua eyes the exact color of his beamed at him through fringed lashes. Not only the exact color of his, but both Will and their late mother shared the rare shade.

His world tilted and slid quickly off the rails. The paternity test would be superfluous, obviously.

He couldn't tear his gaze away from the baby. His baby. It was real. This was his child, and until five minutes ago he'd had no idea she existed. He'd missed his daughter's birth, along with a ton of other milestones, which he mourned all at once. Chelsea could never rectify that crime.

"Why now, Chelsea? You should have bloody well shown up long before today with this news."

"I thought she was Hugh's." Chelsea shrugged nonchalantly as if they were discussing a pair of pants she'd found in her closet after they'd broken up. "He's the guy I left you for. I must have miscalculated my conception date, but I didn't realize it until recently when her eyes changed color. And I knew I couldn't keep this from you."

There was so much wrong with all of that, he hardly knew where to start. "What happened when her eyes changed color, Chelsea? Did you see dollar signs that Hugh couldn't match?"

"No." She frowned, pulling her full lips into a pout. "I thought it was right that you know about Maisey."

Maisey. His daughter's name was Maisey. And he'd had no say in it. Not that it was a horrible name, but if Chelsea had told him when she got pregnant, he might have been able to participate in the selection process. He'd have liked to name his daughter after his mum. Yet another thing this woman had stolen from him.

"If you thought about me at all, I'm sure it had more to do with things like child support."

He had to get over it and figure this out. Chelsea was his daughter's mother. Period. Like it or not, they were going to have some type of relationship for the next eighteen years, at least. Maybe longer.

Before she could deny her selfishness again, he eyed her. "What did Hugh think about your little error in calculation? Bet he wasn't so thrilled."

Chelsea looked away quickly but not before he saw the flash of guilt in her expression.

"He left you," James concluded grimly. "And you're skint."

She sighed. "Hugh refused to keep taking care of a kid that wasn't his and he might have been slightly ticked to find out that I fudged the details a little about the last time you and I slept together. So yeah, I'm low on money."

God, did the string of dumb decisions this woman had made ever end? This was his daughter's life Chelsea was playing around with, but she seemed to be treating it all like a big game.

The baby made a noise that sounded like a cross between a sob and a sigh and she captivated his attention instantly.

"What was that? Is she okay?" he whispered.

"She's a baby," Chelsea snapped impatiently. "That's what they do. Make noise. And cry. And poop."

This conversation had passed surreal ten minutes ago.

"What do you want from me?" he demanded.

Well, hell. It hardly mattered what she wanted. If this little breathing bundle of hair and pink outfit was his daughter, there was a lot more to consider than what the woman who'd given birth to her hoped to achieve. He had rights. He had options. And he would exercise both.

"I want you to be her father," Chelsea said simply.

"Done. We need to discuss child support and custody arrangements."

Reality blasted him like a freight train whistle. What was his life going to look like from now on? Did he need to reconsider Liverpool so he could be close to Chelsea in England? How would Bella feel about spending weekends with his infant daughter from now on?

He scrubbed at his face. *Bella*. God, this was going to be exactly what her father had predicted—a disaster. She deserved so much more than to be saddled with a boyfriend who had a kid. And what kind of new problems might this cause for her? An illegitimate child surely wasn't going to make her father suddenly approve of James.

"Nothing to discuss." Chelsea shook her head. "I don't want either one. I want you to take her. Forever. I'm signing over all my rights to you."

"You…what?"

Arms crossed mutinously like the immature woman she was, Chelsea scowled. "I'm done being a mum. I hate it. This is your fault, so you take her."

She said it as if they were discussing a stray dog. And she was making his choice easy. He didn't want such a selfish mum raising his daughter anyway. Sickened that he could have ever been intimate with this woman, he nodded grimly. "Seems like the best idea all the way around, then."

Single dad. The voice in his head wouldn't stop screaming that phrase, over and over, and the place in his heart that belonged to Bella ached at this new reality. Just as he'd accepted that he not only *could* do a long-term, roots-into-the-ground relationship, he wanted to. But not like this, with such a huge complication as a surprise baby.

The timing was horrific. Because he'd just realized why this was so difficult, why he couldn't take the Liverpool contract. Why he was so worried about dropping this news on Bella—he was in love with her.

Eleven

By evening, James hadn't called.

Bella tried not to think about it. He was busy with Liverpool. She got that. The one time she'd tried to call him, it went straight to voice mail. Maybe his cell phone had died and he'd forgotten his charger.

If not that, there was a simple explanation for his silence and when he got her message, he'd call. No one would willingly face down her father without having some skin in the game. James had said he'd call and he would. He cared about her. She knew he did.

After a long night of tossing and turning, she had to find something to do to keep busy and the farmhouse still needed work. It kept her mind off the disloyal thoughts that had crept in overnight—that the distance between here and England had given James some perspective and his feelings had cooled after all. Just as she'd feared.

Or he'd decided a princess with a scandal-averse family was too much work for a guy who liked to play the field.

Discovering a bird's nest in the tree close to the back

steps finally pulled her attention from her morose thoughts. She missed her own birds— she'd moved the macaws James had given her to the Playa Del Onda house since she hadn't planned to continue traveling back and forth. These baby birds filled the silence with high-pitched cheeps and she smiled as she watched them from an upstairs window.

It was a much-needed sign. Regardless of what happened with James and the news regarding his contract with Liverpool, she should go forward with conservation work. Birds would always need her and she liked having a purpose.

When she returned to Playa Del Onda, a maid met her in the foyer and announced Bella had a visitor in the salon.

James. Her heart did a twisty dance move in her chest. Of course she'd blown his silence out of proportion and they'd laugh over her silliness. Maybe he'd come straight from the airport and somehow she'd missed his call. As she dashed into the salon, she palmed her phone, already checking for the errant message.

It wasn't James, though, and the man standing by the window almost rendered her speechless. But she found her manners somehow.

"Mr. Rowling," Bella greeted James's father cautiously. "How nice to see you."

They'd met formally once before and she'd greeted him at Will's party, but this was the first time they'd spoken without others in attendance. Did James know he was here? Had he already talked to his father? If Gabriel had spoken to Mr. Rowling, he would have mentioned it to her. She was flying completely blind and nothing good could possibly come of this surprise meeting.

James's father didn't offer his hand but instead bowed as if they'd stumbled into a formal setting without her realizing it. "Princess Isabella. Thank you for seeing me on short notice."

"Of course." Mindful of her father's warning to watch

her step when dealing with matters important to the crown, she inclined her head graciously. "What can I do for you?"

"May we take a seat?" Mr. Rowling indicated the overstuffed and incredibly uncomfortable couch.

Sure, why not add more formality on top of the already overbearing deference of the elder Rowling? She perched on the cushion and waited for Patrick Rowling to get to the point.

He cleared his throat. "I realize that you and Will have agreed to part ways and that you are seeing my other son. You've made a terrible mistake and I'm here to ensure you understand the full extent of it."

Geez, first her father and now Patrick Rowling? It was as if everyone thought she could be talked out of her feelings if they just tried hard enough. "Will would be a bigger mistake. We aren't interested in each other."

Mr. Rowling held up a conciliatory hand. "I'm not here to talk about Will. Granted, there is sound sense in a match between you and my son, but even I understand that the heart isn't always sensible."

Confused and suspicious, she eyed James's father. "Then why are you here?"

That had come out a little more bluntly than intended, but he didn't seem bothered by her lack of decorum.

Clearing his throat, he leaned forward as if about to impart a secret. "The mistake you're making, the one I'm here to help you avoid, is putting your faith in James. He is not a good choice for any woman, least of all you."

Her temper boiled over but she schooled her features and bit back the nasty phrase she'd been about to say. This man didn't know her and he had a lot of nerve assuming he had insight into what kind of man would be good for her.

But the worse crime was that he didn't know his own son either. That, she could correct.

"James is an amazing man. I'm shocked his own father doesn't recognize that, but since it's clear you don't, despite ample opportunity to come to know your son, I'll tell you. He has a good heart, a generous nature and most of all, he cares about me."

Her voice rang with sincerity. Because she believed what she was saying. He'd call soon and they'd talk about the future. Everything was going to work out.

Mr. Rowling frowned. "I do so hate to disagree. But my son is a notorious womanizer with little regard for anyone's feelings other than his own. Surely you're aware of his indiscretions." He swept her with a pitying once-over. "God help you if you're not."

Foreboding slid down her spine and raised the hair on the back of her neck.

"You mean the photographs in the tabloids?" She crossed her arms, wondering if it would actually protect her against this man's venom. "I'm aware of them."

James had been very upfront about his brush with scandal. Whatever his father thought he was going to accomplish by bringing up the pictures wasn't going to work.

"Oh, no, Princess Isabella." He shook his head with a *tsk*. "I'm talking about James's illegitimate daughter."

Bella's skin iced over. "His…what?" she whispered.

Mr. Rowling watched her closely through narrowed eyes, and she suspected he'd finally come to the meat of the reason he'd casually dropped by.

"James has an infant daughter he fathered with his last girlfriend. Shall I assume from your reaction that he hasn't mentioned any of this to you?"

"No," she admitted quietly as her pulse skipped a whole lot of beats. "I wasn't aware."

And of course there was a reason James hadn't told her. There had to be. Her mind scrambled to come up with one. But without James here to explain, she was only left with huge question marks and no answers.

In all that time at the farmhouse together, he'd never once thought to mention a baby he'd fathered with the girlfriend he'd stopped seeing nearly two years ago? Had she completely misread what he'd confessed to her about his feelings? None of this made any sense. Why would he talk about the implications of moving to England but not tell her he had a daughter?

It was a lie. Mr. Rowling was trying to cause problems. That was the only explanation.

Mr. Rowling eyed her and she didn't miss the crafty glint in his gaze. Neither of his sons took after this schemer in any way and it was a testament to James that he'd ended up with such an upstanding character.

"It's true," he said, somehow correctly interpreting the set of her jaw. "James will confirm it and then you might ask why he's kept it from you. It's a consideration for a woman when choosing whom she has a relationship with, don't you think?"

Yes, a huge consideration. That's what he'd meant by James not being a good choice for her. Because he wasn't trustworthy.

She shook her head against the rebellious thoughts. This was a campaign to poison her against James, plain and simple, but why, she couldn't fathom. "He has his reasons for not telling me. Whatever they are, I can forgive him."

Because that's what people in a relationship did. Not that she had any practice—she'd never had one, never dreamed she'd have one that tested her in quite this way. But James was worth figuring it out.

"You realize, of course, that his daughter is illegitimate." Mr. Rowling countered smoothly. "You're still in line for the throne should something happen to Gabriel. Alma doesn't cater to that sort of impropriety in its monarchy, and citizens have no patience for royal scandals. Frankly, neither do I."

It was a veiled threat, one she understood all too well after the discussion with Gabriel and her father about business between the crown and Rowling Energy. And blast it, he wasn't overstating the point about her position or potential to be queen one day. A princess couldn't drag an illegitimate child through the world's headlines.

Her head started to pound as her father's warning played over and over on an endless loop in her mind. Gabriel wouldn't be on her side with this one, not after what happened with Rafe and Emily and their unexpected pregnancy. Not after she'd already forced her brother to renegotiate agreements with Rowling, which would be very difficult to wade through indeed if Mr. Rowling's threat was to be believed.

If she continued to be with James, the entire future of Gabriel's reign—and indeed perhaps her own—might be in jeopardy.

"Let me ask you another question, Princess Isabella."

The way he said that made her spine crawl but she didn't correct him. Only her friends called her Bella and this man was not in that group. A shame since she'd hoped he would become her father-in-law someday. That dream had rapidly evaporated under his onslaught.

She nodded, too miserable to figure out how to make her voice work.

"What if she's not the only illegitimate child out there?"

God, he was right. The reality of it unleashed a wave of nausea through her stomach. James had made no secret of his playboy past. Since she'd never sat around in virginal white gowns either, it hadn't troubled her. Until now.

She very much feared she might throw up.

"If you weren't aware of the baby, you also probably aren't aware that her mother is here in Playa Del Onda visiting James." Mr. Rowling leaned forward, apparently oblivious to the hot poker he'd just shoved through Bella's chest. "I know you'd like to think that you're special. James has a particular talent with women. But the fact of the matter is that he still has very deep feelings for the mother of his child. Their relationship is far from over."

"That's not true," Bella gasped out. It couldn't be. She wasn't that naïve. "Anyway, James is in England."

The pitying look Mr. Rowling gave her nearly stopped her heart. "He's been back in Alma since yesterday."

"I trust James implicitly," she shot back and cursed the wobble in her voice. She did. But he'd come home from England and *hadn't called* and his silence was deafening. "Why are you telling me all of this?"

Mr. Rowling pursed his lips. "I'm simply making sure you are aware of what you are getting yourself into by refusing to see the truth about James. I have your best interests at heart."

She doubted that very much. But it didn't negate the accusations he'd brought against James. Her throat burned as she dragged breath into her lungs.

No. This was propaganda, plain and simple. She shook her head again as if she could make it all go away with the denial. "I need to talk to James."

"Of course," he agreed far too quickly. "I've said my piece. But before I go, please note that Will is still open to honoring the original marriage agreement."

With that parting comment, Mr. Rowling followed the butler out of the salon, leaving Bella hollowed out. She crawled onto her bed to lie in a tight ball, but nothing could ease the sick waves still sloshing through her abdomen.

Lies. All of it was lies. James could—and would—straighten all of this out and then they'd deal with the issue of his illegitimate child. Somehow.

Except he still didn't answer her call. Twice.

This silence…it was killing her. If he was done with her, she deserved to hear it from him, face-to-face. Not from his father.

She had to know, once and for all. If he wouldn't answer the phone, she'd go to his house.

The Montoro town car had long been on the list of instantly admitted vehicles at the Rowling Mansion gates, so the driver didn't have to announce Bella's presence. As Mr.

Rowling had said, James's green Lamborghini sat parked in the circular drive of the Rowling mansion.

Bella climbed out of the car, her gaze fastened to the Lamborghini, her heart sinking like a stone. James was home. And hadn't called. Nor would he answer his phone. The truth of Mr. Rowling's revelations burned at the back of her eyes but she refused to let the tears fall.

James would explain.

A woman's laugh floated to her on the breeze and Bella automatically turned toward the gazebo down the slope from the main drive. It was partially obscured by foliage but James was easy to make out. Even if she couldn't plainly see the watch on James's arm, Will didn't live here, and neither would he be at his father's house in the middle of the work day when he had a company to run.

The dark haired woman sitting in the gazebo with James faced away from Bella, but she'd bet every last euro in the royal treasury it was his former girlfriend. It didn't mean anything. They were probably talking about the daughter they shared. Patrick Rowling wasn't going to ruin her relationship with James.

Bella had come for answers and now she'd get them.

Feeling like a voyeur but unable to stop herself, she moved closer to catch what they were saying but the murmurs were inaudible. And then James threaded his fingers through the woman's hair and pulled her into a scorching kiss.

And it was a *kiss*, nothing friendly about it.

The back of Bella's neck heated as she watched the man she loved kiss another woman.

James was kissing another woman.

Brazenly. Passionately. Openly. As if he didn't care one bit whether anyone saw him.

His watch glinted in the late afternoon sun as he pulled the dark-haired woman closer, and the flash blinded Bella. Or maybe her vision had blurred because of the tears.

How long had she been playing the fool in this scenario—and was she truly the last to find out? Was everyone giggling behind their hands at her naïvety? Mr. Rowling had certainly known. This was going on in his house and as many times as she'd accused him of not knowing his son... *she* was the one who didn't know James.

It all swirled through her chest, crushing down with so much weight she thought her heart would cease to beat under the pressure.

Whirling, she fled back to the car, only holding back the flood of anguish long enough to tell the driver to take her home.

But when she finally barricaded herself in her room, it didn't feel like home at all. The only place she'd ever experienced the good, honest emotions of what a home should feel like was at the farmhouse. But it had all been a complete lie.

Still blinded by tears, she packed as much as she could into the bag she'd lived out of during those brief, precious days with James as they cleaned up the Montoro legacy. Alma could make do without her because she couldn't stay here.

Everything is moving too fast, he'd said. He'd meant *she* was, with her expectations and ill-timed confessions. The whole time, he'd had a woman and a baby on the side. Or was *Bella* the side dish in this scenario?

Horrified that she'd almost single-handedly brought down the monarchy with her own gullibility, she flung clothes into bags faster. New York. She'd go to New York where there were no bad memories. Her friends in Miami would only grill her about James because she'd stupidly kept them up to the minute as things unfolded with her new romance.

And her brother Rafe would see through her instantly. She couldn't stand to be around people who knew her well.

Within an hour, she'd convinced Gabriel to concoct

some story explaining her absence and numbly settled into the car as it drove her to the private airstrip where the Montoro jet waited to take her to New York. It was the perfect place to forget her troubles among the casual acquaintances she planned to look up when she got there.

The shorter her time in Alma grew, the more hollowed out she felt.

When her phone beeped, she nearly hurled it out the window. *James*. Finally, he'd remembered that she existed. She didn't care what he had to say, couldn't even bear to see his name on the screen. But a perverse need to cut her losses, once and for all, had her opening up the text so she could respond with something scathing and final.

I'm home. Came by, but Gabriel said you left. When will you be back? We need to talk.

She just bet he'd come by—to tell her he was in love with his daughter's mother. Or worse, to lie to her some more.

Bella didn't think twice before typing in her reply.

Not coming back. Have a nice life with your family.

Now she could shake Alma's dust off her feet and start over somewhere James and his new family weren't. New York was perfect, a nonstop party, and she intended to live it up. After all, she'd narrowly escaped making a huge mistake and now she had no responsibilities to anyone other than herself. Exactly the way she liked it.

But Bella cried every minute of the flight over the Atlantic. Apparently, she'd lost the ability to lie to herself about losing the man she loved.

Twelve

The Manhattan skyline glowed brightly, cheering Bella slightly. Of course, since leaving Alma, the definition of cheer had become: *doesn't make me dissolve into a puddle of tears.*

She stared out over the city that never slept, wishing there was one person out there she could connect with, who understood her and saw past the surface. None of her friends had so much as realized anything was wrong. They'd been partying continuously since this time last night. It was a wonder they hadn't dropped from exhaustion yet.

"Hey, Bella!" someone called from behind her in the crowded penthouse. "Come try these Jell-O shots. They're fab."

Bella sighed and ignored whomever it was because the last thing she needed was alcohol. It just made her even more weepy. Besides, they'd go back to their inane conversations about clothes and shoes whether she joined them or not, as they'd been doing for hours. That was the problem with hooking up with casual acquaintances—they didn't have anything in common.

But neither did she want to call her friends in Miami. The problem was that she didn't really fit in with the wealthy, spoiled crowd she used to run around with in Miami either. Maybe she hadn't for a long time and that was why she'd felt so much like a hurricane back home— she'd never had enough of a reason to slow down and stop spinning.

In Alma, she'd found a reason. Or at least she'd thought she had. But apparently her judgment was suspect.

The party grew unbearably louder as someone turned up the extensive surround sound system that had come with the condo when Rafael had purchased it from a music executive. A Kanye West song beat through the speakers and Bella's friends danced in an alcohol-induced frenzy. All she wanted to do was lie on the wooden floor of a farmhouse eating grapes with a British football player who'd likely already forgotten she existed.

Barricading herself in her room—after kicking out an amorous couple who had no sense of boundaries—she flopped onto the bed and pulled the bag she'd carried from the farmhouse into her arms to hold it tight.

The bag was a poor substitute for the man it reminded her of. But it was all she had. When would she stop missing him so much? When would her heart catch a clue that James had not one, but two females in his life who interested him a whole lot more than Bella?

Something crumpled inside the bag. Puzzled, she glanced inside, sure she'd emptied the bag some time ago.

The letters.

She'd totally forgotten about finding the cache of old, handwritten letters under the floorboards of the farmhouse. She'd meant to give them to Tía Isabella and with everything that had happened…well, it was too late now. Maybe she could mail them to her aunt.

When she pulled the letters from the bag, the memories of what had happened right after she'd found the letters flooded her and she almost couldn't keep her grip on the string-bound lot of paper.

James holding her, loving her, filling her to the brim. They'd made love on that gorgeous bed with the carved flowers not moments after discovering the hiding place under the boards.

She couldn't stand it and tossed the letters onto the bedside table, drawing her knees up to her chest, rocking in a tight ball as if that alone would ward off the crushing sense of loss.

The letters teetered and fell to the ground, splitting the ancient knotted string holding them together. Papers fluttered in a semicircle. She groaned and crawled to the floor to pick them up.

Indiscretion. Illegitimate. Love.

The words flashed across her vision as she gathered the pages. She held one of the letters up to read it from the beginning, instantly intrigued to learn more about a story that apparently closely mirrored her own, if those were the major themes.

She read and read, and flipped the letter over to read the back. Then, with dawning horror and apprehension, she read the rest. *No!* It couldn't be. She must have misread.

With shaking fingers, she fumbled for her phone and speed-dialed Gabriel before checking the time. Well, it didn't matter if it was the middle of the night in Alma. Gabriel needed to make sense of this.

"What?" he growled and she heard Serafia murmur in the background. "This better be good."

"Rafael Montoro II wasn't the child of the king," she blurted out. "Grandfather. Our father's father. He wasn't the king's son. The letters. The queen's lover died in the war. And this means he was illegitimate. They were in love, but—"

"Bella. Stop. Breathe. What are you talking about? What letters?" Gabriel asked calmly.

Yes. Breathing sounded like a good plan. Maybe none of this would pan out as a problem. Maybe she'd read too much into the letters. Maybe they were fake and could be fully debunked. She gulped sweet oxygen into her lungs but her brain was still on Perma-Spin.

"I found some old letters. At the farmhouse. They say that our grandfather, Rafael the Second, wasn't really the king's son by blood. Wait." She pulled her phone from her ear, took snapshots of the most incriminating letter and sent the pictures to Gabriel. "Okay, read the letter and tell me I misunderstood. But I couldn't have. It says they kept the queen's affair a secret because the war had just started and the country was in turmoil."

Gabriel went quiet as he waited for the message to come through and then she heard him talking to Serafia as he switched over to speakerphone to examine the photo.

"These letters are worth authenticating," he concluded. "I'm not sure what it means but if this is true, we'll have to sort out the succession. I might not be the next in line."

"Why do you sound so thrilled?" Bella asked suspiciously. That was not the reaction she'd been expecting. "This is kind of a big deal."

"Because now there's a possibility that after the wedding, I might be able to focus on getting my wife pregnant instead of worrying about how to hold my head so the crown doesn't fall off."

Serafia laughed and she and Gabriel apparently forgot about Bella because their conversation was clearly not meant for outsiders.

"Hey, you guys, what do we do now?" she called loudly before things progressed much further. Geez, didn't they ever give the lovey-dovey stuff a rest? "We need to know if this is for real, preferably before the coronation. But who would be the legitimate heir if it's not you?"

God, what a mess. Thankfully, she wasn't in Alma, potentially about to be swept into a much larger scandal than any she'd ever created on her own.

"Juan Carlos," Serafia confirmed. "Of course. If Rafael's line is not legitimate, the throne would fall to his sister, Isabella. I don't think she'd hesitate to pass it to her grandson. It's perfect, don't you think? Juan Carlos has long been one of the biggest advocates of the restoration of the monarchy. He'll be a great king."

Gabriel muttered his agreement. "Bella, send me the letters overnight, but make copies of everything before you do. Can you send them tonight?"

"Sure." It wasn't as if she had anything else to do.

And that was how an Alman princess with a broken heart ended up at an all-night Kinkos on Fifth Avenue, while her so-called friends drank her vodka and ruined her furniture.

When she got home, she kicked them all out so she could be alone with her misery.

JFK Airport had it in for James. This was the ninth time he'd flown into the airport and the ninth time his luggage had been lost.

"You know what, forget it," he told the clerk he'd been working with for the past hour to locate his bags. "I'll call customer service later."

After two delays at Heathrow, all James wanted to do was crawl into a hole and sleep, but he'd spent close to thirty-six hours already trying to get to Bella. He wasn't flaking out now.

The car service ride to the address Gabriel had given him took another forty-five minutes and he almost got out and walked to Bella's building four times. He worried his lip with his teeth until he reached the building and then had to deal with the doorman, who of course wasn't expecting anyone named James Rowling.

"Please," he begged the doorman. "Buzz Ms. Montoro and tell her I'm here."

It was a desperate gamble, and she might very well say, *James who?* But he had to see her so he could fix things. He might be too late. His father might have ruined everything, but he had to take this shot to prove to Bella that she could trust him. That he'd absolutely planned to tell her about Maisey but everything had happened too fast.

"No need. Here I am."

Bella's voice washed over him and he spun around instantly. And there she was, wearing one of those little dresses that killed him every time, and he wanted to rush to her to sweep her up in his arms.

But he didn't. Because he didn't understand why she'd left Alma without at least letting him explain what was happening with Maisey or why his life had spiraled out of control so quickly that he'd managed to lose her or why just looking at her made everything seem better without her saying a word.

"Hi," he said, and then his throat closed.

He'd practiced what he'd say for a day and a half, only to buckle when it mattered most. Figured.

"Hi," she repeated, and glanced at the doorman, who was watching them avidly. "Thanks, Carl. It's okay."

She motioned James over to the side of the lobby, presumably so she could talk to him with a measure of privacy. "What are you doing here?"

"I wanted to talk to you." *Obviously.*

Off kilter, he ran a hand over his rumpled hair. Now that he was here, flying to New York without even calling first seemed like a stupid plan.

But when his father had smugly told him that he'd taken the liberty of informing Bella about Maisey, James had kind of lost it. And he'd never really regained his senses, especially not after his father made it clear that Bella wasn't interested in a bloke with an illegitimate child. As though it was all sorted and James should just bow out.

That wasn't happening. Because if Bella was indeed no longer interested in him because of Maisey, he wanted to hear it from Bella.

"So talk." She crossed her arms and he got another clue that things between them had progressed so far past the point of reasonable, there might be no saving their relationship. He was on such unfamiliar, unsteady ground, it might as well be quicksand.

The damage was far more widespread than he'd hoped. "Why did you leave before I could explain about Maisey?"

"Maisey? Is that your girlfriend's name?" Her eyes widened and she huffed out a little noise of disgust. "Surely you didn't expect me to sit around and wait for you to give me the boot."

"Maisey is my daughter," he countered quietly. "Chelsea is her mother. I'm sorry I didn't get a chance to tell you about this myself. I'm very unhappy with my father for interfering."

"Well, that couldn't have happened if you'd just told me from the beginning." He could tell by her narrowed gaze that she'd already tried and convicted him. "Why couldn't you be honest with me?"

"I was going to tell you. But you left first." With no clue as to where she was going. Was that her way of saying a lover with a kid was *no bueno*? Sweat dripped between his shoulder blades as he scrambled for the right thing to say. "Why didn't you wait for me to call like we discussed?"

"Wait for you to—are you mad at *me*? You're the one who should be on your knees begging my forgiveness. And you know what else? I don't have to explain myself to you!"

She stormed to the elevator and he followed her, only just squeezing through the doors before they closed.

Obviously *that* hadn't been the right thing to say. And she was far more furious than he'd have ever dreamed.

Yeah, he'd messed up by giving his father an opportunity to get between them, but hadn't he just flown thousands of miles to fix it? Shouldn't he at least get two minutes to make his case?

Or was it too late and was he just wasting his time?

"Actually," he countered as anxiety seized his lungs. "An explanation would be smashing. Because I don't understand why you don't want to hear what I have to say. I thought we were a couple who dealt with things together."

And now he was shouting back at her. Good thing the elevator was empty.

He'd thought they were headed for something permanent. He had little experience with that sort of thing, but he didn't think jetting off to another continent without so much as a conversation about the potential complexities was how you did it.

He'd *wanted* to talk to her about Maisey. To share his fears and ask her opinion. To feel less alone with this huge life-altering role change that had been dropped on him. Even the simple logistics of flying to New York hadn't been so simple, not the way it used to be. It had required him to sweet-talk Catalina, one of the Rowling maids, into babysitting Maisey—totally not her job, but Cat was the only person James trusted implicitly since they'd grown up together. As soon as he got back, finding a nanny for his daughter was priority number one.

She wheeled on him, staring down her nose at him, which was an impressive feat since he was a head taller. "A couple? Really? Do you tell Chelsea the same thing? I saw you two together. You must have had a good laugh at my expense."

"You saw me and *Chelsea* together? When?"

"The day I left Alma. Don't shake your head at me. I *saw* you. You were very cozy in that gazebo."

Gazebo? He'd never set foot in any gazebo.

"That would be a little difficult when Chelsea and I

were in my lawyer's office signing paperwork to give me sole custody of Maisey." They'd obtained the results of the fastest paternity test available and then James had spent a good deal more cash greasing the works so he could be rid of Chelsea as soon as possible. "And then she immediately left to go back to England."

He'd been relieved to have it done. The meeting with his lawyers had taken far longer than he'd expected but he had to deal with that for his daughter's sake before he could untangle himself to go talk to Bella. Unfortunately, those few hours had given his father the perfect window of opportunity to drive a wedge between James and Bella.

"She…what?" For the first time since he'd entered the elevator, Bella's furious expression wavered.

"Yeah. I came to tell you everything but you'd apparently just left. Gabriel gave me some lame explanation, so I texted you, remember?"

The elevator dinged and the doors opened but Bella didn't move, her expression shell-shocked. Gently, he guided her out of the elevator and she led him to the door of one of the apartments down the hall.

Once they were alone in the condo, James raised his brows in silent question.

"I remember your text message. Clearly," Bella allowed. "If Chelsea left, who were you kissing in the gazebo?"

"Kissing? You thought I was kissing someone?" His temper rose again. "Thanks for the lack of trust, Bella. That's why you took off? Because you thought I was two-timing you?"

Suddenly furious he'd spent almost two days in pursuit of a woman who thought so little of him, he clasped his aching head and tried to calm down.

"What was I supposed to think, James?" she whispered and even in his fit of temper he heard the hurt and pain behind it. "Your father told me you still had feelings for Chelsea. I thought he was lying, so I went to the Rowling mansion to talk to you. Only to see you kissing a dark-haired woman. I wouldn't have believed it except for your watch."

She glanced at his bare arm and her face froze as he held it up. "You mean the watch I gave to Will?"

"Oh, my God."

In a flash, she fell to the ground in a heap and he dashed to her, hauling her into his arms before he thought better of it.

"Are you okay?" he asked as he helped her stand, his heart hammering. "Did you faint?"

"No. My knees just gave out." She peered up, her gaze swimming with tears as she clutched his shoulders, not quite in his embrace but not quite distancing herself either. "It was Will. The whole time."

He nodded grimly. Such was the reality of having a brother who looked like you. People often mistook them for each other, but not with such devastating consequences. "Welcome to the world of twins."

Now he understood her animosity. No wonder he'd felt as if he was on the wrong side of a raging bull. His father's interference had caused even more damage than James had known.

And who the hell had *Will* been kissing in the gazebo?

"Why didn't you tell me you gave him your watch? You always wore it. I know how much it means to you and I just…well, I never would have thought you'd…" Her eyes shut for a beat. "I know, I left before you could tell me. I'm sorry. I shouldn't have jumped to conclusions."

"Yeah, on that note. Why did you?"

His temper hadn't fully fled but it had been so long since he'd been this close to her, he couldn't quite make himself let her go. So he sated himself on the scent of her and let that soothe his riled nerves.

"You said everything was moving too fast," she reminded him. "It's not that I didn't trust you. You've always been honest with me, but… Chelsea's your child's mother. You didn't call and your father said you were home from England. Your car was in the drive and he dropped the news about a baby and tells me you have feelings for your old girlfriend. Maybe you thought it was the right thing to try again with her."

That was so far off the mark…and yet he could see the logic from her perspective. It was maddening, impossible, ridiculous. "Not for me. I love *you*."

"You do?" The awe in her face nearly undid him. Until she whacked his shoulder with her fist. "Then why didn't you call me when you got back from England?"

"Blimey, Bella. I'd just had the news about the baby dropped on me, too."

She recoiled. "Wait. You mean you *just* found out you had a daughter?" Her eyelids flew shut for a moment. "I thought…"

"What, you mean you thought I knew from the very beginning?" He swore. Everything made so much more sense. Scowling, he guided her to the couch. "We need to get better at communication, obviously. Then my father wouldn't have been able to cause all of these problems."

She nodded, chagrin running rampant across her expression. "I'm sorry. I told you I wasn't any good at relationships."

"We're supposed to be figuring it out together. Remember?" Without taking his gaze from hers, he held out his hand. "I promised not to let go. I plan to stick to that."

She clasped his hand solemnly, no hesitation. "Are you really in love with me?"

"Completely." Tenderly, he smoothed a stray hair from her cheek. "I'm sorry, too, sweetheart. I was trying to get everything settled in my barmy life before I settled things with you. I jumbled it all up."

This was entirely his fault. If he'd told her every minute what she meant to him, she might have very well marched up to Will and demanded to know what he was doing. And realized it wasn't James. None of this would have happened.

He'd been missing this goal since day one, yet kept kicking the ball exactly the same way. No wonder she'd assumed he didn't want her anymore.

"So are things settled?" She searched his gaze and a line appeared between her eyes. "What did you mean about Chelsea signing over custody? What happened?"

And then reality—his new reality—crashed over him. They'd only dealt with the past. The future was still a big, scary unknown.

James shook his head. "She dumped the diaper bag in my lap and told me she was too young to be tied down with a baby she hadn't asked for. Being a mum is apparently too hard and it's interfering with her parties."

"Oh, James." Her quiet gasp of sympathy tugged at something in his chest.

"I'm quite gobsmacked." This was the conversation he'd intended to have when he went to her house in Playa Del Onda. Only to find that she'd taken off for New York. "I have a daughter I never knew existed and now she's mine. I'm a single father."

And he'd have to relinquish his title as the king of un-complicating things. There was no way to spin the situation differently. No matter how much he loved Bella, she had to decide if he was worth all the extra stuff that came along with the deal.

Now the question was…would she?

James was a single father.

When she'd seen James across the lobby, she'd assumed he'd come to grovel and planned to send him packing. But then the extent of his father's lies and manipulation had come out, changing everything. The instant James had held up his bare wrist, she'd known. He wasn't the man his father made him out to be. The explanation she'd sought, the forgiveness she knew she could offer—it had all been right there, if only she'd stayed in Alma.

Part of the fault in all of this lay with her. She shouldn't have been so quick to judge, so quick to believe the worst in him. So quick to whirl off and leave broken pieces of her relationship with James in her wake.

And still James had said he loved her. Those sweet words…she'd wanted to fall into his arms and say them back a hundred times. If only it were that simple.

But it wasn't.

"That's…a lot to take in," Bella allowed with a small smile. Her mind reeled in a hundred directions and none of them created the type of cohesion she sought. "How old is she?"

"Around ten months. I wish I knew what that meant in terms of development. When will she start walking, for example? It's something I *should* know, as a father. But I don't." He shut his eyes for a beat. "I'm learning as I go."

Her heart dipped. This must be so hard. How did you learn to be a father with no warning? James would have to get there fast and probably felt ill-equipped and completely unready. "You'll be a great father."

He'd stepped up. Just as she would have expected. James always did the right thing.

"I'd like you to meet her. If you want to."

"I do," she said eagerly and then the full reality of what was happening hit her.

Dear God, was *she* ready to be the mate of a single father? She barely felt like an adult herself half the time. When she'd confronted her father to demand her right to see James, she'd taken huge steps to become the settled, responsible person she wanted to be.

But she wouldn't exactly call herself mother material, not yet. Maybe in the future she could be, after she'd spent time alone with James and they'd both figured out how to be in a relationship. But they didn't have the luxury of that time. She couldn't decide in a few months that it was too much responsibility and whirl away, leaving a broken family in her wake. Like her own mother had.

She loved James. After everything, that was still true.

But was love enough when their relationship had so many complications, so many things going against it? Adding a child into the mix—an illegitimate one at that, which would reflect poorly on the royal family—only made it worse.

And in the spirit of figuring it out together, they had to talk about it.

"Your daughter is a…" She'd almost said a *problem*. "A blessing. But I'm a princess in a country very unforgiving of indiscretions. I'm still in line for the throne. You realize there's a potential for our relationship to…go over very badly, right?"

The tabloids would have a field day, eviscerating the royal family in the press. She was supposed to be forging alliances and solidifying the new monarchy in the country of her heritage. Not constantly dodging scandals.

"Yeah." He sighed as she gripped his hand tighter. "I know. We don't make any sense together and you should toss me to the curb this minute. I'm a lot of trouble."

Her heart fluttered in panic at the thought. But that's what they were talking about. Either they'd make a go of it or they'd part ways.

"Seems like you warned me how much trouble you were once upon a time."

Continually. He'd told her he was bad news from the start. She hadn't believed him then and she still didn't. James Rowling had character that couldn't be faked. His father couldn't see it, but Bella did. He was every inch her hero and the rest of the world would see that, too. She'd *help* them see it. And that decided it.

She smiled as she cupped James's face. The face of her

future. "Turns out I like my man with a side of trouble. We have a lot of obstacles to leap. We always have. But I think you're worth it, James Rowling. Jump with me."

"Are you sure?" he asked cautiously even as he pressed his jaw more firmly into her hand. "You don't worry about losing out on your fun lifestyle and how Maisey will tie you down?"

Once, that might have been her sole consideration. No longer.

"The party scene is empty and unfulfilling." As she said the words, they felt right. She'd been growing up all along, becoming a woman she could be proud of, one ready for new challenges. "Maybe someone who hadn't had a chance to sow her wild oats might feel differently. But I don't regret moving on to a new phase of life. Just don't let go of my hand, okay?"

"Never." He grinned back. "You're right, by the way. My grandfather's watch is very special to me. Will bet me that I would ask you to marry me before Gabriel's coronation and the watch was the prize. I fought like hell to keep it, but in the end, it was only fair to hand it over."

"But you haven't asked me to marry you." Because she'd run off and almost ruined everything.

"No, I haven't. Allow me to rectify that." He dropped to one knee and captured her hand. "Isabella Montoro, I love you. I don't deserve a minute of your time, let alone forever, but I'm so lost without you. I have sole custody of my daughter and it's selfish to ask you to be an instant mother. Despite all of that, I'm asking you to marry me anyway. Let me treat you like a princess the rest of your life."

Just when she'd thought he couldn't possibly get any more romantic, he said something like that. How could she say no? "Before I decide, I have a very important question to ask."

"Anything," he said solemnly.

"Do I have to move to England?"

His laugh warmed her. "No. I turned down Liverpool. My heart is in Alma. With you."

"Oh." And then her ability to speak completely fled as she internalized what she'd almost missed out on—an amazing man who'd quietly been making her his top priority all along. "Then yes," she whispered. "The answer is always yes."

He yanked on her hand, spilling her into his lap, and kissed her breathless, over and over until she finally pushed on his chest.

"I love you, too," she proclaimed. "Even though you made a stupid bet with your brother that lost you a watch and almost lost you a fiancée. What if I'd said no? Would you still ha—?"

He kissed her. It was a very effective way to end an argument and she hoped he planned to use it a whole lot in the future.

Epilogue

Bella still loved Miami. Thanks to the double Montoro wedding that had concluded a mere hour ago, she'd gotten an opportunity to come back, see her friends and spend some alone time with James. Which was much needed now that they were settling into life with a baby.

James's arm slipped around her waist as he handed her a glass of champagne. Still a little misty from the ceremony where her brothers had married their brides, she smiled at the man she loved.

Bella sighed a little over the romantic kiss her brother Rafe shared with his new wife, Emily, as they stole a few moments together in a secluded corner. Of course, they probably didn't intend for anyone to see them, but Bella had been keeping her eye on her new sister-in-law. She'd been a little unsteady due to her pregnancy.

Serafia Montoro, Bella's other new sister-in-law, toasted Gabriel and laughed at something her new husband said. They were going to be just as happy together as Rafe and Emily, no question.

The reception was in full swing. Five hundred of the world's most influential people packed the party. The governor of Florida chatted with Bella's father, Rafael III, near the bar and many other of Montoro Enterprises' key partners were in attendance.

"You ready to do this with me soon?" James murmured in her ear.

She shivered, as she always did when he touched her. Looked at her. Breathed in her general direction. Oh, she had it bad and it was delicious.

But who could blame her when she'd fallen in love with the only man in the world who got her? The only man who settled the hurricane in her heart. She'd returned to Alma to meet his daughter, who was the most precious thing in the world. And she looked just like her father, which was a plus in Bella's book. She'd instantly bonded with the little sweetheart.

Then James had helped Bella launch a fledgling organization dubbed the Alma Wildlife Conservation Society. A graphic with twin macaws served as the logo and no one had to know she'd secretly named them Will and James.

It was a healthy reminder that things weren't always what they seemed. As long as she always communicated with James, no one could tear them apart. It was their personal relationship credo and they practiced it often.

Bella smiled at James. "I'm afraid I'm out of siblings so our wedding ceremony will have to star only us. And Maisey."

James cocked his head. "You'd want her to participate? Babies and weddings don't necessarily mix."

"Of course," Bella insisted fiercely. "She's my daughter, too."

Maisey had surprised everyone by uttering her first word last week—*bird*. Her proud father couldn't stop smiling and Bella had decided then and there to have another baby as soon as possible. *After* she and James got married.

The Montoros didn't need any new scandals.

Not long after she'd returned to Alma, Gabriel had appointed a royal committee to authenticate the letters Bella had found at the farmhouse. After careful and thorough examination and corroborating evidence culled from the official archives, the letters proved valid.

The late Rafael Montoro II wasn't the legitimate royal heir, which meant no one in his line was either. His grandson, Gabriel, and granddaughter, Bella, weren't eligible for the throne. The legitimate line for the throne shifted to Isabella Salazar nee Montoro, Rafael's sister, who was unfortunately too ill to take on her new role. Therefore, her grandson, Juan Carlos II, long the only Montoro with the right heart to lead his country, became the sole legitimate heir.

Despite Bella's willingness to brave the tabloids with James, to weather the storm over the unfortunate circumstances of his daughter's birth, in the end, no one paid much attention to Bella and James as the world's focus shifted to Juan Carlos.

Bella wasn't the only Montoro to express relief. Gabriel looked forward to spending time with his new wife instead of balancing his personal life with his public reign. Their cousin would take the throne of Alma, leaving the three Montoro siblings to their happily-ever-afters.

* * * * *

MAID FOR A MAGNATE

BY
JULES BENNETT

Award-winning author **Jules Bennett** is no stranger to romance—she met her husband when she was only fourteen. After dating through high school, the two married. He encouraged her to chase her dream of becoming an author. Jules has now published nearly thirty novels. She and her husband are living their own happily-ever-after while raising two girls. Jules loves to hear from readers through her website, www. julesbennett. com, her Facebook fan page or on Twitter.

A huge thanks to the Harlequin Desire team for including me in this amazing continuity. And a special thanks to Janice, Kat, Katherine, Andrea and Charlene. I loved working with you all on this project.

One

JUAN CARLOS SALAZAR II TRUE HEIR
TO THRONE

Will Rowling stared at the blaring headline as he sipped his coffee and thanked every star in the sky that he'd dodged marrying into the royal family of Alma. Between the Montoro siblings and their cousin Juan Carlos, that was one seriously messed up group.

Of course his brother, James, had wedded the beautiful Bella Montoro. Will's father may have had hopes of Will and Bella joining forces, but those devious plans obviously had fallen through when James fell in love with Bella instead.

Love. Such a fickle thing that botched up nearly every best laid plan. Not that Will had ever been on board with the idea of marrying Bella. He'd rather remain single than marry just to advance his family's business interests.

The Montoros were a force to be reckoned with in Alma, now that the powerful royal family was being restored to the throne after more than seventy years in exile. And Patrick Rowling was all too eager to have his son marry into such prestige, but thankfully that son was not to be Will.

Bella's brother had been heading toward the throne, until shocking letters were discovered in an abandoned family farmhouse, calling into question the lineage of the Montoros and diverting the crown into the hands of their cousin.

Secrets, scandal, lies... Will was more than happy to turn the reins over to his twin.

And since Will was officially single, he could carry out his own devious plan in great detail—his plot didn't involve love but a whole lot of seduction.

First, though, he had to get through this meeting with his father. Fortunately, Will's main goal of taking back control of his life involved one very intriguing employee of his father's household so having this little meeting at the Rowling home in Playa del Onda instead of the Rowling Energy offices was perfectly fine with him. Now that James had married and moved out and Patrick was backing away from working as much, Patrick used his weekend home more often.

"Rather shocking news, isn't it?"

Still clutching the paper in one hand and the coffee mug in the other, Will turned to see his father breeze into the den. While Patrick leaned more toward the heavier side, Will prided himself on keeping fit. It was just another way he and his father were different though some around them felt Will was a chip off the old block.

At one time Will would've agreed with those people, but he was more than ready to show everyone, including his father, he was his own man and he was taking charge.

"This bombshell will certainly shake things up for Alma." Will tossed the newspaper onto the glossy mahogany desktop. "Think parliament will ratify his coronation?"

Patrick grunted as he sank into his leather desk chair. "It's just a different branch of the Montoro family that will be taking the throne, so it really doesn't matter."

Will clutched his coffee cup and shook his head. Anything to do with the Montoros was not his problem. He had his own battles to face, starting with his father right now.

"What did you need to see me so early about?" his father asked, leaning back so far in the chair it squeaked.

Will remained standing; he needed to keep the upper hand here, needed to stay in control. Even though he was going up against his father's wishes, Will had to take back control of his own life. Enough with worrying about what his father would say or do if Will made the wrong move.

James had never bowed to their father's wishes and Will always wondered why his twin was so against the grain. It may have taken a few years to come around, but Will was more than ready to prove himself as a formidable businessman.

Will was a master at multitasking and getting what he wanted. And since he'd kissed Cat a few weeks ago, he'd thought of little else. He wanted her…and he would have her. Their intense encounter would allow for nothing less.

But for right this moment, Will was focusing on his

new role with Rowling Energy and this meeting with his father. Conquering one milestone at a time.

"Up till now, you've had me dealing with the company's oil interests," Will stated. "I'm ready to take total control of the real estate division, too."

His father's chest puffed out as he took in a deep breath. "I've been waiting for you to come to me with this," Patrick said with a smile. "You're the obvious choice to take over. You've done a remarkable job increasing the oil profits. They're up twelve percent since you put your mark on the company."

Will intended to produce financial gains for all of the company's divisions. For years, he'd wanted to get out from under his father's thumb and take control, and now was his chance. And that was just the beginning of his plans where Rowling Energy was concerned.

Finally, now that Will was seeing clearly and standing on his own two feet, nothing would stand in his way. His father's semiretirement would just help ease the path to a beautiful life full of power and wealth... and a certain maid he'd set in his sights.

"I've already taken the liberty of contacting our main real estate clients in London," Will went on, sliding his hands into his pockets and shifting his weight. "I informed them they would be dealing with me."

Will held his father's gaze. He'd taken a risk contacting the other players, but Will figured his father would be proud and not question the move. Patrick had wanted Will to slide into the lead role of the family business for years. Slowly Will had taken over. Now he was ready to seal every deal and hold all the reins.

"Another man would think you're trying to sneak behind his back." Patrick leaned forward and laced his fingers together on the desktop. "I know better. You're taking charge and that's what I want. I'll make sure my assistant knows you will be handling the accounts from here on out. But I'm here anytime, Will. You've been focused on this for so long, your work has paid off."

Will nodded. Part one of his plan was done and had gone just as smoothly as he'd envisioned. Now he needed to start working on the second part of his plan. And both aspects involved the same tactic…trust. He needed to gain and keep the trust of both his father and Cat or everything would blow up in his face.

Will refused to tolerate failure on any level.

Especially where Cat was concerned. That kiss had spawned an onslaught of emotions he couldn't, wouldn't, ignore. Cat with her petite, curvy body that fit perfectly against his. She'd leaned into that kiss like a woman starved and he'd been all too happy to give her what she wanted.

Unfortunately, she'd dodged him ever since. He didn't take that as a sign of disinterest. Quite the opposite. If she wasn't interested, she'd act as if nothing had happened. But the way she kept avoiding him when he came to visit his father at the Playa del Onda estate only proved to Will that she was just as shaken as he was. There was no way she didn't feel something.

Just one kiss and he had her trembling. He'd use that to his advantage.

Seeing Cat was another reason he opted to come to his father's second home this morning. She couldn't avoid him if he cornered her at her workplace. She'd been the maid for his twin brother, James, but James had often been away playing football—or as the Yanks called it, soccer—so Cat hadn't been a temptation thrust right in Will's face. But now she worked directly under Patrick. Her parents had also worked for Patrick, so

Cat had grown up around Will and James. It wasn't that long ago that Will had set his sights on Cat. Just a few years ago, in fact, he'd made his move, and they'd even dated surreptitiously for a while. That had ended tragically when he'd backed down from a fight in a moment of weakness. Since their recent kiss had brought back their scorching chemistry, Will knew it was time for some action.

Will may have walked out on her four years ago, but she was about to meet the new Will…the one who fought for what he wanted. And he wanted Cat in his bed and this time he wouldn't walk away.

Will focused back on his father. "I'll let myself out," he stated, more than ready to be finished with this part of his day. "I'll be in touch once I hear back from the investors and companies I contacted."

Heading for the open double doors, Will stopped when his father called his name.

"You know, I really wanted the thing with you and Bella to work," Patrick stated, as he stared at the blaring, boldface headline.

"She found love with my brother. She and I never had any type of connection. You'd best get used to them together."

Patrick focused his attention back on Will. "Just keep your head on your shoulders and don't follow the path your brother has. Getting sidetracked isn't the way to make Rowling Energy grow and prosper. Just do what you've been doing."

Oh, he intended to do just that.

Will gave his father a brief nod before heading out into the hallway. Little did his father know, Will was fully capable of going after more than one goal at a time. He had no intention of letting the oil or real estate businesses slide. If anything, Will fully intended to expand both aspects of the business into new territory within the next year.

Will also intended to seduce Cat even sooner. Much sooner. And he would stop at nothing to see all of his desires fulfilled.

That familiar woodsy scent assaulted her…much like the man himself had when he'd kissed her a few weeks ago.

Could such a full-on assault of the senses be called something so simple as a kiss? He'd consumed her from the inside out. He'd had her body responding within seconds and left her aching and wanting more than she should.

Catalina kept her back turned, knowing full well who stood behind her. She'd managed to avoid running into him, though he visited his father more and more lately. At this point, a run-in was inevitable.

She much preferred working for James instead of Patrick, but now that James was married, he didn't stay here anymore and Patrick did. Catalina had zero tolerance for Patrick and the fact that she worked directly for him now only motivated her more to finish saving up to get out of Alma once and for all. And the only reason she was working for Patrick was because she needed the money. She knew she was well on her way to leaving, so going to work for another family for only a few months didn't seem fair.

Years ago her mother had moved on and still worked for a prestigious family in Alma. Cat prayed her time here with Patrick was coming to an end, too.

But for now, she was stuck here and she hadn't been able to stop thinking about that kiss. Will had silently taken control of her body and mind in the span of just a few heated moments, and he'd managed to thrust her directly into their past to the time when they'd dated.

Unfortunately, when he'd broken things off with her, he'd hurt her more than she cared to admit. Beyond leaving her when she hadn't even seen it coming, he'd gone so far as to say it had all been a mistake. His exact words, which had shocked her and left her wondering how she'd been so clueless. Catalina wouldn't be played for a fool and she would never be his "mistake" again. She had more pride than that…even if her heart was still bruised from the harsh rejection.

Even if her lips still tingled at the memory of their recent kiss.

Catalina continued to pick up random antique trinkets on the built-in bookshelves as she dusted. She couldn't face Will, not just yet. This was the first encounter since that night three weeks ago. She'd seen him, he'd purposely caught her eye a few times since then, but he'd not approached her until now. It was as if the man enjoyed the torture he inflicted upon her senses.

"You work too hard."

That voice. Will's low, sultry tone dripped with sex appeal. She didn't turn around. No doubt the sight of him would still give her that swift punch of lust to the gut, but she was stronger now than she used to be…or she'd been stronger before he'd weakened her defenses with one simple yet toe-curling kiss.

"Would that make you the pot or the kettle?" she asked, giving extra attention to one specific shelf because focusing on anything other than this man was all that was holding her sanity together.

His rich laughter washed over her, penetrating any

defense she'd surrounded herself with. Why did her body have to betray her? Why did she find herself drawn to the one man she shouldn't want? Because she hadn't forgotten that he'd recently been the chosen one to wed Bella Montoro. Bella's father had put out a false press release announcing their engagement, but of course Bella fell for James instead and Will ended up single. James had informed Cat that Bella and Will were never actually engaged, but still. With Will single now, and after that toe-curling kiss, Cat had to be on her guard. She had too much pride in herself to be anybody's Plan B.

"That spot is clean." His warm, solid hand slid easily onto her shoulder. "Turn around."

Pulling in a deep breath, Catalina turned, keeping her shoulders back and her chin high. She would not be intimidated by sexy good looks, flawless charm and that knowing twinkle in Will's eye. Chemistry wouldn't get her what she wanted out of life…all she'd end up with was another broken heart.

"I have a lot on my list today." She stared at his ear, trying to avoid those piercing aqua eyes. "Your dad should be in his den if you're looking for him."

"Our business is already taken care of." Will's hand dropped, but he didn't step back; if anything, he shifted closer. "Now you and I are going to talk."

"Which is just another area where we differ," she retorted, skirting around him to cross in front of the mantel and head to the other wall of built-in bookcases. "We have nothing to discuss."

Of course he was right behind her. The man had dropped her so easily four years ago yet in the past few weeks, he'd been relentless. Perhaps she just needed to be more firm, to let him know exactly where she stood.

"Listen." She spun back around, brandishing her feather duster at him. Maybe he'd start sneezing and she could make a run for it. "I've no doubt you want to talk about that kiss. We kissed. Nothing we hadn't done before."

Of course this kiss was so, so much more; it had penetrated to her very soul. Dammit.

"But I'm not the same girl you used to know," she continued, propping her hand on her hip. "I'm not looking for a relationship, I'm not looking for love. I'm not even interested in you anymore, Will."

Catalina nearly choked on that lie, but she mentally applauded herself for the firmness in her delivery and for stating all she needed to. She wasn't about to start playing whatever game Will had in mind because she knew one thing for certain…she'd lose.

Will stepped closer, took hold of her wrist and pulled her arm gently behind her back. Her body arched into his as she gripped her feather duster and tried to concentrate on the bite of the handle into her palm and not the way those mesmerizing eyes were full of passion and want.

"Not interested?" he asked with a smirk. "You may be able to lie to yourself, Cat, but you can never lie to me. I know you too well."

She swallowed. "You don't know me at all if you think I still like to be called Cat."

Will leaned in until his lips caressed the side of her ear. "I want to stand out in your mind," he whispered. "I won't call you what everyone else does because our relationship is different."

"We have nothing but a past that was a mistake." She purposely threw his words back in his face and she didn't care if that was childish or not.

Struggling against his hold only caused her body to respond even more as she rubbed against that hard, powerful build.

"You can fight this all you want," he said as he eased back just enough to look into her eyes. "You can deny you want me and you can even try to tell yourself you hate me. But know this. I'm also not the same man I used to be. I'm not going to let you get away this time."

Catalina narrowed her gaze. "I have goals, Will, and you're not on my list."

A sultry grin spread across his face an instant before he captured her lips. His body shifted so that she could feel just how much he wanted her. Catalina couldn't stop herself from opening her mouth for him and if her hands had been free, she probably would've fully embarrassed herself by gripping his hair and holding him even tighter.

Damn this man she wanted to hate, but couldn't.

He demanded her affection, demanded desire from her and she gave it. Mercy, she had no choice.

He nipped at her, their tongues tangling, before he finally, finally lifted his head and ran a thumb across her moist bottom lip.

"I have goals, too, Cat," he murmured against her mouth. "And you're on the top of *my* list."

The second he released her, she had to hurry to steady herself. By the time she'd processed that full-on arousing attack, Will was gone.

Typical of the man to get her ready for more and leave her hanging. She just wished she still wasn't tingling and aching all over for more of his touch.

Two

William sat on his patio, staring down at his boat and contemplating another plan of action. Unfortunately his cell phone rang before he could fully appreciate the brilliant idea he'd just had.

His father's name popped up on the screen and Will knew without answering what this would be about. It looked as if Patrick Rowling had just got wind of Will's latest business actions.

"Afternoon," he greeted, purposely being more cheerful than he assumed his father was.

"What the hell are you doing with the Cortes Real Estate company?"

Will stared out onto the sparkling water and crossed his ankles as he leaned back in his cushioned patio chair. "I dropped them."

"I'm well aware of that seeing as how Dominic called me to raise hell. What were you thinking?" his father demanded. "When you steamrolled into the head position, I thought you'd make wise moves to further the family business and make it even more profitable into the next generation. I never expected you to sever ties with companies we've dealt with for decades."

"I'm not hanging on to business relationships based on tradition or some sense of loyalty," Will stated, refusing to back down. "We've not gained a thing in the past five years from the Corteses and it was time to cut our losses. If you and Dom want to be friends, then go play golf or something, but his family will no longer do business with mine. The bottom line here is money, not hurt feelings."

"You should've run this by me, Will. I won't tolerate you going behind my back."

Will came to his feet, pulled in a deep breath of ocean air and smiled because he was in charge now and his father was going to start seeing that the "good" twin wasn't always going to bend and bow to Patrick's wishes. Will was still doing the "right thing," it just so happened the decisions made were Will's version of right and not his father's.

"I'm not sneaking at all," Will replied, leaning against the scrolling wrought iron rail surrounding his deck. "I'll tell you anything you want to know, but since I'm in charge now, I'm not asking for permission, either."

"How many more phone calls can I expect like the one I got from Cortes?"

His father's sarcasm wasn't lost on Will.

"None for the time being. I only let one go, but that doesn't mean I won't cut more ties in the future if I see we aren't pulling any revenue in after a period of time."

"You run your decisions by me first."

Giving a shrug even though his father couldn't see him, Will replied, "You wanted the golden son to take over. That's exactly what I'm doing. Don't second-guess me and my decisions. I stand to gain or lose like you do and I don't intend to see our name tarnished. We'll come out on top if you stop questioning me and let me do this job the way it's meant to be done."

Patrick sighed. "I never thought you'd argue with me."

"I'm not arguing. I'm telling you how it is."

Will disconnected the call. He wasn't going to get into a verbal sparring match with his father. He didn't have time for such things and nothing would change Will's mind. He'd gone over the numbers and cross-referenced them for the past years. Though that was a job his assistant could easily do, Will wanted his eyes on every report since he was taking over. He needed to know exactly what he was dealing with and how to plan accordingly.

His gaze traveled back to his yacht nestled against his private dock. Speaking of planning accordingly, he had more personal issues to deal with right now. Issues that involved one very sexy maid.

It had taken a lifeless, arranged relationship with Bella to really wake Will up to the fact his father had his clutches so tight, Will had basically been a marionette his entire life. Now Will was severing those strings, starting with the ridiculous notion of his marrying Bella.

Will was more than ready to move forward and take all the things he'd been craving: money and Cat. A beautiful combo to start this second stage of his life.

And it would be soon, he vowed to himself as he stalked around his outdoor seating area and headed inside. Very soon he would add to his millions, secure his place as head of the family business by cementing its leading position in the oil and real estate industries and have Cat right where he wanted her…begging.

Catalina couldn't wait to finish this day. So many things had come up that hadn't been on her regular schedule…just another perk of working for the Rowling patriarch. She had her sights set on getting home, taking off her ugly, sensible work shoes and digging into another sewing project that would give her hope, get her one step closer to her ultimate goal.

This next piece she'd designed late last night would be a brilliant, classy, yet fun outfit to add to her private collection. A collection she fully intended to take with her when she left Alma very soon.

Her own secret goal of becoming a fashion designer had her smiling. Maybe one day she could wear her own stylish clothes to work instead of boring black cotton pants and button-down shirt with hideous shoes. Other than her mother, nobody knew of Catalina's real dream, and she had every intention of keeping things that way. The last thing she needed was anyone trying to dissuade her from pursuing her ambitions or telling her that the odds were against her. She was fully aware of the odds and she intended to leap over them and claim her dream no matter how long it took. Determination was a hell of a motivator.

She came to work for the Rowlings and did her job— and that was about all the human contact she had lately. She'd been too wrapped up in materials, designs and fantasies of runway shows with her clothing draped on models who could fully do her stylish fashions justice.

Not that Catalina hated how she looked, but she

wasn't blind. She knew her curvy yet petite frame wasn't going to get her clothing noticed. She merely wanted to be behind the scenes. She didn't need all the limelight on her because she just wanted to design, no more.

As opposed to the Rowling men who seemed to crave the attention and thrive on the publicity and hoopla.

Adjusting the fresh arrangement of lilacs and white calla lilies in the tall, slender crystal vase, Catalina placed the beautiful display on the foyer table in the center of the open entryway. There were certain areas where Patrick didn't mind her doing her own thing, such as choosing the flowers for all the arrangements. She tended to lean toward the classy and elegant…which was the total opposite of the man she worked for.

James on the other hand had more fun with her working here and he actually acknowledged her presence. Patrick only summoned her when he wanted to demand something. She hated thinking how much Will was turning into his father, how business was ruling him and consuming his entire life.

Will wasn't in her personal life anymore, no matter how much she still daydreamed about their kisses. And Patrick would only be her employer for a short time longer. She was hoping to be able to leave Alma soon, leave behind this life of being a maid for a man she didn't care for. At least James was pleasant and a joy to work for. Granted, James hadn't betrayed Cat's mother the way Patrick had. And that was just another reason she wanted out of here, away from Patrick and the secret Cat knew about him.

Catalina shoved those thoughts aside. Thinking of all the sins from Patrick's past wouldn't help her mood.

Patrick had been deceitful many years ago and Catalina couldn't ignore her mother's warning about the Rowling men. Even if Will had no clue how his father had behaved, it was something Catalina would never forget. She was only glad she'd found out before she did something foolish like fall completely in love with Will.

Apparently the womanizing started with Patrick and trickled down to his sons. James had been a notorious player before Bella entered his life. After all, there was nothing like stealing your twin brother's girl, which is what James had done to Will. But all had worked out in the end because Bella and James truly did love each other even if the way they got there was hardly normal. Leave it to the Rowlings and the Montoros to keep life in Alma interesting.

Catalina just wished those recent kisses from Will weren't overriding her mother's sound advice and obvious common sense.

Once the arrangement was to her liking—because perfection was everything whether you were a maid or a CEO—Catalina made her way up the wide, curved staircase to the second floor. The arrangements upstairs most likely needed to be changed out. At the very least, she'd freshen them up with water and remove the wilting stems.

As she neared the closed door of the library, she heard the distinct sound of a woman sobbing. Catalina had no clue who was visiting. No women lived here, and she'd been in the back of the house most of the morning and hadn't seen anyone come in.

The nosy side of her wanted to know what was going on, but the employee side of her said she needed to mind her own business. She'd been around the Rowling family enough to know to keep her head down, do her job and remember she was only the help.

Inwardly she groaned. She hated that term. Yes, she was a maid, but she was damn good at her job. She took pride in what she did. No, cleaning toilets and washing sheets wasn't the most glam of jobs, but she knew what she did was important. Besides, the structure and discipline of her work was only training her for the dream job she hoped to have someday.

The rumble of male voices blended in with the female's weeping. Whatever was going on, it was something major. Catalina approached the circular table in the middle of the wide hall. As she plucked out wilted buds here and there, the door to the library creaked open. Catalina focused on the task at hand, though she was dying to turn to see who came from the room.

"Cat."

She cringed at the familiar voice. Well, part of her curiosity was answered, but suddenly she didn't care what was going on in that room. She didn't care who Will had in there, though Catalina already felt sorry for the poor woman. She herself had shed many tears over Will when he'd played her for a fool, getting her to think they could ignore their class differences and have a relationship. "I need to see you for a minute."

Of course he hadn't asked. Will Rowling didn't ask... he demanded.

Stiffening her back, she expected to see him standing close, but when she turned to face him, she noted he was holding onto the library door, with only the top half of his body peeking out of the room.

"I'm working," she informed him, making no move to go see whatever lover's spat he was having with the unknown woman.

"You need to talk to Bella."

Bella? Suddenly Catalina found herself moving down

the hall, but Will stepped out, blocking her entry into the library. Catalina glanced down to his hand gripping her bicep.

"Her aunt Isabella passed away in the middle of the night," he whispered.

Isabella Montoro was the grand matriarch of the entire Montoro clan. The woman had been around forever. Between Juan Carlos being named the true heir to the throne and now Isabella's death, the poor family was being dealt one blow after another.

Will rubbed his thumb back and forth over Catalina's arm. "You know Bella enough through James and I figured she'd want another woman to talk to. Plus, I thought she could relate to you because…"

Swallowing, she nodded. When she and Will had dated briefly, Catalina had just lost her grandmother, a woman who had been like a second mother to her. Will had seen her struggle with the loss…maybe the timing of the loss explained why she'd been so naïve to think she and Will could have a future together. For that moment in time, Catalina had clung to any hope of happiness and Will had shown her so much…but it had all been built on lies.

Catalina started to move by him, but his grip tightened. "I don't want to bring up bad memories for you." Those aqua eyes held her in place. "As much as Bella is hurting, I won't sacrifice you, so tell me if you can't go in there."

Catalina swallowed as she looked back into those eyes that held something other than lust. For once he wasn't staring at her as if he wanted to rip her clothes off. He genuinely cared or at least he was playing the part rather well. Then again, he'd played a rather impressive role four years ago pretending to be the doting boyfriend.

Catalina couldn't afford to let her guard down. Not again with this man who still had the power to cripple her. That kiss weeks ago only proved the control he still had and she'd never, ever let him in on that fact. She could never allow Will to know just how much she still ached for his touch.

"I'll be fine," she replied, pulling her arm back. "I'd like to be alone with her, though."

Will opened his mouth as if to argue, but finally closed it and nodded.

As soon as Catalina stepped inside, her heart broke. Bella sat in a wingback chair. James rested his hip on the arm and Bella was curled into his side sobbing.

"James." Will motioned for his twin to follow him out.

Leaning down, James muttered something to Bella. Dabbing her eyes with a tissue, Bella looked up and saw she had company.

Catalina crossed to the beautiful woman who had always been known for her wild side. Right now she was hurting over losing a woman who was as close as a mother to her.

The fact that Will thought Catalina could offer comfort, the fact that he cared enough to seek her out, shouldn't warm her heart. She couldn't let his moment of sweetness hinder her judgment of the man. Bella was the woman he'd been in a relationship with only a month ago. How could Catalina forget that? No matter the reasons behind the relationship, Catalina couldn't let go of the fact that Will would've said *I do* to Bella had James not come along.

Will had an agenda, he always did. Catalina had no

clue what he was up to now, but she had a feeling his newfound plans included her. After all this time, was he seriously going to pursue her? Did he honestly think they'd start over or pick up where they'd left off?

Catalina knew deep down he was only after one thing...and she truly feared if she wasn't careful, she'd end up giving in.

Three

Will lifted the bottle of scotch from the bar in the living room, waving it back and forth slightly in a silent invitation to his brother.

James blew out a breath. "Yeah. I could use a drink."

Neither mentioned the early time. Sometimes life's crises called for an emergency drink to take the edge off. And since they'd recently started building their relationship back up, Will wanted to be here for his brother because even though Bella was the one who'd suffered the loss, James was no doubt feeling helpless.

"Smart thinking asking Catalina to help." James took the tumbler with the amber liquid and eased back on the leather sofa. "Something going on there you want to talk about?"

Will remained standing, leaning an elbow back against the bar. "Nothing going on at all."

Not to say there wouldn't be something going on very

soon if he had his way about it. Those heated kisses only motivated him even more…not to mention the fact that his father would hate knowing "the good twin" had gone after what he wanted, which was the total opposite of Patrick's wishes.

James swirled the drink as he stared down into the glass. "I know Isabella has been sick for a while, but still, her death came as a shock. Knowing how strong-willed she was, I'd say she hung on until Juan Carlos was announced the rightful heir to the throne."

Will nodded, thankful they were off the topic of Cat. She was his and he wasn't willing to share her with anyone right now. Only a month ago, Bella had caught Will and Cat kissing, but at the time she'd thought it was James locking lips with the maid. The slight misunderstanding had nearly cost James the love of his life. "How is Bella dealing with the fact her brother was knocked off the throne before he could fully take control?"

The Montoro family was being restored to the Alma monarchy after decades of harsh dictatorship. First Rafael Montoro IV and then, when he abdicated, his brother Gabriel were thought to be the rightful heirs. However, their sister, Bella, had then uncovered damning letters in an old family farmhouse, indicating that because of a paternity secret going back to before World War II, Juan Carlos's line of the family were the only legitimate heirs.

"I don't think that title ever appealed to Gabriel or Bella, to be honest." James crossed his ankle over his knee and held onto his glass as he rested it on the arm of the sofa. "Personally, I'm glad the focus is on Juan Carlos right now. Bella and I have enough media attention as it is."

In addition to the fact that James had married a member of Alma's royal family, he was also a star football player who drew a lot of scrutiny from the tabloids. The newlyweds no doubt wanted some privacy to start building their life together, especially since James had also recently taken custody of his infant baby, Maisey—a child from a previous relationship.

"Isabella's passing will have the media all over the Montoros and Juan Carlos. I'm probably going to take Bella and Maisey back to the farmhouse to avoid the spotlight. The renovations aren't done yet, but we need the break."

"What can I do to help?" Will asked.

James tipped back the last of the scotch, and then leaned forward and set the empty tumbler on the coffee table. "Give me back that watch," he said with a half smile and a nod toward Will's wrist.

"Nah, I won this fair and square," Will joked. "I told, you that you wouldn't be able to resist putting a ring on Bella's finger."

James had inherited the coveted watch from their English grandfather and wore it all the time. It was the way people told the twins apart. But Will had wanted the piece and had finally won it in a bet that James would fall for Bella and propose. Ironically, it had almost ended James and Bella's relationship because Will had been wearing the watch that night he'd kissed Cat in the gazebo. Bella had mistaken him for James and jumped to conclusions.

"Besides the watch, what else can I do?" Will asked.

"I have no idea." James shook his head and blew out a sigh. "Right now keeping Dad out of my business would be great."

Will laughed. "I don't think that will be a problem.

He's up in arms about some business decisions I've made, so the heat is off you for now."

"Are you saying the good twin is taking charge?"

"I'm saying I'm controlling my own life and this is only the first step in my plan."

Leaning forward, James placed his elbows on his knees. "Sounds like you may need my help. I am the black sheep, after all. Let me fill you in on all the ways to defy our father."

"I'm pretty sure I'm defying him all on my own." Will pushed off the bar and shoved his hands in his pockets. "I'll let you know if I need any tips."

James leveled his gaze at Will. "Why do I have a feeling this new plan of yours has something to do with the beautiful maid?"

Will shrugged, refusing to rise to the bait.

"You were kissing her a few weeks ago," James reminded him. "That little escapade nearly cost me Bella."

The entire night had been a mess, but thankfully things ultimately worked out the way they should have.

"So Catalina…"

Will sighed. "You won't drop it, will you?"

"We practically grew up together with her, you dated before, you were kissing a few weeks ago. I'm sure dear old Dad is about to explode if you are making business decisions that he isn't on board with and if you're seducing his maid."

"I'm not seducing anyone." Yet. "And what I do with my personal life is none of his concern."

"He'll say different once he knows you're after the maid. He'll not see her as an appropriate match for you," James countered, coming to his feet and glancing toward the ceiling as if he could figure out what was going on upstairs between the women. "What's taking them so long? Think it's safe to go back?"

Will nodded. "Let's go see. Hopefully Cat was able to calm Bella down."

"Cat, huh?" James smiled as he headed toward the foyer and the staircase. "You called her that years ago and she hated it. You still going with that?"

Will patted his brother on the shoulder. "I am going for whatever the hell I want lately."

And he was. From this point on, if he wanted it, he was taking it…that went for his business and his bedroom.

The fact that the maid was consoling a member of the royal family probably looked strange from the outside, and honestly it felt a bit weird. But Catalina had been around Bella enough to know how down-to-earth James's wife was. Bella never treated Catalina like a member of the staff. Not that they were friends by any means, but Catalina was comfortable with Bella and part of her was glad Will had asked her to come console Bella over the loss of her aunt.

"You're so sweet to come in here," Bella said with a sniff.

Catalina fought to keep her own emotions inside as she hugged Bella. Even though years had passed, Catalina still missed her grandmother every single day. Some days were just more of a struggle than others.

"I'm here anytime." Catalina squeezed the petite woman, knowing what just a simple touch could do to help ease a bit of the pain, to know you weren't alone in your grief. "There will be times memories sneak up on you and crush you all over again and there will be days you are just fine. Don't try to hide your emotions.

Everyone grieves differently so whatever your outlet is, it's normal."

Bella shifted back and patted her damp cheeks. "Thank you. I didn't mean to cry all over you and bring up a bad time in your life."

Pushing her own memories aside, Catalina offered a smile. "You didn't do anything but need a shoulder to cry on. I just hope I helped in some small way to ease the hurt and I'm glad I was here."

"Bella."

The sound of James's voice had Catalina stepping back as he came in to stand beside his wife. Tucking her short hair behind her ears, Catalina offered the couple a brief smile. James hugged Bella to his side and glanced at Catalina.

"I didn't want to interrupt, but I know you need to work, too," James said. "We really appreciate you."

Those striking Rowling eyes held hers. This man was a star athlete, wanted by women all over the world. Yet Catalina felt nothing. He looked exactly like Will, but in Catalina's heart...

No. Her heart wasn't involved. Her hormones were a jumbled mess, but her heart was sealed off and impenetrable...at least where Will was concerned. Maybe when she left Alma she'd settle somewhere new and find the man she was meant to be with, the man who wouldn't consider her a mistake.

Those damning words always seemed to be in the forefront of her mind.

"I'm here all day through the week," Catalina told Bella. "You can always call me, too. I'm happy to help any way I can."

"Thank you." Bella sniffed. She dabbed her eyes again and turned into James's embrace.

Catalina left the couple alone and pulled the door shut behind her. She leaned against the panel, closed her eyes and tipped her head back. Even though Catalina still had her mother, she missed her grandmother. There was just something special about a woman who enters your life in such a bold way that leaves a lasting impression.

Catalina knew Bella was hurting over the loss of her aunt, there was no way to avoid the pain. But Bella had a great support team and James would stay by her side.

A stab of remorse hit her. Bella's and Catalina's situations were so similar, yet so different. Will had comforted her over her loss when they'd first started dating and Catalina had taken his concern as a sign of pure interest. Unfortunately, her moments of weakness had led her to her first broken heart.

The only good thing to come out of it was that she hadn't given him her innocence. But she'd certainly been tempted on more than one occasion. The man still tempted her, but she was smarter now, less naïve, and she had her eyes wide open.

Pushing off the door, she shoved aside the thoughts of Will and their past relationship. She'd jumped from one mistake to another after he broke things off with her. Two unfortunate relationships were more than enough for her. Focusing on turning her hobby and passion for making clothes into a possible career had kept her head on straight and her life pointed in the right direction. She didn't have time for obstacles…no matter how sexy.

She made her way down the hall toward the main bathroom on the second floor. This bathroom was nearly the size of her little flat across town. She could afford something bigger, but she'd opted to keep her place small because she lived alone and she'd rather save her money for fabrics, new sewing machines, investing in her future and ultimately her move. One day that nest egg she'd set aside would come in handy and she couldn't wait to leave Alma and see how far her dreams could take her. Another couple months and she truly believed she would be ready. She still couldn't pinpoint her exact destination, though. Milan was by far the hot spot for fashion and she could head there and aim straight for the top. New York was also an option, or Paris.

Catalina smiled at the possibilities as she reached beneath the sink and pulled out fresh white hand towels. Just as she turned, she collided with a very hard, very familiar chest.

Will gripped her arms to steady her, but she wasn't going anywhere, not when she was wedged between his solid frame and the vanity biting into her back.

"Excuse me," she said, gripping the terrycloth next to her chest and tipping her chin up. "I'm running behind."

"Then a few more minutes won't matter." He didn't let up on his hold, but instead leaned back and kicked the door shut with his foot. "You're avoiding me."

Hadn't she thought this bathroom was spacious just moments ago? Because now it seemed even smaller than the closet in her bedroom.

"Your ego is getting in the way of common sense," she countered. "I'm working. Why are you always here lately anyway? Don't you have an office to run on the other side of town?"

The edge of his mouth kicked up in a cocky half smile. "You've noticed. I was beginning to think you were immune."

"I've been vaccinated."

Will's rich laugh washed over her and she cursed the goose bumps that covered her skin. Between his touch, his masculine scent and feeling his warm breath on her, her defenses were slipping. She couldn't get sucked back into his spell, not when she was so close to breaking free once and for all.

"Come to dinner with me," he told her, smile still in place as if he truly thought she'd jump at the chance. "Your choice of places."

Now Catalina laughed. "You're delusional. I'm not going anywhere with you."

His eyes darkened as they slid to her lips. "You will."

Catalina pushed against him, surprised when he released her and stepped back. She busied herself with changing out the hand towels on the heated rack. Why wouldn't he leave? Did he not take a hint? Why suddenly was he so interested in her when a few years ago she'd been "a mistake"? Plus, a month ago he'd almost been engaged to another woman.

Being a backup plan for anybody was never an option. She'd rather be alone.

Taking more care than normal, Catalina focused on making sure the edges of the towels were perfectly lined up. She needed to keep her shaking hands busy.

"You can't avoid this forever." Will's bold words sliced through the tension. "I want you, Cat. I think you know me well enough to realize I get what I want."

Anger rolled through her as she spun around to face him. "For once in your life, you're not going to be able to have something just because you say so. I'm not just a possession, Will. You can't buy me or even work your charm on me. I've told you I'm not the same naïve girl I used to be."

In two swift steps, he'd closed the gap between them

and had her backed against the wall. His hands settled on her hips, gripping them and pulling them flush with his. This time she didn't have the towels to form a barrier and his chest molded with hers. Catalina forced herself to look up into his eyes, gritted her teeth and prayed for strength.

Leaning in close, Will whispered, "I'm not the man I used to be, either."

A shiver rippled through her. No, no he wasn't. Now he was all take-charge and demanding. He hadn't been like this before. He also hadn't been as broad, as hard. He'd definitely bulked up in all the right ways…not that she cared.

"What would your father say if he knew you were hiding in the bathroom with the maid?" she asked, hoping the words would penetrate through his hormones. He'd always been yanked around by Daddy's wishes… hence their breakup, she had no doubt.

Will shifted his face so his lips were a breath away from hers as his hands slid up to her waist, his thumbs barely brushing the underside of her breasts. "My father is smart enough to know what I'd be doing behind a closed door with a sexy woman."

Oh, man. Why did she have to find his arrogance so appealing? Hadn't she learned her lesson the first time? Wanting Will was a mistake, one she may never recover from if she jumped in again.

"Are you saying you're not bowing down to your father's commands anymore? How very grown up of you."

Why was she goading him? She needed to get out of here because the more he leaned against her, the longer he spoke with that kissable mouth so close to hers, the harder he was making her life. Taunting her, making her ache for things she could never have.

"I told you, I'm a different man." His lips grazed hers as he murmured, "But I still want you and nobody is going to stand in my way."

Why did her hormones and need for his touch override common sense? Letting Will kiss her again was a bad, bad idea. But she couldn't stop herself and she'd nearly arched her body into his just as he stepped back. The heat in his eyes did nothing to suppress the tremors racing through her, but he was easing backward toward the closed door.

"You're leaving?" she asked. "What is this, Will? A game? Corner the staff and see how far she'll let me take things?"

He froze. "This isn't a game, Cat. I'm aching for you, to strip you down and show you exactly what I want. But I need you to literally hurt for wanting me and I want you to be ready. Because the second I think we're on the same level, you're mine."

And with that, he turned and walked out, leaving the door open.

Catalina released a breath she hadn't realized she'd been holding. How dare he disrupt her work and get her all hot and bothered? Did he truly think she'd run to him begging to whisk her off to bed?

As much as her body craved his touch, she wouldn't fall into his bed simply because he turned on the sex appeal. If he wanted her, then that was his problem.

Unfortunately, he'd just made his wants her problem as well because now she couldn't think of anything else but how amazing he felt pressed against her.

Catalina cursed herself as she gathered the dirty towels. If he was set on playing games, he'd chosen the wrong opponent.

Four

Catalina lived for her weekends. Two full days for her to devote to her true love of designing and sewing. There was nothing like creating your own masterpieces from scratch. Her thick portfolio binder overflowed with ideas from the past four years. She'd sketched designs for every season, some sexy, some conservative, but everything was timeless and classy in her opinion.

She supposed something more than just heartache and angst had come from Will's exiting her life so harshly. She'd woken up, finally figured out what she truly wanted and opted to put herself, her dreams as top priority. And once she started achieving her career goals, she'd work on her personal dreams of a family. All of those were things she couldn't find in Alma. This place had nothing for her anymore other than her mother, who worked for another family. But her mother had already said she'd follow Catalina wherever she decided to go.

Glancing around, Catalina couldn't remember where she put that lacy fabric she'd picked up in town a few weeks ago. She'd seen it on the clearance table and had nothing in mind for it at the time, but she couldn't pass up the bargain.

Now she knew exactly what she'd use the material for. She had the perfect wrap-style dress in mind. Something light and comfortable, yet sexy and alluring with a lace overlay. The time would come when Catalina would be able to wear things like that every single day. She could ditch her drab black button-down shirt and plain black pants. When she dressed for work every morning, she always felt she was preparing for a funeral.

And those shoes? She couldn't wait to burn those hideous things.

Catalina moved around the edge of the small sofa and thumbed through the stack of folded materials on the makeshift shelving against the wall. She'd transformed this spare room into her sewing room just last year and since then she'd spent nearly all of her spare time in the cramped space. One day, though… One day she'd have a glorious sewing room with all the top-notch equipment and she would bask in the happiness of her creations.

As she scanned the colorful materials folded neatly on the shelves, her cell rang. Catalina glanced at the arm of the sofa where her phone lay. Her mother's name lit up the screen.

Lunging across the mess of fabrics on the cushions, Catalina grabbed her phone and came back to her feet as she answered.

"Hey, Mum."

"Sweetheart. I'm sorry I didn't call earlier. I went out to breakfast with a friend."

Catalina stepped from her bedroom and into the cozy

living area. "No problem. I've been sewing all morning and lost track of time."

"New designs?" her mother asked.

"Of course." Catalina sank down onto her cushy sofa and curled her feet beneath her. "I actually have a new summery beach theme I'm working on. Trying to stay tropical and classy at the same time has proven to be more challenging than I thought."

"Well, I know you can do it," her mother said. "I wore that navy-and-gray-print skirt you made for me to breakfast this morning and my friend absolutely loved it. I was so proud to be wearing your design, darling."

Catalina sat up straighter. "You didn't tell her—"

"I did not," her mother confirmed. "But I may have said it was from a new up-and-coming designer. I couldn't help it, honey. I'm just so proud of you and I know you'll take the fashion world by storm once you leave Alma."

Just the thought of venturing out on her own, taking her secret designs and her life dream and putting herself out there had a smile spreading across her face as nerves danced in her belly. The thought of someone looking over her designs with a critical eye nearly crippled her, but she wouldn't be wielding toilet wands for the rest of her life.

"I really think I'll be ready in a couple of months," Catalina stated, crossing back to survey her inventory on the shelves. "Saying a timeframe out loud makes this seem so real."

Her mother laughed. "This is your dream, baby girl. You go after it and I'll support you all the way. You know I want you out from under the Rowlings' thumb."

Catalina swallowed as she zeroed in on the lace and

pulled it from the pile. "I know. Don't dwell on that, though. I'm closer to leaving every day."

"Not soon enough for me," her mother muttered.

Catalina knew her mother hated Patrick Rowling. Their affair years ago was still a secret and the only reason Catalina knew was because when she'd been dumped by Will and was sobbing like an adolescent schoolgirl, her mother had confessed. Maria Iberra was a proud woman and Catalina knew it had taken courage to disclose the affair, but Maria was dead set on her daughter truly understanding that the Rowling men were only after one thing and they were ruthless heart-breakers. Feelings didn't exist for those men, save for James, who seemed to be truly in love and determined to make Bella happy.

But Patrick was ruthless in everything and Will had followed suit. So why was he still pursuing her? She just wanted a straight answer. If he just wanted sex, she'd almost wish he'd just come out and say it. She'd take honesty over adult games any day.

Before she could respond to her mother, Catalina's doorbell rang. "Mum, I'll call you back. Someone is at my door."

She disconnected the call and pocketed her cell in her smock pocket. She'd taken to wearing a smock around her waist to keep pins, thread, tiny scissors and random sewing items easily accessible. Peeking through the peephole, Catalina only saw a vibrant display of flowers.

Flicking the deadbolt, she eased the door open slightly. "Yes?"

"Catalina Iberra?"

"That's me."

The young boy held onto the crystal vase with two hands and extended it toward her. "Delivery for you."

Opening the door fully, she took the bouquet and soon realized why this boy had two hands on it. This thing was massive and heavy.

"Hold on," she called around the obscene arrangement. "Let me give you a tip."

"Thank you, ma'am, but that was already taken care of. You have a nice day."

Catalina stepped back into her apartment, kicked the door shut with her foot and crossed the space to put the vase on her coffee table. She stood back and checked out various shades and types of flowers. Every color seemed to be represented in the beautiful arrangement. Catalina couldn't even imagine what this cost. The vase alone, made of thick, etched glass, appeared to be rather precious.

A white envelope hung from a perfectly tied ribbon around the top of the vase. She tugged on the ribbon until it fell free and then slid the small envelope off. Pulling the card out and reading it, her heart literally leapt up into her throat. *Think of me. W.*

Catalina stared at the card, and then back at the flowers. Suddenly they weren't as pretty as they'd been two minutes ago. Did he seriously think she'd fall for something as cliché as flowers? Please. And that arrogant message on the card was utterly ridiculous.

Think of him? Lately she'd done little else, but she'd certainly never tell him that. What an ego he'd grown since they were last together. And she thought it had been inflated then.

But because no one was around to see her, she bent down and buried her face in the fresh lilacs. They smelled so wonderful and in two days they would still look amazing.

A smile spread across her face as her plan took shape. Will had no idea who he was up against if he thought an expensive floral arrangement was going to get her to drop her panties or common sense.

As much as she was confused and a bit hurt by his newfound interest in her now that he wasn't involved with Bella, she had to admit, toying with him was going to be fun. Only one person could win this battle...she just prayed her strength held out and she didn't go down in the first round.

Will slid his cell back into his pocket and leaned against the window seat in his father's office at his Playa del Onda home. "We've got them."

Patrick blinked once, twice, and then a wide smile spread across his face. "I didn't think you could do it."

Will shrugged. "I didn't have a doubt."

"I've been trying to sign with the Cherringtons for over a year." Patrick shook his head and pushed off the top of his desk to come to his feet. "You're really making a mark here, Will. I wondered how things would fair after Bella, but business is definitely your area of expertise."

Will didn't tell his father that Mrs. Cherrington had tried to make a pass at Will at a charity event a few months back. Blackmail in business was sometimes not a bad thing. It seemed that Mrs. Cherrington would do anything to keep her husband from learning she'd had too much to drink and gotten a little frisky. She apparently went so far as to talk him into doing business with the Rowlings, but considering both families would prosper, Will would keep her little secret.

In Will's defense, he didn't let her advances go far. Even if she weren't old enough to be his mother and if she hadn't smelled as if she bathed in a distillery, she was married. He may not want any part of marriage for himself, but that didn't mean he was going to home in on anybody else's, either.

Before he could say anything further, Cat appeared in the doorway with an enormous bouquet. The arrangement reminded him of the gift he'd sent her. He'd wondered all weekend what she'd thought of the arrangement. Had she smiled? Had she thought about calling him?

He'd end this meeting with his father and make sure to track her down before he headed back to the Rowling Energy offices for an afternoon meeting. He had an ache that wasn't going away anytime soon and he was starting to schedule his work around opportunities to see Cat. His control and priorities were becoming skewed.

"I'm sorry to interrupt," she stated, not glancing Will's way even for a second. "I thought I'd freshen up your office."

Patrick glanced down at some papers on his desk and motioned her in without a word. Will kept his eyes on Cat, on her petite, curvy frame tucked so neatly into her black button-down shirt and hip-hugging dress pants. His hands ached to run over her, *sans* clothing.

She was sporting quite a smirk, though. She was up to something, which only put him on full alert.

"I don't always keep flowers in here, but I thought this bouquet was lovely." She set it on the accent table nestled between two leather wingback chairs against the far wall. "I received these the other day and they just did a number on my allergies. I thought about trashing them, but then realized that you may want something fresh for your office, Mr. Rowling."

Will stood straight up. She'd received those the other day? She'd brought his bouquet into his father's office and was giving it away?

Apparently his little Cat had gotten feisty.

"I didn't realize you had allergies," Will stated, drawing her attention to him.

She tucked her short black hair behind her ears and smiled. "And why should you?" she countered with a bit more sass than he was used to from her. "I'll leave you two to talk."

As she breezed out just as quickly as she'd come, Will looked at his father, who was staring right back at him with a narrowed gaze. Why did Will feel as if he'd been caught doing something wrong?

"Keep your hands off my staff," his father warned. "You already tried that once. I hesitated keeping her on, but James swore she was the best worker he'd ever had. Her mother had been a hard worker, too, so don't make me regret that decision."

No way in hell was he letting his father, or anybody else for that matter, dictate what he could and couldn't do with Cat. Listening to his father's instructions about his personal life was what got Will into this mess in the first place.

"Once we've officially signed with the Cherringtons, I'll be sure to send them a nice vintage wine with a personalized note."

Patrick came to his feet, rested his hands on his desk and leaned forward. "You're changing the subject."

"The subject of your staff or my personal life has no relevance in this meeting," Will countered. "I'll be sure to keep you updated if anything changes, but my assistant should have all the proper paperwork emailed by the end of the day."

Will started to head out the door, but turned to glance over his shoulder. "Oh, and the next time Cat talks to you, I suggest you are polite in return and at least look her in the eye."

Leaving his father with his mouth wide open, Will turned and left the office. Perhaps he shouldn't have added that last bit, but Will wasn't going to stand by and watch his father dismiss Cat like that. She was a person, too—just because she cleaned for Patrick and he signed her checks didn't mean he was more important than she. Will had no doubt that when Cat worked for James, he at least treated her with respect.

Dammit. Why was he getting so defensive? He should be pissed she'd dumped his flowers onto his father. There was a twisted irony in there somewhere, but Will was too keyed up to figure it out. What was it about her blatantly throwing his gift back in his face that had him so turned on?

Will searched the entire first and second floors, but Cat was nowhere to be found. Granted, the house was twelve thousand square feet, but there weren't that many people on staff. How could one petite woman go missing?

Will went back to the first floor and into the back of the house where the utility room was. The door was closed and when he tried to turn the knob, he found it locked. That was odd. Why lock a door to the laundry? He heard movement, so someone was in there.

He tapped his knuckles on the thick wood door and waited. Finally the click of a lock sounded and the door eased open. Cat's dark eyes met his.

"What do you want?" she asked.

"Can I come in?"

"This isn't a good time."

He didn't care if this was good or bad. He was here and she was going to talk to him. He had to get to another meeting and wasn't wasting time playing games.

Will pushed the door, causing her to step back. Squeezing in, he shut the door behind him and flicked the lock into place.

Cat had her back to him, her shoulders hunched. "What do you want, Will?"

"You didn't like the flowers?" he asked, crossing his arms over his chest and leaning against the door.

"I love flowers. I don't like your clichéd way of getting my attention or trying to buy me."

He reached out, grabbed her shoulder and spun her around. "Look at me, dammit."

In an instant he realized why she'd been turned away. She was clutching her shirt together, but the swell of her breasts and the hint of a red lacy bra had him stunned speechless.

"I was trying to carry a small shelf into the storage area and it got caught on my shirt," she explained, looking anywhere but at his face as she continued to hold her shirt. "I ran in here because I knew there was a sewing kit or maybe even another shirt."

Everything he'd wanted to say to her vanished from his mind. He couldn't form a coherent thought at this point, not when she was failing at keeping her creamy skin covered.

"I'd appreciate it if you'd stop staring," she told him, her eyes narrowing. "I don't have time for games or a pep talk or whatever else you came to confront me about. I have work to do and boobs to cover."

Her snarky joke was most likely meant to lighten the mood, but he'd wanted her for too long to let anything deter him. He took a step forward, then another, until he'd backed her up against the opposite wall. With her hands holding tight onto her shirt, her eyes wide and her cheeks flushed, there was something so wanton yet innocent about her.

"What do you like?" he asked.

Cat licked her lips. "What?" she whispered.

Will placed a hand on the wall, just beside her head, and leaned in slightly. "You don't like flowers. What do you like?"

"Actually, I love flowers. I just took you for someone who didn't fall into clichés." She offered a slight smile, overriding the fear he'd seen flash through her eyes moments ago. "But you're trying to seduce the maid, so maybe a cliché is all we are."

Will slid his other hand across her cheek and into her hair as he brought his mouth closer. "I don't care if you're the queen or the maid or the homeless person on the corner. I know what I want and I want you, Cat."

She turned her palms to his chest, pushing slightly, but not enough for him to think she really meant for him to step back…not when she was breathless and her eyes were on his mouth.

"I'm not for sale," she argued with little heat behind her words.

He rubbed his lips across hers in a featherlight touch that instantly caused her to tremble. That had to be her body, no way would he admit those tremors were from him.

"Maybe I'll just sample, then."

Fully covering her mouth, Will kept his hand fisted in her hair as he angled her head just where he wanted it. If she didn't want him at all, why did she instantly open for him?

The sweetest taste he'd ever had was Cat. No woman compared to this one. As much as he wanted to strip her naked right here, he wanted to savor this moment and simply savor her. He wanted that familiar taste only Cat could provide, he wanted to reacquaint himself with every minute sexy detail.

Delicate hands slid up his chest and gripped his shoulders, which meant she had to have released her hold on her shirt. Will removed his hand from the wall and gripped her waist as he slid his hand beneath the hem of her shirt and encountered smooth, warm skin. His thumb caressed back and forth beneath the lacy bra.

Cat arched into him with a slight moan. Her words may have told him she wasn't interested, but her body had something else in mind...something much more in tune with what he wanted.

Will shifted his body back just enough to finish unbuttoning her shirt. He parted the material with both hands and took hold of her breasts. The lace slid beneath his palm and set something off in him. His Cat may be sweet, somewhat innocent, but she loved the sexy lingerie. Good to know.

Reluctantly breaking the kiss, Will ached to explore other areas. He moved down the column of her throat and continued to the swell of her breasts. Her hands slid into his hair as if she were holding him in place. He sure as hell wasn't going anywhere.

Will had wanted this, wanted her, four years ago. He'd wanted her with a need that had only grown over the years. She'd been a virgin then; he'd known it and respected her for her decisions. He would've waited for her because she'd been so special to him.

Then his father had issued an ultimatum and Will had made the wrong choice. He didn't fight for what he wanted and he'd damn well never make that mistake again.

Now Cat was in his arms again and he'd let absolutely nothing stand in the way of his claiming her.

"Tell me you want this," he muttered against her heated skin. "Tell me."

His hands encircled her waist as he tugged her harder against his body. Will lifted his head long enough to catch the heat in her eyes, the passion.

A jiggling of the door handle broke the spell. Will stepped back as Cat blinked, glanced down and yanked her shirt together.

"Is someone in there?" a male voice called.

Cat cleared her throat. "I got something on my shirt," she called back. "Just changing. I'll be out shortly, Raul."

Will stared down at her. "Raul?" he whispered.

Cat jerked her shirt off and stalked across the room. Yanking open a floor-to-ceiling cabinet, she snagged another black shirt and slid into it. As she secured the buttons, she spun back around.

"He's a new employee, not that it's any of your business." When she was done with the last button, she crossed her arms over her chest. "What just happened here, as well as in the bathroom the other day, will not happen again. You can't come in to where I work and manhandle me. I don't care if I work for your family. That just makes this even more wrong."

Will couldn't suppress the grin. "From the moaning, I'd say you liked being manhandled."

He started to take a step forward but she held up her hand. "Don't come closer. You can't just toy with me, Will. I am not interested in a replay of four years ago. I have no idea what your agenda is, but I won't be part of it."

"Who says I have an agenda?"

Her eyes narrowed. "You're a Rowling. You all have agendas."

So she was a bit feistier than before. He always loved a challenge—it was impossible to resist.

"Are you still a virgin?"

Cat gasped, her face flushed. "How dare you. You have no right to ask."

"Considering I'm going to take you to bed, I have every right."

Cat moved around him, flicked the lock and jerked the door open. "Get the hell out. I don't care if this is your father's house. I'm working and we are finished. For good."

Will glanced out the door at a wide-eyed Raul. Before he passed, he stopped directly in front of Cat. "We're not finished. We've barely gotten started."

Crossing into the hall, Will met Raul's questioning stare. "You saw and heard nothing. Are we clear?"

Will waited until the other man silently nodded before walking away. No way in hell did he need his father knowing he'd been caught making out in the damn laundry room with the maid.

Next time, and there would be a next time, Will vowed she'd be in his bed. She was a willing participant every time he'd kissed her. Hell, if the knock hadn't interrupted them, they'd probably both be a lot happier right now.

Regardless of what Cat had just said, he knew full well she wanted him. Her body wasn't lying. What kind of man would he be if he ignored her needs? Because he sure as hell wasn't going to sit back and wait for another man to come along and explore that sexual side.

She was his.

Five

Alma was a beautiful country. Catalina was going to miss the island's beautiful water and white sandy beaches when she left. Swimming was her first love. Being one with the water, letting loose and not caring about anything was the best source of therapy.

And tonight she needed the release.

For three days she'd managed to dodge Will. He had come to Patrick's house every morning, holed himself up in the office with his father and then left, assumedly to head into the Rowling Energy offices.

Will may say he'd changed, but to her he still looked as if he was playing the perfect son, dead set on taking over the family business. Apparently he thought he could take her over as well. But she wasn't a business deal to close and she certainly wouldn't lose her mind again and let him devour her so thoroughly no matter how much she enjoyed it.

Lust was something that would only get her into trouble. The repercussions of lust would last a lifetime; a few moments of pleasure wouldn't be worth the inevitable heartache in the end.

Catalina sliced her arms through the water, cursing herself for allowing thoughts of Will to infringe on her downtime when she only wanted to relax. The man wanted to control her and she was letting him because she had no clue how to stop this emotional roller coaster he'd strapped her into.

Heading toward the shoreline, Catalina pushed herself the last few feet until she could stand. Shoving her short hair back from her face, she took deep breaths as she sloshed through the water. With the sun starting to sink behind her, she crossed the sand and scooped up her towel to mop her face.

He'd seriously crossed the line when he'd asked about her virginity. Yes, she'd gotten carried away with him, even if she did enjoy those stolen moments, but her sexual past was none of his concern because she had no intention of letting him have any more power over her. And she sure as hell didn't want to know about all of his trysts since they'd been together.

Cat wrapped the towel around her body and tucked the edge in to secure the cloth in place. This small stretch of beach wasn't far from her apartment, only a five-minute walk, and rarely had many visitors in the evening. Most people came during the day or on weekends. On occasion, Catalina would see families playing together. Her heart would always seize up a bit then. She longed for the day when she could have a family of her own, but for now, she had her sights set on fashion.

Giving up one dream for another wasn't an option. Who said she couldn't have it all? She could have her ideal career and then her family. She was still young. At twenty-four some women were already married and had children, but she wasn't like most women.

And if Will Rowling thought he could deter her from going after what she wanted, he was delusional. And sexy. Mercy, was the man ever sexy.

No, no, no.

Will and his sexiness had no room in her life, especially her bed, which he'd work his way into if she wasn't on guard constantly.

Catalina pulled out her tank-style sundress and exchanged the towel for the modest coverup. After shoving the towel into her bag, she slid into her sandals and started her walk home. The soft ocean breeze always made her smile. Wherever she moved, she was going to need to be close to water or at least close enough that she could make weekend trips.

This was the only form of exercise she enjoyed, and being so short, every pound really showed. Not that she worried about her weight, but she wanted to feel good about herself and she felt her best when she'd been swimming and her muscles were burning from the strain. She wanted to be able to throw on anything in her closet and have confidence. For her, confidence came with a healthy body.

Catalina crossed the street to her apartment building and smiled at a little girl clutching her mother's hand. Once she reached the stoop leading up to her flat, she dug into her bag for her keys. A movement from the corner of her eye caught her attention. She knew who was there before she fully turned, though.

"What are you doing here, Will?"

She didn't look over her shoulder, but she knew he

followed her. Arguing that he wasn't invited was a moot point; the man did whatever he wanted anyway.

"I came to see you."

When she got to the second floor, she stopped outside her door and slid her key into the lock. "I figured you'd given up."

His rich laughter washed over her chilled skin. Between the warm water and the breezy air, she was going to have to get some clothes on to get warm.

"When have you known me to give up?" he asked.

Throwing a glance over her shoulder, she raised a brow. "Four years ago. You chose your career over a relationship. Seeing me was the big mistake. Ring any bells?"

Will's bright aqua-blue eyes narrowed. "I didn't give up. I'm here now, aren't I?"

"Oh, so I was just put on hold until you were ready," she mocked. "How silly of me not to realize."

"Can I come in?" he asked. "I promise I'll only be a couple minutes."

"You can do a lot of damage in a couple minutes," she muttered, but figured the sooner she let him in, the sooner he'd leave…she hoped.

Catalina pushed the door open and started toward her bedroom. Thankfully the door to the spare room was closed. The last thing she needed was for Will to see everything she'd been working on. Her personal life was none of his concern.

"I'm changing and you're staying out here."

She slammed her bedroom door, hoping he'd get the hint he wasn't welcome. What was he doing here? Did he think she'd love how he came to her turf? Did he think she'd be more comfortable and melt into a puddle at his feet, and then invite him into her bed?

Oh, that man was infuriating. Catalina jerked off

her wet clothes and draped them over her shower rod in her bathroom. Quickly she threw on a bra, panties and another sundress, one of her own designs she liked to wear out. It was simple, but it was hers, and her confidence was always lifted when she wore her own pieces.

Her damp hair wasn't an issue right now. All she wanted to know was why he was here. If he only came for another make-out scene that was going to leave her frustrated and angry, she wanted no part of it. She smoothed back a headband to keep her hair from her face. It was so short it would be air-dried in less than an hour.

Padding barefoot back into her living room, she found Will standing near the door where she'd left him. He held a small package in his hands that she hadn't noticed before. Granted she'd had her back to him most of the time because she didn't want to face him.

"Come bearing gifts?" she asked. "Didn't you learn your lesson after the flowers?"

Will's smile spread across his face. "Thought I'd try a different tactic."

On a sigh, Catalina crossed the room and sank into her favorite cushy chair. "Why try at all? Honestly. Is this just a game to see if you can get the one who got away? Are you trying to prove to yourself that you can conquer me? Is it a slumming thing? What is it, Will? I'm trying to understand this."

He set the box on the coffee table next to a stack of the latest fashion magazines. After taking a seat on her couch, Will rested his elbows on his knees and leaned forward.

Silence enveloped them and the longer he sat there, the more Catalina wondered what was going through his mind. Was he planning on lying? Was he trying to figure out how to tell her the truth? Or perhaps he was second-guessing himself.

She studied him—his strong jawline, his broad frame taking up so much space in her tiny apartment. She'd never brought a man here. Not that she'd purposely brought Will here, but having such a powerful man in her living room was a new experience for her.

Maybe she was out of her league. Maybe she couldn't fight a force like Will Rowling. But she was sure as hell going to try because she couldn't stand to have her heart crushed so easily again.

Catalina curled her feet beside her in the spacious chair as Will met her gaze. Those piercing aqua eyes forced her to go still.

"What if I'm here because I've never gotten over you?"

Dammit. Why did he let that out? He wasn't here to make some grand declaration. He was here to soften her, to get her to let down that guard a little more because he was not giving up. He'd jump through whatever hoop she threw in front of him, but Cat would be his for a while. A steamy affair that no one knew about was exactly what they needed whether she wanted to admit it or not.

When he'd been given the ultimatum by his father to give up Cat or lose his place in Rowling Energy, Will hadn't had much choice. Oh, and his father had also stated that he'd make sure Catalina Iberra would never work anywhere in Alma again if Will didn't let her go.

He'd had to protect her, even though she hated him at the time. He'd do it all over again. But he didn't want to tell her what had happened. He didn't want her to feel guilty or to pity him. Will would win her back just as he'd won her the first time. He'd be charming and wouldn't take no for an answer.

His quiet, almost vulnerable question still hung heavy in the space between them as he waited for her response. She hadn't kicked him out of her flat, so he was making progress. Granted, he'd been making progress since that spur-of-the-moment kiss a month ago, but he'd rather speed things along. A man only had so much control over his emotions.

"You can have any woman you want." Catalina toyed with the edge of the hem on her dress, not making eye contact. "You let me go, you called me a mistake."

He'd regret those words until he died. To know he'd made Cat feel less than valuable to him was not what he'd wanted to leave her with, but once the damning words were out, he couldn't take them back. Anything he said after that point would have been moot. The damage had been done and he'd moved on...or tried to. He'd said hurtful things to get her to back away from him; he'd needed her to stay away at the time because he couldn't afford to let her in, not when his father had such a heavy hand.

Will had been devastated when she'd started dating another man. What had he expected? Did he think a beautiful, vibrant woman was just going to sit at home and sulk about being single? Obviously she had taken the breakup better than he had. And how sick was that, that he wished she'd been more upset? He wanted her to be happy...he just wanted it to be with him.

"I can't have any woman," he countered. "You're still avoiding me."

She lifted her dark eyes, framed by even darker lashes, and focused on him. Every time she looked at him, Will felt that punch to the gut. Lust. It had to be lust because he wouldn't even contemplate anything else. They'd been apart too long for any other emotion to have settled in. They were two different people now and he just wanted to get to know her all over again, to prove himself to her. She deserved everything he had to give.

Will came to his feet. He couldn't stay here because the longer he was around her, the more he wanted her. Cat was going to be a tough opponent and he knew all too well that the best things came from patience and outlasting your opponent. Hadn't it taken him four years to best his father? And he was still in the process of doing that.

"Where are you going?" she asked, looking up at him.

"You want me to stay?" He stepped forward, easing closer to the chair she sat in. "Because if I stay, I'm going to want more than just talking."

"Did you just come to see where I lived? Did you need this reminder of how opposite we are? How I'm just—"

Will put his hand over her mouth. Leaning down, he gripped the arm of her chair and rested his weight there. He eased in closer until he could see the black rim around her dark eyes.

"We've been over this. I don't care what you are. I know what I want, what I need, and that's you."

Her eyes remained locked on his. Slowly he drew his hand away and trailed his fingertips along the thin tan line coming down from behind her neck.

"You're getting red here," he murmured, watching her shiver beneath his touch. "I haven't seen you out of work clothes in years. You need to take better care of your skin."

Cat reached up, grabbed his hand and halted his movements. "Don't do this, Will. There's nothing for you here and I have nothing to give. Even if I gave you my body, I'd regret it because you wouldn't give me any more and I deserve so much. I see that now and I won't lose sight of my goals just because we have amazing chemistry."

Her pleading tone had him easing back. She wanted him. He'd broken her down enough for her to fully admit it.

What goals was she referring to? He wanted to know what her plans were because he wouldn't let this go. He'd waited too long for this second chance and to finally have her, to finally show his father he was in control now, was his ultimate goal.

"I'm not about to give up, Cat." Will stood straight up and kept his eyes on hers. "You have your goals, I have mine."

As he turned and started walking toward the door, he glanced back and nodded toward the package on the table. "You didn't like flowers. This may be more practical for you."

Before she could say a word, he let himself out. Leaving her flat was one of the hardest things he'd done. He knew if he'd hung around a bit longer she would give in to his advances, but he wanted her to come to him. He wanted her to be aching for him, not reluctant.

Cat would come around. They had too much of a history and a physical connection now for her to ignore her body. He had plenty to keep him occupied until she decided to come to him.

Starting with dropping another bomb on his father where their investments and loyalties lay.

Six

Damn that man.

Catalina resisted the urge to march into the Rowling Energy offices and throw Will's gift back in his face.

But she'd used the thing all weekend. Now she was back at the Playa del Onda estate cleaning for his father. Same old thing, different day.

Still, the fact that Will had brought her a sewing kit, a really nice, really expensive sewing kit, had her smiling. She didn't want to smile at his gestures. She wanted to be grouchy and hate them. The flowers had been easy to cast aside, but something as personal as the sewing kit was much harder to ignore.

Will had no idea about her love of sewing, he'd merely gotten the present because of the shirt she'd ripped the other day. Even though he had no clue of her true passion, he thought outside the proverbial box and took the time to find something to catch her attention... as if he hadn't been on her radar already.

Catalina shoved a curtain rod through the grommets and slid it back into place on the hook. She'd long put off laundering the curtains in the glass-enclosed patio room. She'd been too distracted since that initial kiss nearly a month ago.

Why, after four years, why did Will have to reawaken those feelings? Why did he have to be so bold, so powerful, making her face those desires that had never fully disappeared?

The cell in her pocket vibrated. Pulling the phone out, she glanced down to see Patrick's name on the screen. She wasn't afraid of her boss, but she never liked getting a call from him. Either she'd done something wrong or he was about to unload a project on her. He'd been so much more demanding than James had. Granted James had traveled all over the world for football and had rarely been home, but even when he was, he treated Catalina with respect.

Patrick acted as if the dirt on his shoe had a higher position in the social order than she did.

But she needed every dime she could save so that she could leave once she'd finished all her designs. She made a good income for a maid, but she had no idea how much she'd need to start over in a new country and get by until she got her big break.

"Hello?" she answered.

"Come to my office."

She stared at the phone as he hung up. So demanding, so controlling...much like his son.

Catalina made her way through the house and down the wide hall toward Patrick's office. Was Will here today? She didn't want to pry or ask, but she had a feeling Patrick was handing over the reins to the twin he'd groomed for the position.

The office door stood slightly ajar, so Catalina tapped her knuckles against the thick wood before entering.

"Sir," she said, coming to stand in front of Patrick's wide mahogany desk.

The floral arrangement she'd brought a few days ago still sat on the edge. Catalina had to suppress her grin at the fact that the gift a billionaire purchased for a maid now sat on said billionaire's father's desk.

When Patrick glanced up at her, she swallowed. Why did he always make her feel as if she was in the principal's office? She'd done nothing wrong and had no reason to worry.

Oh, wait. She'd made out with his son in the laundry room and there had been a witness outside the door. There was that minor hiccup in her performance.

"I'm going to have the Montoro family over for a dinner," Patrick stated without preamble. "With the passing of Isabella, it's fitting we extend our condolences and reach out to them during this difficult time."

Catalina nodded. "Of course. Tell me what we need."

"The funeral will be Wednesday and I know they will have their own gathering. I'd like to have the dinner Friday night."

Catalina pulled out her cell and started typing in the notes as he rattled off the details. Only the Montoros and the Rowlings would be in attendance. Patrick expected her to work that day preparing the house and that evening cleaning up after the party... Long days like that were a killer for her back and feet. But the double time pay more than made up for the aches and pains.

"Is that all?" she asked when he stopped talking.

He nodded. "There is one more thing."

Catalina swallowed, slid her phone into her pocket and clasped her hands in front of her body. "Yes, sir?"

"If you have a notion of vying for my son's attention, it's best you stop." Patrick eased back in his chair as if he had all the power and not a worry in the world. "He may not be marrying Bella as I'd hoped, but that doesn't mean he's on the market for you. Will is a billionaire. He's handling multimillion dollar deals on a daily basis and the last thing he has time for is to get tangled up in the charms of my maid."

The threat hung between them. Patrick wasn't stupid; he knew exactly what was going on with his own son. Catalina wasn't going to be a pawn in their little family feud. She had a job to do. She'd do it and be on her way in just a few months. Patrick and Will would still be bringing in money and she'd be long forgotten.

"I have no claim on your son, Mr. Rowling," she stated, thankful her voice was calm and not shaky. "I apologize if you think I do. We dated years ago but that's over."

Patrick nodded. "Let's make sure it stays that way. You have a place here and it's not in Will's life."

Even though he spoke the truth, a piece of her heart cracked a bit more over the fact.

"I'll get to work on these arrangements right away," she told Patrick, purposely dropping the topic of his son.

Catalina escaped the office, making it out to the hall before she leaned back against the wall and closed her eyes. Deep breaths in and out. She forced herself to remain calm.

If Patrick had known what happened in the laundry room days ago, he would've outright said so. He wasn't a man known for mincing words. But he knew something was up, which was all the more reason for her to stay clear of Will and his potent touch, his hypnotizing kisses and his spellbinding aqua eyes.

Pushing off the wall, Catalina made her way to the kitchen to speak to the head chef. They had a dinner to discuss and Catalina needed to focus on work, not the man who had the ability to destroy her heart for a second time.

He'd watched her bustle around for the past hour. She moved like a woman on a mission and she hadn't given him one passing glance.

Will wouldn't tolerate being ignored, especially by a woman he was so wrapped up in.

Slipping from the open living area where Cat was rearranging seating and helping the florist with new arrangements, Will snuck into the hallway and pulled his phone from his pocket. Shooting off a quick text, he stood in a doorway to the library and waited for a reply.

And waited. And waited.

Finally after nearly ten minutes, his phone vibrated in his hand. Cat hadn't dismissed him completely, but she wasn't accepting his offer of a private talk. What the hell? She was just outright saying no?

Unacceptable.

He sent another message.

Meet me once the guests arrive. You'll have a few minutes to spare once you're done setting up.

Will read over his message and quickly typed another. I'll be in the library.

Since he hadn't seen his father yet, Will shot his dad a message stating he may be a few minutes late. There was no way he could let another opportunity pass him by to be alone with Cat.

He'd worked like a madman these past few days and

hadn't even had a chance to stop by for a brief glimpse of her. He knew his desires ran deep, but he hadn't realized how deep until he had to go this long without seeing her, touching her, kissing her.

In the past two days Will had severed longstanding ties with another company that wasn't producing the results he wanted. Again he'd faced the wrath of his father, but yet again, Will didn't care. This was his time to reign over Rowling Energy and he was doing so by pushing forward, hard and fast. He wasn't tied to these companies the way his father was and Will intended to see the real estate division double its revenues in the next year.

But right now, he didn't want to think about finances, investments, real estate or oil. He wanted to focus on how fast he could get Cat in his arms once she entered the room. His body responded to the thought.

She wasn't even in the same room and he was aching for her.

Will had plans for the weekend, plans that involved her. He wanted to take her away somewhere she wouldn't expect, somewhere they could be alone and stop tiptoeing around the chemistry. Stolen kisses here and there were getting old. He felt like a horny teenager sneaking around his father's house copping a feel of his girl.

Will took a seat on the leather sofa near the floor-to-ceiling windows. He kept the lights off, save for a small lamp on the table near the entryway. That soft glow was enough; he didn't want to alert anyone who might be wandering outside that there was a rendez-vous going on in here.

Finally after he felt as if he'd waited for an hour,

the door clicked softly and Cat appeared. She shut the door at her back, but didn't step farther into the room.

"I don't have much time," she told him.

He didn't need much…yet. Right now all he needed was one touch, just something to last until he could execute his weekend plans.

Will stood and crossed the spacious room, keeping his eyes locked on hers the entire time. With her back to the door, he placed a hand on either side of her face and leaned in.

His lips grazed over hers softly. "I've missed kissing you."

Cat's body trembled. When her hands came up to his chest, he thought she'd take the initiative and kiss him, but she pushed him away.

"I know I've given mixed signals," she whispered. "But this has to end. No matter how much I enjoy kissing you, no matter how I want you, I don't have the energy for this and I can't lose my j—"

Cat put a hand over her mouth, shook her head and glanced away.

"Your job?" he asked, taking hold of her wrist and prying her hand from her lips. "You think you're going to lose your job over what we have going?"

Her deep eyes jerked back to his. "We have nothing going, Will. Don't you get that? You can afford to mess around. You have nothing at stake here."

He had more than she realized.

"I need to get back to the guests. Bella and James just arrived."

He gripped her elbow before she could turn from him. "Stop. Give me two minutes."

Tucking her hair behind her ears, she nodded. "No more."

Will slid his thumb beneath her eyes. "You're exhausted. I don't like you working so hard, Cat."

"Some of us don't have a choice."

If she were his woman, she'd never work a day in her life.

Wait. What was he saying? She wasn't his woman and he wasn't looking to make her his lifelong partner, either. Marriage or any type of committed relationship was sure as hell not something he was ready to get into. Yes, he wanted her and wanted to spend time with her, but anything beyond that wasn't on his radar just yet.

Gliding his hands over her shoulders, he started to massage the tense muscles. His thumbs grazed the sides of her neck. Cat let out a soft moan as she let her head fall back against the door.

"What are you doing to me?" she groaned.

"Giving you the break you've needed."

Will couldn't tear his gaze from her parted lips, couldn't stop himself from fantasizing how she would look when he made love to her…when, not if.

"I really need to get back." Cat lifted her head and her lids fluttered open. "But this feels so good."

Will kept massaging. "I want to make you feel better," he muttered against her lips. "Let me take you home tonight, Cat."

On a sigh, she shook her head and reached up to squeeze his hands, halting his movements. "You have to know your father thinks something is going on with us."

Will stilled. "Did he say something to you?"

Her eyes darted away. "It doesn't matter. What matters is I'm a maid. You're a billionaire ready to take on the world. We have different goals, Will."

Yeah, and the object of his main goal was plastered against his body.

Will gripped her face between his palms and forced her to look straight at him. "What did he say?"

"I'm just fully aware of my role in this family and it's not as your mistress."

Fury bubbled through Will. "Patrick Rowling does not dictate my sex life and he sure as hell doesn't have a clue what's going on with us."

The sheen in her eyes only made Will that much angrier. How dare his father say anything? He'd done that years ago when Will had let him steamroll over his happiness before. Not again.

"There's nothing going on between us," she whispered.

Will lightened his touch, stroked her bottom lip with the pads of his thumbs. "Not yet, but there will be."

Capturing her lips beneath his, Will relaxed when Cat sighed into his mouth. Will pulled back because if he kept kissing her, he was going to want more and he'd be damned if he had Cat for the first time in his father's library.

When he took Cat to bed, it would be nowhere near Patrick Rowling or his house.

"Get back to work," he muttered against her lips. "We'll talk later."

"Will—"

"Later," he promised with another kiss. "I'm not done with you, Cat. I told you once, I've barely started."

He released her and let her leave while he stayed behind.

If he walked out now, people would know he'd been hiding with Cat. The last thing he ever intended was to get her in trouble or risk her job. He knew she took pride in what she did and the fact she was a perfection-ist only made Will respect her more. She was so much more, though. She was loyal and determined. Qualities he admired.

Well, he was just as determined and his father would never interfere with his personal life again. They'd gone that round once before and Patrick had won. This time, Will intended to come out, not only on top, but with Rowling Energy and Cat both belonging to him.

Seven

William stared over the rim of his tumbler as he sipped his scotch. The way Cat worked the room was something he'd seen in the past, but he hadn't fully appreciated the charm she portrayed toward others during such a difficult time.

There were moments where she'd been stealthy as she slipped in and out of the room, removing empty glasses and keeping the hors d'oeuvre trays filled. Will was positive others hadn't even noticed her, but he did. He noticed every single thing about her.

The dinner was due to be served in thirty minutes and the guests had mostly arrived. Bella stood off to the side with her brother Gabriel, his arm wrapped around her shoulders.

"Your maid is going to get a complex if you keep drilling holes into her."

Will stiffened at James's words. His brother came to stand beside him, holding his own tumbler of scotch.

"I'm not drilling holes," Will replied, tossing back the last of his drink. He welcomed the burn and turned to set the glass on the accent table. "I'm making sure she's okay."

James's brief laugh had Will gritting his teeth to remain quiet and to prevent himself from spewing more defensive reasons as to why he'd been staring at Cat.

"She's used to working, Will. I'd say she's just fine."

Will turned to face his twin. "Did you come over here to hassle me or did you actually want to say something important?"

James's smile spread across his face. Will knew that smile, dammit. He'd thrown it James's way when he'd been in knots over Bella.

"Shut up," Will said as he turned back to watch Cat.

If his brother already had that knowing grin, then Will's watching Cat wouldn't matter at this point. She was working too damn hard. She'd been here all day to make sure the house was perfect for the Montoros and she was still busting her butt to make everyone happy. The chef was really busting it, too, behind the scenes. Cat was definitely due for a much needed relaxing day away from all of this.

"You appear to be plotting," James commented. "But right now I want to discuss what Dad is in such a mood about."

Will threw his brother a glance. "He's Patrick Rowling. Does he need a reason?"

"Not necessarily, but he was a bit gruffer than usual when I spoke with him earlier."

Will watched his father across the room as the man approached Bella and Gabriel. As they all spoke, Will knew his father was diplomatic enough to put on a front of being compassionate. He wouldn't be his stiff, grouchy self with those two.

"I may have made some business decisions he wasn't happy with," Will stated simply.

"Business? Yeah, that will do it." James sighed and finished his scotch. "He put you in charge, so he can't expect you to run every decision by him."

"That's what I told him. I'm not one of his employees, I'm his son and I'm the CEO of Rowling Energy now."

"Plus you're trying to seduce his maid," James added with a chuckle. "You're going to get grounded."

Will couldn't help but smile. "You're such an ass."

"It's fun to see the tables turned and you squirming over a woman for once."

"I'm not squirming, dammit," Will muttered.

But he wouldn't deny he was using Cat as another jab at his father. Yes, he wanted Cat and always had, but if being with her still irritated the old man, so much the better.

Part of him felt guilty for the lack of respect for his father, but that went both ways and the moment Patrick had issued his ultimatum years ago, Will had vowed then and there to gain back everything he deserved, no matter what the cost to his relationship with his father.

Bella's oldest brother, Rafe, and his very pregnant wife, Emily, crossed the room, heading for Will and James. Since he'd abdicated, Rafe and Emily had lived in Key West. But they'd traveled back to be with the family during this difficult time.

"This was a really nice thing for Patrick to do," Rafe stated as he wrapped an arm around his wife's waist. "Losing Isabella has been hard."

"I'm sorry for your loss," Will said. "She was definitely a fighter and Alma is a better place because of her."

"She was quite stubborn," Emily chimed in with a smile. "But we'll get through this because the Montoros are strong."

Will didn't think this was the appropriate time to bring up the subject of Rafe resigning from his duties before his coronation. It was the proverbial elephant in the room.

"I'm going to save my wife from my father," James told them. "Excuse me."

Rafe and Emily were talking about the funeral—how many people had turned out and how supportive the country was in respecting their time of mourning. But Will was only half listening. Cat glanced his way once and that's all it took for his heart to kick up and his body to respond. She didn't smile, she merely locked those dark eyes on him as if she knew his every thought.

Tension crackled between them and everyone else in the room disappeared from his world. Nobody existed but Cat and he knew without a doubt she would agree to his proposal.

He wouldn't accept no for an answer.

Her feet were absolutely screaming. Her back wasn't faring much better. The Montoros lingered longer than she'd expected and Catalina had stuck around an hour after the guests had left.

This fourteen-hour workday would certainly yield a nice chunk of change, but right now all Catalina could think of was her bed, which she hoped to fall into the moment she got home. She may not even take the time to peel out of her clothes.

Catalina nearly wept as she walked toward her car.

She'd parked in the back of the estate near the detached garage where Patrick kept his sporty cars that he only brought out on special occasions. The motion light popped on as she approached her vehicle.

Instantly she spotted Will sitting on a decorative bench along the garage wall. Catalina stopped and couldn't help but smile.

"Are you hiding?" she asked as she started forward again.

"Waiting." He unfolded that tall, broad frame and started coming toward her. "I know you're exhausted, but I just wanted to ask something."

Catalina crossed her arms and stared up at him. "You could've called or texted me your question."

"I could've," he agreed with a slight nod. "But you could say no too easily. I figure if you're looking me in the eye—"

"You think I can't resist you?" she laughed.

Exhaustion might have been consuming her and clouding her judgment, but there was still something so irresistible and charming about this overbearing man…and something calculating as well. He'd purposely waited for her, to catch her at a weak moment. He must really want something major.

"I'm hoping." He reached out, tucking her hair behind her ears before his fingertips trailed down her jawline. "I want to take you somewhere tomorrow afternoon. Just us, on my yacht for a day out."

Catalina wanted to give in to him, she wanted to forget all the reasons they shouldn't be together in any way. She wished her head and her heart would get on the same page where Will Rowling was concerned. She had goals, she had a job she needed to keep in order to reach those goals…yet everything about Will made her want to entertain the idea of letting him in, even if just for one night.

"I even have the perfect spot chosen for a swim," he added, resting his hands on her shoulders. Squeezing her tense muscles, Will smiled. "I'll be a total gentleman."

"A total gentleman?" Catalina couldn't help but laugh. "Then why are you so eager to go?"

"Maybe I think it's time someone gives back to you." His hands stilled as he held her gaze and she realized he wasn't joking at all. "And maybe it's time you see that I'm a changed man."

Her heart tumbled in her chest. "I'm so tired, Will. I'm pretty sure I'm going to spend the next two days sleeping."

"You won't have to do a thing," he promised. "I'll bring the food. All you have to do is wear a swimsuit. I promise this will be a day of total relaxation and pampering."

Catalina sighed. "Will, your father—"

"He's not invited."

She laughed again. "I'm serious."

"I am, too."

Will backed her up to her car and towered over her with such an intense gaze, Catalina knew she was fighting a losing battle.

"This has nothing to do with my father, your job or our differences." His strong jaw set firm, he pressed his gloriously hard body against hers as he stared into her eyes. "I want to spend time with you, Cat. I've finally got my sights set on what is important to me and I'm not letting you get away again. Not without a fight."

"That's what scares me." She whispered the confession.

"There's nothing to be afraid of."

"Said the big bad wolf."

Will smiled, dropped his hands and eased back. "No pressure, Cat. I want to spend time with you, but if you're not ready, I understand. I'm not going anywhere."

The man knew exactly what to say and his delivery was flawless. In his line of work, Will was a master at getting people to see things his way, to ensure he got what he wanted at the end of the day.

No matter what common sense tried to tell her, Catalina wasn't about to start in on a battle she had no chance of winning.

"I'll go," she told him.

The smile that spread across his face was half shadowed by the slant of the motion lights, but she knew all too well how beautiful and sexy the gesture was.

"I'll pick you up at your apartment around noon," he told her. "Now, go home. I'm going to follow you to make sure you get there safely since you're so tired."

"That's not necessary."

Will shrugged. "Maybe not, but I wasn't kidding when I said someone needed to take care of you and pamper you for a change. I'm not coming in. I'll just follow, and then be on my way home."

"I live in the opposite direction from your house," she argued.

"We could've been halfway to your flat by now." He slid his arm around her and tugged on her door handle. "Get in, stop fighting me and let's just save time. You know I'll win in the end anyway."

That's precisely what she feared the most. Will having a win over her could prove more damaging than the last time she'd let him in, but she wanted to see this new side of him. She wanted to take a day and do absolutely nothing but be catered to.

Catalina eased behind the wheel and let Will shut her door. Tomorrow would tell her one of two things: either she was ready to move on and just be his friend or she wanted more with him than stolen kisses behind closed doors.

Worry and panic flooded Catalina as she realized she already knew what tomorrow would bring.

Will had been meaning to see his niece, Maisey, and this morning he was making her his top priority. Before he went to pick up Cat for their outing, he wanted to surprise his adorable niece with a gift…the first of many. He had a feeling this little girl was going to be spoiled, which was better than a child being ignored.

Maisey Rowling would want for nothing. Will's brother had given up being a playboy and was growing into his family-man role rather nicely, and Bella was the perfect stepmother to the infant. Will figured since he and his twin were growing closer, he'd stop in and offer support to James. This complete one-eighty in lifestyles had to be a rough transition for James, but he had Bella and the two were completely in love. And they both loved sweet Maisey.

A slight twinge of jealousy speared through Will, but not over the fact that his brother had married Bella. There had been no chemistry between Will and Bella. She was sweet and stunning, but Will only had eyes for one woman.

The jealousy stemmed from the thought of his brother settling down with his own family. Will hadn't given much thought to family before. He'd been raised to focus solely on taking over Rowling Energy one day.

Will tapped on the etched glass front door to James and Bella's temporary home. They were living here until they knew for sure where they wanted to be permanently. They were in the middle of renovating the old farmhouse that belonged to the Montoros and James had mentioned that they'd probably end up there.

But for now, this house was ideal. It was near the beach, near the park and near Bella's family. Family was important to the Montoros…and yet Will was still thrilled he'd dodged that clan.

The door swung open and Bella greeted him with a smile. "Will, this is a surprise. Come on in."

Clutching the doll he'd brought as a present, Will stepped over the threshold. "I should've called, but I really thought of this last-minute."

Bella smoothed her blond hair behind her shoulders. "This is fine. Maisey and James are in the living room. They just finished breakfast and they're watching a movie."

Her blue eyes darted down to his hands. "I'm assuming that's for Maisey?"

Will nodded. "I haven't played the good uncle yet. Figured it was time I started spoiling her."

Bella's smile lit up her face. "She's going to love it."

The thought of being married to this woman did nothing for Will. Yes, she was stunning, but he'd never felt the stirrings of lust or need when he'd been around her. Their fathers never should have attempted to arrange their engagement, but thankfully everything had worked out for the best…at least where Bella and James were concerned. They were a unified family now.

The thought of his black sheep, playboy brother snuggling up with a baby girl and watching some kid flick was nearly laughable. But Will also knew that once James had learned he had a child, his entire life had changed and his priorities had taken on a whole new order, Maisey being at the top.

Bella led Will through a wide, open-arched doorway to a spacious living room. Two pale yellow sofas sat facing each other with a squat, oversized table between them. An array of coloring books and crayons were scattered over the top of the glossy surface.

James sat on one of the sofas, legs sprawled out before him with Maisey on his lap. James's short hair was all in disarray. He still wore his pajama bottoms and no shirt, and Maisey had a little pink nightgown on; it was obvious they were enjoying a morning of laziness.

As Will stepped farther into the room, James glanced over and smiled. "Hey, brother. What brings you out?"

Bella sat at the end of the couch at her husband's feet. Maisey crawled over her father's legs and settled herself onto Bella's lap. Will looked at his niece and found himself staring into those signature Rowling aqua eyes. No denying who this baby's father was.

"I brought something for Maisey." Will crossed the room and sat on the edge of the coffee table. "Hey, sweetheart. Do you like dolls?"

What if she didn't like it? What if she didn't like him? Dammit. He should've planned better and called to see what Maisey actually played with. He'd just assumed a little girl would like a tiny stuffed doll.

"Her dress matches your nightgown," Bella said softly to the little girl.

Maisey kept her eyes on him as she reached for the toy. Instantly the blond hair went into Maisey's mouth.

"She likes it." James laughed. "Everything goes into her mouth these days."

Will continued to stare at his niece. Children were

one area where he had no clue, but if James said Maisey liked it, then Will had to assume she did.

James swung his legs to the floor and leaned forward. "You hungry?" he asked. "We still have some pancakes and bacon in the kitchen."

"No, I'm good. I'm getting ready to pick up Cat, so I can't stay anyway."

James's brows lifted as he shot Bella a look. "Is this a date?"

Will hadn't intended on telling anyone, but in growing closer with James over the past couple months, he realized he wanted this bond with his twin. Besides, after their conversation last night, James pretty much knew exactly where Will stood in regards to Cat.

He trusted James, that had never been an issue. The issue they'd had wedged between them stemmed from their father always doting on one brother, molding him into a disciple, while ostracizing the other one.

"I'm taking her out on my yacht," Will told him. "We're headed to one of the islands for the day. I'm hoping for total seclusion. Most tourists don't know about them."

There was a small cluster of islands off the coast of Alma. He planned on taking her to Isla de Descanso. The island's name literally meant Island of Relaxation. Cat deserved to be properly pampered and he was going to be the man to give her all of her needs...every single one.

"Sounds romantic." Bella shifted Maisey on her lap as she stared at Will. "I wasn't aware you and Catalina were getting more serious."

James laughed. "I think they've been sneaking."

"We're not serious and we're not sneaking," Will

defended himself. "Okay, fine. We were sneaking, but she's private and she's still leery of me."

"You can't blame her," James added.

Will nodded. "I don't, which is why we need this time away from everything. Plus she's working like crazy for Dad and she's never appreciated."

James snorted. "He barely appreciates his sons. You think he appreciates a maid? I was worried when he moved into my old house. I tried to warn her, but she said she could handle it and she needed the job."

Will hated the thought of her having to work. Hated how much she pushed herself for little to no praise and recognition.

"Well, I appreciate her," Bella chimed in. "I saw how hard she worked the dinner last night. I can't imagine the prep that she and the cooks went through, plus the cleanup after. Catalina is a dedicated, hard worker."

"She won't stay forever," James stated as he leaned over and ruffled Maisey's hair.

Will sat up straighter. "What do you mean?"

His brother's eyes came back to meet his. "I'm just saying someone who is such a perfectionist and self-disciplined surely has a long-term goal in mind. I can't imagine she'll want to play maid until she's old and gray. She hinted a few times when she worked for me that she hoped to one day leave Alma."

Leave Alma? The thought hadn't even crossed Will's mind. Would Cat really go somewhere else? Surely not. Her mother still worked here. She used to work for Patrick, but years ago she had suddenly quit and gone to work for another prominent family. Cat had been with the Rowlings for five years, but James was right. Someone as vibrant as Cat wouldn't want to dust and wash sheets her entire life. He'd already seen the toll her end-less hours were taking on her.

Will came to his feet, suddenly more eager than ever to see her, to be alone with her. "I better get going. I just wanted to stop by and see Maisey before I headed out."

James stood as well. "I'll walk you to the door."

Bidding a goodbye to Bella and Maisey, Will fol-lowed his brother to the foyer.

"Don't say a word about Cat and me," Will said.

Gripping the doorknob, James nodded. "I'm not say-ing a word. I already know Dad would hate the idea and he's interfered enough in our personal lives lately. And I'm not judging you and Catalina. I actually think you two are a good match."

"Thanks, man, but don't let this happily-ever-after stuff you have going on filter into my world. I'm just spending time with Cat. That's all." Will gave his brother a one-armed man hug. "I'll talk to you next week."

Will headed toward his car, more than ready to pick up Cat and get this afternoon started. He planned to be in complete control, but he'd let her set the tone. As much as he wanted her, he wasn't going to pressure her and he wasn't going to deceive her.

Yes, there was the obvious appeal of the fact that his father would hate Will bedding the maid, but he wouldn't risk her job that way even to get petty revenge on his domineering father.

Besides, Cat was so much more than a romp. He couldn't figure out exactly what she was…and that ir-ritated him.

But now he had another worry. What was Cat's ul-timate goal in life? Would she leave Alma and pursue something more meaningful? And why did he care? He wasn't looking for a ring on his finger and he wasn't about to place one on hers, either.

Still, the fact that she could leave bothered him more than he cared to admit.

Will pushed those thoughts aside. Right now, for today, all he was concerned with was Cat and being alone with her. All other world problems would have to wait.

Eight

Nerves kicked around in Catalina's belly as she boarded the yacht. Which seemed like such a simple word for this pristine, massive floating vessel. The fact that the Rowlings had money was an understatement, but to think that Will could own something this amazing…it boggled her mind. She knew he would make a name for himself, knew he'd climb to the top of Rowling Energy. There was never any doubt which twin Patrick was grooming for the position.

But she wasn't focusing on or even thinking of Patrick today. Will wanted her to relax, wanted her to enjoy her day off, and she was going to take full advantage.

Turning toward Will, Catalina laughed as he stepped on board. "I'm pretty sure my entire flat would fit on this deck."

Near the bow, she surveyed the wide, curved outdoor seating complete with plush white pillows. There was even a hot tub off to the side. Catalina couldn't even imagine soaking in that warm water out under the stars. This yacht screamed money, relaxation…and seduction.

She'd voluntarily walked right into the lion's den.

"Let me show you around." Will took hold of her elbow and led her to the set of steps that went below deck. "The living quarters are even more impressive."

Catalina clutched her bag and stepped down as Will gestured for her to go first. The amount of space in the open floor plan below was shocking. It was even grander than she'd envisioned. A large king-sized bed sat in the distance and faced a wall of curved windows that overlooked the sparkling water. Waking up to a sunrise every morning would be heavenly. Waking up with your lover beside you would simply be the proverbial icing on the cake.

No. She couldn't think of Will as her lover or icing on her cake. She was here for a restful day and nothing else. Nookie could not play a part in this because she had no doubt the second he got her out of her clothes, she'd have no defense against him. She needed to stay on guard.

A deep, glossy mahogany bar with high stools separated the kitchen from a living area. The living area had a mounted flat-screen television and leather chairs that looked wide enough for at least two people.

The glossy fixtures and lighting only added to the perfection of the yacht. It all screamed bachelor and money…perfect for Will Rowling.

"You've done well for yourself," she told him as she placed her tote bag on a barstool. "I'm impressed."

Will's sidelong smile kicked up her heart rate. They hadn't even pulled away from the dock and he was already getting to her. This was going to be a day full of her willpower battling her emotions and she didn't know if she'd have the strength to fight off Will's advances.

Who was she kidding? Catalina already knew that if Will tried anything she would succumb to his charms. She'd known this the moment she'd accepted his invitation. But that didn't mean she'd drop her wall of defenses so easily. He'd seriously hurt her before and if he wanted to show her what a changed man he was now, she was going to make him work for it.

"Did you think I was taking you out in a canoe for the day?"

"I guess I hadn't given much thought to the actual boat," she replied, resting her arm on the smooth, curved edge of the bar. "I was too worried about your actions."

"Worried you'd enjoy them too much?" he asked with a naughty grin.

"More like concerned I'd have to deflate your ego," she countered with a matching smile. "You're not seriously going to start putting the moves on me now, are you?"

Will placed a hand over his heart. "You wound me, Cat. I'm at least going to get this boat on course before I rip your clothes off."

Catalina's breath caught in her throat.

Will turned and mounted the steps to go above deck, and then froze and threw a sexy grin over his shoulder. "Relax, Cat. I won't do anything you don't want."

The playful banter had just taken a turn, a sharp turn that sent shivers racing through her entire body. Was she prepared for sex with this man? That's what everything leading up to this moment boiled down to.

Cat would be lying to herself if she tried to say she

didn't want Will physically. That had been proven each time he'd kissed her recently.

I won't do anything you don't want, he'd said.

And that was precisely what scared her the most.

With the ocean breeze sliding across his face, Will welcomed the spittle of spray, the taste of salt on his lips. He needed to get a damn grip. He hadn't meant to be so teasing with Cat.

Okay, he had, but he hadn't meant for her to get that panicked look on her face. He knew full well she was battling with herself where he was concerned. There wasn't a doubt in his mind she wanted him physically and that was easy to obtain. But there was part of Will that wanted her to see that he wasn't at all the same man he used to be.

She would get to see that side of him today. He intended to do everything for her, to prove to her just how appreciated she was and how valued. Will had fully stocked the yacht when he'd had this idea a couple days ago. He'd known he would take her out at some point, but it wasn't until he saw her working the crowd, with circles under her eyes and a smile on her face at the dinner last night, that he decided to invite her right away.

With all of the recent upheaval in Alma—the Montoro monarchy drama and Isabella's passing, not to mention Will's taking the reins of Rowling Energy—there was just too much life getting in the way of what he wanted. Too many distractions interfering with his main goal…and his goal was to have Cat.

He may be the good son, the twin who was raised to follow the rules and not question authority. But Will wasn't about to make the same mistake with Cat as he had in the past. The moment he'd let her walk away

years ago, he'd already started plotting to get her back.
Then the whole debacle with Bella had happened and
Will knew more than ever that it was time to make his
move with Rowling Energy and Cat.

Spending the day together on his yacht, however, was
something totally unrelated to everything else that had
happened in their past. Today was all about them and
nothing or nobody else. Everything that happened with
Cat from here on out was going to be her call…he may
just silently nudge and steer her in the right direction.
Those initial kisses had reignited the spark they'd left
burning long ago and he knew without a doubt that she
felt just as passionate as he did.

He didn't blame her one bit for being leery. He'd
done some major damage before and she wouldn't let
him forget it anytime soon. Not that he could. He'd
never forget that look on her face when he'd told her
they'd been a mistake and then walked away. That moment had played over and over in his mind for the past
several years. Knowing he'd purposely hurt Cat wasn't
something he was likely to ever forget.

Still, if she ever discovered the truth, would she see
that he'd done it for her? He'd best keep that secret to
himself and just stay on course with his plan now. At
least she was here, she was talking and she was coming around. The last thing Will wanted to do was rehash the past when they could be spending their time
concentrating on the here and now.

Will steered the yacht toward the private island not
too far from Alma. In just under an hour he'd have Cat
on a beach with a picnic. He wondered when the last
time was that she'd had someone do something like
that for her, but quickly dismissed the thought. If an-

other man had pampered her, Will sure as hell didn't want to know.

Of course, there was no man in her life now. Will was the one kissing her, touching her. She was his for at least today so he needed to make the most of every moment they were alone. He truly hoped the tiny island was deserted. He'd come here a few times to think, to get away from all the pressure and stress. Only once had he run into other people.

Cat stayed below for the duration of the trip. Perhaps she was trying to gather her own thoughts as well. Maybe she was avoiding him because she thought that taking her out to a private island for sex was so cliché, so easy to read into.

But for reasons Will didn't want to admit or even think about, this day was so much more than sex. *Cat* was more than sex. Yes, he wanted her in the fiercest way imaginable, but he also wanted more from her... he just didn't know what.

No, that was wrong. The first thing he wanted was for her to see him in a different light. He wanted her to see the good in him she'd seen when they'd grown up together, when they'd laughed and shared secrets with each other. He wanted her to see that he wasn't the monster who had ripped her heart out and diminished their relationship into ashes with just a few damning words.

Perhaps this outing wasn't just about him proving to her what a changed man he was, but for him to try to figure out what the hell to do next and how far he wanted to take things with her once they got back to reality.

When he finally pulled up to the dock and secured the yacht, he went below deck. He hoped the last forty-five minutes had given Cat enough time to see that he wasn't going to literally jump her. The playful banter had taken a sexual turn, but he wasn't sorry. He was only sorry Cat hadn't come up once to see him. This initial space was probably for the best. After all, today was the first time they'd been fully alone and not sneaking into the bathroom or laundry area of his father's home for a make-out session.

Yeah, his seduction techniques needed a bit of work to say the least. But he'd had four years to get control over just how he wanted to approach things once he finally got his Cat alone. And now he was ready.

As he stepped below, Will braced his hands on the trim overhead and froze on the last step. Cat lay sideways, curled into a ball on his bed. The innocent pose shouldn't have his body responding, but…well, he was a guy and this woman had had him tied in knots for years.

Will had wanted Cat in his bed for too long. All his fantasies involved the bed in his house, but the yacht would do. At this point he sure as hell wasn't going to be picky. He'd waited too damn long for this and he was going to take each moment he could get, no matter the surroundings.

And the fact that she was comfortable enough to rest here spoke volumes for how far they'd come. Just a few weeks ago he'd kissed her as if she was his next breath and she'd run away angry. Though Will was smart enough to know her anger stemmed from arousal.

Passion and hate…there was such a fine line between the two.

Slowly, Will crossed the open area and pulled a small throw from the narrow linen closet. Gently placing the thin blanket over her bare legs and settling it around her waist, Will watched the calm rise and fall of her chest. She was so peaceful, so relaxed and not on her guard.

For the first time in a long time, Will was finally seeing the woman he knew years ago, the woman who was more trusting, less cautious.

Of course, he'd helped shape her into the vigilant person she was today. Had he not made such bad choices when they'd been together the first time, perhaps she wouldn't have to feel so guarded all the time. Perhaps she'd smile more and laugh the way she used to.

Cat shifted, let out a throaty moan and blinked up at Will. Then her eyes widened as she sat straight up.

"Oh my. Was I asleep?"

Will laughed, crossing his arms over his chest. "Or you were playing dead."

Cat smoothed her short hair away from her face and glanced toward the wall of windows. "I was watching the water. I was so tired, so I thought I'd just lie here and enjoy the scenery."

"That was the whole point in having my bed right there. It's a breathtaking view."

When she turned her attention back to him, she gasped. That's right, he hadn't been discussing the water. The view of the woman was much more enticing.

"Why don't you use the restroom to freshen up and change into your suit?" he suggested. "I'll get our lunch set up."

The bright smile spreading across her face had something unfamiliar tugging on his heart. He may not be able to label what was going on between them, but he couldn't afford to be emotional about it.

Dammit. He didn't even know what to feel, how to act anymore. He wanted her, but he wasn't thinking of forever. He wanted now. He needed her to see he was a different man, yet he was more than ready to throw this relationship into his father's face.

Sticking to business would have been best; at least he knew exactly what he was getting into with real estate and oil. With Cat, he had no clue and the fact that she had him so tied in knots without even trying was terrifying.

Once his mission had been clear—to win back Cat to prove he could and to show his father who was in charge. But then, somewhere along the way, Will had shifted into needing Cat to see the true person he'd come to be, the man who still had feelings for her and cared for her on a level even he couldn't understand.

Cat came to her feet and started folding the throw. "I'm sorry I fell asleep on you."

Stepping forward and closing the space between them, Will pulled the blanket from her hands, wadded it up and threw it into the corner. "You aren't cleaning. You aren't folding, dusting, doing dishes. Your only job is to relax. If you want a nap, take a nap. The day is yours. The cleaning is up to me. Got it?"

Her eyes widened as she glanced at the crumpled blanket. "Are you just going to leave that there?"

Will took her chin between his thumb and finger, forcing her to look only at him. "You didn't answer my question."

Her wide, dark eyes drew him in as she merely nodded. "I can't promise, but I'll try."

Unable to help himself, Will smacked a kiss on her lips and pulled back as a grin spread across his face. "Go freshen up and meet me on the top deck."

Will watched as Cat grabbed her bag off the barstool and crossed to the bathroom. Once the door clicked shut, he let out a breath.

He'd sworn nobody would ever control him or hold any power over him again. Yet here was a petite, doe-eyed maid who had more power over him than any business magnate or his father ever could.

Will raked a hand through his hair. He'd promised Cat a day of relaxation and he intended to deliver just that. If she wasn't ready for more, then he'd have to pull all of his self-control to the surface and honor her wishes.

What had he gotten himself into?

Nine

Maybe bringing this particular swimsuit had been a bad idea. When she'd grabbed the two-piece black bikini, Catalina had figured she'd make Will suffer a little. But, by wearing so little and having him so close, she was the one suffering.

Catalina pulled on a simple red wrap dress from her own collection and slipped on her silver flip-flops.

One glance in the mirror and she laughed. The bikini would at least draw attention away from the haggard lines beneath her eyes and the pallor of her skin. Over the past few months, if she wasn't working for James or Patrick, she was working for herself getting her stock ready to showcase when the opportunity presented itself. She believed in being prepared and the moment she saw an opening with any fashion design firm, she was going to be beating down their doors and promoting her unique styles.

Catalina tossed her discarded clothes back into her tote and looked around to make sure she hadn't left anything lying around in the bathroom. Could such a magnificent room be a simple, mundane bathroom?

With the polished silver fixtures, the glass wall shower and sparkling white tile throughout, Catalina had taken a moment to appreciate all the beauty before she'd started changing. The space screamed dominance…male dominance.

Will was pulling out all the stops today. He'd purposely invited her aboard his yacht because he knew that given her love of water she'd never be able to say no. He was right. Anything that got her away from her daily life and into the refreshing ocean was a no-brainer.

Exiting the bathroom, Catalina dropped her bag next to the door and headed up to the top deck. The sun warmed her skin instantly as she turned and spotted Will in a pair of khaki board shorts and a navy shirt he'd left completely unbuttoned. The man wasn't playing fair…which she assumed was his whole plan from the start.

Fine. She had a bikini and boobs. Catalina figured she'd already won this battle before it began. Men were the simplest of creatures.

Will had transformed the seating area into a picnic. A red throw covered the floor, a bucket with ice and wine sat to one side and Will was pulling fruit from a basket.

"Wow. You really know how to set the stage."

He threw her a smile. "Depends on the audience."

"It's just me, so no need to go to all the trouble." She edged around the curving seats and stood just to the side of the blanket. "I'd be happy with a simple salad."

"There is a need to go to all this trouble," he corrected her as he continued to pull more food from the basket. "Have a seat. The strawberries are fresh, the wine is chilled and I have some amazing dishes for us."

Catalina couldn't turn down an invitation like that. She eased down onto the thick blanket and reached for a strawberry. She'd eaten three by the time Will came to sit beside her.

With his back resting against the sofa, he lifted his knee and wrapped his arm around it. "I have a variety of cheese, salmon, baguettes, a tangy salad my chef makes that will make you weep and for dessert…"

He reached over and pulled the silver lid from the dish. "Your favorite."

Catalina gasped as she stared at the pineapple upside-down cheesecake. "You remembered?"

"Of course I did." He set the lid back down. "There's not a detail about you that I've forgotten, Cat."

When she glanced over at him, she found his eyes locked on hers and a small smile dancing around his lips. "I remembered how much you love strawberries and that you will always pick a fruity dessert over a chocolate one. I also recall how much you love salmon, so I tried to incorporate all of your favorites into this lunch."

Strawberry in hand, she froze. "But you just asked me last night. How did you get all of this together?"

Will shrugged and made up a plate for her. "I knew I wanted to take you out on my yacht at some point. I was hoping for soon, but it wasn't until yesterday that I realized how hard you've been working."

He passed her the plate with a napkin. "You need this break and I want to be the one to give it to you. Besides, there's a lot I can do with a few hours and the right connections."

Catalina smiled as she picked up a cube of cheese.

"I'm sure your chef was making the cheesecake before the crack of dawn this morning."

Will shrugged. "Maybe. He did have nearly everything else done by the time I headed out to James and Bella's house this morning."

"You visited James already, too?"

Will settled back with his own plate and forked up a bite of salmon before answering. "I wanted to see Maisey before James heads back out on the road for football. I haven't really bonded with her much, especially with the strain on my relationship with James. But we're getting there and I wanted to see my niece. I'm sure she and Bella will accompany James on the road when they can."

Something inside Catalina warmed at the image of Will playing the doting, spoiling uncle. A family was definitely in her future plans, but knowing Will was taking an active part in little Maisey's life awakened something in her she hadn't yet uncovered.

But no. Will couldn't be father material. He wasn't even husband material. No matter how much, at one time, she'd wished he was. Will was a career-minded, power-driven man who valued family, but he didn't scream minivan and family portraits.

"How did the bonding go?" she asked, trying to concentrate on her food and not the fact that the image had been placed in her head of Will with a baby. Was there anything sexier than a big, powerful man holding an innocent child?

"She seemed to like the doll I brought her."

Of course he'd brought a doll. Now his "aww" level just exploded. Why did the man have to be so appealing on every single level? She didn't want to find him even more irresistible. She couldn't afford to let her heart get tangled up with him again.

Catalina couldn't handle the struggle within her. "You took her a doll? Did your assistant or someone on your staff go buy it?"

Will glanced at her, brows drawn in. "No, I bought it the other day when I was out and just got the chance to take it to her this morning. Why?"

The man was gaining ground and scaling that wall of defenses she'd so carefully erected. And in unexpected ways. He'd wanted to have a special moment with his niece, which had nothing to do with Catalina. Yet here she sat, on his boat, eating her favorite foods that he'd remembered while listening to him talk of his love for his baby niece.

Why was she keeping him at a distance again?

Oh, yeah. That broken heart four years ago.

They ate the rest of their lunch in silence, except when she groaned like a starved woman as she inhaled her piece of cheesecake. As promised, Will cleaned up the mess and took everything back down to the galley. Once he returned, he extended his hand to her.

"Ready to go for a walk?" he asked.

Catalina placed her hand in his, allowing him to pull her up. "I'm not sure I can walk after that, but I can waddle. I'm pretty stuffed."

Will laughed as he led her from the boat. Once they stepped off the wooden dock, Catalina slipped out of her sandals to walk on the warm, sandy beach. The sand wasn't too hot to burn her feet and as the soft grains shifted beneath her, she found herself smiling. She couldn't remember the last time she'd done absolutely nothing by way of working in one form or another.

"I hope that smile has something to do with me,"

Will stated, again slipping his hand into hers as they walked along the shoreline.

"I'm just happy today. I needed a break and I guess I didn't realize it."

"From one workaholic to another, I recognized the signs."

His confession had her focusing on the words and not how powerful and wonderful his fingers felt laced with hers.

"I never thought you took a break," she replied.

Catalina looked at all the tiny seashells lining the shore and made a mental note to find some beautiful ones to take back with her.

"I've had breaks," he replied. "Not many, mind you, but I know when I need to step back so I don't get burnt out."

Catalina turned her face toward the ocean. She'd been burnt out on cleaning since she started. But sewing and designing, she could never imagine falling out of love with her passion.

They walked along in silence and Catalina let her thoughts run wild. What would've happened between them had Will not succumbed to his father's demands that he drop her? Would they have these romantic moments often? Would he make her take breaks from life and put work on hold for her?

She really couldn't see any of that, to be honest. Will was still under his father's thumb, whether he admitted it or not. He'd been at the house most mornings going over Rowling Energy stuff, which Catalina assumed was really just Will checking in.

"Why did you give up on us before?" she asked before she could think better of it.

Will stopped, causing Catalina to stop as well. She dropped his hand and turned to fully face him.

"Never mind," she said, shaking her head. "It doesn't matter now."

The muscle in Will's jaw ticked as he stared back at her. "It does matter. Our breakup damaged both of us."

Catalina pushed her hair behind her ears, which was useless as the wind kept whipping it out. "I'm pretty sure you weren't damaged, seeing as how ending our relationship was your decision."

When she started to walk on, Will gripped her elbow. "You think seeing you move on and dating another man wasn't crushing to me? You think knowing you were in another man's arms, maybe even in his bed, didn't tear me up?"

She'd tried not to think about Will when she threw herself into another relationship to mask the hurt. From the angst in his tone and the fire in his eyes, though… *had* Will been hurt over the breakup? How could that be when he was the one who had ultimately ended things? Did he not want the split? Was he doing it to appease his father? If that was the case then she was doubly angry that he hadn't fought for them.

"You thought I'd sit around and cry myself to sleep over you?" she retorted, refusing to feel guilt over a decision he'd made for both of them.

And so what if she'd shed tears over him? Many tears, in fact, but there was no way she'd admit such a thing. As far as he knew she was made of steel and stronger than her emotions.

"Besides, you had moved on quite nicely. You ended up in a relationship with a Montoro princess."

Dammit. She hadn't meant for that little green monster to slip out. Catalina knew just how much Bella and

James loved each other, yet there was that sliver of jealousy at the fact that Will had been all ready to put a ring on Bella's finger first.

Will laughed. "That fake engagement was a mistake from all angles. James and Bella have found something she never would've had with me."

"But you would've married her."

And that fact still bothered Catalina. She hated the jealousy she'd experienced when she'd discovered Will was engaged. Not that she ever thought she stood a chance, but how could anyone compete with someone as beautiful and sexy as Bella Montoro? She was not only royalty, she was a humanitarian with a good heart.

On a sigh, Catalina started walking again, concentrating on the shells lining the shore. "It doesn't matter, honestly. I shouldn't have brought it up."

She reached down to pick up an iridescent shell, smoothing her finger over the surface to swipe away the wet sand. Catalina slid the shell into the small hidden pocket on the side of her dress and kept walking, very much aware of Will at her side. He was a smart man not to deny her last statement. They both knew he would've married Bella because that's what his father had wanted. Joining the fortunes of the two dynamic families was Patrick's dream...the wrong son had fallen for the beauty, though.

They walked a good bit down the deserted beach. Catalina had no idea how Will had managed to find such a perfect place with total privacy, but he had no doubt planned this for a while. On occasion he would stop and find a shell for her, wordlessly handing it to her as they walked on. The tension was heavier now that she'd opened up the can of worms. She wished she'd kept her feelings to herself.

What did it matter if he was going to marry Bella? What man wouldn't want to spend his life with her? Not only that, had Catalina truly thought Will would remain single? Had she believed he was so exclusively focused on work that he wouldn't want to settle down and start the next generation of Rowling heirs?

The warm sun disappeared behind a dark cloud as the wind kicked into high gear. Catalina looked up and suppressed a groan. Of course a dark cloud would hover over her. The ominous sky was starting to match her mood.

"Should we head back to the yacht?" she asked, trying to tuck her wayward strands of hair behind her ears as she fought against the wind.

"I don't think it's going to do anything major. The forecast didn't show rain."

That nasty cloud seemed to indicate otherwise, but she wasn't going to argue. They already had enough on their plate.

Catalina glanced through the foliage, squinting as something caught her eye. "What's that?"

Will stopped and looked in the direction she'd indicated. "Looks like a cabin of sorts. I've not come this far inland before. Let's check it out."

Without waiting for her, Will took off toward the small building. Catalina followed, stepping over a piece of driftwood and trailing through the lush plants that had nearly overtaken the property.

"I wonder who had this cabin built," he muttered as he examined the old wood shack. "The island belongs to Alma from what I could tell when I first started coming here."

The covered porch leaned to one side, the old tin roof had certainly seen better days and some of the wood around the door and single window had warped. But the place had charm and someone had once cared enough to put it here. A private getaway for a couple in love? A hideout for someone seeking refuge from life? There was a story behind this place.

Will pushed on the door and eased inside. Catalina couldn't resist following him. The musty smell wasn't as bad as she'd expected, but the place was rather dusty. Only a bit of light from outside crept in through the single window, but even that wasn't bright because of the dark cloud covering.

"Careful," he cautioned when she stepped in. "Some of those boards feel loose."

There was enough dim light coming in the front window for them to see a few tarps, buckets and one old chair sitting against the wall.

"Looks like someone was working on this and it was forgotten," Catalina said as she walked around the room. "It's actually quite cozy."

Will laughed. "If you like the rustic, no-indoor-plumbing feel."

Crossing her arms over her chest, she turned around. "Some of us don't need to be pampered with amenities. I personally enjoy the basics."

"This is basic," he muttered, glancing around.

The sudden sound of rain splattering on the tin roof had Catalina freezing in place. "So much for that forecast."

Will offered her a wide smile. "Looks like you get to enjoy the basics a bit longer unless you want to run back to the yacht in the rain."

Crossing the room, Catalina sank down onto the old, sheet-covered chair. "I'm good right here. Will you be able to handle it?"

His aqua eyes raked over her, heating her skin just as effectively as if he'd touched her with his bare hands. "Oh, baby, I can handle it."

Maybe running back to the yacht was the better option after all. How long would she be stranded in an old shack with Will while waiting out this storm?

Catalina wasn't naïve. She knew full well there were only so many things they could talk about and nearly every topic between them circled back to the sexual tension that had seemed to envelop them and bind them together for the past several weeks.

Her body trembled as she kept her gaze locked onto his.

There was only one way this day would end.

Ten

Will stared out the window at the sheets of rain coming down. He didn't need to look, though; the pounding on the roof told him how intense this storm was.

So much for that flawless forecast.

Still, staying across the room from Cat was best for now. He didn't need another invisible push in her direction. He glanced over his shoulder toward the woman he ached for. She sat as casual as you please with her legs crossed, one foot bouncing to a silent beat as her flip-flop dangled off her toes. Those bare legs mocked him. The strings of her bikini top peeking out of her dress mocked him as well. Every damn thing about this entire situation mocked him.

What had he been thinking, inviting her for a day out? Why purposely resurrect all of those old, unresolved feelings? They'd gone four years without bringing up their past, but Will had reached his breaking

point. He needed to know if they had a chance at…
what? What exactly did he want from her?

He had no clue, but he did know the need for Cat had
never lessened. If anything, the emptiness had grown
without her in his life. He'd let her go once to save her,
but he should've fought for them, fought for what he
wanted and found another way to keep her safe. He'd
been a coward. As humiliating as that was to admit,
there was no sugarcoating the truth of the boy he used
to be.

"You might as well have a seat," she told him, meeting his gaze. "The way you're standing across the room
is only making the tension worse. You're making me
twitchy."

Will laughed. Leave it to Cat to call him on his actions, though he didn't think the tension could get worse.

He crossed the room and took a seat on the floor in
front of the chair.

"This reminds me of that time James, you and I were
playing hide-and-seek when it started raining," she said.
"You guys were home from school on break and I had
come in to work with my mum."

Will smiled as the memory flooded his mind. "We
were around eight or nine, weren't we?"

Cat nodded. "James kept trying to hold my hand
when we both ran into the garage to hide and get dry."

Will sat up straighter. "You never told me that."

"Seriously?" she asked, quirking a brow. "You're
going to get grouchy over the actions of a nine-year-old?"

"I'm not grouchy. Surprised, but not grouchy."

"James was only doing it because he knew I had a
thing for you."

The corner of Will's mouth kicked up. "You had a
thing for me when you were that young?"

Cat shrugged, toying with the edge of her dress. "You were an older man. Practically worldly in all of your knowledge."

"It was the Spanish, wasn't it?" he asked with a grin.

Cat rolled her eyes and laughed. "James was fluent in Spanish as well. You two both had the same hoity-toity schooling."

Will lifted his knee and rested his arm on it as he returned her smile. "Nah. I was better. We would sometimes swap out in class because the teacher couldn't tell us apart. She just knew a quiet blond boy sat in the back. As long as one of us showed up, she didn't pay much attention to the fact there were really supposed to be two."

"Sneaky boys. But, I bet if I asked James about the Spanish speaking skills he'd say he was better," she countered.

"He'd be wrong."

Cat tipped her head, shifting in her seat, which only brought her bare legs within touching distance. "You tricked your teachers and got away with it. Makes me wonder how many times you two swapped out when it came to women."

Will shook his head. "I'm not answering that."

"Well, I know that watch nearly cost James the love of his life," Cat said, nodding toward the gold timepiece on his wrist.

"It was unfortunate Bella saw you and me kissing. I truly thought we were secluded." Will sighed and shifted on the wood floor. "She had every right to think James was kissing someone else because she had no clue about the bet."

The rain beat against the window as the wind kicked up. Cat tensed and her eyes widened.

"Hope this old place holds up," she said. "Maybe running back to the yacht would have been a better idea."

"Too late now." Will reached over, laying his hand on her knee. "We're fine. It's just a pop-up storm. You know these things pass fast."

With a subtle nod, she settled deeper into the seat and rested her head on the back cushion. Guilt rolled through Will. He'd planned a day for her, and had been hopeful that seduction would be the outcome. Yet here they sat in some abandoned old shack waiting out some freak storm. Even Mother Nature was mocking him.

But there was a reason they were here right now, during this storm, and Will wasn't going to turn this chance away. He planned on taking full advantage and letting Cat know just how much he wanted her.

Shifting closer to her chair, Will took Cat's foot and slid her shoe off. He picked up her other foot and did the same, all while knowing she had those dark, intoxicating eyes focused on his actions. It was her exotic eyes that hypnotized him.

Taking one of her delicate feet between his hands, Will started to massage, stroking his thumb up her arch.

"I'll give you ten minutes to stop that," she told him with a smile.

The radiant smile on her face was something he hadn't realized he'd missed so much. Right now, all relaxed and calm, even with the storm raging outside, Cat looked like the girl he once knew…the girl he'd wanted something more with.

But they were different people now. They had different goals. Well, he did; her goals were still unclear to him. He suddenly found himself wanting to know about those dreams of hers, and the fact that she'd hinted to James that she wouldn't stay in Alma forever.

But all of those questions could come later. Right now, Cat's comfort and happiness were all that mattered. Tomorrow's worries, issues and questions could be dealt with later. He planned on enjoying Cat for as long as she would allow.

Damn. When had this petite woman taken control over him? When had he allowed it? There wasn't one moment he could pinpoint, but there were several tiny instances where he could see in hindsight the stealthy buildup of her power over him.

Cat laughed as she slid down a bit further in the chair and gazed down at him beneath heavy lids. "If your father could see you on the floor rubbing his maid's feet, you'd lose your prestigious position at Rowling Energy."

Will froze, holding her gaze. It may have been a lighthearted joke, but there was so much truth to her statement about how angry this would make his father. But Will had already set in motion his plan to freeze his father out of the company.

Besides, right now, Will didn't care about Patrick or Rowling Energy. What he did care about was the woman who was literally turning to putty in his hands. Finally, he was going to show her exactly what they could be together and anticipation had his heart beating faster than ever.

"Does this feel good?" he asked.

Her reply was a throaty moan, sexy enough to have his body responding.

"Then all of the other stuff outside of this cabin doesn't matter."

Blinking down at him, Cat replied, "Not to me, but I bet if your father made you choose, you'd be singing a different tune."

Just like last time.

The unspoken words were so deafening, they actually drowned out the beating of the rain and the wind against the small shelter.

Will's best option was to keep any answer to himself. He could deny the fact, but he'd be lying. He'd worked too hard to get where he was to just throw it all away because of hormones.

At the same time, he planned on working equally as hard to win over Cat. There was no reason he had to give up anything.

His hand glided up to her ankle, then her calf. She said nothing as her eyes continued to hold his. He purposely watched her face, waiting for a sign of retreat, but all that was staring back at him was desire.

There was a silent message bouncing between them, that things were about to get very intimate, very fast.

The old cabin creaked and groaned against the wind's force. Cat tensed beneath him.

"You're safe," he assured her softly, not wanting to break this moment of trust she'd settled into with him. "This place is so old. I know it has withstood hurricanes. This little storm won't harm the cabin or us."

And there weren't any huge trees around, just thick bushes and flowers, so they weren't at risk for anything falling on them.

Right now, the only thing he needed to be doing was pushing through that line of defense Cat had built up. And from her sultry grin and heavy lids, he'd say he was doing a damn fine job.

Catalina should tell him to stop. Well, the common sense side of her told her she should. But the female side, the side that hadn't been touched or treasured in more time than she cared to admit, told her common sense to shut up.

Will had quite the touch. She had no idea the nerves in your feet could be so tied into all the girly parts. She certainly knew it now. Every part of her was zipping with ache and need. If he commanded her to strip and dance around the room naked, she would. The power he held over her was all-consuming and she was dying to know when he was going to do more.

She'd walked straight into this with her eyes wide open. So if she was having doubts or regrets already, she had no one to blame but herself. Though Catalina wasn't doubting or regretting. She was aching, on the verge of begging him to take this to the next level.

Catalina's head fell back against the chair as his hands moved to her other calf, quickly traveling up to her knee, then her thigh. She wanted to inch down further and part her legs just a tad, but that would be a silent invitation she wasn't quite brave enough for.

Yet.

"I've wanted to touch you for so long," he muttered, barely loud enough for her to hear over the storm. "I've watched you for the past four years, wondering if you ever thought of me. Wondering if you ever fantasized about me the way I did you."

Every. Single. Night.

Which was a confession she wasn't ready to share. The ball was in his court for now and she planned on just waiting to see how this played out.

He massaged her muscles with the tips of his fingers and the room became hotter with each stroke. If the man could have such power over her with something so simple as a foot massage, how would her body react once Will really started showing her affection?

"Do you remember that time your mother caught us making out?" he asked with a half laugh.

At the time, Catalina had been mortified that her mother caught them. But it wasn't until after the breakup that she realized why her mother had been so disappointed.

Patrick Rowling had really done a number on Catalina's mum. And it was those thoughts that could quickly put a bucket of cold water on this encounter, but she refused to allow Patrick to steal one more moment of happiness from her life…he'd already taken enough from her.

Will may not be down on his knees proposing marriage, but he was down on his knees showing her affection. And maybe she hoped that would be a stepping-stone to something more… But right now, that was all she wanted. She'd fought this pull toward him for too long. She hadn't wanted to let herself believe they could be more, but now she couldn't deny herself. She couldn't avoid the inevitable…she was falling for Will all over again.

"She didn't even know we were dating," Catalina murmured, her euphoric state suddenly overtaking her ability to speak coherently.

"Not many people did. That's when I realized I didn't want to keep us a secret anymore."

And that had been the start of their spiral toward the heartbreak she'd barely recovered from.

Once they were an "official" item, Patrick had intervened and put a stop to his good son turning to the maid. Shocking, since turning to the staff for pleasure certainly hadn't been below Patrick at one time. Not that what Catalina and Will shared had been anything like that. But the idea that Patrick could act as if he were so far above people was absolutely absurd.

"Don't tense on me now," Will warned. "You're supposed to be relaxing."

Catalina blew out a breath. "I'm trying. It's just hard when I'm stuck between the past and whatever is happening to us now."

Will came up to his knees, easing his way between her parted legs, his hands resting on the tops of her thighs, his fingertips brushing just beneath the hem of her dress.

"It's two different times. We're two different people. There's nothing to compare. Focus on now."

She stared down at those bright blue eyes, the wide open shirt and something dark against his chest. Was that...

"Do you have a tattoo?" she asked, reaching to pull back the shirt.

He said nothing as she eased the material aside. The glimpse she got wasn't enough. Catalina didn't ask, she merely gripped the shirt and pushed it off his shoulders. Will shifted until it fell to the floor.

Sure enough, black ink swirled over the left side of his chest and over his shoulder. She had no idea what the design was. All she knew was that it was sexy.

Without asking, she reached out and traced a thin line over his heart, then on up. The line thickened as it curled around his shoulder. Taut muscles tensed beneath her featherlight touch.

Catalina brought her gaze up to Will's. The intensity of his stare made her breath catch in her throat and stilled her hand.

"Don't stop," he whispered through clenched teeth. "Will..."

His hand came up to cover hers. "Touch me, Cat."

He'd just handed her the reins.

With just enough pressure, he flattened her hand between his palm and his shoulder. The warmth of his skin penetrated her own, the heat sliding through her entire body.

"I—I want to but—"

She shook her head, killing the rest of her fears before they could be released and never taken back.

"But what?" he muttered, pushing her hair behind her ear, letting his fingertips trail over her cheek, her jawline and down her neck until she trembled.

"I'm not sure I can go any farther than that," she confessed. "I don't want to tease you."

"I've fantasized about you touching me like this for years. You're not teasing, you're fulfilling a fantasy."

Catalina stared into those aqua eyes and knew without a doubt he was serious. The fact that he'd been dreaming of her for this long confused her further, brought on even more questions than answers.

"Don't go there," he warned as if he knew where her thoughts were headed. "Keep touching me, Cat. Whatever happens here is about you and me and right this moment. Don't let past memories rob us of this time together."

Catalina opened her mouth, but Will placed one finger over her lips. "I have no expectations. Close your eyes."

Even though her heart beat out of control from anticipation and a slither of fear of the unknown, she did as he commanded.

"Now touch me. Just feel me, feel this moment and nothing else."

His tone might have been soft, but everything about

his words demanded that she obey. Not that he had to do much convincing. With her eyes closed, she wasn't forced to look at the face of the man who'd broken her heart. She wanted this chance to touch him, to ignore all the reasons why this was such a bad idea. But she couldn't look into those eyes and pretend that this was normal, that they were just two regular people stranded in an old shack.

With her eyes closed she actually felt as if they were regular people. She could pretend this was just a man she ached for, not a man who was a billionaire with more power than she'd ever see.

With her eyes closed she could pretend he wanted her for who she was and not just because she was a challenge.

Catalina brought her other hand up and over his chest. If she was given the green light to explore, she sure as hell wanted both hands doing the job. Just as she smoothed her palms up and over his shoulders, over his thick biceps, she felt the knot on her wrap dress loosen at her side.

Her eyes flew open. "What are you doing?"

"Feeling the moment."

The dress parted, leaving her torso fully exposed. "You don't play fair."

The heat in his eyes was more powerful than any passion she'd ever seen. "I never will when it comes to something I want."

"You said—"

"I'd never force you," he interrupted, gliding his fingertips over the straps of her bikini that stretched from behind her neck to the slopes of her breasts. "But that doesn't mean I won't try to persuade you."

As the rain continued to beat against the side of the

shack, Catalina actually found herself happy that she was stuck here. Perhaps this was the push she needed to follow through with what she truly wanted. No, she wasn't looking for happily-ever-after, she'd never be that naïve again where Will was concerned. But she was older now, was going into this with both eyes wide open.

And within the next couple months, hopefully she'd be out of Alma and starting her new life. So why not take the plunge now with a man she'd always wanted? Because he was right. This was all about them, here and now. Everything else could wait outside that door.

For now, Catalina was taking what she'd wanted for years.

Eleven

Catalina came to her feet. From here on out she was taking charge of what she'd been deprived of and what she wanted…and she wanted Will. Whatever doubts she had about sleeping with him wouldn't be near as consuming as the regret she'd have if she moved away and ignored this opportunity.

The moment she stood before him, Will sank back down on the floor and stared up at her as her dress fell into a puddle around her feet. As she stepped away and kicked the garment aside, his eyes roamed over her, taking in the sight of the bikini and nothing else.

The image of him sitting at her feet was enough to give her a sense of control, a sense of dominance. The one time when it counted most, she didn't feel inferior.

Will could've immediately taken over, he could've stood before her and taken charge, but he'd given her the reins.

"That bikini does some sinful things to your body." He reached out, trailed his fingertips over the sensitive area behind her knee and on up to her thigh. "Your curves are stunning, Cat. Your body was made to be uncovered."

"How long have you wanted me, Will?" she asked, needing to know this much. "Did you want me when we were together before?"

"More than anything," he rasped out, still sliding his fingers up and down the backs of her legs. "But I knew you were a virgin and I respected you."

"What if I were a virgin now?" she asked, getting off track. "Would you still respect me?"

"I've always respected you." He came up to his knees, putting his face level with her stomach. He placed a kiss just above her bikini bottoms before glancing up at her. "And I don't want to discuss if there's been another man in your bed."

With a move she hadn't expected, he tossed her back into the chair and stood over her, his hands resting on either side of her head. "Because I'm the only man you're going to be thinking of right now."

"I've only been with one other, but you're the only man I've ever wanted in my bed," she admitted. "I need you to know that."

Maybe she was naïve for letting him in on that little piece of information she'd kept locked in her heart for so long, but right now, something more than desire was sparking between them. He was too possessive for this to just be something quick and easy.

They weren't just scratching an itch, but she had no clue what label to put on what was about to happen. Which was why she planned on not thinking and just feeling. This bond that was forming here was something she'd have to figure out later…much later.

"All I need to know is that you want this as much as I do," he told her. "That you're ready for anything that happens because I can't promise soft and gentle. I've wanted you too long."

A shiver of arousal speared through her. "I don't need gentle, Will. I just need you."

In an instant his lips crushed hers. She didn't know when things had shifted, but in the span of about two minutes, she'd gone from questioning sex with Will to nearly ripping his shorts off so she could have him.

Will's strong hands gripped her hips as he shifted the angle of his head for a deeper kiss. Cat arched her body, needing to feel as much of him as possible. There still didn't seem to be enough contact. She wanted more… she wanted it all. The need to have everything she'd deprived herself of was now an all-consuming ache.

"Keep moaning like that, sweetheart," he muttered against her lips. "You're all mine."

She hadn't even realized she'd moaned, which just proved how much control this man had over her actions.

Gripping his shoulders, she tried to pull him down further, but he eased back. With his eyes locked onto hers, he hooked his thumbs in the waistband of his board shorts and shoved them to the floor. Stepping out of them he reached down, took her hand and pulled her to her feet.

Keeping her eyes on his, she reached behind her neck and untied her top. It fell forward as she worked on the knot. Soon they'd flung the entire scrap of fabric across the room. Will's eyes widened and his nostrils flared.

Excitement and anticipation roiled through her as she shoved her bottoms down without a care. She had no clue who reached for whom first, but the next second she was in his arms, skin to skin from torso to knees and she'd never felt anything better in her entire life.

Will's arms wrapped around her waist, his hands splaying across her bare back. He spun her around and sank down into the chair, pulling her down with him. Instinctively her legs straddled his hips. Catalina fisted her fingers in his hair as his lips trailed down her throat.

"So sexy," he murmured against her heated skin. "So mine."

Yes. She was his for now…maybe she always had been.

When his mouth found her breast, his hands encircled her hips. She waited, aching with need.

"Will," she panted, not recognizing her own voice. "Protection."

With his hair mussed, his lids heavy, he looked up. "I don't have any with me. Dammit, they're on the yacht. I didn't expect to get caught out here like this." Cursing beneath his breath, he shook his head. "I'm clean. I swear I wouldn't lie about something like that. I haven't been with a woman in…too long, and I recently had a physical."

"I know I'm clean and I'm on birth control."

He gave her a look, silently asking what she wanted to do. Without another word she slowly sank down onto him, so that they were finally, fully joined after years of wanting, years of fantasizing.

Their sighs and groans filled the small room. Wind continued to beat against the window as rain pelted the tin roof. Everything about this scenario was perfect. Even if they were in a rundown shed, she didn't care. The ambiance was amazingly right. The storm that had swept through them over the years only matched Mother

Nature's fury outside the door. This was the moment they were supposed to be together, this was what they'd both waited for so long.

"Look at me," he demanded, his fingertips pressing into her hips.

Catalina hadn't realized she'd closed her eyes, but she opened them and found herself looking into Will's bright, expressive aqua eyes. He may be able to hold back his words, but those eyes told her so much. Like the fact that he cared for her. This was sex, but there was so much more going on…so much more they'd discuss later.

As her hips rocked back and forth against his, Will continued to watch her face. Catalina leaned down, resting her hands on his shoulders. The need inside her built so fast, she dropped her forehead against his.

"No," he stated. "Keep watching me. I want to see your face."

As she looked back into his eyes, her body responded to every touch, every kiss, every heated glance. Tremors raced through her at the same time his body stilled, the cords in his neck tightened and his fingertips dug even further into her hips.

His body stiffened against hers, his lips thinned as his own climax took control. Catalina couldn't look away. She wanted to see him come undone, knowing she caused this powerful man to fall at the mercy of her touch.

Once their bodies eased out of the euphoric state, Catalina leaned down, rested her head on his shoulder and tried to regain some sense of normal breathing. She didn't know what to say now, how to act. They'd taken this awkward, broken relationship and put another speed bump in it. Now all they had to do was figure out how to maneuver over this new hurdle since they'd moved to a whole new, unfamiliar level.

Will trailed his hand up and down Cat's back, which was smooth and damp with sweat. Damn, she was sexier than he'd ever, *ever* imagined. She'd taken him without a second thought and with such confidence. Yet she'd been so tight…had she not slept with anyone? How had that not happened? Surely she wasn't still a virgin.

Had Cat kept her sexuality penned up all this time? For completely selfish reasons, this thought pleased him.

As much as Will wanted to know, he didn't want to say a word, didn't want to break the silence with anything that would kill the mood. The storm raged on outside, the cabin creaked and continued to groan under the pressure, but Cat was in his arms, her heart beating against his chest, and nothing could pull him from this moment.

The fact that he was concentrating on her heartbeat was a bit disconcerting. He didn't want to be in tune with her heart, he couldn't get that caught up with her, no matter how strong this invisible force was that was tugging him to her. Having her in his arms, finally making love to her was enough.

So why did he feel as if there was more to be had?

Because when he'd originally been thinking of the here and now, he'd somehow started falling into the zone of wanting more than this moment. He wanted Cat much longer than this day, this week, even. Will wanted more and now he had to figure out just how the hell that would work.

"Tell me I wasn't a substitute for Bella."

Will jerked beneath her, forcing her to sit up and meet his gaze. "What?"

Cat shook her head, smoothing her short hair away from her face. "Nothing," she said, coming to her feet. "That was stupid of me to say. We had sex. I'm not expecting you to give me anything more."

As she rummaged around the small space searching for her bikini and dress, Will sat there dumbfounded. So much for not letting words break the beauty of the moment.

What was that about Bella? Seriously? Did Cat honestly think that Will had had a thing for his brother's fiancée?

"Look at me," he demanded, waiting until Cat spun around, gripping her clothing to her chest. "Bella is married to James. I have no claim to her."

"It's none of my business."

Will watched as she tied her top on and slid the bikini bottoms up her toned legs. "It is your business after what we just did. I don't sleep with one woman and think of another."

Cat's dark eyes came up to his. A lock of her inky black hair fell over her forehead and slashed across her cheek.

"You owe me no explanations, Will." Hands on her hips, she blew the rogue strand from her face. "I know this wasn't a declaration of anything to come. I'm grown up now and I have no delusions that things will be any different than what they are. We slept together, it's over."

Okay, that had originally been his mindset when he'd gone into this, but when the cold words came from her mouth, Will suddenly didn't like the sound of it. She wasn't seeing how he'd changed at all and that was his fault. She still believed he was a jerk who had no cares at all for her feelings. But he did care…too damn much.

"I know you saw me as a challenge," she went on as she yanked the ties together to secure her dress. "A conquest, if you will. It's fine, really. I could've stopped you, but I was selfish and wanted you. So, thanks for—"

"Do not say another word." Pushing to his feet, Will jerked his shorts from the floor and tugged them on before crossing to her. "You can't lie to me, Cat. I know you too well. Whatever defense mechanism you're using here with ugly words isn't you. You're afraid of what you just felt, of what just happened. This wasn't just sex and you damn well know it."

Her eyes widened, her lips parted, but she immediately shut down any emotion he'd just seen flash across her face. No doubt about it, she was trying to cut him off before he did anything to hurt her…again. He should have seen this coming.

Guilt slammed into him. Not over sleeping with her just now, but for how she felt she had to handle the situation to avoid any more heartache.

"Will, I'm the maid," she said softly. "While I'm not ashamed of my position, I also know that this was just a onetime thing. A man like you would never think twice about a woman like me for anything more than sex."

Will gripped her arms, giving her a slight shake. "Why are you putting yourself into this demeaning little package and delivering it to me? I've told you more than once I don't care if you're a maid or a damn CEO. What just happened has nothing to do with anything other than us and what we feel."

"There is no us," she corrected him.

"There sure as hell was just a minute ago."

Why was he so dead set on correcting her? Here he

stood arguing with her when she was saying the same exact thing he'd been thinking earlier.

"And I have no clue why you're bringing Bella into this," he added.

Cat lifted her chin in a defiant gesture. "I'm a woman. Sometimes my insecurities come out."

"Why are you insecure about her?"

Cat laughed and broke free from his hold, taking a step back. "You were with one of the most beautiful women I've ever seen. Suddenly when that relationship is severed, you turn to me. You haven't given me any attention in nearly four years, Will. Forgive me if suddenly I feel like leftovers."

"Don't downgrade what just happened between us," he demanded. "Just because I didn't seek you out in the past few years doesn't mean I didn't want you. I wanted the hell out of you. And I was fighting my way back to you, dammit."

He eased closer, watching as her eyes widened when he closed the gap and loomed over her. "Seeing you all the time, being within touching distance but knowing I had no right was hell."

"You put yourself there."

As if he needed the reminder of the fool he'd been.

Will smoothed her hair back from her forehead, allowing his hand to linger on her jawline. "I can admit when I was wrong, stubborn and a jerk. I can also admit that I have no clue what just happened between us because it was much more than just sex. You felt it, I felt it, and if we deny that fact we'd just be lying to ourselves. Let's get past that. Honesty is all we can have here. We deserve more than something cheap, Cat."

Cat closed her eyes and sighed. When her lids lifted,

she glanced toward the window. "The rain has let up. We should head back to the yacht."

Without another word, without caring that he was standing here more vulnerable than he'd ever been, Cat turned, opened the door and walked out.

Nobody walked out on Will Rowling and he sure as hell wasn't going to let the woman he was so wrapped up in and had just made love to be the first.

Twelve

Catalina had known going into this day that they'd most likely end up naked and finally giving into desires from years ago.

And she hadn't been able to stop herself.

No matter what she felt now, no matter what insecurities crept up, she didn't regret sleeping with Will.

This was a one and done thing—it had to be. She couldn't afford to fall any harder for this man whom she couldn't have. She was planning on leaving Alma anyway, so best to cut ties now and start gearing up for her fresh start. Letting her heart interfere with the dreams she'd had for so long would only have her working backward. She was so close, she'd mentally geared up for the break from Alma, from Will…but that was before she'd given herself to him.

But what had just transpired between them was only closure. Yes, that was the term she'd been looking for.

Closure. Nothing else could come from their intimacy and finally getting each other out of their systems was the right thing to do...wasn't it?

While the rain hadn't fully stopped, Catalina welcomed the refreshing mist hitting her face. She had no clue of the amount of time that had passed while they'd been inside the cabin lost in each other. An hour? Three hours?

The sand shifted beneath her bare feet as she marched down the shore toward the dock. Sandals in her hand, she kept her focus on the yacht in the distance and not the sound of Will running behind her. She should've known he'd come chasing after her, and not just because he wanted to get back to the yacht.

She'd left no room for argument when she'd walked out, and Will Rowling wouldn't put up with that. Too bad. She was done talking. It was time to move on.

Too bad her body was still humming a happy tune and tingling in all the areas he'd touched, tasted.

Figuring he'd grab her when he caught up to her, Catalina turned, ready to face down whatever he threw her way. Will took a few more steps, stopping just in front of her. He was clutching his wadded up shirt at his side. Catalina couldn't help but stare at his bare chest and the mesmerizing tattoo as he pulled in deep breaths.

"You think we're done?" he asked as he stared her down. "Like we're just heading back to the yacht, setting off to Alma and that's it? You think this topic is actually closed? That I would accept this?"

Shrugging, Catalina forced herself to meet his angry gaze. "You brought me here to seduce me. Wasn't that the whole plan for getting me alone? Well, mission accomplished. The storm has passed and it'll start getting dark in a couple hours. Why wait to head back?"

"Maybe because I want to spend more time with you," he shouted. "Maybe because I want more here than something cheap and easy."

As the misty rain continued to hit her face, Catalina wanted to let that sliver of hope into her heart, but she couldn't allow it...not just yet. "And what do you want, Will? An encore performance? Maybe in your bed on the yacht so you can have a more pampered experience?"

His lips thinned, the muscle in his jaw tightened. "What made you so harsh, Cat? You weren't like this before."

Before when she'd been naïve, before when she'd actually thought he may love her and choose her over his career. And before she discovered a secret that he still knew nothing about.

Beyond all of that, she was angry with herself for allowing her emotions to get so caught up in this moment. She should've known better. She'd never been someone to sleep around, but she thought for sure she could let herself go with Will and then walk away. She'd been wrong and now because of her roller coaster of emotions, she was taking her anger out on him.

Shaking her head, Catalina turned. Before she could take a step, she tripped over a piece of driftwood she hadn't seen earlier. Landing hard in the sand, she hated how the instant humiliation took over.

Before she could become too mortified, a spearing pain shot through her ankle. She gasped just as Will crouched down by her side.

"Where are you hurt?" he asked, his eyes raking over her body.

"My ankle," she muttered, sitting up so she could look at her injury.

"Anywhere else?" Will asked.

Catalina shook her head as she tried to wiggle her ankle back and forth. Bad idea. She was positive it wasn't broken—she'd broken her arm as a little girl and that pain had been much worse—but she was also sure she wouldn't be able to apply any pressure on it and walk. The piercing pain shot up her leg and had her wincing. She hoped she didn't burst into tears and look even more pathetic.

So much for her storming off in her dramatic fit of anger.

Will laid his shirt on her stomach.

"What—?"

Before she could finish her question, he'd scooped her up in his arms and set off across the sand. Catalina hated how she instantly melted against his warm, bare chest. Hated how the image of them in her mind seemed way more romantic than what it was, with Will's muscles straining as he carried her in his arms—yeah, they no doubt looked like something straight out of a movie.

"You can't carry me all the way to the yacht," she argued. "This sand is hard enough to walk in without my added weight."

"Your weight is perfect." He threw her a glance, silently leaving her no room for argument. "Relax and we'll see what we're dealing with once I can get you on the bed in the cabin."

Those words sent a shiver of arousal through her that she seriously did not want. Hadn't she learned from the last set of shivers? Hadn't she told herself that after they slept together she'd cut ties? She had no other choice, not if she wanted to maintain any dignity and sanity on her way out of his life for good.

As they neared the dock, Will was breathing hard,

but he didn't say a word as he trudged forward. Her ankle throbbed, which should have helped shift her focus, but being wrapped in Will's strong arms pretty much overrode any other emotion.

Catalina had a sinking feeling that in all her pep talks to herself, she'd overlooked the silent power Will had over her. She may have wanted to have this sexcapade with him and then move on, but she'd seriously underestimated how involved her heart would become.

And this hero routine he was pulling was flat-out sexy...as if she needed another reason to pull her toward him.

Will quickly crossed toward the dock, picking up his pace now that he was on even ground. When he muttered a curse, Catalina lifted her head to see what the problem was. Quickly she noted the damage to the yacht and the dock. Apparently the two had not played nice during the freak storm.

"Oh, Will," she whispered.

He slowed his pace as he carefully tested the weight of the dock. Once his footing was secure, and it was clear that the planks would hold them, he cautiously stepped forward.

"I need to set you down for a second to climb on board, but just keep pressure off that ankle and hold onto my shoulders."

She did as he asked and tried not to consider just what this damage meant for their return trip home. When Will was on deck, he reached out, proceeded to scoop her up again and lifted her onto the yacht.

"I can get down the steps," she told him, really having no clue if she could or not. But there was no way they could both fit through that narrow doorway to get below deck. "Go figure out what happened."

He kept his hold firm. "I'm going to get you settled, assess your ankle and then go see what damage was done to the yacht."

Somehow he managed to get her down the steps and onto the bed without bumping her sore, now swollen ankle along the way. As he adjusted the pillows behind her, she slid back to lean against the fluffy backdrop. Will took a spare pillow and carefully lifted her leg to elevate her injury.

"It's pretty swollen," he muttered as he stalked toward the galley kitchen and returned with a baggie full of ice wrapped in a towel. "Keep this on it and I'll go see if I can find some pain reliever."

"Really, it'll be fine," she lied. The pain was bad, but she wanted him to check on the damage so they could get back to Alma… She prayed they could safely get back. "Go see how bad the destruction is. I'm not going anywhere."

Will's brows drew in. With his hands on his hips, that sexy black ink scrolling over his bare chest and the taut muscles, he personified sex appeal.

"Staring at my ankle won't make it any better," she told him, suddenly feeling uncomfortable.

His unique blue eyes shifted and held her gaze. "I hate that I hurt you," he muttered.

So much could be read from such a simple statement. Was he referring to four years ago? Did he mean the sexual encounter they'd just had or was he referencing her fall?

No matter what he was talking about, Catalina didn't want to get into another discussion that would only take them in circles again. They were truly getting nowhere…well, they'd ended up naked, but other than that, they'd gotten nowhere.

"Go on," she insisted. "Don't worry about me."

He looked as if he wanted to argue, but ended up nodding. "I'll be right back. If you need something, just yell for me. I'll hear you."

Catalina watched as he ascended the steps back up to the deck. Closing her eyes, she dropped her head against the pillows and pulled in a deep breath. If the storm had done too much damage to the yacht, she was stuck. Stuck on a glamorous yacht with an injured ankle with the last person she should be locked down with.

The groan escaped before she could stop it. Then laughter followed. Uncontrollable laughter, because could they be anymore clichéd? The maid and the millionaire, stranded on a desert island. Yeah, they had the makings for a really ridiculous story or some skewed reality show.

Once upon a time she would've loved to have been stranded with Will. To know that nothing would interrupt them. They could be who they wanted to be without pretenses. Just Will and Catalina, two people who l—

No. They didn't love each other. That was absurd to even think. Years ago she had thought they were in love, but they couldn't have been. If they'd truly been in love, wouldn't he have fought for everything they'd discussed and dreamed of?

Maybe he'd been playing her the entire time. A twenty-year-old boy moving up the ladder of success really didn't have much use for a poor staff member. She was a virgin and an easy target. Maybe that's all he'd been after.

But she really didn't think so. She'd grown up around Will and James. James was the player, not Will. Will had always been more on the straight and narrow, the rule follower.

And he'd followed those rules right to the point of breaking her heart. She should have seen it coming, really. After their mother passed away, Will did every single thing he could to please his father, as if overcompensating for the loss of a parent.

Yet there was that little girl fantasy in her that had held out hope that Will would see her as more, that he would fall in love with her and they could live happily ever after.

Catalina sighed. That was long ago; they were different people now and the past couldn't be redone…and all those other stupid sayings that really didn't help in the grand scheme of things.

And it was because she was still so tied up in knots over this man that she needed to escape Alma, fulfill her own dreams and forget her life here. She was damn good at designing and she couldn't wait to burn her uniforms and sensible shoes, roast a marshmallow over them and move on.

"We're not going anywhere for a while."

Catalina jerked her head around. Will was standing on the bottom step, his hands braced above him on the doorframe. The muscles in his biceps flexed, drawing her attention to his raw masculinity. No matter how much the inner turmoil was caused by their rocky relationship, Catalina couldn't deny that the sight of his body turned her on like no other man had ever been able to do.

"There's some major damage to the starboard side. I thought maybe I could get it moving, but the mechanics are fried. I can only assume the boat was hit by lightning as well as banging into the dock repeatedly."

Catalina gripped the plush comforter beneath her palms. "How long will we be stuck here?"

"I have no clue."

He stepped farther into the room and raked a hand over his messy hair. Will always had perfectly placed hair, but something about that rumpled state made her hotter for him.

"The radio isn't working, either," he added as he sank down on the edge of the bed, facing her. "Are you ready for some pain medicine since we're going to be here awhile?"

She was going to need something a lot stronger if she was going to be forced to stick this out with him for too long. Hours? Days? How long would she have to keep her willpower on high alert?

"I probably better," she admitted. "My ankle's throbbing pretty good now."

Will went to the bathroom. She heard him rummaging around in a cabinet, then the faucet. When he strode back across the open room, Catalina couldn't keep her eyes off his bare chest. Why did he have to be so beautiful and enticing? She wanted to be over her attraction for this man. Anything beyond what happened in that cabin would only lead to more heartache because Will would never choose anyone over his father and Rowling Energy and she sure as hell wasn't staying in Alma to clean toilets the rest of her life waiting to gain his attention.

Catalina took the pills and the small paper cup of water he offered. Hoping the medicine kicked in soon, she swallowed it as Will eased back down beside her on the bed.

"Dammit," he muttered, placing his hand on the shin of her good leg. "If we hadn't been arguing—"

"We've argued for weeks," she told him with a half smile. "It was an accident. If anyone is to blame it's me for not watching where I was going and for trying to stomp off in a fit."

"Were you throwing a fit?" he asked. "I don't remember."

Catalina lifted an eyebrow. "You're mocking me now."

Shaking his head, he slid his hand up and down her shin. "Not at all. I just remember thinking how sexy you looked when you were angry. You have this red tint to your cheeks. Or it could've been the great sex. Either way, you looked hot."

"Was that before or after I was sprawled face first in the sand?" she joked, trying to lighten the mood.

"You can't kill sexy, Cat, even if you're eating sand."

The slight grin he offered her eased her worry. Maybe they could spend the day here and actually be civil without worrying about the sexual tension consuming them. Maybe they had taken the edge off and could move on.

Well, they could obviously move on, but would this feeling of want ever go away? Because if anything, since they'd been intimate, Catalina craved him even more.

So now what could she do? There was nowhere to hide and definitely nowhere to run in her current state.

As she looked into Will's mesmerizing eyes, her worry spiked once again because he stared back at her like a man starved…and she was the main course.

Thirteen

Thankfully the kitchen was fully stocked and the electricity that fed the appliances hadn't been fried because right now Will needed to concentrate on something other than how perfect Cat looked in his bed.

He'd come to the kitchen a while ago to figure out what they should do for dinner. Apparently the pain pills had kicked in because Cat was resting peacefully, even letting out soft moans every now and then as she slept.

It was those damn moans that had his shorts growing tighter and his teeth grinding as he attempted to control himself. He'd heard those groans earlier, up close and personal in his ear as she'd wrapped her body around his.

The experience was one he would never forget.

Will put together the chicken and rice casserole that his mother used to make. Yes, they'd had a chef when he was a child, but James and Will had always loved this dish and every now and then, Will threw it together just to remember his mother. He still missed her, but it was the little things that would remind him of her and make him smile.

Setting the timer on the oven, Will glanced back to the sleeping beauty in his bed. His mother would have loved Cat. She wouldn't have cared if she was the maid or—

What the hell? How did that thought sneak right in without his realizing the path his mind was taking? It didn't matter what his mother would have thought of Cat. He wasn't getting down on one knee and asking her into the family.

He needed to get a grip because his hormones and his mind were jumbling up all together and he was damn confused. Sleeping with Cat should have satisfied this urge to claim her, but instead of passing, the longing only grew.

With the casserole baking for a good bit, Will opted to grab a shower. He smelled like sex, sand and sweat. Maybe a cold shower would help wake him up to the reality that he'd let Cat go once. Just because they slept together didn't mean she was ready to give this a go again. And was that what he wanted? In all honesty did he want to try for this once more and risk hurting her, hurting himself, further?

He was making a damn casserole for pity's sake. What type of man had he become? He'd turned into some warped version of a homemaker and, even worse, he was perfectly okay with this feeling.

Before he went to the shower, he wanted to try the radio one more time. There had to be a way to communicate back to the mainland. Unfortunately, no matter which knobs he turned, which buttons he hit, nothing sparked to life. Resigned to the fact they were indeed stuck, Will went to his master suite bathroom.

As he stripped from his shorts and stepped into the spacious, open shower, he wondered if maybe being stranded with Cat wasn't some type of sign. Maybe they were supposed to be together with no outside forces hindering their feelings or judgment.

And honestly, Will wanted to see what happened with Cat. He wanted to give this another chance because they were completely different people than they were before and he was in total control of his life. She was that sliver of happiness that kept him smiling and their verbal sparring never failed to get him worked up.

No other woman matched him the way she did and he was going to take this opportunity of being stranded and use every minute to his advantage. He'd prove to her he was different because just telling her he was really wouldn't convince her. He needed to show her, to let her see for herself that he valued her, that he wanted her. He'd never stopped wanting her.

While he may want to use this private time to seduce the hell out of her, Will knew those hormones were going to have to take a back seat because Cat was worth more and they were long overdue for some relaxing, laid back time. And then maybe they could discuss just what the hell was happening between them.

Whatever that smell was, Catalina really hoped she wasn't just dreaming about it. As soon as she opened her eyes, she was greeted with a beautiful orange glow across the horizon. The sun was setting, and lying in this bed, Will's bed, watching such beauty was a moment she wanted to lock in her mind forever.

She rolled over, wincing as the pain in her ankle reminded her she was injured. The ice bag had melted and slid off the pillow she'd propped it on. As soon as she sat up, she examined her injury, pleased to see the swelling had gone down some.

"Oh, good. Dinner is almost ready."

Catalina smoothed her hair away from her face and smiled as Will scooped up something from a glass pan.

"I tried the radio again," he told her. "It didn't work. The whole system is fried."

Catalina sighed. As much as she wanted to get back home, she couldn't deny the pleasure she'd experienced here, despite the injury. She had a feeling she was seeing the true Will, the man who wasn't all business and power trips, but a man who cared for her whether he was ready to admit it or not.

"Someone will come for us," she told him. "Besides, with you cooking and letting me nap, you're spoiling me. Dinner smells a lot like that chicken dish you made me for our first date."

Will grinned back at her and winked. *Winked.* What had she woken to? Will in the kitchen cooking and actually relaxed enough to wink and smile as if he hadn't a care in the world.

"It is," he confirmed. "I'll bring it to you so don't worry about getting up."

"I actually need to go to the restroom."

In seconds, Will was at her side helping her up. When he went to lift her in his arms, she pushed against him.

"Just let me lean on you, okay? No need to carry me."

Wrapping an arm around her waist, Will helped her stand. "How's the ankle feeling?"

"Really sore, but better than it was." She tested it, pulling back when the sharp throbbing started again.

"Putting weight on it still isn't a smart move, but hopefully it will be much better by tomorrow."

Will assisted her across the room, but when they reached the bathroom doorway, she placed a hand on his chest. "I can take it from here."

No way was he assisting her in the bathroom. She'd like to hold onto some shred of dignity. Besides, she needed a few moments to herself to regain mental footing since she was stuck playing house with the only man she'd ever envisioned spending forever with.

"I'll wait right here in case you need something," he told her. "Don't lock the door."

With a mock salute, Catalina hobbled into the bathroom and closed the door. The scent of some kind of masculine soap assaulted her senses. A damp towel hung over the bar near the shower. He'd made use of the time she'd been asleep. Her eyes darted to the bathtub that looked as if it could seat about four people. What she wouldn't give to crawl into that and relax in some hot water, with maybe a good book or a glass of wine. When was the last time she'd indulged in such utterly selfish desires?

Oh, yeah, when she'd stripped Will naked and had her way with him in the old cabin earlier today.

A tap on the door jerked her from her thoughts. "Are you okay?"

"Yeah. Give me a minute."

A girl couldn't even fantasize in peace around here. She still needed time to process what their intimacy meant and the new, unexpected path their relationship had taken. Will had most likely thought of what happened the entire time she'd been asleep. Of course he was a man, so he probably wasn't giving their encounter the amount of mind space she would.

Minutes later, Catalina opened the door to find Will leaning against the frame. Once again he wrapped an arm around her and steered her toward the bed.

"I can eat at the table." She hated leaning on him, touching him when her nerves were still a jumbled up mess. "I'm already up. That bed is too beautiful to eat on."

In no time he'd placed their plates on the table with two glasses of wine…again, her favorite. A red Riesling.

"If I didn't know better, I'd say you stocked this kitchen just for me," she joked as she took her first sip and knew it wasn't the cheap stuff she kept stocked in her fridge.

"I did buy a lot of things I knew you liked." His fork froze midway to his mouth as he looked up at her. "At least, you liked this stuff four years ago."

For a split second, he seemed unsure. Will was always confident in everything, but when discussing her tastes, he suddenly doubted himself. Why did she find that so adorable?

She felt a shiver travel up her spine. She didn't have time for these adorable moments and couldn't allow them to influence her where this man was concerned. That clean break she wanted couldn't happen if she let herself be charmed like that.

They ate in silence, but Catalina was surprised the strain wasn't there. Everything seemed…normal. Something was up. He wasn't trying to seduce her, he wasn't bringing up the past or any other hot topic.

What had happened while she'd been asleep? Will had suddenly transformed into some sort of caretaker with husbandlike qualities.

But after a while she couldn't take the silence anymore. Catalina dropped her fork to her empty plate.

"That was amazing. Now, tell me what's going through your mind."

Will drained his glass before setting it back down and focusing on her. "Right now I'm thinking I could use dessert."

"I mean why are you so quiet?"

Shrugging, he picked up their plates and put them in the kitchen. When he brought back the wine bottle, she put a hand over hers to stop him from filling her glass back up.

"If I need more pain pills later, it's best I don't have any more even though I only took a half pill."

Nodding, he set the bottle on the table and sat across from her again.

"Don't ignore the question."

A smile kicked up at the corners of his mouth. "I'm plotting."

Catalina eased back in her seat, crossing her arms over her chest. "You're always plotting. I take it I'm still in the crosshairs?"

His eyes narrowed in that sexy, toe-curling way that demanded a woman take notice. "You've never been anywhere else."

Her heart beat faster. When he said those things she wanted to believe him. She wanted to be the object of his every desire and fantasy. And when he looked at her as if nothing else in the world mattered, she wanted to stay in that line of sight forever, though she knew all of that was a very naïve way of thinking.

"I only set out to seduce you," he went on, toying with the stem on his glass. "I wanted you in my bed more than anything. And now that I've had you..."

Catalina wished she'd had that second glass of wine after all. "What are you saying?"

His intense stare locked onto her. "We're different people. Maybe we're at a stage where we can learn from the past and see…"

It took every ounce of her willpower not to lean forward in anticipation as his words trailed off yet again. "And see what?" she finally asked.

"Maybe I want to see where we could go."

Catalina gasped. "You're not serious."

Those heavy-lidded eyes locked onto her. "I can't let you go now that I know how right we are together."

Her eyes shifted away and focused on the posh living space while she tried to process all he was saying.

Her mother's words of warning from years ago echoed in Catalina's mind. How could she fall for this man with his smooth words and irresistible charm? Hadn't her mother done the same thing with Patrick?

No. Will wasn't Patrick and Catalina was not her mother.

To her knowledge, Will, even to this day, had absolutely no idea what had transpired when he'd been a young boy right around the time of his mother's death. That hollow pit in Catalina's stomach deepened. Had the affair been the catalyst in Mrs. Rowling's death?

"Why now?" she asked, turning back to face him. "Why should I let you in now after all this time? Is it because I'm convenient? Because I'm still single or because you're settling?"

Why was fate dangling this right in front of her face when she'd finally decided to move on? It had taken her years to get up the nerve to really move forward with her dream and now that she'd decided to take a chance, Will wanted back in?

"Trust me, you're anything but convenient," he laughed.

"I've busted my butt trying to think of ways to get your attention."

Catalina swallowed. "But why?"

"Because you want this just as much as I do," he whispered.

Catalina stared down at her hands clasped in her lap. "We're at the age now that our wants don't always matter." Letting her attention drift back up, she locked her eyes on him. "We both have different goals, Will. In the end, nothing has really changed."

"On that we can agree." Will came to his feet, crossed to her side of the table and loomed over her. His hands came to rest on the back of her chair on either side of her shoulders. "In the end, I'll still want you and you'll still want me. The rest can be figured out later."

Before she could say anything, he'd scooped her up in his arms. "Don't say a word," he chided. "I want to carry you, so just let me. Enjoy this moment, that's all I'm asking. Don't think about who we are away from here. Let me care for you the way you deserve."

His warm breath washed over her face as she stared back at him. He didn't move, he just waited for her reply.

What could she say? He was right. They both wanted each other, but was that all this boiled down to? There were so many other outside factors driving a wedge between them. Did she honestly believe that just because he said so things would be different?

Catalina stared into those eyes and for once she saw hope; she saw a need that had nothing to do with sex.

Resting her head on his shoulder, Catalina whispered, "One of us is going to get hurt."

Fourteen

Catalina leaned back against Will's chest as they settled onto the oversized plush sofa on the top deck. The full moon provided enough light and just the perfect ambiance; even Will couldn't have planned it better.

Granted he didn't like that the yacht was damaged or that Catalina had been injured, but the feel of her wrapped in his arms, their legs intertwined, even as he was careful of her ankle, was everything he'd wanted since he let her walk away so long ago.

Will laced his hands over her stomach and smiled when she laid her hands atop his.

"It's so quiet and peaceful," she murmured. "The stars are so vibrant here. I guess I never pay much attention in Alma."

"One of these days you're going to have your own maid, your own staff," he stated firmly. "You deserve to be pampered for all the hours you work without asking for anything in return. You work too hard."

"I do," she agreed. "I have so many things I want to do with my life and working is what keeps me motivated."

A strand of her hair danced in the breeze, tickling his cheek, but he didn't mind. Any way he could touch her and be closer was fine with him. She wasn't trying to ignore this pull and she'd actually relaxed fully against him. This is what they needed. The simplicity, the privacy.

"What are your goals, Cat?"

"I'd love a family someday."

The wistfulness in her tone had him wanting to fulfill those wishes. Will knew he'd never be able to sit back and watch her be with someone else, make a life and a family with another man.

"What else?" he urged. "I want to know all of your dreams."

She stiffened in his arms. Will stroked her fingers with his, wanting to keep her relaxed, keep her locked into this euphoric moment.

"It's just me, Cat." He purposely softened his tone. "Once upon a time we shared everything with each other."

"We did. I'm just more cautious now."

Because of him. He knew he'd damaged that innocence in her, he knew full well that she was a totally different woman because of his selfish actions. And that fact was something he'd have to live with for the rest of his life. All he could do was try to make things better now and move forward.

"I shouldn't have let you go," he muttered before he could think.

"Everything happens for a reason."

Will didn't miss the hint of pain in her tone. "Maybe so, but I should've fought for you, for us."

"Family has always been your top priority, Will. You've been that way since your mother passed. You threw yourself into pleasing your father and James ran wild. Everyone grieves differently and it's affected your relationships over the years."

Will shouldn't have been surprised that she'd analyzed him and his brother so well. Cat had always been so in tune with other people's feelings. Had he ever done that for her? Had he ever thought of her feelings if they didn't coincide with his own wants and needs?

"I never wanted you hurt." Yet he'd killed her spirit anyway. "I have no excuse for what I did. Nothing I say can reverse time or knock sense into the man I was four years ago."

"Everything that happened made me a better person." She shifted a bit and lifted her ankle to resettle it over the edge of the sofa. "I poured myself into new things, found out who I really am on my own. I never would've done that had I been with you."

Will squeezed her tighter. "I wouldn't have let you lose yourself, Cat. Had you been with me I would've pushed you to do whatever you wanted."

She tipped her head back and met his gaze. "You wouldn't have let me work. You would've wanted the perfect, doting wife."

There was a ring of truth to her words. He most likely would have tried to push her into doing what he thought was best.

"I wasn't good to you." He swallowed. "You were better off without me, but it killed me to let you go, knowing you'd be fine once you moved on."

Silence settled heavily around them before she finally said, "I wasn't fine."

"You were dating a man two months after we broke up."

Cat turned back around, facing the water. "I needed to date, I needed to move on in any way that I could and try to forget you. When I was alone my mind would wander and I'd start to remember how happy I was with you. I needed to fill that void in any way I possibly could."

Will swallowed. He'd hated seeing her with another man, hated knowing he was the one who drove her into another's arms.

"I slept with him."

Her words cut through the darkness and straight to his heart. "I don't want—"

"I slept with him because I was trying to forget you," she went on as if he hadn't said a word. "I was ready to give myself to you, then you chose to obey your father once again at my expense. When I started dating Bryce, I mistook his affection for love. I knew I was on the rebound, but I wanted so badly to be with someone who valued me, who wanted to be with me and put me first."

Those raw, heartfelt words crippled him. He'd had no idea just how much damage he'd caused. All this time, she'd been searching for anyone to put her at the top of their priority list when he'd shoved her to the bottom of his.

"Afterward I cried," she whispered. "I hated that I'd given away something so precious and I hated even more that I still wished I'd given it to you."

Her honesty gutted him. Will wished more than anything he could go back and make changes, wished he could go back and be the man she needed him to be.

But he could be honest now, he could open up. She'd shared such a deep, personal secret, he knew she deserved to know why he'd let her go so easily.

"I had to let you go."

"I know, your father—"

"No." Will adjusted himself in the seat so he could face her better. "I need you to know this, I need you to listen to what I'm saying. I let you go because of my father, but not for the reasons you think."

The moon cast enough of a glow for Will to see Cat's dark eyes widen. "What?"

"I let you go to save you. My father's threats…" Will shook his head, still angry over the way he'd let his father manipulate him. "As soon as I let you go, I was plotting to get you back, to put my father in his place. I didn't care how long it took, didn't care what I had to do."

Cat stared back at him, and he desperately wanted to know what was swirling around in her head. There was so much hurt between them, so many questions and years of resentment. Will hated his father for putting him in this position, but he hated even more the way Cat had been the victim in all of this.

"Your father threatened me, didn't he?" Cat asked, her voice low, yet firm. "He held me over your head? Is that why you let me go?"

Swallowing the lump of guilt, Will nodded.

Cat sat up, swung her feet over the side and braced her hands on either side of her hips. Will lifted his leg out of her way and brought his knee up to give her enough room to sit. He waited while she stared down at the deck. Silence and moonlight surrounded them, bathing them in a peace that he knew neither of them felt.

"Talk to me." He couldn't handle the uncertainty. "I don't want you going through this alone."

A soft laugh escaped her as she kept her gaze averted. "But you didn't care that I went through this alone four years ago."

"Dammit, Cat. I couldn't let you get hurt. He had the ability to ruin you and I wasn't going to put my needs ahead of yours."

When she threw him a glance over her shoulder, Will's gut tightened at the moisture gathered in her eyes. "You didn't put my needs first at all. You didn't give me a chance to fight for us and you took the easy way out."

Raking a hand over his hair, Will blew out a breath. "I didn't take the easy way," he retorted. "I took the hardest way straight through hell to keep you safe and to work on getting you back."

She continued to stare, saying nothing. Moments later her eyes widened. "Wait," she whispered. "How did Bella come into play?"

"You know I never would've married her. That was all a farce to begin with." Will shifted closer, reaching out to smooth her hair back behind her ear. "And once I kissed you, I knew exactly who I wanted, who I needed."

Cat started to stand, winced and sat back down. Will said nothing as he pushed his leg around her, once again straddling her from behind. He pulled her back against his chest and leaned on the plush cushions. Even though she remained rigid, he knew the only way to get her to soften was for him to be patient. He'd waited four years; he was the epitome of patient.

Wrapping his arms around her, he whispered in her ear. "I messed up," he admitted. "I only wanted to protect you and went about it the wrong way. Don't shut me out now, Cat. We have too much between us. This goes so much deeper than either of us realizes and I won't let my father continue to ruin what we have."

Dammit, somewhere along the way to a heated affair Will had developed stronger feelings, a deeper bond with Cat than he'd anticipated. And now that he knew he wanted more from her, he was close to losing it all.

"And what do we have, Will?" Her words came out on a choked sob.

"What do you want?"

What do you want?

Catalina couldn't hold in the tension another second. There was only so much one person could handle and Will's simple question absolutely deflated her. Melting back against his body once more, she swallowed the emotion burning her throat.

"I want…" Catalina shut her eyes, trying to figure out all the thoughts fighting for head space. "I don't know now. Yesterday I knew exactly what I wanted. I was ready to leave Alma to get it."

Will's fingertips slid up and down her bare arms, causing her body to tremble beneath his delicate touch. "And now? What do you want now, Cat?"

Everything.

"I don't want to make things harder for you," he went on. "But I'm not backing down. Not this time."

And there was a portion of her heart that didn't want him to. How could she be so torn? How could two dreams be pulling her in completely different directions?

Because the harder she'd tried to distance herself from him, the more she was being pulled back in.

"I'm afraid," she whispered. "I can't make promises and I'm not ready to accept them from you, either."

His hands stilled for the briefest of moments before he kissed the top of her head. Catalina turned her cheek to rest against his chest, relishing the warmth of his body, the strong steady heartbeat beneath her. Part of her wanted to hate him for his actions years ago, the other part of her wanted to cry for the injustice of it all.

But a good portion of her wanted to forgive him, to believe him when he said that he'd sacrificed himself to keep her safe. Why did he have to be so damn noble and why hadn't he told her to begin with? He didn't have to fight that battle all on his own. Maybe she could have saved him, too.

Catalina closed her eyes as the yacht rocked steadily to the soothing rhythm of the waves. She wanted to lock this moment in time and live here forever. Where there were no outside forces trying to throw obstacles in their way and the raw honesty…

No. She still carried a secret that he didn't know and how could she ever tell him? How could she ever reveal the fact that his father had had an affair with her mother? Would he hate her for knowing?

"Will, I need—"

"We're done talking. I just want to hold you. Nothing else matters right now."

Turning a bit more in his arms, Catalina looked up into those vibrant eyes that had haunted her dreams for years. "Make love to me, Will. I don't care about anything else. Not when I can be with you."

In one swift, powerful move, he had her straddling his lap. Catalina hissed a breath when her ankle bumped his thigh.

"Dammit. Sorry, Cat."

She offered him a smile, stroking the pad of her thumb along the worry lines between his brows. "I'm fine," she assured him as she slid the ties at the side of her dress free. "I don't want to think about my injury, why we're stuck here or what's waiting for us when we get back. All I want is to feel you against me."

Will took in the sight of her as she continued to work out of her clothing. When his hands spanned her waist, she arched against his touch.

He leaned forward, resting his forehead against her chest as he whispered, "You're more than I deserve and everything I've ever wanted."

Framing his face with her hands, Catalina lifted his head until she could look him in the eyes. "No more talking," she reminded him with a soft kiss to his lips. "No more talking tonight."

Tomorrow, or whenever they were able to get off this island, she'd tell him about his father. But for now, she'd take this gift she'd been given and worry about the ugly truth, and how they would handle it, later.

Fifteen

By the second day, Catalina still hadn't told Will the truth. How could she reveal such a harsh reality when they'd been living in passionate bliss on a beautiful island in some fantasy?

They'd both fiddled with the radio and tried their cell phones from various spots on the island, but nothing was going through. She wasn't going to panic quite yet. They had plenty of food and for a bit, she could pretend this was a dream vacation with the man she'd fallen in love with.

Will rolled over in bed, wrapping his arm around her and settling against her back. "I'd like to say I can't wait to get off this island, but waking up with you in my arms is something I could get used to."

His husky tone filled her ear. The coarse hair on his chest tickled her back, but she didn't mind. She loved the feel of Will next to her.

"I'm getting pretty spoiled, too." She snuggled deeper into his embrace. "I'm never going to want to leave."

"Maybe that's how I want you to be," he replied, nipping her shoulder.

"We can't stay here forever," she laughed.

"As long as you don't leave Alma, I'm okay with going back."

A sliver of reality crept back in. Catalina shifted so that she could roll over in his arms and face him.

"I don't plan on working as a maid forever," she informed him, staring into his eyes. "And after what you told me about your father, I think it's best if I don't work there anymore. I can't work for a man who completely altered my future. I stayed with James because I adore him and I moved on to Patrick because I needed the job, but now that I know the full truth, I can't stay there."

Will propped himself up on his elbow and peered down at her. "I understand, but stay in Alma. Stay with me."

"And do what?" she asked, already knowing this conversation was going to divide them. "I have goals, Will. Goals that I can't ignore simply because we're… I don't even know what this is between us right now."

"Do you need a label?" he asked.

Part of her wanted to call this something. Maybe then she could justify her feelings for a man who'd let her go so easily before.

She had no idea what she was going to do once she got back to Alma. Working for Patrick was not going to happen. She'd put up with his arrogance for too long. Thankfully she'd only worked for him a short time because up until recently, James had been the one occupying the Playa del Onda home. Catalina had had a hard enough time working for Patrick knowing what she did about her mother, but now knowing he'd manipulated his son and crushed their relationship, Catalina couldn't go back there. Never again.

So where did that leave her? She didn't think she was quite ready to head out with her designs and start pursuing her goal. She had a few more things she'd like to complete before she made that leap.

"What's going through your mind?" Will asked, studying her face.

"You know the sewing set you got me?"

Will nodded.

"You have no idea how much that touched me." Catalina raked her hand through his blond hair and trailed her fingertips down his jaw, his neck. "I've been sewing in my spare time. Making things for myself, for my mother. It's been such a great escape and when I saw what you'd gotten me, I…"

Catalina shook her head and fell back against the bed. She stared up at the ceiling and wished she could find the right words to tell him how much she appreciated the gift.

"So you're saying it was a step up from the flowers?" he joked.

Shifting her gaze to him, her heart tightened at his playful smile. "I may have cried," she confessed. "That was the sweetest gift ever."

Will settled over her, his hands resting on either side of her head. "It was meant more as a joke," he said with a teasing smile. "And maybe I wanted to remind you of what we did in the utility room."

Cat smacked his chest. "As if I could've forgotten. That's all I could think about and you know it."

He gave her a quick kiss before he eased back. "It's all I could think of, too, if that helps."

Catalina wrapped her arms around his neck, threading her fingers through his hair. "What are we going to do when we get back?"

"We're going to take this one day at a time because I'm not screwing this up again."

"We can't seem to function in normal life."

Will's forehead rested against hers as he let out a sigh. "Trust me, Cat. I've fought too hard to get you back. I'm going to fight just as hard to keep you."

Catalina prayed that was true, because all too soon she was going to have to reveal the final secret between them if she wanted a future with this man.

Cat lay on the deck sunbathing in that skimpy bikini, which was positively driving him out of his mind. Right now he didn't give a damn that the radio was beyond repair or that their phones weren't getting a signal. For two days they'd made love, stayed in bed and talked, spending nearly every single moment together.

Perhaps that's why he was in such agony. He knew exactly what that lush body felt like against his own. He knew how amazingly they fit together with no barriers between them.

Will couldn't recall the last time he'd taken this much time away from work. Surprisingly he wasn't getting twitchy. He'd set his plan into motion a couple months ago for Rowling Energy and it shouldn't be too much longer before everything he'd ever wanted clicked into place like a perfectly, methodically plotted puzzle.

Will folded his arms behind his head and relaxed on the seat opposite Cat. But just as he closed his eyes, the soft hum of an engine had him jumping to his feet.

"Do you hear that?" he asked, glancing toward the horizon.

Cat sat up, her hand shielding her eyes as she glanced in the same direction. "Oh, there's another boat."

Will knew that boat and he knew who would be on board. Good thing his brother hadn't left to go back to training for football yet because that meant he could come to their rescue. Which was what he was doing right now.

"Looks like our fairy tale is over," Catalina muttered.

He glanced her way. "It's not over," he corrected. "It's just beginning."

As James's yacht closed the distance between them, Will slid his shoes back on. "Stay here. I'll wave James to the other side of the dock where the damage isn't as bad. And I'll carry you on board once we're secure."

Cat rolled her eyes and reached for her wrap draped across the back of the white sofa. "I can walk, Will. My ankle is sore, but it's much better than it was."

Will wasn't going to argue. He'd win in the end regardless.

As soon as James was near enough, Will hopped up onto the dock and made his way toward the other end. By the time James came to a stop, Bella was at his side, a worried look etched across her face.

"Coast guard has arrived," James said, coming up behind his wife.

"I figured you'd come along sooner or later," Will replied.

James took in the damage to the dock and the yacht. "Damn, you've got a mess. That must've been one hell of a storm. It rained and there was some thunder and wind in Alma, but no damage."

"Let me go get our things," Will told his brother. "I need to carry Cat, too. She's hurt."

"Oh no," Bella cried. "What happened?"

"I fell."

Will turned to see Cat leaning over the side of the yacht. "You're supposed to be sitting down," he called back.

"I'm fine. I will need some help off this thing, but I can walk if I go slow."

Will shook his head. "I'll carry her," he told his brother. "Give me a few minutes to get our personal stuff gathered."

Once they transferred everything Will and Cat needed to his brother's yacht and Will carried a disgruntled Cat on board, they were ready to head out. The trip back to Alma was filled with questions from Bella and James. Their worry was touching and Will actually found himself loving this newfound bond he and his brother shared. This is what he'd been missing for years. This is what their grief had torn apart after their mother had died. But now they were slowly making their way back to each other.

"I wasn't quite sure which island you went to," James said as they drew nearer to Alma's coastline. "I went to two last night and had to start again today when I couldn't find you."

"Did you tell anyone what was going on?" Will asked.

"No." James maneuvered the boat and pulled back on the throttle. "Bella and I are the only ones who know where you were."

Will was relieved nobody else knew. He didn't want to share Cat or their relationship with anyone just yet. He wanted to bask in their privacy for a bit longer.

"Dammit," James muttered as they neared what was supposed to be a private dock where Alma's rich and famous kept their boats. "The damn press is here."

"What for?" Cat asked, her eyes widening.

"There were a few reporters here when I left earlier,"

James stated as he steered the yacht in. "They were speculating because Will's yacht had been missing for a few days and they knew a storm had come through. They asked me where you were and I ignored them."

Will groaned. So much for that privacy he'd been clinging to. "Don't they have anything better to cover? Like the fact Juan Carlos is going to be crowned king in a few weeks? Do they seriously have to focus on me?"

Cat's eyes remained fixed on the throng of reporters and cameras turning in their direction.

Will crouched down before her seat and smoothed her hair back from her face. "Ignore them. No matter what they say, do not make a comment. They'll forget about this by tomorrow and we can move on."

Her eyes sought his and she offered him a smile. "Ignore them. That I can do."

Will stood back up and offered her his hand. "I'm going to at least put my arm around you so you can put some of your weight on me. Anyone looking will just think I'm helping you."

"I'll carry her bag," Bella offered. "I'll go first. Maybe they'll focus on James and me. I can always just start discussing my upcoming fund-raiser for my foundation next weekend. I'm okay with yanking the reporters' chains, too."

Will couldn't help but laugh at Bella's spunk. She was the perfect match for his brother.

As they made their way down the dock, Will kept his arm secured around Cat's waist. James and Bella took the lead, holding hands as they wedged through the sea of nosy people.

The reporters seemed to all start shouting at once.

"Where have you been for three days?"

"Was your yacht damaged by the storm?"

"Were you stranded somewhere?"

"Who is with you, Will?"

The questions kept coming as Will tried to shield Cat from the press. The whispers and murmurs infuriated him. Seriously? Wasn't there other newsworthy stuff happening in Alma right now? Dammit, this was one major drawback to being a wealthy, well-known businessman. And if he thought for a second he could have any privacy with Cat now that they were back, he was living in a fantasy.

When he heard someone say the word "staff" he clenched his jaw. He wouldn't respond. That's what they wanted: some type of reaction. He heard his father's name and for reasons unbeknownst to Will, the gossipmongers were starting to piece things together rather quickly. Where the hell would they have seen Cat? On occasion his father would allow a few press members to attend certain parties thrown by the Rowlings if there was a charity involved. Cat had been James's maid, too, though.

Will groaned as he kept his sights on his brother's back as the foursome pushed through to the waiting car in the distance. They couldn't get there fast enough for Will.

"Is your mistress a member of your family's staff, Mr. Rowling?"

The rude question had Cat stiffening at his side. "Keep going," he murmured. "Almost there."

"Wasn't she working for your brother?"

"Is she on Patrick's staff?"

"How long have you been seeing your father's maid?"

"Weren't you just engaged to your brother's wife?"

"What does your father think about you and his maid?"

Will snapped. "This isn't like that. You're all making a mistake."

Catalina's gasp had him jerking his gaze toward her. "Dammit," he muttered beneath his breath. "You know that's not what I mean."

Those damn words echoed from the last time he'd said them to her. And this time they were just as damaging when taken out of context.

Easing back from his side, Cat kept her eyes on his. "I'm not sure, Will. Because only moments ago you said ignore them and you said we'd take this one day at a time. We've only been back in Alma five minutes and you're already referring to me as a mistake."

Will raked a hand through his hair. From the corner of his eye he spotted James and Bella standing close. For once the reporters weren't saying a word. They waited, no doubt hoping to really get something juicy for their headlines.

"Marry me."

Okay, he hadn't meant to blurt that out there, but now that the words hovered between them, he wasn't sorry. Maybe Cat would see just how serious he was about them.

"Marry you?" she asked, her brows drawn in. "You're not serious."

He stepped forward and took her hand. "We are not a mistake, Cat. You know we're perfect together. Why wouldn't you?"

Cat stared back at him, and then shook her head and let out a soft laugh. "This is ridiculous. You don't mean this proposal so why would you do this to me? Why would you ask that in front of all these people? To prove them wrong? Because you got caught with the maid and you're trying to glamorize it?"

"Dammit, Cat, this has nothing to do with anyone else. We can talk later, in private."

He didn't want to hash this out here in front of the press. And he sure as hell didn't want to sound as if he was backpedaling because he'd chosen the worst possible time to blurt out a proposal.

Crossing her arms over her chest, she tipped her chin up just a notch, but enough for him to know she was good and pissed. "Would you have proposed to me if all of these people hadn't been around? Later tonight when we were alone, would you have asked me to marry you?"

Will gritted his teeth, clenched his fists at his side and honestly had no reply. He had absolutely no idea what to say. He didn't want to have such an intimate talk in front of the whole country, because that's exactly what was happening. The press would no doubt splash this all over the headlines.

"That's what I thought." Cat's soft tone was full of hurt. "I'd say it's officially over between us."

When she turned, she winced, but just as Will reached to help her, Bella stepped forward and slowly ushered Cat to the car. James moved in next to Will and ordered the press away. Will didn't hear much, didn't comprehend what was going on because in the span of just a few minutes, he'd gone from deliriously happy and planning his future, to seeing that future walk away from him after he'd hurt her, called her a mistake, once again.

This time, he knew there would be no winning her back.

Sixteen

"What the hell is this?"

Will turned away from his office view to face his father, who stood on the other side of his desk with a folder in his hand. Will had been waiting for this moment. But he hadn't expected to feel this enormous pit of emptiness inside.

"I see you received the notice regarding your shares in Rowling Energy." Will folded his arms across his chest and leveled his father's gaze. "Your votes in the company are no longer valid. I held an emergency meeting with the other stockholders and we came to the decision."

Patrick's face reddened. "How dare you. What kind of son did I raise that he would turn around and treat his father like this?"

"You raised the son who fought for what he wanted." Will's blood pressure soared as he thought of all he'd lost and all he was still fighting for. "You raised a son who watched his father put business first, above family, and to hell with the rest of the world. I'm taking Rowling Energy into new territory and I need sole control. I'm done being jerked around by you."

Patrick rested his palms on the desk and leaned in. "No, you'd rather be jerked around by my maid. You two made quite a scene yesterday—it made headlines. You're becoming an embarrassment and tarnishing the Rowling name."

Will laughed. "What I do in my personal life is not your concern. You poked your nose in years ago when you threatened to dismiss Catalina if I didn't dump her. I won't be manipulated ever again and you will leave Cat alone. If I even think you've tried to—"

"Knock off the threats," his father shouted as he pushed off the desk. "Your little maid quit on me and has really left me in a bind. If you were smart, you'd stay away from her. You two get cozy and she quits. I don't believe in coincidences. Those Iberra women are nothing but gold diggers."

Will stood up straighter, dropped his arms to his sides. "What did you say?"

Patrick waved a hand in the air, shaking his head. "Forget it."

"No. You said 'those Iberra women.' What did you mean?"

Will knew Cat's mother had worked for Patrick years ago. Maria had been around when James and Will had been young, when their mother was still alive.

"What did Maria do that you would call her a gold digger?" Will asked when his father remained silent.

Still, Patrick said nothing.

Realization dawned on Will. "No. Tell me you didn't have an affair with Maria."

"Every man has a moment of weakness," Patrick stated simply. "I expect this past weekend was yours."

Rage boiled to the surface. Will clenched his fists. "You slept with Cat's mother while my mother was still alive? Did Mum know about the affair?"

The thought of his sweet, caring mother being betrayed tore through Will's heart. Part of him prayed she never knew the ugly acts his father had committed.

"She found out the day she died." Patrick let out a sigh, his eyes darting to the ground. "We were arguing about it when she left that night."

For once the great Patrick Rowling looked defeated. Which was nothing less than he deserved. Will's heart was absolutely crushed. He reached out, gripped the back of his desk chair and tried to think rationally here. Finding out your father had an affair with the mother of a woman you had fallen for was shocking enough. But to add to the intensity, his mother had died as a result of the affair.

Dread settled deep in Will's his gut. Did Cat know of this affair? Surely not. Surely she would have told him or at least hinted at the knowledge. Would this crush her, too?

"Get out," Will said in a low, powerful tone as he kept his eyes on the blotter on his desk. "Get the hell out of my office and be glad my freezing your voting rights in this company is all I'm doing to you."

Patrick didn't move. Will brought his gaze up and glared at the man he'd once trusted.

"You have one minute to be out of this building or I'll call security."

"I never thought you'd turn on me," his father replied.

"I turned on you four years ago when you threatened the woman I love."

Will hadn't meant to declare his love for Cat, but it felt good to finally let the words out. And now more than ever he wasn't giving up. He was going to move heaven and earth to win her back because he did love her. He'd always loved her if he was honest with himself. And he wanted a life with her now more than ever.

Bella was having a fund-raiser this coming weekend and Will knew he was going to need reinforcements. He wasn't letting Cat go. Not this time. Never again.

"I figured you'd be at work today." James sank down onto the chaise longue on his patio as Maisey played in her sandbox. "You look like hell, man."

Will shoved his hands in his pockets and glanced toward the ocean. "I feel like hell. Thanks for pointing it out."

"You still haven't talked to Catalina?"

Maisey squealed, threw her toy shovel and started burying her legs beneath the sand. Will watched his niece and wondered if there could ever be a family for Cat and him. She wanted a family and the more he thought of a life with her, the more he wanted the same thing.

"No, I haven't seen her." Will shifted his focus to his brother and took a seat on the edge of a chair opposite him. "Bella's fund-raiser is going to be at the Playa del Onda house this weekend, right?"

"Yes. Dad will be out of town and that house is perfect for entertaining. Why?"

"I want you to ask Cat to help with the staff there." Will held up a hand before his brother could cut him off. "I have my reasons, but I need your help in order to make this work."

James shook his head and stared down at his daughter for a minute before he looked back at Will. "This could blow up in your face."

Will nodded. "It's a risk I'm willing to take."

"What's in it for me?" James asked with a smirk.

Will laughed. Without even thinking twice, he unfastened the watch on his wrist and held it up. "This."

James's eyes widened. "I was joking."

"I'm not." Will reached out and placed the watch on the arm of his brother's chair. "You deserve it back. This has nothing to do with you helping me with Cat. The watch is rightfully yours."

James picked it up and gripped it in his hand. "We've really come a long way," he muttered.

Will had one more piece of business to take care of and he was not looking forward to this discussion at all. There was no way James knew of the affair or he definitely would've said something. Will really hated to crush his brother with the news, but James deserved to know.

"I need to tell you something." Will glanced at Maisey. "Is your nanny here or is Bella busy?"

James sat up in his seat, slid his watch on and swung his legs around to the deck. "Bella was answering emails, but she can watch Maisey. Is everything okay?"

Will shook his head. "Not really."

Worry and concern crossed James's face as he nodded. After taking Maisey inside, he returned moments later, closing the patio doors behind him.

"This must really be something if it has you this upset." James sat back down on the edge of his chair. "What's going on?"

Will took in a deep breath, blew it out and raked a hand through his hair. "This is harder than I thought," he said on a sigh. "Do you remember the night Mum died? Dad woke us and said she'd been in an accident?"

James nodded. "I heard them arguing earlier that evening. I was heading downstairs to get some water and heard them fighting so I went back upstairs."

Will straightened. "You heard them arguing?"

James nodded. "Dad raised his voice, and then Mum was crying and Dad was saying something else but in a lower tone. I didn't hear what all he said."

Will closed his eyes and wished like hell he could go back and...what? What could he have done differently? He'd been a kid. Even if James had gone downstairs and interrupted the fight, most likely their mother still would've walked out to get away from their father.

"What is it?" James prodded. "What aren't you telling me?"

Will opened his eyes and focused on his brother. "Dad had an affair. They were arguing about that."

"What?" James muttered a curse. "Has that man ever valued his family at all?"

"There's more." Will hesitated a moment, swallowed and pushed forward. "The affair was with Maria. Cat's mum."

Will started to wonder if James had heard him, but suddenly his brother jumped to his feet and let out a chain of curses that even had Will wincing. James kicked the leg of the chair, propped his hands on his hips and dropped his head between his shoulders.

"If I'd have gone downstairs that night..." he muttered.

"Mum still would've left," Will said softly. "We can't go back in time and you're not to blame. Our dad is the one whose selfish needs stole our mother. He crushed her. She would've done anything for him and he threw it all away."

James turned. "Does Cat know this?"

Shaking his head, Will came to his feet. "I doubt it. She's never said a word to me."

"Do you think once she knows the truth she'll take you back?"

Yeah, the odds were more than stacked against him, but he refused to back down. Nobody would steal his life again. And Cat was his entire life.

"I don't even know what to say about this," James said, staring out to the ocean. "I never had much respect for Dad, but right now I hate that man."

"I've made his life hell." Will was actually pleased with the timing. "As CEO of Rowling Energy, I've frozen his shares. He can no longer vote on any company matters that come before the board."

James smiled. "If this action were directed to an enemy, dear old Dad would be proud of your business tactics."

"Yeah," Will agreed, returning the grin. "He's not too proud right now, though. But I have more pressing matters to tend to."

James reached out, patted Will on the back. "I'll do what I can where Cat is concerned. I know what this is like to be so torn over a woman."

Torn wasn't even the word.

"I never thought either of us would fall this hard." Will pulled in a deep breath. "Now we need Bella to convince Cat to work the party. I can take it from there. I just need you guys to get her there."

Seventeen

If Catalina didn't adore Bella and her valiant efforts to raise money for the Alma Wildlife Conservation Society which she'd recently founded, Catalina wouldn't have stepped foot back into this house.

But Patrick was out of town and Bella and James had caught Catalina at a weak moment, offering her an insane amount of money to help set up for the event.

In the past week since she'd last seen Will, she'd not heard one word from him. Apparently she wasn't worth fighting for after all. Not that she would have forgiven him, but a girl likes to at least know she's worth something other than a few amazing sexual encounters.

Catalina hurried through the house, hoping to get everything set up perfectly before the first guests arrived.

Okay, fine. There was only one person on the guest list she was trying like hell to avoid.

She'd spent this past week furiously working on her

final designs. She didn't have the amount of money saved up that she wanted before she left Alma, but it would just have to be enough. Alma had nothing left to offer her. Not anymore.

Catalina took a final walkthrough, adjusting one more floral arrangement on the foyer table before she was satisfied with everything. She'd already double-checked with the kitchen to make sure the food was ready and would be served according to the set schedule. She'd also told Bella she would be back around midnight to clean up. There was just no way she could stay during the party. That had been her only condition for working tonight, and thankfully Bella had agreed.

Catalina checked her watch. Only thirty minutes until guests were due to arrive. Time to head out. She'd opted to park near the side entrance off the utility room. Just as she turned into the room to grab her purse and keys, she ran straight into a very hard, very familiar chest.

Closing her eyes, she tried like hell not to breathe in, but Will's masculine aroma enveloped her just as his strong arms came around to steady her.

"Running away?" he whispered in her ear.

Knowing she'd never get out without talking, Catalina shored up all of her courage and lifted her gaze to his. "I'm not the one who usually runs."

Keeping his aqua eyes on her, Will reached around, slammed the door and flicked the lock. "Neither of us is getting out of here until we talk."

"I don't need you to hold onto me," she told him, refusing to glance away. No way was he keeping the upper hand here just because her heart was in her throat.

"I want to make sure you'll stay put."

He dropped his hands but didn't step back. The

warmth from his body had hers responding. She wished she didn't fall so easily into the memories of their love-making, wished she didn't get swept away by such intriguing eyes. Even through their rocky moments, Catalina couldn't deny that all the good trumped the bad…at least in her heart.

"I'll stay." She stepped back until she was flat against the door. "If I don't listen now, I know you'll show up at my apartment. Might as well get this over with."

Why couldn't he be haggard or have dark circles beneath his eyes? Had he not been losing sleep over the fact he'd been a jerk? Why did he have to be so damn sexy all the time and why couldn't she turn off her hormones around this man who constantly hurt her?

"There's so much I want to say," he muttered as he ran a hand over his freshly shaven jaw. "I don't know where to start."

Catalina tapped her watch. "Better hurry. The party starts soon."

"I don't give a damn about that party. I already gave Bella a check for the foundation."

"Of course you did," she muttered. "What do you want from me, Will?"

He stepped forward until her body was firmly trapped between his and the door. Placing a hand on either side of her head, he replied, "Everything."

Oh, mercy. She wasn't going to be able to keep up this courage much longer if he kept looking at her like that, if he touched her or used those charming words.

"You can't have everything." She licked her lips and stared up at him. "You can't treat everything like a business deal, only giving of yourself when it's convenient for you or makes you look good in the public eye."

Will smoothed her hair away from her face and she

simply couldn't take it anymore. She placed her hands on his chest and shoved him back, slipping past him to get some breathing room before she lost her mind and clung to him.

"I'm actually glad you cornered me," she went on, whirling around to face him. "I didn't want to run into you tonight, but we both need closure. I don't want to leave Alma with such awkwardness between us."

"Leave Alma," he repeated. "You're not leaving Alma."

Catalina laughed. "You know you can't control everyone, right? I am leaving. In two weeks, actually. My mother and I have tickets and we're heading to Milan."

"What's in Milan?"

Catalina tucked her hair behind her ears and crossed her arms. "My new life. I've been working for nearly four years and I'm finally ready to take my clothing designs and see what I can do in the world. I may not get far, but I'm going to try."

Will's brows drew in as he listened. Catalina actually liked the fact that she'd caught him off guard. He'd been knocking the air out of her lungs for a good while now and it was only appropriate she return the favor.

"I know you're angry with me for blurting out the proposal in front of such an audience, but you have to listen to me now."

"I'll listen, but you're wasting your time if you're trying to convince me of anything. We're not meant to be, Will. We've tried, and we weren't successful either time. I don't want to keep fighting a losing battle."

"I've never lost a battle in my life," he informed her as he took a step closer. "I don't intend to lose this one."

"You already lost," she whispered. "On the island we were so happy and for that time I really thought we could come back here and build on that. But once again, I was naïve where you were concerned. As soon as we stepped foot back in Alma, you turned into that take-charge man who didn't want to look like a fool in front of the cameras. You were embarrassed to be seen with the maid, and then when you realized just how much of a jerk you were being, you opted to propose? Did you honestly think I'd accept that?"

Will was close enough to touch, but he kept his hands propped on his hips. "I reacted without thinking. Dammit, Cat we'd just had the best few days together and I was scared, all right? Everything about us terrifies me to the point I can't think straight. I've never wanted anything or anyone the way I want you and I've never been this afraid of losing what I love forever."

Catalina gasped. He didn't just say… No, he didn't love her. He was using those pretty words to control her, to trick her into…

What? What was his end game here?

"You don't love me, Will." Oh, how she wished he did, but that was still the naïve side of her dreaming. "You love power."

"I won't deny power is important to me. But that also means I can use that power to channel some pretty damn intense emotions." He leaned in, close enough for her to feel his breath on her face, yet he still didn't touch her. "And I love you more than any business deal, more than any merger or sale. I love you, Catalina."

She didn't want to hear this. He'd used her full name so she knew he was serious, or as serious as he could be.

"I don't want this," she murmured, trying to look away, but trapped by the piercing gaze. "I have plans, Will, and I can't hinge my entire life around a man who may or may not put me above his career."

And even if she could give in and let him have her heart, she carried this secret inside of her that would surely drive another sizeable wedge between them.

"Listen to me." He eased back, but reached out and placed his hands on either side of her face. "Hear every single word I'm about to tell you. For the past four years I've fought to get you back. At first I'll admit it was because my father wanted something else for my life and I was being spiteful, but the longer you and I were apart, the more I realized there was an empty ache inside of me that couldn't be filled. I poured myself into work, knowing the day would come when I'd take over Rowling Energy. Even through all of that, I was plotting to get you back."

He stared at her, his thumb stroking back and forth along the length of her jawline as if he was putting her into some type of trance.

"Just the thought of you with another man was crushing, but I knew if I didn't fight for you, for us, then you'd settle down and I'd lose you forever. I've always put you first, Cat. Always. Even when we weren't together, I was working my way back to you."

When she started to glance away, he tipped her head up, forcing her to keep her eyes on his. "You think I was working this long to win you back just to have sex with you? I want the intimacy, I want the verbal sparring matches we get into, I want to help you pick up those little seashells along the beach and I want to wake up with you beside me every day for the rest of my life. Rowling Energy and all I have there mean nothing in the grand scheme of things. I want the money and the power, but I want you more than any of that."

Catalina chewed on her bottom lip, trying to force her chin to stop quivering. She was on the verge of losing it and once the dam burst on her tears, she might never regain control.

"Before you decide, I don't want anything coming between us again," he went on. "I need to tell you something that is quite shocking and I just discovered myself."

Catalina reached up, gripped his wrists and eased his hands away from her face. She kept hold of him, but remained still. "What is it?"

"There's no easy way to tell you this without just saying it."

Fear pumped through her as her heart kicked up the pace. What on earth was he going to reveal? Whatever it was, it was a big deal. And once he told her his shocking news, she had a bombshell of her own to drop because she also couldn't move forward, with or without him, and still keep this secret.

"I found out that my father and your mother had an affair."

When Catalina stared at him for a moment, his eyes widened and he stepped back. She said nothing, but the look on his face told her all she needed to know.

"You already knew?" he asked in a whisper. "Didn't you?"

Cat nodded. Will's heart tightened. How had she known? How could she keep something so important from him?

"You've known awhile," he said, keeping his eyes on her unsurprised face. "How long?"

Cat blinked back the moisture that had gathered in her dark eyes. "Four years."

Rubbing the back of his neck, Will glanced down at

the floor. He couldn't look at her. Couldn't believe she'd keep such a monumental secret from him.

"I didn't know when we were together," she told him. "My mom told me after we broke up. I was so upset and she kept telling me how the Rowling men… Never mind. It's not important."

Everything about this was important, yet the affair really had nothing to do with how he felt for Cat. The sins of their parents didn't have to trickle down to them and ruin their happiness.

"I still can't believe you didn't say anything."

Cat turned, walked to the door and stared out into the backyard. Will took in her narrow shoulders, the exposed nape of her neck. She wasn't wearing her typical black shirt and pants. Right now she had on a pair of flat sandals, a floral skirt and some type of fitted shirt that sat right at the edge of her shoulders. She looked amazing and she was just out of his reach, physically and emotionally.

"I wanted to tell you on the island," she said, keeping her back to him. "I tried once, but we got sidetracked. That's an excuse. I should've made you listen, but we were so happy and there was no such thing as reality during those few days. I just wanted to stay in that euphoric moment."

He couldn't fault her for that because he'd felt the exact same way.

"There's just so much against us, Will." She turned back around and the lone tear on her cheek gutted him. "Sometimes people can love each other and still not be together. Sometimes love isn't enough and people just need to go their own way."

Will heard what she was saying, but how could he not hone in on the one main point to her farewell speech?

"You love me?" He couldn't help but smile as he crossed to her. "Say it, Cat. I want to hear the words."

She shook her head. "It doesn't mean anything."

"Say it." His hands settled around her waist as he pulled her flush against him. "Now."

"I love you, Will, but—"

He crushed his lips to hers. Nothing else mattered after those life-altering words. Nothing she could say would erase the fact that she loved him and he loved her, and he'd be damn it if he would ever let her walk away.

Her body melted against his as her fingers curled around his biceps. Will lifted his mouth from hers, barely.

"Don't leave, Cat," he murmured against her lips. "Don't leave Alma. Don't leave me."

"I can't give up who I am, Will." She closed her eyes and sighed. "No matter how much I love you, I can't give up everything I've worked for and I wouldn't expect you to give up your work for me. We have different goals in different directions."

The fear of losing her, the reality that if he didn't lay it all on the line, then she would be out of his life for good hit him hard.

"I'm coming with you."

Cat's eyes flew open as Will tipped his head back to see her face better. "What?"

"I meant what I said. I won't give you up and you're more to me than any business. But I can work from anywhere and I can fly to Alma when I need to."

"You can't be serious." Panic flooded her face. "This is rushed. You can't expect me to just say okay and we'll be on our way to happily-ever-after. It's too fast."

Will laughed. "I've known you since you were a little girl. I dated you four years ago and last weekend you spent nearly three days in my bed. You said you love me and I love the hell out of you and you think this is too fast? If we move any slower we'll be in a nursing home by the time you wear my ring on your finger."

"I can't think." Once again she pushed him aside and moved past him. "I can't take all this in. I mean, your dad and my mom…all of the things that have kept us apart. And then you corner me in a laundry room of all places to tell me you want me forever."

"So we don't do things the traditional way." He came up behind her, gripped her shoulders and kissed the top of her head. "I'm done with being by the book and boring. I want adventure, I want to be on a deserted island with the only woman in the world who can make me angry, laugh and love the way you do. I want to take care of you, I want to wear out the words *I love you* and I want to have no regrets from here on out where we are concerned."

Cat eased back against him, her head on his shoulder. "I want to believe all of that is possible. I want to hold on to the hope that I can still fulfill my dreams and I can have you. But I won't give up myself, no matter how much I love you, Will."

Wrapping his arms around her waist, he leaned his cheek on her head. "I wouldn't ask you to give up anything. I just didn't want you leaving Alma without me. We can live wherever you want. I have a jet, I have a yacht…well, I'll have a new one soon. I can travel where I need to be for work and I can take you where you need to go in order to fulfill this goal of yours. I want to be with you every step of your journey."

"I want to do it on my own," she stated, sliding her hands over his.

"I wouldn't dream of interfering," he replied. "I'll

support you in any way you need. I'll be the silent financial backer or I'll be the man keeping your bed warm at night and staying out of the business entirely. The choice is yours."

Cat turned in his arms, laced her hands behind his neck and stared up at him. "Tell me this is real. Tell me you don't hate me for keeping the secret and that you will always make me first in your life."

"It's real." He kissed her forehead. "I could never hate you." He kissed her nose. "And you'll never question again whether you're first in my life."

He slid his mouth across hers, gliding his hands down her body to the hem of her shirt. Easing the hem up, he smoothed his palms up over her bare skin, pleased when she shivered beneath his touch.

"Are you seriously trying to seduce me in a laundry room all while your sister-in-law is throwing a party to raise money for her foundation a few feet away?"

Will laughed as his lips traveled down the column of her throat. "I'm not trying. I'm about to succeed."

Cat's body arched back as her fingers threaded through his hair. "I hope no partygoers take a stroll through the backyard and glance in the window of the door," she panted when his hands brushed the underside of her breasts.

"We already made headlines." He jerked the shirt up and over her head, flinging it to the side without a care. "Another one won't matter at this point."

"What will your brother think if you don't show at the party?"

Will shrugged. "James is pretty smart. I'd say he'll know exactly where I am."

Cat started working on the buttons of his shirt and

soon sent the shirt and his jacket to the floor. "We still don't have a solid plan for our future."

Hoisting her up, Will sat her on the counter and settled between her legs. "I know how the next several minutes are going to play out. Beyond that I don't care so long as you're with me."

Will kissed her once more and eased back. "But I already have the perfect wedding present for you."

Cat laughed as her arms draped over his shoulders. "And what's that?"

"A maid. You'll not lift a finger for me ever. I want you to concentrate on your design career and the babies we're going to have in the future."

When Cat's smile widened and she tightened her hold on him, Will knew the four years he'd worked on getting back to her were worth it. Everything he'd sacrificed with his father and personal life was worth this moment, knowing he was building a future with the only woman he'd ever loved.

* * * * *

A ROYAL TEMPTATION

BY
CHARLENE SANDS

Charlene Sands is a *USA TODAY* bestselling author of more than thirty-five romance novels, writing sensual contemporary romances and stories of the Old West. Her books have been honored with a National Readers' Choice Award, a CataRomance Reviewers' Choice Award, and she's a double recipient of the Booksellers' Best Award. She belongs to the Orange County chapter and the Los Angeles chapter of RWA.

Charlene writes "hunky heroes with heart." She knows a little something about true romance—she married her high school sweetheart! When not writing, Charlene enjoys sunny Pacific beaches, great coffee, reading books from her favourite authors and spending time with her family. You can find her on Facebook and Twitter. Charlene loves to hear from her readers! You can write her at PO Box 4883, West Hills, CA 91308, USA or sign up for her newsletter for fun blogs and ongoing contests at www.charlenesands.com.

To Allyson Pearlman, Robin Rose,
Mary Hernandez and Pam Frendian. You're my crew,
my Best Friends Forever. Your friendship puts
lightness in my heart and a smile on my face every
day. I am surrounded by the best and I love you dearly.

One

Juan Carlos Salazar II stood at the altar in Saint Lucia's Cathedral, holding his head high as he accepted the responsibility and honor of being crowned King Montoro of Alma. In a dreamlike state he went through the motions that would bring the monarchy back to what it had once been decades ago. He'd been orphaned at a young age and taken in by his uncle. Since then, he'd lived a life filled with determination and dignity. He'd always known great things would come to him if he worked hard and kept his focus. But king? Never in his life would he have guessed his own true destiny.

With the golden orb and blessed scepter in his hands, he saw the austere ceremony in the cathedral was coming to a close. Prime Minister Rivera had given a speech full of renewed hope for the country, the small set of islands off the coast of Spain that had been ravaged by the now overthrown dictatorship of the Tantaberras. Seventy years of oppression overturned by loyal citizens, who looked to Juan Carlos for the reinstatement of a monarchy that would capture their hearts and minds.

Archbishop Santiago placed the royal robe over Juan Carlos's shoulders. As he took his seat on the throne, the archbishop set the jeweled crown of Alma upon his head. All of the tradition, ritual and protocol of the coronation had been observed, and he was now King Montoro of

Alma, the true heir to the throne. He spoke an oath and vowed to be much more than a figurehead as he promised to restore order and hope to the country.

It was a monumental time in Alma's history and he was happy to have the support of his cousins, Gabriel, Rafe and Bella. They were smiling and nodding their approval from their seats, Bella with tears in her eyes. They'd all lived and thrived in the United States before this, and forgive him, but heaven knew Rafe and Gabriel, who were once thought to be first in line to the throne but had been disqualified for separate and unique reasons, were not cut out for the rigors and sacrifice of royal life. They were only too glad to see Juan Carlos accept the position of sovereign.

A woman seated several rows behind his cousins caught his attention. Deep cerulean-blue eyes, clear and large, stood out against her porcelain face and white-blond hair. She reminded him of a snow queen from a fairy tale in his youth. And as he was ushered down the aisle after the coronation their gazes locked for an instant and her one eyelid closed in a wink. Was it for him? His lips immediately quirked up at the notion and he forced the smile from his expression. Still, his heart did a little tumble as it had been doing all day, but this time it was the woman, and not the ceremony, that had caused the commotion.

The next hour passed, again in dreamlike wonder, as he was escorted out of the cathedral by Alma's finest royal guards, to be met with unrestrained jubilation all along the parade route. He sat atop a convertible car and waved with gloved hands, as they made their way toward the palace. And there, on the top steps of Alma's regal old-world palace, Juan Carlos began his first speech as king.

"Citizens of Alma, as your new king, I promise to honor the sovereignty of our nation, to always put the country first and to work alongside our parliament to restore our democracy. It is a vow I take with an open but steady heart and a determination to see that our freedoms are never threatened again."

Cheers went up. "Viva Juan Carlos!"

Juan Carlos waited until the crowd calmed to finish a speech that was interrupted three more times by applause.

He left the palace steps energized, instilled with the very same hope he saw in the eyes of his fellow countrymen. He was a foreigner, by all rights, an American, and yet, they'd accepted him and looked to him to help establish a newer, brighter Alma.

He would not let them down.

As austere as his day was, he took a moment to reflect on the coronation and picture the beautiful woman in the light blue chiffon gown, her eyes as vibrant as deep ocean waters. He'd searched for her during the procession, the parade and the speech that followed, only to be disappointed.

She'd been a diversion from the gravity of the day.

Winking at him had brought a smile to his lips.

Who was she?

And would she have his children?

"Do I need to call you Your Highness?" his cousin Rafe asked as he pumped Juan Carlos's hand. They stood off to the side in the palace's grand ballroom. The coronation gala was well underway and the orchestra played lively tunes. An array of fresh flowers decorated the arched entryways, aisles and tables.

"You mean, as opposed to Squirt, Idiot and Bonehead like when we were kids?"

"Hey, I wasn't that bad."

"You were a year older and that gave you bullying rights."

"Okay, guilty as charged. But now you can have me hung by the neck until dead."

"I could've done that to you back then, too."

"Ha, funny."

"Call me Juan Carlos or cuz, just like you do now. Your Highness comes into play only on formal occasions or royal business."

All amusement on his cousin's face disappeared. "Seriously, Juan Carlos, congratulations. The family is proud of you. You're the only one of the lot who was cut out for this. You are honoring our aunt Isabella's final wishes by restoring the monarchy."

Juan Carlos came to the throne quite by accident, after Bella discovered a secret cache of letters that revealed Rafe, Gabriel and Bella's late grandfather, Raphael Montoro II, was illegitimate and not the true heir to the throne. As such, neither of Juan Carlos's cousins would have been the rightful king. The former queen's indiscretion had been kept hidden all these years until her great-grandchildren had uncovered it.

"Thank you, cousin. I've thought about my grandmother these past few weeks and I think she would approve. It means a great deal to me." He sighed. "I hope to make a diff—" He caught a glimpse of a woman in blue and craned his neck to get a better look.

It was her. She was attending the gala. Only dignitaries, friends and family members along with the royal photographers and journalists had been invited to the party, two hundred strong.

"Hey," Rafe asked. "What are you stretching your neck to see?"

"She's here," he muttered, without shifting his gaze. She was standing near an archway leading to the foyer, looking to make an escape.

"Juan Carlos?"

"Oh, uh, I saw a woman at the coronation and I haven't stopped thinking about her."

"This I've got to see. Any woman who can take your

mind off a day as big as this has got to be something special. Where is she?"

"I'm not going to point. Just look for the most beautiful woman in the room and you'll find her."

"Emily is right there, talking to Bella."

"Spoken like a besotted newlywed. Okay, yes, Emily is gorgeous, now find a woman in blue who is not your wife."

"If you'd agreed to a formal receiving line, you'd have met her already."

He hadn't wanted a stiff, awkward line of people congratulating him. He'd make his way over to his guests and speak with them during the course of the evening. He'd vowed to be a king *of* the people and *for* the people and that started right now. "Do you see her?"

"Ah, I do see her now. Very blonde, nice body, great eyes."

"That's her. Do you know who she is?"

"No, but apparently she knows Alex and Maria Ramon. They just walked up to her and they appear friendly."

"Well, then, I think it's time I spoke with Alma's deputy prime minister of commerce and his wife, don't you?"

Juan Carlos moved swiftly across the ballroom and as he approached, Alex spotted him and smiled. "Your Highness." Juan Carlos nodded. It would take some time getting used to that greeting.

Maria, not one to stand on ceremony, hugged his neck. She and Alex had just married and postponed their honeymoon to attend the coronation. "I'm happy to see this day, Your Highness. You are just what Alma needs."

"Thank you, Maria."

As he made eye contact with the blonde woman, it felt as if something quick and sharp had pierced his body. Her eyes were large, shaped like perfect twin almonds, the sparkle in them as bright as any star. Mesmerized, he couldn't look away.

"And please, let me introduce you to Portia Lindstrom, Princess of Samforstand."

Princess?

She *could* have his children.

Juan Carlos offered her his hand and at the touch of her delicate palm, he once again felt that quick, sharp sensation. "Nice to meet you, Princess. I'm glad you could make the coronation. It's a good day for Alma, I hope."

"I'm sure it will be, Your Majesty. And please, call me Portia."

"I will," he said. "If you call me Juan Carlos."

A pink cast tinged her porcelain skin. "I couldn't."

"Why not?"

"Because, you're the king."

"I'll let you in on a secret. Up until a few months ago, I was living in Miami and running a rather large business conglomerate. I'm afraid I still have American ties and king is not in their vocabulary, unless we're talking about Elvis."

She smiled. "I live in America, too. I'm on the west coast right now. My family was from a tiny country near Scandinavia."

"Well, then, we have a lot in common. As you can see, Alma is not a large country, either."

Maria and Alex exchanged looks and excused themselves. He'd forgotten they were there. It was rude of him. But now, he was alone with Portia.

"You are a curiosity. You won't call me Juan Carlos, but yet you wink at me just as I am crowned king."

Portia froze. Surely the king didn't believe she'd actually winked at him. It was that darn nervous twitch of hers. It would have to happen at the exact moment she'd first made eye contact with him. She should be immune to royalty—she'd met enough princes and princesses in her twenty-eight years—but Juan Carlos Salazar seemed different, strikingly handsome and down to earth. Before she could explain about the wink, the orchestra began playing a lovely Latin waltz.

He bowed in old world fashion. "Princess Portia, I'd be honored if you danced with me."

"I'm afraid I don't waltz."

"Neither do I," he replied. "We can wing it and set a new trend."

She chuckled. He didn't act like the stuffed-shirt royals she'd met in the past, and when he took her hand and led her to the unoccupied dance floor, she didn't protest. He was a better dancer than he let on, and she glided across the floor with him, fully aware every set of eyes in the room were on them.

"We're the only ones out here," she whispered.

He grinned, flashing white teeth against golden-brown skin. He was tall and dashing and at the moment, charming her silly by staring into her eyes as if she was the only person who existed in the world. It was quite flattering.

"Don't worry. Other guests will join in after the king's first dance. It's tradition."

"Then I should be honored you picked me."

"After that wink, how could I not pick you?" He held her possessively and spoke with authority, as if he'd been king all of his life.

"It was a twitch. I had something in my eye."

"I choose to believe it was a wink."

"Yes, Your Highness."

He smiled again and moved her across the dance floor as if she were light as air.

When the dance ended, he didn't release her hand. "Will you take a walk with me?"

"You want to leave your own gala?"

He shrugged and didn't appear worried. "It's been a long, monumental day. I could use a little break."

Portia couldn't very well say no. And getting some fresh air did sound good. Because of her title, she'd been invited to the gala, and to refuse such a high honor would've been unheard of. Her mother and father's greatest wish, as her grandmother told it, was for her to remain true to her royal bloodlines, even while having a career and life of her own. So she juggled her time accordingly, to honor her deceased parents' wishes. She hadn't had enough time with them, but she'd hoped to make them proud. "Well, then, yes. I'll walk with you."

They strode off the dance floor in silence. His hand pressed to her back, he guided her toward a small back door and they ducked out to a deserted foyer. "There are private gardens just outside where we can sit."

He opened a door she was sure only royals were privy to, and a gust of cool autumn air hit her. Without a second's hesitation, Juan Carlos removed his tuxedo jacket and placed it around her shoulders. "Better?"

"Yes, thank you." She tugged the lapels closed and kept her hands there, away from the king's tempting grasp. His dark eyes were on her every move, and when he touched her, her pulse raced in a way it hadn't in a very long time.

He led her to grounds surrounded by lattices covered with vines. "Would you like to sit down?"

"Okay."

She sat on a delicately woven rattan love seat and he lowered down beside her, his six-foot presence looming large next to her. Aware of the solid breadth of his shoulders and the scent of his skin, she found the new king of Alma a little too appealing. "It's nice here. Quiet," she said. "You must be exhausted."

"Yes, but invigorated, too. If that makes any sense to you."

"It does. When I'm researching a piece of art for a client, I might work sixteen-hour days, but I always get excited when I locate it." His brows came together as if he were puzzled. "I'm an art advisor," she explained. "I help collectors build their collections."

"Impressive. And do you work in your country?"

"I'm based out of Los Angeles and New York. I don't spend any time in Samforstand."

"That's how it was for me. I worked out of Miami and New York, but now, Alma will be my permanent home. My duty is here and I will adjust. The country is beautiful, so it won't be a hardship."

"Excuse me, Your Highness," said a voice from behind the bench.

"Yes?" Juan Carlos turned around.

"I'm sorry to interrupt, but Chancellor Benoit has been called away and insists on saying his farewells to you personally. He is waiting in the antechamber."

"All right, thank you. Please tell the chancellor I will be in to see him shortly."

The man gave a curt nod and walked off.

"Well, looks like duty calls. I'm sorry." He rose and extended his hand. "Please save another dance for me tonight, Portia. There's more I want to learn about...*art advising*." He smiled.

Her heart hammered. She didn't know what to make of the cocoon-like hold he had on her. She'd only just met him and already he was wrapping himself around her thoughts with his silent compliments and easy ways. "I will."

She rose and he walked her back to the ballroom, depositing her exactly where he'd found her, beside Maria and Alex.

"I will be back," he said.

Portia's throat hitched and she nodded.

"Looks like the king is smitten." Maria kept her voice

low enough for only Portia's ears. She was sure Maria, a public relations expert and friend, had been instrumental in her receiving an invitation to the coronation and gala.

"He's being gracious, Maria."

Maria seemed to ignore her comment. "He's a good man."

"Perfect for Alma. But not for me." She was attracted to Juan Carlos. Any woman with blood running through her veins would be, but talk about high profile. You couldn't get much higher, and that's the last thing Portia needed in her life. It had taken her three years to climb out of the hole she'd dug for herself by getting involved with the Duke of Discourse, Travis Miles, LA's favorite talk show host.

Charming, debonair and controversial, he'd dragged her into his limelight from the start of their love affair to the bitter, heartbreaking end. Her career had suffered as the details of his neglect and wandering eye came into play. She'd almost lost all credibility with her clients. Luckily, she'd managed her way out of that situation, vowing to keep a low profile, stay in the small circle of the art world and not allow another high-profile charmer to get to her. And that included the king of Alma.

"I don't know about that," Maria said, matter-of-factly.

"I do," she said, convincing herself of that very thing. "I have an important meeting in Los Angeles with a client in a few days."

"A lot could happen in a few days, Portia."

But the conversation ended when a nice-looking gentleman approached, introduced himself as Alma's secretary of defense, and asked her to dance.

Portia accepted, and as she was being led to the dance floor, shot an over-the-shoulder glance at Maria.

Only to find Juan Carlos standing there, his gaze following her every movement.

He had indeed come back for her.

* * *

Gnashing his teeth, Juan Carlos ran a hand down his face to cover the tightness in his jaw. Princess Portia had danced nonstop with three men since he'd returned from seeing Chancellor Benoit off. Every time Juan Carlos thought to approach, he was interrupted or summoned into a conversation with a group of dignitaries. He couldn't fall short of his duties on his coronation day, yet the beautiful snow queen consumed his thoughts, and as he spoke with others, he kept one eye on Portia.

Finally free from conversations, he had an aide approach the orchestra and suggest that they take a five-minute break. The music died instantly and Juan Carlos strode over to the table where Portia had just taken a seat. "Hello again."

Those startling blue eyes lifted to him. "Hello."

"I'm happy to see you having a good time."

"I am," she said. "Would you like to sit down?"

"I have a better idea."

Her eyes twinkled. "Really? What would that be?"

He offered his hand again, hoping she'd take it. "Come with me and find out."

Her hesitation rattled his nerves. "Where?"

"Trust me and I'll show you."

She rose then, and as they walked out of the ballroom again with her hand in his, she watched him carefully. She had no reason not to trust him. He would never steer her wrong.

"In here," he said.

He tugged her into a spacious office and shut the door. It was black as coal at first, but the light of the full moon streamed in and his eyes adjusted so that he could make out Portia's silhouette. He took her gently into his arms and overwhelming sensations rushed through his body. Silently, with a look, she questioned his actions, but with his eyes he assured her she had nothing to fear. Then the orchestra began playing and as music piped into the room through the air ducts, he began to move her along to the beat. She tossed her head back and laughed. "You aren't serious."

He grinned. "It's the only way I can assure us not being interrupted again."

"You are resourceful, Your Highness. We have an entire dance floor all to ourselves."

"What would make it perfect would be if you'd call me Juan Carlos."

"But you've earned the right to be called king."

"Tonight, for now, think of me as a man, and not a king."

"I'll try, but you have to understand, after all the adoration, the photos and parades and galas in your honor, it's not easy for me."

He did understand, but pressed his reasoning a little further. "Think of it this way. How would you like it if everyone you knew called you Princess Portia?"

She gave it some thought and nodded. "I see your point."

He drew her inches closer, so that her sweet breaths touched his face, but he didn't dare do more. Though he wanted to crush her against him, feel her body sway with his, he couldn't rush her or scare her off. These feelings pulsed through him with near desperation. He'd never been so…besotted. Such an old-world word, but that's exactly how he felt.

"How long will you be in Alma?" he asked.

"I leave for the States in two days. I'm due back at work."

News he didn't want to hear. "Are you working with a client?"

"Yes, he's someone very influential and I'm thrilled to have the chance to meet with him for the first time. He's new to collecting, and I have an interview with him to see where his tastes lie."

"I see. It's a good opportunity for you. I would imagine being Princess Portia of Samforstand carries some weight in your line of work."

"I'll admit, using my royal heritage has helped me attain clients, but it's my expertise that has earned their trust."

"Trust is important," he said.

"You have the trust of the entire country right now."

"Yes," he said, sighing. "It's a big responsibility. I'm sure you take your responsibility seriously."

"I do. My reputation earns me that trust and I guard it like a mother would her child."

He smiled at the image gathering in his mind, of Portia, mother of his child.

Dios. He was in deep. How was it possible? He had known her less than a day.

And already, he was naming their first-born child.

Two

Stately and grand, Portia's hotel in Del Sol was just a short distance from the palace. The big bed in her room was cushy and comfy. The morning sunlight streamed in to warm her and the air was sweetened by a bouquet of roses, compliments of the hotel manager. It was all fit for a princess. Yet she hadn't slept well.

Last night, as Juan Carlos bid her farewell, he'd almost kissed her. She was sure he would have if they hadn't been surrounded by his guests. She'd thought about that non-kiss during the night. How would his lips feel against hers? Heavens, she hadn't had so much as a date with a man in almost a year, and it had been even longer since she was ravaged by a kiss. Which, she was sure, would have happened had they been alone.

She was thankful that he hadn't locked lips with her in front of the attendees at the gala. Yet, lightbulbs had flashed and pictures had been snapped of the two of them. It was last thing she needed and she'd dashed out as rapidly as Cinderella racing against the midnight hour.

When he'd asked her to join him for brunch this morning, she'd quickly agreed, despite her tingling nerves and fuzzy brain.

Her brunch "date" with the King of Montoro would happen precisely at ten o'clock and he'd promised they wouldn't be interrupted.

She heard the familiar Bruno Mars ringtone of her cell phone and grabbed it from the nightstand. Her assistant's name popped up on the screen and she smiled. From the very beginning, her assistant had been her closest friend. "Hello, Jasmine."

"Hi, Portia. I hope I didn't wake you?"

"No, not at all. I'm getting ready to have brunch. It's good to hear your voice."

"Did you survive the coronation?" Jasmine Farr never minced words. "I know you weren't thrilled about attending."

"Actually, it wasn't so bad." The newly named king was quite a man. "And it's my lot in life to attend these functions every so often."

"That's what you get for being a princess." She chuckled. "I saw some of the coronation on YouTube."

"That was fast."

"It always is. Anyway, I'm calling to tell you that Mr. Greenboro had to cancel your meeting this week. He's flying out of the country and won't be back for three months. He sends his apologies, of course, and he did reschedule. I hope it's okay that I took the liberty of making that appointment. I didn't think you'd want to let him get away."

"Oh, I'm disappointed. I'd set the entire week aside to work with him, but I'm glad you're on the ball and rescheduled with him. Text me that date and I'll mark it on my calendar."

"Will do. So, now you don't have to rush back. There's really nothing else going on this week."

"Right."

"You've worked hard these past few months and you've been meaning to pencil in a vacation. Seems like a perfect opportunity."

"It is beautiful here."

"From the pictures I'm seeing, the beaches are to die for. I wish I could join you. I'd come in an instant."

"Why don't you come? We could have spa days together."

"I can't. I'm flying to Maryland for my cousin's wedding at the end of the week. "

"I'd forgotten about that. Darn."

"But that doesn't mean you can't stay on. I can book you a villa suite in Playa del Onda. The beach resort is top notch. You'll get lots of R&R."

"Let me think about it. I'll get back to you later on today."

After she ended the call, she stripped off her pajamas and entered the shower. The pounding water rained down and woke her up to the possibility of an actual vacation: away from phones, away from the hectic pace of gallery openings, away from the pressures of making art selections for her obscenely rich or drastically eccentric clients. Her schedule was a busy one, and this did seem like a perfect opportunity to unwind.

When she was finished with her shower, she slipped into a white dress with red polka dots that belted at the waist, slid on navy patent leather shoes and tossed her hair up into a ponytail. She applied light makeup, including eyeliner and soft pink lip gloss.

The jewelry she chose was delicate: a thin strand of pearls around her neck and wrist. She fastened her watch on her left arm and noted the time. Juan Carlos was sending a car for her in ten minutes. She grabbed her purse and left the hotel room.

In the lobby, she was greeted by a uniformed driver who escorted her to an ink-black limousine. She played the role of princess well, but she would rather be wearing a pair of jeans and going to the local café for a bite of breakfast.

"Your Highness," the driver said, as he opened the door for her, "allow me."

She slid into the backseat and bumped legs with Juan Carlos. Her breath hitched in her throat. He took in her wide-eyed surprise and grinned. "Good morning, Portia."

"Excuse me, but I didn't expect you to come to pick me up."

Should she worry about the implications? This wasn't a date. At least, not in any real sense.

"It's a nice morning for a drive. After yesterday's events, I thought you might like to join me to see some of the city. I hope you don't mind, but I've changed our brunch plans for today."

He wore dark slacks and a casual white silk shirt, opened slightly at the collar. She glimpsed his tanned chest and gulped for air.

"Of course not."

"Great. You look very pretty this morning."

"Thank you." *And you look dynamic, powerful and gorgeous.*

He issued directions to the driver and they took off.

"How were your first twenty-four hours as king?" she asked.

He rubbed his chin, thinking for a second. "It's strange that I don't feel any different. I keep expecting a big transformation, but I'm just me."

She smiled at his earnest answer. "I thought it would be an adjustment for you. Every move you make now will be documented somehow." She glanced out the window, expecting to see photographers following the limo, snapping pictures. She'd had experience with her ex-boyfriend's fame and it had gotten old very fast. No one should be followed and photographed at every turn for entertainment's sake. "How did you escape the palace?"

He chuckled. "You make it seem like prison."

"No, no. I'm sorry. That's not what I meant."

"I know what you meant, Portia." Her name slid effortlessly from his lips. "There are some advantages to being king."

"Such as?" she probed.

"Such as, I didn't make my intentions known. No one expected me to take a drive this morning. No one questioned me. I had the car ready to pick you up, and then I merely slipped into the backseat before anyone at the palace got wind of it."

"You snuck out."

He laughed again and she joined in. "Okay, yes. I snuck out."

Speaking to him put her at ease and she settled back in her seat. "Do you have bodyguards?"

"Yes, they are following behind somewhere."

"You're not worried?"

He shook his head. "No. I'm not worried. And neither should you be."

"Okay, I'll trust you." She'd never traveled with bodyguards, but her situation was quite different. As an exiled princess, she'd grown up in America and never had what Juan Carlos now had: a citizenry eager to reinstate their monarchy. "But you must have dozens of dignitaries and family members waiting to speak with you at the palace."

"Which I will do later. But for now," he said, reaching for her hand, "I find being with you more important."

Juan Carlos held her hand during the tour of the city. He showed her sites of great historical significance and some trendy new hot spots that were cropping up. The rise of democracy was good for enterprise, he explained.

As he spoke, the tone of his deep and sincere voice brought a smile to her lips more times than she could count. It was intimate in a way, hearing the love he had for a country that was almost as new to him as it was to her. He kept her hand locked in his as if it was precious. As if he needed the connection. To hear him say that being with her was important did wonders for her ego.

Yet she only indulged him because nothing could possibly come of it. And because it had been a long time since she'd enjoyed a man's company so much.

Tomorrow, she would leave Del Sol.

The limo stopped at a tiny café off the main street of town. "I hear Matteo's is fantastic."

"You've never eaten here before?" she asked.

"No, I haven't. We'll experience it together. Do you mind?"

"I love adventure."

He nodded, a satisfied glimmer in his eyes. "I thought you might."

They exited the limo, which looked out of place on the backstreets of the royal city. Once inside, they were escorted to their table by the owner. He was sweating, nervous and fidgety. Juan Carlos clapped him on the back gently to reassure him. "Bring us your specials, Matteo. I hear they are the best in all of Del Sol."

"*Si, si.* I will be glad to serve you myself, Your Majesty."

Juan Carlos nodded. "Thank you."

Though the café walls showed signs of age, it was a clean, modest place. "Are you sure the food is good here?" she asked.

His brows gathered. "It comes highly recommended. Why?"

"We're the only ones seated."

Juan Carlos looked around the empty café. "My bodyguards. They called ahead to announce my arrival. I'll make it up to Matteo. I can't have him losing business on my account."

"I'm sure he'll be boasting that King Montoro of Alma dined in his café. His business will double by next week."

Juan Carlos sharpened his gaze on her. "I hadn't thought of that."

"You're new to this royal thing."

"Yes, I guess I am."

Just wait, she wanted to say. He was an intelligent man, from all she'd read about him. He managed the sizable personal accounts of the Montoros and had helped build a fortune for the family. He had wits and smarts, but nothing would prepare him for the limelight he'd just entered. He'd have to experience it himself, the good, the bad, the ugly. His life would be under a microscope now.

And she didn't want to be the amoeba next to him.

Coffee was served, along with fresh handmade tortillas, butter and a bowl of cut fruit. "Looks delicious," Juan Carlos said to Matteo.

"Please, is there anything else I can bring you while the meal is cooking?"

"This is perfect. Don't you agree, Portia?"

She nodded and smiled at the owner.

When Matteo left the room she continued to smile. "You're kind. He will always remember this day because you put him at ease."

Travis Miles had been kind, too, in the beginning.

"Now who is being kind?" he asked.

"I'm just speaking the truth. You'll impact a great many lives."

"In a positive way, I hope and pray."

"Kind," she repeated. "You care about the people in the country."

"Thank you." His incredibly warm brown eyes softened and her stomach did a little flip.

She buttered a tortilla, rolled it up and took a few bites. She sipped coffee and asked Juan Carlos a few pointed questions about his life to keep the conversation flowing and her mind off the fact that King Montoro was a hunk.

The meal was delivered with fanfare. Matteo and his staff put out the dishes in sweeping motions and finally left them to dine privately. The food was delicious. The main dish consisted of bits of sautéed pork topped with eggs and lathered with a creamy, mildly spicy sauce. There was also some type of sweet corn soufflé served inside the husks, as well as caramelized plantains. Every bite she took rewarded her taste buds. "Mmm…this is heavenly."

Juan Carlos nodded, his mouth full.

As he chewed, his gaze remained on her. He had warm, luxurious, intense eyes that didn't stray. Goose bumps rode up and down her arms. As far as men went, Juan Carlos had it all, except for one thing. His fatal flaw. He was king. And that meant after today, she couldn't see him again.

"So what are your plans for the rest of the day?" he asked.

"Oh, I'm, uh, going to…" She really didn't have any plans. Maybe do a little shopping. Check out the only art museum in the city. "I'll be packing."

"That can't take all day."

"I wouldn't think so."

"Would you consider having dinner with me?"

No. No. No. "I really shouldn't."

Juan Carlos leaned back in his seat, studying her. "Do you have a man in your life, Portia?"

Slowly, she shook her head. She felt a trap coming.

"No one? I find that hard to believe. Do you date?"

"Rarely. My career is demanding. And it's very important to me. I've worked hard to get where I am."

"Admirable. Are you working tonight?"

"No, but I…"

He grinned. "I'm only asking for a dinner date, Portia."

Her shoulders sagged an inch. A barely noticeable move,

but she felt the defeat all the way down to her toes. She couldn't insult the king. "Then, yes, I'll have dinner with you."

After the meal, Juan Carlos escorted her to the limo. She took a seat at the far window and he climbed in after her. To his credit, he didn't crowd her, leaving a modest amount of space between them. But as the car took off, he placed his hand over hers on the empty seat, and wild pings of awareness shot through her body.

Don't let him get to you, Portia.

He's not the man for you.

As the limo pulled up to the hotel, Juan Carlos spoke to the driver. "Give us a minute please, Roberto."

The driver's door opened and closed quietly. Silence filled the air and suddenly she did feel crowded, though Juan Carlos hadn't made a move toward her. "I cannot walk you to your door, Princess."

"I understand."

"Do you? Do you know how much I want to?" His eyes were down, gazing at her hand as his thumb worked circles over her fingers. Her nerves jumped, like kernels of corn popping in a fry pan, one right after the other. "I don't want to cause you any inconvenience."

"I...know."

He tugged her hand gently and she fell forward, closing the gap between them. His dark-fringed eyelids lifted; she was struck by all-consuming heat. He wasn't moving a muscle, but leaving it up to her. As if she had a choice now. As if she could deny him. His mesmerizing hunger was contagious; years of abstinence made her hungry, as well. Her gaze lowered to his mouth. Lord in heaven, she wanted his kiss.

She moistened her lips and his eyes drew down immediately. "You leave me no choice, Princess."

He used a finger to tilt her chin, and then bent his head

toward her. Anticipation pulsed through her veins. Every single second was an unnerving kind of torture. And finally, his mouth was on hers, his hand coming to wrap more firmly around her jaw, as if he couldn't get enough, as if he would devour her.

Long live the king!

Her tummy ached from goodness and she indulged like a miser finding a hidden supply of cash. She touched his face, his jaw steel under her fingertips, and a groan erupted from his throat.

A whimpering mewling sound came from hers. Mortification would have set in, if the king wasn't equally as needy. But there was no shame, just honesty, and it was, after all, the kiss to end all kisses. Juan Carlos didn't let up, not for a moment. His lips worked hers hard, then soft, then hard again. Under her dress, her nipples ached. She was pretty sure the king was experiencing the same agony, but farther south on his body.

She didn't know whose mouth opened first, or whether it was at the exact same instant, but suddenly she was being swept up and hollowed out, his tongue doing a thorough job of ravaging her. Any second now, she'd be out of her head with lust. But Juan Carlos placed his hands on her shoulders and, she sensed, with great reluctance, moved her away from him.

He leaned back against the seat, breathing hard. "I've never made love to a woman in a limo before, Princess. It wouldn't take much to change that," he said. He tried for amusement, tried to chuckle, but a serious tone had given away his innermost thoughts.

"It would be a first for me, too," she said, coming up for air.

A rumpled mess, she tried her best to straighten herself out before she exited the limo.

He pressed a button and the window rolled down. Roberto appeared by the car door. "See Princess Portia to her hotel room," Juan Carlos said calmly. He'd gotten his emotions in check already, while she was still a ravaged jumble of nerves.

Again, those warm brown eyes lit upon her. "I'll send a car to pick you up for dinner at seven."

She swallowed. "Maybe...we shouldn't," she squeaked.

"Are you afraid of me?" he asked, though his confident tone indicated that it wasn't even a concern.

She shook her head. "I'm leaving in the morning."

"And you love your job. Your career means a lot to you. Yes, that's clear."

He'd made her refusal seem silly. And it was. Nothing would happen unless she wanted it to happen. She already knew Juan Carlos was that type of man.

"I'll see you tonight," she said finally. When the driver opened the car door, she rushed out.

She hadn't exactly lied to him, had she?

She said she'd be gone, and he thought she meant back to the States. But she'd made up her mind to vacation on the shores of Alma, at least until the end of the week.

But he didn't need to know that.

After a late lunch, Juan Carlos had a meeting in the city with the prime minister and few of Alma's most trusted and prominent business leaders. He struggled to keep his mind on the topics at hand. The restoration of the entire country was a tall order. But every so often, his mind traveled to that place where Portia was in his arms. The image of her lips locked on his, their bodies pulsing to the same lusty rhythms, knocked him for a loop and sent his brain waves scrambling. She was, in his estimation, perfect. For him. For the country.

Wow. Where had that come from? Why was he thinking of her in terms of permanence? As a queen for Alma, for goodness' sake.

Because aside from the fact that his sensual response was like the national flag being hoisted to full mast every time he looked at her, there was no doubt in his mind that she could take a place by his side at the throne.

As a public figure, he was never alone much anymore, but that didn't mean he wasn't lonely. He hadn't had a serious relationship for years. His ambition had gotten in the way and sure, he'd had a few women in his life, but nothing serious. No one who'd made him feel like this.

Portia's face flashed in his mind, that porcelain skin, those ice-blue eyes, that haughty chin, that mouth that tasted like sweet sin. The snow queen had become important to him in a short time, and…

"Your Majesty? Juan Carlos, are you all right?"

"Huh? Oh, yeah, I'm fine." Prime Minister Rivera was giving him a strange look. "Just deep in thought."

They'd been talking about how to bring new enterprise to Alma and how the rise of the monarchy would bring in tourism. They needed to brand themselves as a free country and show the world that democracy reigned, that new visitors and new businesses were welcome to their stunning Atlantic shores.

"Actually, I have an idea as to how to draw more tourists," Juan Carlos said.

"Really?"

Alex Ramon's ears perked up. As the deputy prime minister of commerce, he was fully immersed in the issue. "Tell us your thoughts."

"It's been rumored in our family for years that our ancestors had stashed a considerable amount of artwork, sculptures and paintings on land that had fallen to ruin. Land that Tantaberra overlooked. Right before the family was deposed, they'd thought to hide the art so it wouldn't fall into the dictator's greedy hands."

Juan Carlos's mind was clicking fast. He didn't know how true those rumors were. He'd only heard the tales while growing up; Uncle Rafael had spoken of hidden treasures the way a master storyteller would about a pirate's bounty. It had all been exciting, the sort of thing that captured a little boy's imagination. But the rumors had held fast and true during his adulthood, and only recently, his cousin Bella had found a hidden cache of letters at one of the family's abandoned farms, letters that proved that he, a Salazar and not a Montoro, was the rightful heir to the throne.

"I have plans to visit the area myself and see what I can find. If it's true, and artwork is indeed on the property, think of the story. The art could be restored, and we could have a special showing or a series of showings to bring awareness to Alma."

"It's genius, Your Highness," Prime Minister Rivera said.

Others around the board table agreed.

The meeting ran long and Juan Carlos didn't get back to the palace until six. He had just enough time to shower and dress for dinner. His pulse sped up as he thought of Portia again, of her sweetly exotic scent and the way she'd filled his body with pleasure when he was near her. She caused him to gasp and sweat and breathe hard. It wasn't ideal. She was a hard case. She didn't seem interested in him. And that worried him, because as far as he was concerned, she was The One.

He came down at precisely six forty-five and bumped into his new secretary at the base of the winding staircase, nearly knocking the clipboard out of her hands. "Oh, sorry, Your Highness." She was out of breath, as if she'd been running a marathon.

"My apologies," he said. "I've been preoccupied and didn't see you."

Alicia was redheaded, shapely and quite efficient. She wore glasses, but under those glasses were pretty, light green eyes. She'd taken on a lot, being a first hire, as there was much ground to cover. "Your seven o'clock appointment is here."

Warmth spread through his body at the mention of his dinner date. "Princess Portia?"

"Oh, uh. No, Your Highness. I'm sorry. I don't see Princess Portia on the books." She studied her clipboard, going over the names. "No, you have appointments every half hour for the next few hours. I penciled in a dinner break for you at nine."

"I thought those were on tomorrow night's schedule." Surely, he hadn't been mistaken, had he? Yet he had to take Alicia at her word. He'd already come to find that she rarely if ever made mistakes. He, on the other hand, had been hypnotized by a pair of deep ocean-blue eyes and was more than distracted.

"I can't possibly make all of those appointments." High-ranking officials and the heads of businesses along with their wives or husbands wanted to meet the new king. It was as simple as that. It was good for commerce to know the pillars of trade in Alma, so he'd agreed to a few evening appointments. Under normal circumstances, he'd rather cut off his right arm than cancel them, but he couldn't break a date with Portia. "See what you can do about cancelling them. Who was first on the schedule?"

"Mr. and Mrs. Rubino. The Rubinos are in the royal study. And your next appointment after that is already here, I'm afraid. They are notoriously early for every occasion, I'm told. They are waiting in the throne room."

He ran his hands through his hair. "Fine. I'll see them. But see what you can do about cancelling the rest."

"Yes, Your Highness. I'll do my best." She bit her lower lip, her eyes downcast. "Sorry for the confusion."

"Alicia?"

"Yes?"

"It's not your doing. I forgot about these appointments. We're all learning here. It's new to all of us."

She had ten years of experience running a duke's household in London, coordinating parties and events with dignitaries and the royal family. She hadn't much to learn. He was the one who had screwed up.

"Yes, Your Highness. I'll get on those cancellations right away."

Juan Carlos rubbed the back of his neck and headed to the study.

With luck, he could salvage the evening.

Portia had been stood up. She'd been delivered to the palace minutes before seven, only to be informed that the king had visitors and to please be patient and wait. She was shown to the dining room and shortly after, the palace chef himself had set dishes of appetizers on the table before her.

Candles were lit and soft music filtered into the room.

The only problem? Her date wasn't here. And she wasn't about to eat a thing until he showed. Call her stubborn.

It was after eight. She knew because her stomach refused to stop growling and finally, she'd glanced at her watch.

She'd already taken in the paintings on the walls, assessing them and noting that they weren't up to par with usual palatial art. Oh, they were lovely pieces, but from contemporary artists. Many of them were replicas of the real thing. It was a curiosity. The monarchy stretched way beyond the years of the dictatorship. There should be older, more authentic works on the walls. But this was only one room. Maybe for security reasons, the gallery held the most valuable pieces.

After wandering the dining hall, she picked a particular patch of space near the fireplace and began pacing.

She couldn't fault Juan Carlos. His secretary had taken the blame, explaining that she'd failed to remind the king of his visitors. She'd tried her best to cancel the meetings, but she was afraid she wasn't as successful as she'd hoped.

But the more Portia thought about it, the more pangs of anger replaced her patience.

How long would he keep her waiting?

Travis is in a meeting. He won't be available for hours. He'd like you to wait, though.

This isn't the same thing, she reminded herself. Her ex-boyfriend wasn't a king. Well, maybe the king of late-night television. And she'd fallen for him. He was funny and charming and kind. It was like a regular Cinderella story, the poor broke comedian hooks up with a real live princess. Travis was far from poor now, although he'd come from humble beginnings and the press loved their story and ate it up.

A new American fairy tale, they'd called it.

Travis had been on top of the world when they were together. Everyone loved him and thought he was worthy of a princess from an obscure little country. Only dating a supermodel would have given him more credibility.

And here she was, doing the same thing. Another American fairy tale, only this time with a real king.

Stupid of her.

Her nerves were jumpy and by the time eight-thirty rolled around, she was royally pissed.

Juan Carlos had twisted her arm to accept this dinner date, the way charming men did. He'd trapped her and then kissed her until every brain cell was lulled into capitulation. God, she'd been looking forward to being alone with him again. That kiss was good. Better than good. It was the best kiss she'd ever had. Not even Travis could kiss like that, and he'd been plenty experienced in that department.

"Sorry, so sorry, Portia."

She jumped. "Oh!" Juan Carlos entered the room, looking dashing in a dark buttoned-up suit but no tie. Another growl emitted from her stomach, this time not due to hunger.

"Did Alicia explain what happened? It was my fault. This is the first chance I've had to—"

"It's been over ninety minutes," was all she could think to say.

"I would've cancelled with you and sent you home, but this is your last night in Alma. Selfishly, I wanted to see you again."

Guilt rose like bile in her throat. She remained silent.

He glanced at the feast of food that had been put before her. "You didn't touch anything Chef prepared. You must be famished."

"I'm not hungry anymore, Your Majesty."

His lips pursed in disapproval.

She still couldn't bring herself to call him by his given name.

"You've been so patient. There's just one more meeting I have to get through. Will you wait?"

She shook her head. "Actually, I think I'd like to go."

"You're angry."

"No, I'm tired and, and…"

"Angry."

She didn't respond. "Will you have your driver take me back to the hotel?"

Juan Carlos closed his eyes briefly. "Yes, of course. I just assumed after we kissed, you'd… Never mind. You're right. I shouldn't have made you wait."

A man who admitted when he was wrong? How rare.

"Duty called. I'm afraid it always will."

That's how it had worked with Travis. The difference? Travis had been building his own personal dynasty, while Juan Carlos was trying to build one for his country. But that still left Portia with the same end result. She'd never be a top priority and while she liked Juan Carlos, she had vowed, after many disappointments with Travis, to never get herself in that situation again.

With that, she wished Juan Carlos a good evening, assured him she wasn't angry and put enough distance between them that he couldn't touch her, couldn't plant his delicious lips on hers again and make her change her mind.

Three

The beach at Playa del Onda was one of the most stunning Portia had ever visited. Warm sand squeezed between her toes as she sat on a lounge chair, reading a book. This morning she'd gotten up early and taken a long jog along the shoreline, the October sun warming her through and through. She'd met a lovely family of tourists and had breakfast with them at a terrace café that overlooked the Atlantic. But their two little children, aged five and three, reminded her that it would probably be a long time before she was blessed with motherhood.

Often, she thought of having a family. She'd been orphaned at a young age. Aside from her great-aunt Margreta, she had no other family. Her grandmother Joanna had died during Portia's sophomore year in college. But she had her work and it fulfilled her, and she had good friends. She wasn't complaining. Yet being here on this beautiful beach was not only relaxing, it was…lonely.

Face it, Portia. How many books can you read this week? How many hot stone spa treatments can you indulge in? How many solo dinners in your room can you enjoy?

It had been three days of torturous relaxation. And it didn't compute. How odd for her to realize while on a vacation in a beautiful locale that she wasn't made for inactivity. She liked to keep active, to busy herself with things that mattered. Yesterday, she'd given herself a mental slap.

You deserve this vacation, so shut up, sit back and enjoy yourself.

Today, the mental slaps weren't working. Her relaxation was even more forced. She fidgeted in her chair; the book in her hands no longer held her interest. Sunglasses shading her eyes, she watched others frolicking on the sand, tossing a Frisbee, their laughter drifting over to her, reminding her how lonely she was. How bored.

She wished Jasmine was here. They would've had a good time with shopping, spa dates and maybe a nightclub or two.

The Frisbee landed at her feet and a teenage boy trotted over and stopped abruptly, blasting sand onto her legs. "Excuse me," he said. He reached for the Frisbee slowly, eyeing her legs, then her bikini-clad body. "Want to play with us?" he asked.

He had Spanish good looks, dark hair, bronzed skin and a charming smile. He was sixteen tops, and she would've actually considered tossing the Frisbee around with him, if he hadn't been so blatant about ogling her breasts.

She was saved from refusing, when the concierge from the Villa Delgado approached. "Excuse me, Princess."

The boy blinked at her title, turned a lovely shade of cherry-blossom pink and bowed, before dashing off. She chuckled under her breath. Her royal status did have some advantages. "Yes," she said to the concierge, removing her sunglasses.

"You have a phone call at the desk. A woman named Jasmine. She says she works for you. Apparently, she hasn't been able to reach you on your cell phone."

"I left my cell in my room," she replied. She didn't want to be interrupted in her state of lonely boredom. Now she realized how silly that seemed. "Sorry you had to track me down."

"Not a problem, Princess Portia."

"Will you tell her that I'll call her as soon as I get to my room?"

"My pleasure," he said.

When he walked off, she gathered up her beach bag, hat and sunglasses and promptly made her way toward the villa. Her suite with its second-floor terrace came into view. It was really quite picturesque, the columns and archways suggesting old-world grace and style. Why couldn't she like being here more? Why wasn't she okay with being idle? Maybe things had changed with Jasmine. Maybe her friend would come join her, after all. Her hope in her throat, Portia hiked a little faster to reach her suite of rooms.

Once inside, she set her things down on the dining table and headed for the bedroom, where she was sure she'd left her phone. It was charging on her nightstand. She unhooked the charger, just as she heard a knock at the door.

She belted her cover-up a little tighter and moved to the door. With a gentle tug on the knob, the door opened and she came face to face with Juan Carlos Salazar. The king.

She blinked and a rush of heat rose up her neck. She trembled at the sight of him, *the gorgeous, unexpected, surprising* sight of him. The phone slipped slightly in her hand and she grabbed at it before it crashed onto the floor.

His eyes were on her, and those dark raised brows made her flush even hotter. With guilt. Piercing disappointment flickered in his eyes. She hadn't told him the absolute truth when she'd left Del Sol.

"Princess," he said.

"Your Majesty," she responded.

His lips twitched. "I see you've decided to stay on in Alma, after all."

"I, uh, yes." She didn't owe him an explanation. One heart-robbing kiss didn't give him that right. "My plans changed."

"Quite unexpectedly, I assume."

"Yes, that's right." The movement of two bodyguards caught her attention. They stayed back, at least five feet away, but she was certain they could hear every word. "Would you like to come in?"

His gaze dipped down to her bikini-clad body, covered only by a soft robe of silk that reached her thighs. "Yes."

She backed up a few steps and he nodded to his bodyguards and then entered. They stood face-to-face again, alone in her suite.

Despite her guilt and a sense of being caught redhanded, this was the most exciting thing that had happened to her in three days. But how did he find out where she was and what did he want from her?

Her cell phone buzzed and she looked down at the screen. A text was coming through from Jasmine. She hadn't had time to call her back yet. Quickly, she scanned the message.

Heads up. I might've made a mistake by giving King Montoro your location. He was charming and said it was a business thing. Apologizing in advance. Love you!

She lifted her lids to him. Okay, so he wasn't psychic. But he was thorough.

"It's good to see you again," he said.

Warmth swelled inside her like an overflowing river. He had too much of an effect on her.

"It's nice to see you, but I do admit, it's quite a surprise."

On this warm day, he was wearing dark trousers and a tan shirt, sleeves rolled up with his hands in his pockets, looking as casual and delicious as any man she'd ever met. Man, *not king*. But she couldn't forget who he was. "I have to admit, I was also surprised to learn you hadn't left the country."

"You were looking for me?"

"Yes, I spoke with your assistant. She's very nice, by the way, and she's loyal to you. But the fact is, I have something of a business venture for you. And after I told her a little about it, she was willing to let me get in touch with you."

His eyes skimmed over Portia's body. Another wave of heat shimmied down to her belly and she turned away from his hot, assessing stare. Man or king, he was dangerous. "Would you like to sit down?" She waved him over to a latte-colored leather chair by the window that faced the Atlantic. "Please give me a minute to change my clothes."

"Only if you have to."

There was a wicked twinkle in his eyes that tweaked something lusty and recently unleashed in her body. It made her run, not walk toward her bedroom. "I'll be a minute, Your Majesty," she called over her shoulder.

His chuckle followed her into her room.

She scrubbed her face clean of sunscreen and removed her hair fastener, combing the tangles away and then gathering the strands back up into a long ponytail. She put on a pair of white capris and an off-the-shoulder cornflower-blue blouse.

A hint of lip gloss, some shading to her eyelids and she was ready. And more than mildly curious as to what was so important that King Juan Carlos had come all the way here to seek her out. She gave a last glance in the mirror and nodded. She felt a little less vulnerable to the king's hungry eyes now.

Juan Carlos stood when Portia entered the room. His heart hammered in his chest at the sight of her. She didn't know it yet, but he was determined to possess her. Aside from his newfound reign over Alma and his duties here, she'd become the most important thing in his life.

In such a short time.

It wasn't rational. He had no explanation for it. He'd never experienced anything quite like this. When she'd left the palace the other night, remorse had plagued him and lingered for days. Was he pathetic? Or simply a man who knows what he wants.

She was perfect, his ideal woman. She was royal, beautiful, smart, but at the moment…quite unattainable.

"Princess," he said.

"Would you like something cold to drink?" she asked.

"No, thank you."

"Okay, then maybe we should sit down and you can tell me what this is all about."

She took a seat, her eyes widening as she waited for him to explain.

"It seems I might have need for your services."

"My services? As an art advisor?"

"Well, yes. In a way. It would be something quite adventurous. You did say you liked adventure, didn't you?"

"I do."

"Well, then, let me explain. I don't know how much you know about the history of Alma, but it's been rumored that right before my family fled the country, they hid artwork dating back before World War II on the grounds of their abandoned farm. It's very run-down and Tantaberra never went there, so it was the perfect hiding place. Now that I'm king, I want to find those treasured pieces belonging to the royal family. It would go a long way in helping the country heal and bring new hope to our people. Imagine what a find that would be."

"It would be monumental," she agreed. Fireworks lit in her eyes at the mention of hidden art.

Good. He had her attention.

"But I see that you're vacationing here, so maybe you'd be too busy to help me locate the treasure."

"You want my help in locating the artwork?"

"Yes, I would need someone to help me hunt for it, and then assess its value. You'd be able to look at something and determine if it's authentic, I would imagine."

"Yes, for the most part. It's what I do. But you plan on doing this by yourself?"

"I can donate a few days of my time, yes. I wouldn't want word to leak out about what I was doing. If I come up empty, or if there are other issues regarding the artwork we find, I would rather it not become public knowledge immediately. Bella and her husband had already begun renovations on the property but given the site's historical significance, they've agreed to allow me to take over and devote the full resources of the crown to the project. As we speak, there is a team working on the grounds, getting it ready for my arrival. So Princess Portia, would you consider helping me? Of course, you'd be paid for your time."

"So, this is a job offer?"

"Yes, I'm offering you a job and an adventure."

She smiled, leaning forward and placing her hands on her crossed knee. "Who else will be there?"

He gathered his brows. "No one but my bodyguards. As I said, I plan to do this discreetly."

"It's intriguing, Your Majesty. But the two us alone, all that time?"

"Is that a problem for you?" God only knew, it was a problem for him. How could he keep his hands off her? It would be a living hell, but not worse than having her living a continent away. A few days was all he was asking of her.

"Maybe. Answer one thing for me, please."

He extended his arms, palms up. "Anything."

"Do you have an ulterior motive in offering me this opportunity? And please don't make me spell it out."

He smiled. She'd made her point and he wouldn't do her a disservice by lying to her. "If you mean, do I value a few more days in your company, then yes. I suppose. But I do honestly have good reason to be asking this of you. You are an expert, are you not?"

"I am."

The sparkle in her eyes evaporated.

"What is it?"

She rose from her seat, and good manners had him rising, too. She walked behind the chair, putting distance between them, and leaned her elbows on the back, a battle raging in her eyes, on her face. "I'm not presuming anything here, but I do have to tell you where I stand. It's… it's complicated. Because I do like you."

Encouraging. He nodded.

"And that kiss we shared…well, it bordered on amazing."

He nodded again. She had something to say and he wanted to hear it.

Or maybe not.

"But the truth is, you're King Montoro of Alma. You're new to this king thing, but you'll find out how demanding a job it will be. And you'll be in the spotlight. All. The. Time."

"Does that worry you?"

"Yes. You see, I'm not one to share heartbreak stories, but in this case, I should probably share with you, why I've been—"

"Playing hard to get?" He couldn't hold back a smile.

"Yes. Only I'm not playing. I'm seriously not interested in getting involved with a man with so much…glitter."

"Glitter?" He laughed. "What's that?"

"You're always going to shine. No matter what." His smile faded. She was dead serious. "And any woman who gets involved with you, will be giving up her identity, her dreams, her heart, to someone who has pledged his life to his country."

"Who was he, Portia? Surely, someone has broken your heart."

"Yes, my heart was broken. I don't like talking about it, but since it's important to our conversation, I'll tell you about Travis Miles. He's like a king in America, a big time Hollywood celebrity."

Juan Carlos nodded. "Of course I know of him. I don't go in much for entertainment news, but he sure has quite a résumé."

"Travis knows everyone of substance in the country from sports figures and superstars to high-ranking politicians. We ran hot for a short time, and then…I became old news to him. He didn't have time for me and we began seeing less and less of each other. Shortly after, I found out he'd been cheating on me with a woman on the staff of his TV show for a long time. Seems that everyone knew about it but poor little gullible me. He'd made me out to be a fool and my career and credibility suffered. It's taken me three years to get my reputation back. Princess or not, I wasn't immune to the blonde-bimbo stigma and so now, I'm cautious. Which is why your royal status isn't a plus in my book."

He stood with hands on hips, silent, taking it all in. He understood her caution. The pain in her eyes, the tremor in her voice were telling, and his heart hurt hearing her confession. He should leave and let her resume her vacation. He shouldn't press her. But his feet were planted and they weren't moving. He couldn't face not seeing her again.

"If things were different, would you accept my offer?"

"Yes," she said, her eyes clear now. "I wouldn't hesitate. It sounds far too exciting to pass up."

"Then let's pretend that we've just met. There was no amazing kiss from before. We haven't danced and spent time together. This is a business meeting. And I promise to keep things completely professional between us."

"Why is it so important to you?" she asked.

"Because, I…I see how much you want to say yes. I see that you'd love to locate the secret artworks."

"And you promise that after we discover this wonderful treasure, we'll just be friends?"

He let a split second go by. He was a man of his word.

If he promised, he'd have to adhere to his vow, regardless of how much he wanted things to be different.

"I promise, Princess."

She nodded. "I know you mean what you say. So yes, I accept your offer."

The next morning, Portia informed the concierge that she'd be checking out earlier than expected from Villa Delgado and offered her thanks for his accommodations. He'd questioned her, hoping she hadn't been disappointed in her stay, and she assured him that was not the case. She'd been called away unexpectedly, she explained. And his brows arched as if he'd suspected King Montoro had something to do with her sudden departure.

And so, her adventure was beginning. Dressed for the search, wearing a pair of Gucci jeans and a red plaid shirt tucked in and belted at the waist, she swopped out her Bruno Magli shoes for tall leather boots and stood outside the villa at precisely eight o'clock. Sunglasses shielding her eyes, her bags packed and ready to go, she gave one last glance to the Atlantic shoreline and the clear azure waters lapping the sands. There would be no five-star accommodations where she was going. She was told to expect rustic and that was fine with her. She'd gone camping before; she knew how to rough it.

Sort of. Jasmine had convinced her once to rent a motor home and they'd trekked as far as Pismo Beach, California. They'd parked the giant thing facing the ocean, and then had gone out for lunch and dinner every night. They'd hit a few clubs, too, dancing until dawn. So maybe that wasn't roughing it per se.

But they had cooked their own breakfasts and hiked the beach in the mornings. Did that count?

One of Juan Carlos's bodyguards drove up in a black SUV, right on time. Poker-faced, he promptly opened the door for her and she got into the backseat as he hoisted her luggage into the cargo space.

As they drove off, she sat quietly in the car, enjoying the sounds of morning, excitement flowing through her veins.

She'd taken Juan Carlos at his word. He would treat her as a professional and so she had nothing to fear and everything to look forward to. Her little heartfelt speech seemed to convince him that she wasn't looking for romantic involvement. Surprisingly, it hadn't been hard admitting her failings to him. He'd put her at ease and that was saying something, since she didn't go around revealing her innermost feelings to anyone but her best friend.

They drove away from the shore, through the streets of Playa del Onda and onto a highway that led inland. "Excuse me. When will we be picking up King Montoro?" she asked Eduardo, the driver-slash-bodyguard.

"His Majesty will be meeting you there," he said.

Ah…discretion.

"Is it a long drive?"

"Not overly so. We should arrive in less than an hour. Is there anything you need, Princess?"

"No, no. I'm perfectly comfortable."

She gazed out the window taking in the scenery, where residential streets were soon replaced by more rural-looking spaces. As the minutes ticked by, the groomed vegetation bordering the road gave way to untamed brush and wildflowers. There was a certain neglected beauty to the land that inspired her. The road though was becoming less and less car friendly. The tires spit broken gravel as they traveled along a bumpy country road.

"Sorry, Princess," Eduardo said. "The road is washed out from here on."

"Is it much longer?"

"No, just another mile or two."

And shortly, he turned onto a path and drove through

wrought-iron gates clawed by fingers of dead branches and vines. Weeds and overgrown scrub led to a two-story house in desperate need of a good solid paint job. Banging sounds reached her ears and she searched for the source as the car came to a stop in front of the house. Juan Carlos appeared on the porch holding a hammer, his shirt slung open and sweat glistening on his beautiful bronzed chest. His dark hair gleaming under the October sunshine, he gave her a wide welcoming smile.

She sucked oxygen in. If she could slither away in a trembling mass, she would. She could order Eduardo to turn the car around, drive and keep on driving until she forgot the exact chestnut color of Juan Carlos's eyes, the deep dark shine of his hair and the powerful rock-solid muscle of his body.

She bit her lower lip until it pained her.

As he made his approach, she bucked up and remembered why she was here, and the promise Juan Carlos had made to her. Now, if she could get her heart to stop racing…

"Welcome," he said, opening the door wide for her. He offered her his hand and helped her out of the car. Eyes shining, his smile broadened. "I hope your trip wasn't too uncomfortable."

"No, no. It was fine," she said, looking beyond him to the house.

"Sorry about my appearance."

She nearly choked on her own saliva. Was he kidding?

"I found some loose planks on the porch. They could be dangerous."

"You're handy with a hammer?"

"You sound surprised. Actually, I had a lot of odd jobs in my younger days. My uncle believed in hard work and I was always employed during my college years."

"Doing?"

"All sorts of things. Remind me to tell you about the time I worked at a strip club in Miami."

"You were a stripper?"

The image of him shedding his clothes made her mouth water.

"I didn't say that. But I sure got a quick education." Her eye fluttered and he squeezed her hand. "There's that wink again. I'm very happy you're here, Portia."

"It's not a wink," she assured him.

He smiled again and released her hand. Breath quietly swooshed out of her mouth.

"Let me assure you, the inside of the house is in better shape than the outside. Bella and James had two bedrooms renovated upstairs and my crew made sure the kitchen and living space are clean and functioning."

She flinched at the mention of the bedrooms and slid a glimpse at Eduardo, who was removing her luggage, appearing stoic as ever. "That's...fine."

She only wished that Juan Carlos would button his shirt so that she could breathe freely again.

Eduardo stopped at the steps with her two suitcases. "Just leave them. I'll take it from here," Juan Carlos said. "Thanks, Eduardo."

The man nodded, but it looked more like a bow. "Your Highness."

Juan Carlos rolled his eyes.

She chuckled. It would take him a while to get used to being royalty.

"Stop laughing," he whispered out of earshot of his bodyguard.

"I'll try," she whispered back. "Not promising anything."

He shook his head but grinned like a schoolboy.

She was up against massive charm and a killer body.

"Let me show you around." Juan Carlos took her arm and guided her inside.

The living room was cozy with a large brick fireplace and old wood floors that looked as though they'd been scoured and polished. A new patterned rug was laid down between two sofas covered with floral tapestry pillows. The smell of fresh drying paint filled the room.

"Come see the kitchen," he said, taking her hand. "It's rustic, but I didn't have the heart to replace everything. I'm assured the oven is in working order." The oven was indeed, quaint and lovely. She could tell it, too, had been scoured to a new brilliance, but it must date back to the 1940s. The refrigerator had been replaced, and the counters were chipped in places but the sink had passed the test of time. A kitchen table sat in front of windows overlooking the backyard grounds. Someone had recently plowed the area and planted a garden of fresh flowers and herbs so the immediate view was quite picturesque.

"It's charming the way it is."

"The refrigerator is stocked. Would you like a cold drink?"

"Sure."

He opened the door and peeked inside. "Lemonade, soda, orange juice and sparkling water."

"Lemonade sounds good. I'll get the glasses." She flipped open a few cupboards and found them. It was obvious the dinnerware and glassware were all new, or imported from the palace. "Here we go." She set two glasses in front of him on the counter and he filled them.

A cool, refreshing swallow quenched her thirst and as she sipped, she strolled through the kitchen, exploring. She passed a utility room and then entered a large bathroom. Juan Carlos was just steps behind her and prickles of awareness climbed up her spine. She felt his eyes on her and as she turned slowly, he didn't even try to look away. He was in the doorway, his arms braced on the doorjamb, his shirt hanging open loosely from his shoulders. All that pure masculinity in one man didn't seem fair.

He stared at her for long seconds, until regret seemed to dull the gleam in his eyes. She had the same regret. If only she was just a woman and he was just a man and they were here together, sharing a grand adventure.

She swiveled around, pretending interest in a claw-foot tub, running a finger along the porcelain edge. "Makes you wonder about what life was like here when the farm was active." She turned to him again. "Do you know if there were animals?"

"Hmm. I think so. There are many outer buildings on the acreage. Supply sheds, barns and feed shacks. They owned livestock. Probably sheep, maybe cattle, but definitely horses. Do you ride?"

"Horses? Yes, I do. I'm no expert but I know how to plant my butt in the saddle."

He smiled.

"Will we be riding?"

"Possibly. There's five thousand acres here to investigate. Between the Jeep and the horses, we should be able to scour the entire grounds. The horses will be here this afternoon."

"Did your family ever live here?"

"I don't think a Salazar ever lived here. But a Montoro must have at some point. This land is all part of the Montoro holdings."

"Do you have any idea where to start looking?"

"I'm thinking we should stick close to the house today and if we come up empty, we can venture out tomorrow."

"Sounds good. I have to admit, I'm eager to start."

"Okay, then I'll get your luggage. Your room is upstairs at the end of the hallway. It's been painted and furniture was brought in yesterday. Take some time to relax. I think you'll like the room, but if there's anything you need, just let me know."

"I'm sure it's fine." She'd roughed it with Jasmine, after

all. She really could handle her own luggage, but His Majesty would never allow that. His sense of gentlemanly duty would become tarnished. And darn, if she didn't find that amazingly appealing. "Thank you."

As she headed upstairs, a sigh escaped from her lips.

Juan Carlos was a big juicy ripe apple, dangling his unabashed charm and beautiful body in front of her.

And the wicked serpent in her head was daring her to take a bite.

Four

Portia's room was more than adequate. A queen-size bed, adorned with Egyptian cotton sheets, a snowy comforter and pale pink pillows took up most of the space. Southern light streamed into the room through twin windows with ruffled curtains and an exquisitely crafted armoire made of inlaid mahogany and cherrywood held the bulk of her clothes.

She glanced out one window to the unkempt grounds below. The Montoros owned all the land as far as her eyes could see. Would they find the hidden artwork somewhere out there? Her belly warmed to the idea. She was grateful for the opportunity to search for it.

And ready.

As she headed for the stairs, movement caught her eye from a room at the opposite end of the landing. Juan Carlos was in his bedroom, changing his shirt. Twenty feet separated them, and she immediately glanced away, but not before she caught sight of bare broad shoulders tapering down to a trim waist. She gulped and scurried down the stairs before she got caught ogling him.

She wandered outside into the yard. Birds flitted between tree branches and flew away. She knew the bodyguards were out here somewhere, watching over the place, but she'd yet to see anyone else since Eduardo had deposited her here this morning.

She heard the door open and close behind her and footsteps crunching the fallen leaves as Juan Carlos approached. "Where are they? I know they are out there somewhere," she said.

He chuckled. "Luis and Eduardo have orders not to disturb us unless there's danger. They're here, trust me."

"I'm not worried." She put on a pair of sunglasses.

"That's good. How do you like your room?" He sidled up next to her. Dressed in jeans and a chambray shirt, with a black felt hat shading his eyes, he looked like a modern-day Spanish vaquero.

"It's better than I imagined, considering the state of the grounds around us. I'm sure you had a hand in making it comfortable for me."

He shrugged. "If you're comfortable, that's all that matters. Let's check out what we can on foot. There's a stable and a few broken-down buildings nearby." He reached into his back pocket and came up with a pair of work gloves. "Here, put these on."

She slipped them on. "I'm ready." And off they went.

The stable was in ruins, like pretty much everything else on the property. As they entered, she spied a wagon wheel, some rusted harnesses and a stack of rotted grain bags. It didn't seem as though anything could be hidden in here, but Juan Carlos touched every wall, kicked clean every stall and scoured the entire area with assessing eyes.

She took his cue, and searched the outside perimeter of the building, looking for anything that could be used as a hiding place.

He met her outside. "Nothing here. I didn't think we'd find anything this close to the house, but we need to be thorough."

"Okay, where next?"

"There's some feed shacks farther out we should check. Are you up for a long walk?"

She stared into his eyes. "You know that pea under my mattress didn't ruin my sleep last night."

He gave her a look of mock concern. "There was a pea under your mattress, Princess? Twenty lashes for the chambermaid who made up your bed last night."

She grinned. "More like fifty lashes for the king who thinks I can't keep up with him."

"Okay, I get your point. You're not frail."

"Not one little bit. But I think your concern is sweet."

"And antiquated."

"That, too. But what woman doesn't dream of a knight in shining armor once in a while?"

He peered directly into her eyes. "Do you?"

"I'm...not going to tell."

With that, she dashed ahead of him and hoped she was heading in the right direction.

Juan Carlos's laughter reached her ears, but he hung back a little, watching her.

She came upon three outer buildings, each one fifty feet or so from the others. She was just about to enter one when Juan Carlos called out, "Portia, wait!"

She whirled around. He came marching toward her, making up their distance in long strides. "Let's do this together."

He was being overprotective again. "I don't see why I can't—"

"Humor me," he said, sweeping up her hand and tugging her inside with him.

The small shed was in better shape than the stable had been. Juan Carlos remarked on how it was a newer building, perhaps added on later as the farm prospered. The open door allowed a sliver of light inside the windowless and otherwise dark space. Juan Carlos released her hand and the tingles streaming down her arm finally eased.

He got down on his knees and scoured the floorboards, looking for a trap door while she tapped at the walls. She tugged at a splintered hoe leaning against the far wall, moving it out of her way. A deafening hiss broke the silence. She looked down and saw a snake coiling around her boot. Panicking, she gasped quietly.

Juan Carlos jumped up. "Don't move!"

She froze. Oh, God, no. "What should I do? What should I do?" The thing was moving up her leg.

"Hold still, sweetheart. Trust me."

Juan Carlos reached into his boot and a glint of silver caught her eye. A knife?

There was a flash of movement as he lunged forward, and she squeezed her eyes shut. He ripped the thing off her in seconds flat. When she opened her eyes, she saw that he'd slashed the snake's neck all the way through. Juan Carlos tossed the dead reptile, head and all, across the shed. It landed with a smack and her stomach recoiled.

She shook uncontrollably and Juan Carlos took her into his arms. "You're okay, Portia. You're okay, sweetheart."

Tears spilled from her eyes and she nodded.

"Let's get outside," he said softly.

"I don't know if I can move."

"You can. I'll help you."

She nodded. "Okay." She clung to him as he guided her into the daylight. Fresh air filled her lungs and helped with her shaking.

"I'm sorry," he said, over and over, kissing her forehead.

She held his neck tight. She'd never been so frightened in her life. It all happened so fast, but the thought of that thing crawling up her body would surely give her nightmares for days to come.

"No, she'll be fine. I've got this," he was saying to someone, shaking his head. Then he turned his attention back to her. "Sweetheart, we'll go back to the house now."

"Who were you talking to?" She glanced past his shoulders and caught Eduardo gazing at her for a second before he lowered his eyes.

"We can walk, unless you want Eduardo to drive us back to the house?"

"No." She clung to Juan Carlos tighter, still shocked. She wasn't ready to let go. "No, we have more to do."

He ran his hand over her ponytail, like a father would a child. "But not today, Portia." His voice was gentle. "Not if you're not up to it."

She glanced to where Eduardo had been standing. He'd disappeared.

"Just hold me a little longer, please."

"Of course." One hand ran comforting circles on her back.

"I…I guess you have your answer." She spoke into his shirt, still too freaked out to back away.

"What do you mean?"

"You're my knight in shining armor today."

"Just today?" There was amusement in his voice and Portia couldn't deny how safe she felt being in his protective arms.

"Hmm." To say more would be too revealing. She was vulnerable right now and had let her guard down with him. She didn't want to let go of him. She needed his strength. He bolstered her courage.

"I guess, I'll settle for that," he said.

She tipped her chin up and gazed into his eyes. It would be so easy to kiss him now, to thank him for saving her from that creature.

"Portia," he whispered. His gaze tumbled down to her lips and the longing in his voice tortured her.

Debating with herself, she closed her eyes.

She heard him sigh deeply as one hand gripped her shoulders. He gave a little shove and she stumbled back and then blinked. He'd set her away deliberately. She focused on the blade he still held in his other hand and the image of that snake's split body flashed again in her mind.

A tick worked at his jaw, beating an erratic rhythm. "You test my honor, Portia. I made you a promise."

"I...know."

He put his head down, not meeting her eyes, and then bent to wipe the blade clean on the grass. One, two, three slashes were all that he needed. Then he stood and sheathed the knife, placing it in his waistband. "Come," he said, reaching for her gloved hand. "We should go."

"Yes. I can make it to the other shacks now."

He nodded and led the way.

"Here." Juan Carlos set a glass of whiskey into her hand. "Take a few sips and drink slowly." She sat on the sofa near the fireplace and kept her eyes focused on the jumping blue-orange flames. They sizzled and popped and brought warmth to the cool evening. "You'll need it to calm down."

"I'm calm." She wasn't really. Her body still quaked inside even as she sipped the numbing whiskey. The thought of that snake wrapped around her made her stomach curl. Yuck, it was disgusting. And frightening. Juan Carlos had been wonderful. He'd stayed by her side and comforted her, and hadn't balked when she'd insisted on continuing on their search. Though he'd made a thorough check of the next two buildings for creatures before he allowed her to step foot inside. He'd told her he was proud of her. It hadn't been courage on her part, but rather sheer stubborn determination that made her put one foot in front of the other and kept her from running back to the house for refuge. They hadn't found a thing in those other sheds, not one clue as to the whereabouts of the treasure, and she'd been ridiculously happy to return to the house after they'd exhausted their foot search.

"How's that going down?" he asked.

"Smooth. I'm not usually a hard drinker."

"But you needed something tonight."

"I'm not usually such a wimp, either," she said, smiling awkwardly. She'd felt like an idiot for panicking after Juan Carlos explained that the snake probably wasn't poisonous or deadly, but her fear was real, and he'd understood that. Rather than take a chance, he'd done the manly thing. He'd killed the culprit. Her knight.

"You were very brave. You kept your cool."

"You mean I froze in panic?"

He stared at her from his perch atop the sofa arm. "I'm sorry you had to go through that. I promise nothing like that will ever happen to you again. I'm very cautious. I'll take care to secure the site before you go pouncing."

"I don't *pounce*," she said.

"Don't you?" He smiled over his glass and sipped whiskey. "I had to stop you from going inside by yourself."

"I didn't know there would be snakes."

He arched his brows. "All the more reason for us to stick closer together."

"Can't get much closer than this," she said, chuckling. Oh, but yes, they could, and Juan Carlos's arched brow, the amusement in his eyes, said he was thinking the same thing. The thought of sleeping just down the hall from him tonight killed her laughter. The alcohol was already affecting her brain, and her rational thinking. She set her glass down, looking into the amber liquid that remained. She needed her wits about her. It would be too easy to fall into lust with the king. "I think I'll be okay now. What's the plan for tomorrow?"

He thought about it a few seconds. "Tomorrow, we go out on horseback. There's some terrain I want to explore that we can't get to with the Jeep."

"Are the horses here?"

He nodded. "They arrived this afternoon. Eduardo and Luis have stabled them."

"You've thought of everything, Your Highness."

"Juan Carlos."

She grinned. "I'm sorry. Still can't get there."

He shrugged, and it dawned on her that she needed that wall of separation in order to remind herself who he was. She'd do better to think of him as a monarch, rather than a man.

"Are you getting hungry?" he asked, and she was glad he didn't press the issue.

"A little." It was after six and up until now, she hadn't thought about food.

"Wait here, I'll be right back."

He rose and entered the kitchen. She heard him rustling around in there, opening the refrigerator door and banging shut the cupboards. The dance of lights in the fireplace mesmerized her for the few minutes he was gone.

Juan Carlos returned with a plate of delicacy cheeses, a bunch of deep red grapes and a loaf of bread. "I hope this will satisfy your hunger. If not, I can cook a few steaks and bake some potatoes."

"No, this is perfect. I don't think I could eat much more."

"Want to sit in front of the fire?"

"Sure." She grabbed a fringy knit throw blanket hanging over the sofa and fanned it out in front of the fireplace. Juan Carlos waited for her to sit, and then handed her the plates before taking his seat facing her.

"This is nice, thank you." She arranged the plates in front of them.

The flickering flames cocooned them in a warm halo of light. She nibbled on the cheese and bread. Miles away from the city, she was at peace in this farmhouse.

She reached for a grape, and met with Juan Carlos's hand as he did the same. Their fingers touched and she lifted her eyes to him. He was staring at her, as if memorizing the way she looked right now. Her heart began to beat faster. Their gazes remained locked for a second, and then she tore a bunch of grapes off and popped one into her mouth.

Outside, breezes blew, making the windows rattle. The distant sound of horses whinnying carried on the wind and she pictured them in their stalls. How long had it been since there was life in those stalls? She hoped the winds wouldn't frighten the animals.

"What is it?" he asked.

"I'm just wondering if the horses are okay out there. The stable walls aren't solid anymore."

"I was going to check on them after you went to bed."

"I'd like to see them."

He pulled air into his lungs and nodded, as if convincing himself of his suggestion. "Then you'll join me."

Juan Carlos held a battery-powered lantern in one hand and Portia's hand in the other. He hadn't planned on spending more time with her tonight. Holding her shaking body and consoling her after the snake incident had stirred a possessive streak in him. He'd wanted to protect her from harm and keep her safe, but having her melt into him, her heartbreaking tears soaking his shirt, had sliced him up inside. He could have held her for hours and not tired of it, yet they'd continued on their search and he'd cursed that damn promise he'd made to her. He'd been desperate to get her to stay on in Alma. And he'd had to agree to her terms with a promise he hoped like hell he could uphold.

Tonight, he'd thought to escape her. Maybe he would have had a drink with Eduardo and Luis or taken a late-night ride, or simply waited until Portia was safely ensconced in her bedroom before making it up to his room. Yet he couldn't refuse Portia her request to join him in the stables.

So here he was, gritting his teeth as she walked beside him under the stars. The stables weren't far and he'd given the bodyguards strict orders to watch without being seen. They were out there somewhere.

The night air had grown cooler, and Portia wrapped both of her arms around herself despite her coat. She might've shivered once or twice.

"Cold?"

"Yes, but I'm okay. I have Scandinavian blood flowing through my veins. Cold weather doesn't bother me."

Juan Carlos hunkered down into his jacket. He'd lived in Miami most of his life. Neither Florida nor Alma got down into freezing temperatures very often. He could tolerate cold weather, but it wasn't his favorite thing. "This is about as cold as it gets here," he said. "At least that's what I'm told."

"It's mostly the wind I don't like."

Right on cue, a howling gust blew from the north. She shivered again and on impulse, he wrapped his free arm over her shoulder and drew her close.

She looked up at him.

"Thanks for keeping me warm," he said.

"Yes, Your Majesty. Anything for the king." A teasing smile played at her lips.

He laughed.

Before long they reached the stables.

"Want me to go in and check for snakes?"

She drew a breath and glanced around the property completely encased in darkness. "I have a feeling it's safer inside than out."

She had a point. There could be all manner of animals roaming the land. Wolves, wild boars and lynx were indigenous to the area. "Okay, then stick close to me."

"You still have your knife?"

"Of course."

"Then you won't be able to shake me."

"I wouldn't even try," he said, quite honestly.

A hum ran through her body. His subtle compliments did crazy things for her ego. After what she'd been through with Miles, that part of her brain had needed nourishment and was now being fed day in and day out by His Hunkiness the King.

She gasped.

"What is it?"

"Oh, nothing. I was just thinking." Jasmine would have a good laugh over this one. Portia was resorting to using terms from a romance novel to describe the handsome, honorable Juan Carlos Salazar II, King of Montoro.

He gripped her hand and led her into the stables. The protective way he held her was another turn-on.

The lantern lit up about five feet of the path in front of them. The place was dank and colder than she'd hoped for the animals. Juan Carlos lifted the lantern to his shoulder and illuminated the stalls. There were shuffling sounds, whinnies and snorts as all four horses came into view. Beauties.

They were curious enough to approach their individual gates. Though she'd been here earlier, Portia could see hints of work done today to make the stable more secure for the horses. The stalls had been shored up, and beds of straw had been laid down. Holes in the walls letting in cold air had been hastily boarded up. Juan Carlos knew how to get things done.

Her eyes darted to the animals' backs. "They're wearing blankets."

"To keep warm. I put Luis on it tonight. They seem comfortable enough, don't they?"

She smiled, relieved. "Yes, I feel better now. They are amazing creatures. Are they yours? I mean do they belong to the palace?"

"We haven't had time to build a remuda of horses for the palace. The transition takes time, but we will have a royal guard on horseback one day soon. These horses belong to me personally, as of two days ago. I have it on good authority they are gentle and trustworthy. I've yet to ride any of them. Tomorrow will be a good test."

"For them or for you?"

His brow arched. "Maybe for all of us."

"Maybe," she agreed. "I've never claimed to be an expert, but I do love animals. What are their names?"

"Come. Let me introduce you." Straw crunched underfoot as they made their way to the first stall. "This is Julio. He's a two-year-old gelding," Juan Carlos said. The sleek charcoal-colored horse had a thick black mane and tail. "He's an Andalusian."

"The horse of kings," she said.

"Yes, I've heard them referred to that way."

"Because they're powerful and sturdy?"

"Because they're intelligent and docile."

She eyed the commanding animal in front of her. He was gorgeous. "Docile?"

"Not as hot-blooded as a thoroughbred. He'll be my mount."

Julio was tall and grand. His curious ink-black eyes watched her. She lifted her hand to him cautiously and he edged closer. She took that as an invitation to stroke the side of his face. "That's it, boy. You and I are going to be good friends," she crooned. Back in Los Angeles, she volunteered at an animal rescue when she wasn't working. Her lifestyle and schedule didn't allow having a pet of her own and she enjoyed donating her time to animals in need.

"You're good with him."

She touched her cheek to Julio's cold nose and he nuzzled her throat eagerly. The force pushed her back a step and she righted herself and giggled. "Oh, he is sweet."

Juan Carlos's gaze touched upon her. Something flickered in his eyes. He swallowed and stroked his hand over his chin. He hadn't shaved today, and his stubble only added to his good looks.

With an inward sigh, she focused back on Julio, giving his mane a solid but loving stroke. She sensed that she had indeed made a new friend today.

Juan Carlos tugged her along to the next stall. "This is Sugar. She's an Arabian. Quick, sharp and good-natured. You'll ride her tomorrow."

"Hello, Sugar. You're a pretty one."

Sugar wasn't as tall or commanding as Julio, but was equally as stately. She had sensitive eyes and seemed friendly. Her chestnut coat glistened under the lantern light. "I'll see you in the morning, girl."

Juan Carlos showed her the other two horses, Arabians named Estrella and Manzana, who were presumably for Eduardo and Luis. Were the king's bodyguards good riders? Was that part of their job description?

New feedbags hung from nails in the walls, replacing the shredded ones from this morning, and a bag of carrots sat on a splintered bench. "Can we give them a treat?"

"Good idea." Juan Carlos went to retrieve the carrots. He dipped his hand inside the bag and came up with four. "One for each."

"Only one?"

"We don't want to spoil them."

"I bet you'd be a tough disciplinarian with your children."

At the mention of children his eyes twinkled and somehow the mischief seemed aimed directly at her. "I'm ready to find out."

Her blood warmed. She hadn't thought along those lines for herself. Parenthood was a long way off for her. But Juan Carlos seemed to know exactly what he wanted. He was resolute, an action taker and at times, he intimated her with his decisiveness. "You want a family one day?"

"Of course...I've lived my life without my parents. I have

no brothers or sisters, although I have my cousins and we have been on good terms. But to have a child of my own, to share that bond with someone I love…it's a dream of mine."

He handed her all four carrots and she walked the stalls, allowing Sugar to nibble at hers first.

"I would think being king would be your dream."

"It's my duty and a role I'm proud to uphold. But a man can have more than one dream, can't he?"

His eyes darkened, his gaze boring into her like a nail being hammered into the wall. He was too close, his expression telling her too much. She couldn't look at him and not see his life all planned out…with her beside him. Were the limited lighting and her silly imagination playing tricks on her?

She turned away from him, taking interest in the horses again. "I suppose." Three beggars were vying for her attention, shuffling their feet, bobbing their heads back and forth. She walked over to Julio next. "Here you go, boy."

Juan Carlos shadowed her to the next two stalls and watched her feed the other Arabians. "Do I make you nervous, Princess?"

Her eyes crinkled as she squeezed them closed. Why did he have to ask her that? She took a breath to steady her nerves and pivoted around. Her back to the stall door, the lie was ready to fall from her lips. Her one eye fluttered, like a wink, but certainly *not* a wink. Oh, boy. She wanted to sink into a black hole. "Y-yes." Damn her honesty. So much for pretending disinterest in him.

Juan Carlos gave her an approving smile as if he'd expected her answer. As if he was pleased with her honesty. "I promised not to pursue you, Portia. But I didn't say I would back off if you came to me. If you decided you wanted me, craved my body as I do yours, I would claim you in an instant and not feel I'd betrayed my vow to you."

He took her hand then, and led her out of the stable. "Come, it's time for bed."

Five

Sugar kept an even pace with Julio as they ambled farther out onto the property. The horse was gentle, took commands well and her sure-footed gait put Portia at ease. She gazed at the cloudless blue sky above. The warmth of the rising sun removed the bite of coolness in the morning air and made the ride pleasant.

Juan Carlos's felt hat shaded his eyes. Portia had put her hat on, too, one that Juan Carlos, who planned for everything, had given her to wear.

"How are you doing?" Juan Carlos asked after five minutes of silence.

"I have no complaints, Your Highness."

He paused. Gosh, why did she goad him? Oh, yeah, to put distance between them. "We've been riding a while now. Is your rear end sore?"

She chuckled. "A little, but I'll survive."

"You just let me know when you want to take a break."

Things had been a little weird between them since last night. Juan Carlos had put a bug in her ear. He'd given her an out. Up until then, her idea to keep their relationship strictly platonic had rested solely on Juan Carlos's shoulders. She'd made him promise to keep his distance. But now he'd tossed the ball into her court. And it had gotten her thinking. But it wasn't a good thing for a woman desperately attracted to a man who was all wrong for her to be given those options.

If you decided you wanted me, craved my body as I do yours...

Those hot words had thrown her. She'd thought of them, of him, all through the night. What would it be like to have Juan Carlos make love to her? What if, here, in this remote, private place, she gave in to temptation and spent the night touching him and being touched. Kissing his perfect mouth, running her cheek along that sexy stubble and nibbling on his throat? What would it be like to have him inside her, the steely velvet of his erection impaling her body?

She squirmed in the saddle, suddenly uncomfortable. Mentally, she forbade Juan Carlos to look over, to see her struggling with thoughts he'd planted inside her head. *Don't look at me. Don't see the expression on my face. Don't see me...wanting you.*

"Portia?"

Darn it. "I'm fine." She stared straight ahead. "Everything's good and dandy."

She sensed him studying her as they rode the length of five football fields until they came upon a graveyard surrounded by a run-down picket fence. The square of ground was full of weeds, unkempt. The neglect was almost sacrilegious. It was out in the middle of nowhere, a place long forgotten.

Juan Carlos slowed his gelding and she did the same. "We'll stop here," he said.

Her rear end rejoiced. She spotted trees that offered perfect shade just yards away. The horses moved toward an oak, massive in size, its roots splayed in all directions.

Juan Carlos dismounted quickly and strode to her. Sugar wasn't as tall as Julio, but Portia still needed help with her dismount. Either that, or run the risk of breaking an ankle when she tried to slide down the horse's left flank.

Juan Carlos's arms were up, reaching for her. She swung her leg over the saddle and his hands found her waist, securing her with a firm grip and guiding her down until her boots hit the ground. He held her for a few beats of time, with her back to his chest, his nose tickling her neck, breathing in her hair. "You smell delicious," he whispered, and then released her.

She sighed. If only she didn't miss his hold on her. Didn't enjoy having him touch her.

I would claim you in an instant and not feel I'd betrayed my vow to you.

He stood beside Julio, gazing at the graveyard as he unlatched a saddlebag and came up with a bottle of water. He walked over to her. "Here," he said. "Take a drink, you must be thirsty."

The water, cool and refreshing, slid down her throat. "That's good." She handed it back to him. His mouth clamped around the lip of the bottle and he tipped it back. He swallowed a big gulp, then another. A trickle of sweat ran down his forehead and he wiped it away.

Simple gestures. Yet her heart raced being near him, sharing water, doing natural things that seemed to bind them together.

"I'd like to check out the graveyard. You can stay here and rest. I'll put a blanket down. You'll be in the shade."

She shook her head. She was curious about the graveyard, too. "I'll come with you."

He nodded and began walking. She followed behind. Wind kicked up and almost blew her hat off. She grabbed it just in time and held it to her head as she approached a wooden gate. Overhead, tree branches made a makeshift archway, and scrolled in wood a sign read: Montoro Family Cemetery.

"So this is where the farm families ended up," she said.

Juan Carlos nodded. "They were probably distant cousins, relatives of my uncles. I'd bet Tantaberra made sure no one has ever come to honor their graves."

They walked through the battered gate. There were many headstones, maybe twenty-five in all. Portia stopped beside Juan Carlos as he bent his head in prayer over one after another. She sent up her own prayers for the lives forgotten here, stepping from one grave site to the next. "Do you know any of these names?" she asked.

"Some sound familiar," he said. The first and middle initials were etched on the headstones along with the last names. "Montoro, of course, and Olivio I've heard mentioned, but many I don't know. I will have this cemetery restored to honor their graves."

Juan Carlos insisted on clearing away the larger of the weeds that had overgrown the area. She bent to help him. "No, please. Your hands will be cut," he said.

"I'll be careful. I want to help." Her chin up, she was ready to do him battle.

He stared at her. "I forgot to bring you gloves." And then he warned, "See that you are careful, Princess."

She smiled and something tugged at her heart. He was angry with himself for the oversight. "I promise to be careful."

He began to pull away tumbleweeds clustered around the graves, staring at the names embedded on the stones as if embedding them into his brain. She, too, had little family. She could see the sadness and the loss in the contoured planes of his face, in the shadows of his dark eyes. The dictatorship had taken so much from his family.

"Let me see your hands," he said when they were all through. They'd cleared away as much as they possibly could. The wind was howling; breezes that had cooled the day's heat were swirling more rapidly now.

She turned her palms up.

Juan Carlos inspected her hands carefully, turning them one way then another.

"See. I'm not a wimpy princess."

He laughed, the shine returning to his eyes. "I'd never describe you that way. I'm grateful for your help."

"You're welcome. But there's one more thing to do."

His right eyebrow shot up. "What would that be?"

"I'll be right back. Don't follow me. I'll only be ten minutes."

She left him in the graveyard. This was something she wanted to do by herself. For his family. He leaned against the post outside the cemetery and watched her march into the fields. Every time she turned, his gaze was glued to her. He wouldn't let her out of his sight. She got that. He was a protector by nature. Gallant. He didn't interfere with her independence though and she appreciated that.

Ten minutes later, she returned to the Montoro family cemetery. Juan Carlos smiled broadly as he gazed at the large bunch of wildflowers she'd gathered in her hands. Some were probably classified as weeds, but they were indisputably pretty anyway. Bluebonnet blues, pale yellows, creamy whites and carnation pinks.

"Would you like to help me lay these down?"

He nodded, a play of deep emotion on his face.

They walked through the cemetery one last time, offering up the flowers to grave sites and headstones to tell the deceased that someone remembered them. Someone cared.

They left the place quietly, Juan Carlos taking her hand. It was a solemn moment, but a sweet one, too. Portia was moved by the care he'd taken with his distant relatives, the honor he'd bestowed upon them.

How many would have just ridden past? How many wouldn't have bothered to stop and clear up the neglect and mess?

This feeling she had for Juan Carlos wasn't going away. It grew stronger each moment she spent in his company.

The horses whinnied upon their return, huffing breaths and stomping hooves. Juan Carlos dipped into the saddlebag again, this time to offer the animals a handful of oats to keep them satisfied. "There, now. You two be quiet. No more complaining." He stroked Julio's head a few times and then turned to Portia. "Let's sit a minute. Take a rest."

"All right."

He grabbed a blanket and spread it out under the tree. The shade was no longer an issue; the weather had cooled and gray clouds were gathering in the skies. She shivered and walked to her saddlebag, picking out a jacket from the things she'd brought along.

"Cold?"

"A little bit."

"We can head back."

It was too early to return to the house. They had more ground to cover and she didn't want to delay their mission because of a little cold weather. Her family hailed from Scandinavia, where food was put out on windowsills to freeze quickly, where the elderly lived over one hundred years because germs couldn't survive the environment. She refused to slow Juan Carlos down.

"Ten minutes is all I need," she said.

She put on the jacket and sat down. He sat next to her and roped his arm around her. It seemed only natural to put her head on his shoulder.

"There is a giant rock formation about half an hour from here. The terrain is rough but these horses can make it up there. I found it on a GPS map of the area." His voice soothed her even as he spoke of a tough task. She closed her eyes. "I think it's a good hiding place for the artwork. I suspect caves have formed between the interlocking rocks. At least, that's what I'm hoping."

"Sounds reasonable. We'll check it out."

"Are you up for it? We can return tomorrow if you're not."

"I'm up for it," she said. "We're already halfway there, aren't we?"

"Yes, but the weather might be a problem."

"It won't be, Juan Carlos. I'm not a wimpy princess, remember?"

Laughter rumbled from his chest. "How can I forget? You keep reminding me."

"Good," she said, snuggling deeper into his arms.

The solid beats of his heart were like the revving of a powerful engine. It was dangerous and thrilling and though she hated to move, it was time to break this cozy moment with him. She slid away from his grip and rose to her feet. "I'm ready when you are."

He bounded up, regret in his eyes, as if she'd taken something precious from him.

From both of them.

The rocks were adobe-red, huge and intimidating. They were also beautiful against the landscape of gray skies and brown earth. The horses treaded with agility through the gravelly terrain, their sure-footed gait assuring her she would not fall to her death as they climbed a plateau that led to the face of the mountain. "This is amazing. It reminds me of Sedona back in the States. Have you ever been there?"

"In Arizona?" Juan Carlos gave his head a shake. "No, but I've seen pictures. It's an artist colony, isn't it?"

"Yes, among other things. There are some wonderful galleries and art exhibits in the area. I studied there one summer."

"Did you ever climb the rocks?"

She nibbled her lower lip. "I'd been tempted a few times, but no, I didn't climb the rocks. I was there for the art. Are we climbing rocks today?" she asked pointedly.

Juan Carlos spread his gaze over the entire mountainside, studying the terrain. "Just like back then, you came here for the art. So no. We don't have to climb the rocks.

The openings seem to be on the lower levels. We can reach them without climbing."

She released a tight breath. She didn't like heights and they didn't like her, so no rock climbing was a good thing. "I'm excited. I have a good feeling about this," she said. "I'm imagining the artwork tucked inside the mountain somewhere, deep inside a cave."

"Then let's go find it," he said.

He dismounted and strode over, lifting his hands to her waist again. Dust kicked up by the strong wind mingled with the potent scent of horseflesh and earth. More threatening clouds gathered above, and a shiver shook her shoulders as she slid into his arms. His hands steadied her until her boots hit the ground. Then he took the reins of both horses and they began walking toward a row of rocks, stacked neatly like building blocks five stories high.

He stopped at the base of a formation where two giant boulders separated and an opening appeared. It wasn't much wider than a double-door refrigerator, but large enough to allow a man to enter. "Wait here," he said. "Stay with the horses. I'll go inside and see if it goes anywhere. It might be a dead end. I'll be back in a minute." He pulled out a flashlight and turned to her. "Okay?"

She took the reins with one hand and stroked Sugar's nose with the other. Eyeing him, Portia confessed, "I'm not very patient."

A grin crossed his features, that gorgeous mouth of his lifting crookedly. "Good to know."

For real? The man had a one-track mind. "Come and get me, if you find anything."

"Will do. We're in this together," he said, and then disappeared into the gap.

Just then, the wind knocked her back against the rocks. It was fierce today. She huddled behind the horses, allowing them to block the sharp bite of cold. Her teeth chattered anyway. Goodness, it seemed as if Juan Carlos had already been gone for hours but it was more like a minute or two.

Then she heard his approach, his footfalls scraping the ground of the cave. Thank God. A thrill shimmied through her belly. She really wasn't patient, not when it came to this. If only they could find the artwork today.

When he emerged from the opening, she took one look at Juan Carlos's expression and her shoulders slumped. "You didn't find it?"

He shook his head. "Not in there." His eyes were solemn as they toured over her face and body. "You're freezing."

"I'm...not."

His lips twisted at her denial. Then he turned away from her and grappled with both of their saddlebags, freeing them from their fasteners and tossing them over his shoulder. "Come," he said, handing her their blankets. "It's warmer inside. Besides, there is something I want to show you."

"Really? What is it?"

"You'll see." He took her frigid hand and immediately the blood began pulsing more warmly through her veins. One would think he was a flaming hot furnace with how easily his touch could heat her up through and through.

He led her into the darkness. The flashlight illuminated the way and she squinted as her eyes adjusted. Around her, stone walls made up a cavelike space, tall enough for them to stand in and wide enough for an entire hunting party to take refuge. The air inside was cool, but without the outside wind gusts it was warmer by a dozen degrees. "You're right, it is warmer in here."

"Take a look at this," he said, aiming his flashlight at a far corner.

Eyes appeared first, round and frightened, and then the light followed the length of the animal, stretched out on the ground nursing her young. "Kittens!"

Five tiny bodies fought for a place at mama's table, eager for their meal. The mother cat, striped in reds, browns and grays, eyed both Juan Carlos and Portia warily. "She's scared," Portia said. "Poor mama." She'd had lots of experience with birthing pups and kittens at the rescue where she volunteered. "She might be feral, though I doubt it. She would've been hissing and scratching her way out of here by now. The babies look to be only a few weeks old."

"You think she's domestic?" he asked.

Portia crouched down, studying the cat from five feet away. "I think she's somewhere in between. She might've been abandoned. She's doing what comes natural and found this place to have her kittens. Cats like dark cool isolated places to give birth."

"Well, she found that," Juan Carlos said, keeping his voice soft. Both of them whispered now, so as not to startle the wary cat.

"I wonder if she's hungry. She looks pretty scrawny."

"About all we've got is water and sandwiches."

"Water, for sure. She'll need that. And we can pull out cheese and bits of meat from our sandwiches. If she's hungry enough, she'll eat it."

"Good idea. I'm getting hungry. Maybe we should stay inside and eat, too."

Portia kept her eyes fixed on the new little family. "I'd like that."

Outside the wind howled. The refuge they'd found would do for now until the weather let up. Portia worked with Juan Carlos to fix the mama cat a meal of beef and cheese, and laid it out on a cloth napkin. She was at a loss as to where to put the water. They had narrow-necked bottles and not much else that would work for a bowl.

"Here," Juan Carlos said, handing her his hat, tipped upside down in his palm. "She needs it more than I do."

Under the dim flashlight rays, his eyes were full of

compassion. He was a problem solver, but it was more than that. He was doing this as much for Portia's sake as he was for the sweet cat family. "You'll freeze your head off when we go back out there."

"Not if we stay here overnight."

Her heart skipped. To be alone with Juan Carlos all night? She couldn't possibly. He didn't mean it. It was hard enough knowing he was sleeping down the hallway at the farmhouse. "Surely, we can't."

His eyes twinkled. "It was a nice thought, though. Being trapped in here with you all night...*to watch over the kittens.*"

Blood rushed to her cheeks. Suddenly, the cold dank cave sizzled with heat. She coughed, to cover errant thoughts of spending the night with Juan Carlos, of wearing nothing but a blanket to keep each other warm. His arms would wrap around her, and then their bare bodies would conform, mesh and he would nudge himself inside her.

"Are you okay, sweetheart?"

He knew. The sparkle in his eyes lit up even brighter.

"I'm fine."

"Are you sure?"

"Perfectly," she snapped. Goodness, she sounded like a witch.

He shrugged a shoulder, a smile teasing his lips as he handed her the cat's meal. "Do you want to take it to her?"

She nodded, recovering from the image that had sprung up in her head. "I'll try. I hope she doesn't run."

Portia took pained steps toward the cat, catching her eye and hoping her slow movements would show her she wasn't a threat. The cat's tail tensed and arched, her head came up and those tigerlike eyes watched her every move. Then she meowed.

"It's okay, sweet mama. I don't want to hurt you. Look, I have food. I hope you'll eat it."

The cat hissed, but she was just protecting her young. "This is as far as I'll go," Portia said softly. "See." She set down the napkin two feet from her and as soon as she backed away, the cat sniffed at it. "Put the hat down carefully," she said to Juan Carlos. He was only half a step behind and he set the water down next to the food. Then his hand clamped over her arm as he guided her several feet back, the beam of light dimming on the mama cat.

"Chances are, she won't eat or drink anything until she gives everything a complete smell test."

"We've done what we could for them," Juan Carlos said. "They are cute."

"Adorable," Portia said. The fuzzy fur babies were nestled against mama cat's underside, many of them satisfied and ready to nap.

Juan Carlos spread the blanket out and they began eating their sandwiches. Nibbling on her sliced steak sandwich sitting cross-legged, her eyes kept darting over to the cats.

"She'll eat eventually," Juan Carlos said.

"She's starving, but she won't make a move until we leave."

"Then we'll go as soon as we finish up here."

She nodded and within a few minutes, Portia was back atop Sugar, waiting for Juan Carlos to take his mount. She was torn about leaving the kittens in there, hoping the mama would survive the cold and be able to care for her young babes. How would she feed herself after the food they left behind was gone?

"Where to next?" Portia asked, blinking away tears, trying to distract herself from the sick feeling in her gut. She was a softie when it came to animals.

He stared into her eyes and smiled. "They'll survive. Don't worry."

He'd read her mind, but unlike most people, Portia didn't believe cats had nine lives. Sometimes, they couldn't beat the odds. If only this wasn't one of those times. She mustered a smile, but her heart wasn't in it.

"Since the wind has died down, I'd like to check out two of the nearby dwellings while we're here. If you stay put, I'll go in and be out quickly." He pointed north. "They aren't far. We'll get home before we lose light."

"I'm fine with that." She really was, though part of her wanted to stay behind and nurture the kittens. But that was impossible. Mama cat wanted no part of them right now. "I like the plan."

He nodded. "Let's go."

After showering and getting dressed, Portia marched downstairs in new jeans and a beige ribbed sweater to start dinner. She wasn't going to have Juan Carlos waiting on her. She planned to do her part. As she reached the bottom stair, she saw the fire crackling in the hearth and warmth settled around her. It was after seven; the darkened sky was lit with a scant few stars tonight. Her stomach grumbled, protesting over only having a light afternoon lunch. Thank God Juan Carlos wasn't around to hear the commotion her belly made.

The blaze in the front room beckoned. She could just as easily plop in a chair and watch the flickering fire, but she moved on and headed for the kitchen.

She found fresh tomatoes, whole garlic cloves, cans of tomato paste and packaged pasta in the cupboard. "Spaghetti it is." She wasn't a bad cook. She could crush tomatoes with the best of them.

Inside the fridge, she also found a covered dish of already cooked meatballs.

It seemed as though Juan Carlos had kitchen minions.

She wasn't complaining.

She turned the stove on, grabbed a cast-iron pan, peeled and mashed two garlic cloves with a butcher knife and poured a little oil in the pan. Garlicky steam billowed up and pungent scents filled the room.

The back door opened and Juan Carlos walked in. "Mmm. Smells great in here."

"I hope you like spaghetti and meatballs."

"Who doesn't?" he said, coming to stand beside her.

"Hand me those tomatoes," she said, fully aware of his freshly groomed presence beside her.

Instead of walking to get them, he grabbed her waist with one hand from behind and stretched the other hand out as far as he could, snapping up three ripe tomatoes from the counter without leaving her side. "Here you go."

His touch sent heat spiraling through her body. "Into the pot with them, please."

"Like this?" He lowered them down gently, his face brushing against her hair.

He was a tease.

"Thank you."

"Don't you have to peel them?"

She shook her head. "The skin will peel off easily later from the heat. And then, you'll get to crush them."

"Me?"

"Yes, you. They need a manly crush."

"Well then, I'm your man."

She stopped and gazed into his eyes. Those words. They could be true. If she allowed it. Juan Carlos had owned up to his deal. He hadn't really come on to her, but every single second of every single minute of the day, he told her in his own silent, heart-melting way that he wanted her.

"Yes, well, uh…just let me get the meatballs."

How was that for a change of subject?

"I can crush those, too," he said.

She laughed. "I'm sure you can."

Dinner was half an hour later. They decided to eat in the kitchen this time, at a wooden table with inlaid painted tiles. One of the nearby windows faced the backyard garden, now bathed in starlight, and if she squinted she could see the plants. It was cozy and nice, and she'd put out a mason jar candle that cast a pretty glow over the room. Juan Carlos kept glancing at his watch as they forked spaghetti into their mouths and spoke of easy simple things. She refused to think any more about the snake with the severed head lying in that shack. Or the cemetery with so many families who'd lived here before.

After his eyes shifted to his watch once again, her curiosity got the better of her. "Am I keeping you from something?"

There was no television in the house. No important soccer games to watch. No distractions. Maybe he couldn't wait to get upstairs to finish the book he'd been reading.

He shook his head. "There's no place I'd rather be than right here."

Oh, she'd stepped into that one.

"The meal is delicious," he said.

"It was all that manly crushing," she remarked, and he put his fork down to grin at her.

She jingled in places that normally jangled. He turned her life upside down. She'd miss him when this adventure was over and she went back to LA.

She rose and grabbed up their empty plates. "Would you like another helping?"

He patted his flat, washboard stomach. "No, I'd better stop here."

"Then no cherry cobbler? It seems the kitchen minions made a trip to the bakery."

"Maybe later, Princess."

She washed dishes and he dried. It was all so domestic. Well, as domestic as she'd seen on the Hallmark Channel. Her life was hardly a typical American tale. What did one do after the dishes were cleaned and the night loomed ahead?

Her gaze slid to Juan Carlos, wiping his hands on a kitchen towel. He folded the towel neatly, set it on the counter and smoothed it out. With a slight tilt of his head, he sought her out, a question on his lips.

Before he could voice his thoughts, the purr of an engine reached her ears. Juan Carlos strode to the kitchen window that faced the side yard. "It's Eduardo. He ran an errand for me. Wait here, I'll be right back."

"Why?"

But he dashed out the door before giving her an answer.

She heard their voices and strained to hear what they were saying, but she couldn't make it out.

The back door opened with the slight kick of Juan Carlos's boot and he strode in holding a wire cage in both hands.

Meeeow.

The cats! Juan Carlos had the mama cat and her kittens.

Eduardo followed behind him, his hair rumpled, drops of blood staining his scratched hands. He looked almost as frazzled as the cat.

"Eduardo, you're bleeding!"

"Hazard of the job," he mumbled.

It took only a second for her to figure out what he'd done. What they'd both done. Juan Carlos had sent Eduardo on a mission to rescue mama cat and her babies.

"He wouldn't let me go," Juan Carlos was saying.

"My job is to protect you, Your Majesty."

"Not from cats." The king appeared annoyed at himself for allowing Eduardo to do the job he'd wanted to do. "I should've gone. Now look at you."

"Better me than you. They're nothing but a few scrapes. She put up a good fight." Eduardo grinned. "She is a feisty one."

Juan Carlos gritted his teeth. "Those injuries should've been on my hands."

"Stop arguing, you two," Portia said. "What you both did was very kind. Juan Carlos, take the cats in the living area. The room is dark and cozy. It might put mama at ease. Eduardo, come with me. I'll take care of your hands." She marched into the bathroom and heard footsteps behind her. Grateful that Eduardo had obeyed her order, she grabbed a washrag, filled a bowl of warm water and pointed for him to sit on the edge of the bathtub.

Goodness.

She sat, too, and took his big hands in hers, scouring over half a dozen scratch marks. "She must've been very frightened."

"That made two of us."

"Oh, Eduardo." She began dabbing at the wounds. He flinched, but took the pain. She dabbed a little more gently, cleansing and dressing his wounds. "There."

"The king is very angry with me. Luis and I both, we convinced him not to go. He wanted to do this thing... for you."

Portia closed her eyes. "I...know."

Her chest tightened. It was the sweetest gesture anyone had ever done for her. Or tried to do.

"He is a proud man. But don't worry, he won't be angry for long."

"He won't?"

"No. I think not. And thank you, Eduardo, for rescuing the animals."

She placed a chaste kiss on his cheek. He was large, built like a block of stone, but his expression softened and as he rose, he bowed to her with his eyes twinkling.

And she felt as though she'd made a new friend.

Six

"Do you think she'll try to escape if we open the cage?" Portia asked as she sat facing Juan Carlos on the floor beside the fire. The cage was between them. The leery mama cat's eyes were guarded and wide. Portia made a move to get a better look at the babies, and a mewling hiss, one born of fear more than anything else, pressed through the feline's tight lips.

Juan Carlos shrugged. "She has nowhere to go. The house is locked up and the doors to this room are closed. Right now, I think she needs to see us and know we won't harm her."

"I think you're right." Portia tilted her head to one side. "You're intuitive when it comes to animals."

While she had been bandaging up Eduardo, Juan Carlos had set out a bowl of water and a plate of leftover cheese bits for when they let the cat out later.

"At least she won't starve tonight," he said.

Outside the wind was howling again, even pushing through the flue of the fireplace. The flames scattered momentarily in the hearth, blazing wildly before returning to a normal easy burn again. "No, she won't starve and the kittens will thrive. Thanks to you."

He kept his eyes on the fire, not commenting, refusing to take any credit for the deed. It didn't matter. He couldn't hide his intentions from her.

"They're the cutest little things," she said, her voice squeaking. She couldn't help it. Babies in all forms brought her voice to a higher pitch. Who in the world didn't love furry new kittens? "I'm glad they're here."

She had a view of his profile, so sharp and defined. Firelight played across his face and when he turned to her, his expression softened. "Me, too."

"Why didn't you tell me your plan to rescue her?" It was what all his watch-glancing had been about. It made sense to her now and she was incredibly relieved to learn the reason for his impatience. "Was it a surprise?"

He nodded. "I didn't want you to be disappointed if Eduardo couldn't bring her back."

And there it was. On his face. Concern. Caring. Almost love.

Something shifted inside her. It wasn't a blunt move, but something that had been tilting and leaning gradually, like dominoes toppling in super slow motion. She could feel each one fall, until every shred of her defenses was being taken down by this good, kind, *sexy* man.

"It's late," he said.

No, it wasn't.

"We should unlatch the cage now and leave her, so she can eat."

"Okay," Portia said, sorely disappointed. She knew that meant saying good night to Juan Carlos and parting ways at the top of the stairs once again.

He sighed as he rose to his feet and strode to the fireplace to take up a metal poker. He slashed at the logs, until only simmering embers heated the brick floor inside.

Portia carefully unlatched the hook on the cage and flipped it away. The wire door swung open but the cat stayed put. "Here you go, Duchess. You're free now."

"Duchess?" Juan Carlos turned to her.

"She needs a name." She shrugged. "It seems fitting somehow."

He smiled, but his eyes remained hooded. "Duchess it is. What's one more royal around here, anyway? Well, I'll say good-night now. We have an early call tomorrow."

They did. They were going even farther out on the grounds in the Jeep.

"Are you coming up?" he asked. He had almost reached the hallway door.

She rose to her feet and stared at him from across the room. Words wouldn't come. Her heart was thumping, drowning out everything else in her world.

"Portia?"

"What if...?" A swallow stole her next words.

He waited, his face in the shadows so she couldn't see his expression.

"What if I said I was a w-wimpy princess, after all?"

He paused. "Would you rather not go out in the Jeep tomorrow?"

"No." She shook her head, her hair falling like a sheet around her shoulders. "Juan Carlos, it means I don't want you to go to bed..."

He stepped out of the shadows, his eyes dark, intense. Waiting.

She froze. Oh, God, she was breaking every rule she'd ever committed to.

"Say it."

The force of his command sent thrills careening through her body.

"Say it, Portia."

He wouldn't break his vow to her. She had to do it. He'd told her as much just the other day. His honor meant that much to him and he wouldn't have it any other way.

"Without me." She nodded, convincing herself. "I don't want you to go to bed without—"

And suddenly, he was there in front her, gazing into her eyes, cupping her head in his hands and brushing his lips over hers. Once. Twice. His hungry mouth devoured her over and over again. His arms wrapped around her, his hand brushing away her hair tenderly, his body trembling as he took her in kiss after kiss.

She was lost in the goodness of him, the thrill of his hands finally on her. The scent of his skin. The power of his body. Tears spilled down her cheeks at the clarity of this moment. She was his. He was hers. It was so easy, so simple. How had she managed to keep this amazing man at bay? How had she not realized earlier how perfect they would be for each other?

"Portia, don't cry," he was murmuring between kisses.

"I'm…happy, Juan Carlos."

"Oh, God. How I've waited for this. For *you*. Say my name again."

"Juan Carlos. Juan Carlos. Juan Carlos."

He grinned, a flash of white teeth in a broad happy smile that branded her heart. His gaze roved over her face and traveled the length of her body, his smile fading into something delicious. Something dangerous. And something she no longer feared. His eyes burned with want, the heat in them back full force. The man knew how to smolder.

"Portia." He breathed her name as if his life depended on it. "I need you."

"I need you, too," she admitted softly. She reached for the hem of his shirt, pushing the material up his torso.

"No," he said, taking her hands in his. "We'll do this right."

And in the next instant, he swooped her up into his arms. She wound her arms around his neck and as he headed upstairs, she pressed her lips to his, kissing him until they reached the threshold to his room.

"Here we are," he said, his voice reverent, as if the next step he took would be monumental. He carried her over the threshold with great ceremony and smiled at her. "I've wanted you since the moment I laid eyes on you."

"You have me," she said softly.

"God. I cannot wait much longer, but I will not rush with you." He lowered her down onto the bed. The mattress cushioned her body and then his hands were there, removing her sweater and unbuttoning her blouse, spreading it out so he could see her breasts. "You are beautiful," he said, planting both hands on the mattress beside her head, trapping her. She may never want to escape. His kiss was rough and hungry, and when she looked up, the sharp lines of his face tightened, a passionate preamble of what was to come. Her skin prickled in anticipation.

His fingertips grazed over her breasts lightly, hovering, teasing the sensitive tips. Hot liquid warmth pooled between her thighs. Then he wound his hands behind her back and she lifted herself up enough for him to unfasten her bra. With his help, she shrugged out of it and then lay back down.

"Fair is fair," he said, rising to grab the hem of his shirt. He pulled it up and over his head. Her mouth gaped open and she took a hard swallow, gazing at the tempting sculpted bronze chest.

"That is totally *unfair*," she whispered.

A smile spread across his face as he bent on his knees to remove her boots, her belt and then slowly, achingly moved the zipper of her pants down. Cool air hit her thighs, but she was too swamped already, too raggedly consumed by heat for that to have any lasting effect. He tugged at one pant leg and then the other, until she was free of them. All that was left on her body was a pair of teeny hot pink panties. "I like your style, Princess," he murmured, sliding up her thighs to hook the hem with his fingers.

"I like yours." She gulped.

He smiled again and dragged her panties down her legs. Then the mattress dipped as he lowered down next to her. Immediately, his scent wafted to her nose: fresh soap and a hint of lime. She squeezed her eyes closed, breathing him in. He cupped her head and kissed her lips, her chin, her throat. "Let me explore you, Portia," he whispered.

She nodded. "If I can explore you."

"Be my guest," he said, his tone once again reverent. He fell back against the bed.

She rose up part of the way to lay a hand on his chest. Heat sizzled under her palm as she slid her fingers over tight skin and muscle. His chest was a work of art and as she continued to explore, he took sharp gasps of breath. Empowered now, she moved more confidently, her fingers flat over his nipples, weaving them through tiny chest hairs and reaching his broad shoulders. She nibbled on him there, nipping his hot skin and breathing the scent of raw sex emanating from his pores. "You are amazing, Juan Carlos," she said. And suddenly she was eager for him to explore her, to touch her in ways she'd secretly dreamed about. "Your turn."

She lay back on the bed and he rose over her to take a leisurely tour of her naked body, his eyes a beacon of light flowing over every inch of her. Then his hands began to trace the contours of her body, caressing her curves and moving effortlessly over her skin. He was thorough, leaving no part of her untouched. Goose bumps rose on her arms and legs, his precision and utmost sensitivity leaving her trembling in his wake.

Next, he covered her trembling body with his, wrapping her in his heat and claiming her with his presence. She bore his weight and peered up at him. He was amazing, so handsome, so incredibly virile. His hands cushioned her breasts, massaging them until the peaks were two sensitive tips. The pads of his thumbs flicked at them gently, and something powerful began to build and throb below her waist.

She had not been with a man in a long time. It felt so good. So right. Being with him.

He pressed her a little harder and she cried out. "Juan Carlos."

It seemed to satisfy him. He took her in an earth-shattering kiss, pressing her mouth open and sweeping into her. She moved under him, arching her hips, that feeling below her waist becoming stronger and stronger the longer the kiss went on.

His hand was moving again, leaving her full breasts and moving down her torso, past her navel and below her waist, where she ached and ached for him. "Trust me," he said.

All she could do was nod.

And his hands and mouth worked magic on her, shredding her into tiny pieces, squeezing tortured moans from her lips and making her squirm until she finally reached a fantastic, bone-melting orgasm.

"Juan Carlos," she breathed, lifting her head to find his eyes on her as he unbuckled his belt. He shucked out of his clothes quickly and sheathed himself, in all his naked glory, with a condom.

He touched her where she was most sensitive, lending her comfort and warmth in the aftermath of her pulsing release. She relaxed and eased back slowly, as another fire began to build. "I've waited for you all of my life, Portia. And now, you're mine."

She was ready for him when he entered her, wanting him this way, taking his weight and watching a fiery veil of passion burn in his eyes. He began to rock back and forth, each thrust a love note, a daring caress and sugary candy for her hungry body. "You are all I will ever need," he murmured.

She smiled as he pressed farther and farther inside her body. She was his. *He* was all she would ever need and as she met his driving rhythm, arching up and down, her breaths heavy, her body primed, she found solace and peace in his arms and lust and desire in his bed.

Juan Carlos drew a deep breath into his lungs. He'd often dreamed of waking up next to Portia, and now his very fantasy had come true. He turned his head and watched her chest rise and fall slowly. Her hair fanned across the pillow. He ached to touch it and sift the strands through his fingers. He wanted to kiss her awake and then make love to her again. But the sun had barely risen and the day would prove a long one. She needed her sleep. He'd worn her out last night. He shook his head at the thoughts running through his mind. He couldn't touch her again this morning and have her think he was lecherous, waking her with only one thing on his mind.

He smiled. He would come to her again sometime today. It would be hard to keep to the task at hand, but they were on a mission. Though a wicked part of him wanted to play hooky today. Why couldn't they just stay in bed all day? The States had snow days. Why couldn't he declare a Royal Day?

A little noise pressed through her lips, a moan that he'd come to know. Last night, she'd moaned plenty and turned his world on end.

She shifted toward him and one hand—warm, delicate and soft—flopped onto his cheek. He moved his head enough to press his lips there and kiss her.

"Hi," she said, smiling, though her eyes were still closed.

"Good morning, sweetheart."

"Is it time to get up?"

"You can stay in bed as long as you'd like."

"With you?"

"Yes, only with me."

Her eyes opened and he gazed into their sleep-hooded amazing blue depths. He could fall into those eyes and never want to return.

"Juan Carlos," she said, "last night was…"

"I know."

"I didn't know it could be that good."

He leaned in and kissed her tenderly. "I'm humbled to hear you say that."

"Humbled? Not over-the-moon, cocky and feeling proud of yourself?"

He chuckled. "Maybe that, too."

"I had…uh, you know. Three times. That's never happened before."

"Keep telling me things like that and we'll never get out of this bed."

She grinned and reached over to move a tendril of hair off his forehead, her delicate fingertips sliding down his cheek. He loved it when she touched him. "You know, that doesn't sound like a bad idea."

He caught her wrist and kissed her pulse point. "We can make that happen, sweetheart."

"If only," she said, sighing, her head falling back against the pillow. "But we need to finish what we started."

She would be leaving soon. She didn't have to say the words. He had only a few more days with her, before she would head back to the States. How quickly reality reared its ugly head. "We will finish it, one way or another."

"I hope we find something today," she said.

"We'll give it a good shot."

"I should get dressed. I'm anxious to see how our little family is doing."

She meant the cats. Juan Carlos had almost forgotten about them. "Right. Let's go check on them together."

She rose from the bed and turned away. As she fitted

her arms through the sleeves of his shirt, he glimpsed her lush blond hair falling down her back, the creamy texture of her skin, her rounded backside and the coltlike legs that had wrapped around him last night.

He sighed, enjoying the view and ignoring his body's immediate reaction to her. He threw on a pair of jeans and a T-shirt. Hand in hand, they strolled out of the bedroom and into the living area.

"Shhh," she said, spying the cat nursing her kittens outside the cage on a loop rug in front of the fireplace. "We don't want to startle her."

Duchess was resting with her head down, her eyes closed, allowing her five offspring to take their morning meal. Juan Carlos was moved by the sweet look on Portia's face as she silently watched mama and babies. He wrapped his arm around her shoulder and drew her closer, kissing the top of her head. How could he ever let this woman go? The answer was simple: he couldn't. It wouldn't be easy but he would convince her to stay. And marry him.

"Do you think Duchess will eat eggs?" she asked Juan Carlos as she scrambled four eggs in a cast-iron skillet. Morning sunshine brightened the kitchen, filling it with warmth. Bacon sizzled on the griddle and toast was cooking under the broiler. "I'll put a little cheese on them."

"You can try," he said, pouring two mugs of coffee. "She'll eat when she gets hungry enough. I'll send Eduardo out this morning for cat food."

She'd managed to get fresh water over to the cat without her running for cover. Duchess was still wary, but the kittens slowed her down or else she probably would've bolted when Portia set the bowl down. In time, Duchess would come to trust her. Sadly, she wouldn't be around long enough to see it.

She had work waiting for her in Los Angeles.

It was for the best that she leave Alma. She couldn't fall in love with Juan Carlos. He didn't fit into her plans for a quiet, unassuming life. Yet spending time with him had been magnificent.

He came up behind her, kissed the side of her throat and ran a hand up her thigh. She tensed in all the good places. He'd asked her not to dress yet, and now she knew why. She was only wearing his shirt, which gave him easy access to her body. Not that she minded. Heavens, no. She loved him touching her. "I'll be right back," he said. "Coffee's ready and on the table."

"Where are you going?" she asked.

"Don't be so nosy. I'll be back before you know it."

She smiled and turned, and his arms automatically wound around her. "See that you are. Breakfast is almost ready."

"Bossy, Princess," he said, staring at her mouth.

Her heart skipped a beat and a moment passed between them before he kissed the tip of her nose.

She shrugged a shoulder. "Kings."

He laughed and exited the back door.

Juan Carlos may have originally been a reluctant king, but there was no doubt in her mind that he was good for Alma and that he would put the country's welfare above all else. As it should be. Alma had been through tough times under a ruthless dictatorship. The country needed a strong man.

So do you.

No, she couldn't go there. The map was already drawn up for both of them, and after this little interlude, their paths wouldn't cross again.

After she set the table, Juan Carlos returned holding a bouquet of tall azure flowers. "For you," he said, handing her all but one stem. "Scilla hispanica."

"They're beautiful." She lifted them to her nose. "Are these from the garden?"

He nodded. "Spanish bluebells. They're almost a perfect match to your eyes, sweetheart." He pinched off the end of the one he still held and fitted it behind her right ear. "There. Now you're perfect."

"Hardly," she said.

"I think so."

"You think I'm bossy."

"Dressed like that, cooking my breakfast and wearing flowers in your hair? I can deal with a little bossiness."

She shook her head. "You're wicked." And so very thoughtful.

"So I'm told."

He took the flowers from her hands, snapped off the tips of the stems and arranged the bouquet in an old thick green glass bottle. After he filled it with water, he placed it on the table. "Have a seat, Princess," he said, pulling out a chair. "I'll serve you."

She had a protest on her lips, but Juan Carlos's expression wouldn't allow arguing. "Yes, Your Highness."

He smiled. "Good. I'm glad you know who the real boss is around here."

Portia's heart swelled. And as they sat down and ate, easy conversation flowed between them. Juan Carlos touched her hand often, as if needing the connection. She leaned over to brush hair from his forehead and he'd steal a kiss or two. They were in sync with each other; nothing had ever been as perfect as it was now, with the two of them doing ordinary everyday things, like cooking breakfast, sharing a meal and worrying over the cat family.

"So what will happen to Duchess and her babies when we have to leave here?" she asked.

"She'll become the official palace cat, of course."

"And the kittens?"

"We'll find them good homes, Portia. Don't worry."

Her eye twitched. "I know you're doing this for me." She covered his hand with hers. "Thank you."

The feelings between them were getting too heavy, too fast. She had no way of stopping it, short of leaving him right here and now. But she couldn't do that. Not only did she not want to, but she'd promised to spend a few days here helping with the search, and with the exception of a snake decapitation, she was having a wonderful time.

"You're welcome. Now, if you'll excuse me, I have to speak with Luis about a few matters."

Juan Carlos rose and began clearing the dishes. What a guy. She bounded up quickly and took the plates from his hands. "I'll take care of that," she said with enough authority to keep prison inmates in line.

"Okay," he said. "Thanks."

He bent his head and took her in a long amazing kiss. When their lips parted and he was through, her head spun. "That was…promising."

He grinned, shaking his head at her understatement. "Get ready. We'll be leaving in a little while. Unless you've changed your mind and want to play hooky today."

He was reaching inside her shirt. She slapped his hand away and pointed. "Go."

He went.

And Portia cleared the dishes and cleaned up the kitchen. She checked on Duchess and her brood; they were all sleeping. What a pretty serene picture they made, a mass of calico colors and balls of fluff all nestled together. She was grateful they'd have a home after they left the farmhouse. Her heart had never been so full.

Thirty minutes later, Portia climbed into the passenger side of the Jeep and Juan Carlos got behind the wheel. They said goodbye to Luis, though that didn't mean anything. He was sure to follow. Eduardo had gone into the local town on a cat food mission.

"All set?" Juan Carlos said, gunning the motor. "Strapped in?"

She nodded. The weather was glorious, the temperature in the mid-seventies with clear blue skies. She wore a lightweight white jacket that billowed in the breeze as Juan Carlos drove off and picked up speed.

"We're going out about five miles," he shouted over the engine's roar.

She sat back and relaxed, enjoying the scenery, excitement stirring her bones. Maybe today they'd find the art treasures.

For four hours they traveled at a snail's pace over lush lands, where wildflowers and lantana grew in abundance, the vista opening up to a prairie as they scoured the grounds looking for possible hiding places. They came upon another shack but after a thorough inspection, with Juan Carlos insisting on going inside first, they found absolutely nothing. Not even a snake.

"We have a little more land to cover before we head back," Juan Carlos said, and she heard the disappointment in his voice. She, too, was disappointed.

"Let's stop for lunch by that little lake we passed a few minutes ago." Maybe regrouping would give them a fresh perspective.

"It wasn't much of a lake," Juan Carlos said. "More like an oversize pond."

She entwined their fingers. "But it's pretty there and I'm getting hungry."

He smiled and gave her hand a squeeze. That was all it took for her heart to do a little flip. "Okay, we'll have a picnic." And he maneuvered the Jeep around, heading for the lake.

Warm breezes ruffled her hair and sweat beaded her

forehead as the sun climbed high overhead. She loved being outdoors. Much of her time in the States was spent indoors at art exhibits, galleries or simply poring over books and surfing the internet. She took a full breath of Alma air and vowed not to let disappointment ruin their day.

They'd packed a lunch and had a blanket. That was all they would need.

Juan Carlos braked the Jeep several yards from the water's edge. There were no shade trees so they used the vehicle to provide a bit of cover. From Luis. They were always being watched, but Portia was starting to get used to the idea and it wasn't as creepy as she'd once thought. Juan Carlos jumped down first as she gathered up the blanket. Then he reached for her and helped her down, crushing her body against his and taking her in a long, slow, deliberate kiss.

When he released her, her breathing sped up, coming in short clips. The blanket between them was her only salvation from being ravaged on the spot. She clung to it and backed away. "I should spread this out."

He backed off, too. "You do that," he said, his voice tight. "I'll get the cooler."

Once everything was in place, they sat down facing the water, their backs propped against the side of the Jeep. "The kitchen minions make great sandwiches," she said, taking a bite of chicken salad.

"I'll remember to thank them."

At some point during the day, either Luis or Eduardo would fill the refrigerator and cupboards with food, much of it readymade. She wasn't entirely sure it didn't come from the palace itself. The King of Montoro had a wonderful cook staff. But she decided the mystery was exciting and she didn't want to know how it magically appeared. She liked that it just did.

"What do we do now?" she asked, taking another bite.

Juan Carlos's throat worked, as he tipped a water bottle back and took a sip. He wiped the back of his hand across his mouth and turned to her, his eyes dark and searching. "I don't know. I think we've exhausted all possibilities. Where else is there to look?"

She had to agree. They'd searched the entire grounds—the prairies, the hills, the outer buildings—and found nothing. "The art could be anywhere and we'd never know it. There are no clues and sadly those secrets have been buried along with your family members."

He nodded. "At least the artwork didn't fall into the hands of the dictator, which was their main intent. I can't say I'm not disappointed. I thought we'd find something, a clue, some hint that would lead us to it. I can only hope it is found one day."

"I'm sorry, Juan Carlos." She set her sandwich down and brought her lips to his mouth. It was a chaste kiss, one of commiseration.

Instantly, his arms wound around her shoulders and he tugged, pulling her practically on top of him, deepening the kiss. "You're the only woman who can make me feel better," he murmured.

A pulse throbbed in her neck. She loved hearing his sweet words, even though they might be some of the last she'd hear from him. Soon, when the search was finally concluded, she'd have to say goodbye to him and all that they'd meant to each other in this short span of time. Yet, right now, she wanted to make him feel better—but she couldn't do it here. Out in the open. "We should go," she said. "Luis is watching."

He kissed her again, and then lifted himself up, pulling his phone out of his pocket. He spent a few seconds texting someone and then returned to her. "He's not watching anymore."

"Juan Carlos! What did you say to him?"

His lips twitched. "I told him to retreat one hundred yards and turn his head away from the Jeep for twenty minutes."

"You didn't!" Her face instantly burned. Her pride was stung. "He's going to know."

Juan Carlos touched her face gently, his fingertips on her cheeks, calming her. "Sweetheart, any man who sees how I look at you *knows*. Luis won't say a word."

"But I'll know he knows."

"It's beautiful here, Portia. And I need you. Do you not need me, too?"

His words worked magic on her. Yes, she needed him, too. She nodded. "But—"

He kissed away her doubts and then lowered her onto the blanket. His mouth was brutally tender, claiming her with each stroke of the tongue as soul-wrenching groans escaped his throat.

Thrills ran up and down her body as he exposed her to the sun's rays. The scent of fresh water and clear skies combined made her forget her inhibitions. She'd never made love outdoors and she only wanted to experience it with this one exciting man.

Firelight created jumping shadows across the living room walls. Juan Carlos sat with Portia beside him on the sofa as they watched Duchess bathe a kitten, her tongue taking long swipes across its furry body. The kitten took a playful swing or two at mama cat, but Duchess didn't relent. She used one paw to hold her charge down, determined to finish the job and lick away the grime of the day before moving on to her next one. She cleansed and fed her young diligently. Duchess, for all her wildness, was a good mama cat.

"You're quiet tonight," Portia said. "Still thinking about the missing art treasure?"

That was part of it. His failure to find it bothered him. He'd been so certain that there were clues here on the property and yet, he felt as if he was missing something important. He couldn't say what, but deep down in his bones he still believed the answers were here.

Yet most of his thoughts concerned Portia. They'd exhausted their search and there was nothing to keep them on the farm any longer. Tomorrow they would head back to Del Sol and then Portia would return to the States. Eventually. Unless he could convince her to stay.

"I'm thinking about us," he answered honestly.

Portia put her head on his shoulder. "What about us?" she asked, her smooth-as-velvet voice tapping into his heart. At least she didn't say, *there is no us.* She recognized that they were edging toward a precarious cliff.

Three sharp raps at the door interrupted their conversation. He gave it a glance and waited for the next two knocks, which would signal him that all was well. Those two knocks came and Juan Carlos rose, striding to the door. "It's either Luis or Eduardo," he said over his shoulder to reassure Portia, and then opened the door. "Eduardo. I trust everything is all right?"

"Yes. But I have something of interest I thought you would want to hear right now."

Eduardo glanced at Portia, who was now sitting on the edge of the sofa, her eyes round with curiosity. "Regarding?"

"Your search, Your Majesty."

Juan Carlos swung the door open wider. "Come in."

"Your Highness," he said to Portia as he made his way inside the room.

"Eduardo." She granted him a beautiful smile, most likely grateful it wasn't his counterpart, Luis, seeking them out. He could see the relief in her eyes. This afternoon, making love under blue skies behind the Jeep, Portia had let go her inhibitions and made a memory that would live forever in his mind. But afterward his Portia had gone on and on about Luis, asking how she could ever face him again.

Juan Carlos had succeeded in kissing away her worries.

"Would you like to sit down?" Portia asked.

"No, thank you. I didn't mean to interrupt." Eduardo regarded the kittens, his expression softening.

"Duchess is coming around," Portia said, her eyes glittering.

One look at Eduardo and the cat's back arched, and a low mewling hiss sprang from her mouth.

Portia rolled her eyes. "*Slowly* she's coming along. She should know better than to bite the hand that feeds her. Sorry, Eduardo. And how are your hands?"

He waved them in the air. "They are fine, Princess. No need to worry."

"What did you find out of interest, Eduardo?" he asked. "Something about the search?"

"Yes, Your Highness. You gave me the list of names on the graves at the Montoro family cemetery."

"Yes, I committed many of them to memory." He'd tasked Eduardo with contacting his uncle Rafe and alerting him about the cemetery. Juan Carlos wanted those family plots cleaned up and the headstones that were damaged beyond repair to be replaced as soon as possible.

"Yes, well, I spoke with your uncle, as you asked. He has no knowledge of those family members or that there even was a Montoro cemetery on the grounds. Not one name seemed to jar his memory."

"We didn't have first names. We only found initials on the headstones. It doesn't matter if he remembered the names or not. We will have that cemetery restored."

"There's more."

Juan Carlos nodded. "I'm listening."

"Your uncle claims that as a rite of passage, every Montoro had the privilege of being buried in the family mausoleum in Alma, whether rich or poor. If they were related to Montoro and had bloodlines, it was an honor to be buried there."

"Yes, I know that. But surely during Tantaberra's reign, that wouldn't hold true anymore. After the war, everything changed. I assumed those graves were there because Tantaberra controlled even where a person would lay to rest."

Portia walked up to take his hand. "But Juan Carlos, think about some of the dates on the headstones. Many were pre-Tantaberra."

He gave it a moment of thought, his mind clicking back to the headstones. "You're right. There were at least four that I remember that dated back to the 1920s and '30s. Before the war, before Tantaberra."

"Yes," Portia said, her voice reaching a higher pitch. "And those initials might've been used to throw people off. They'd have no real way of investigating who was laid to rest there."

"Hold on a second," Juan Carlos said, pulling out his phone. He clicked over to the list he'd brought with him of the known art pieces missing from the palace. His heart racing, he located the titles.

"*Joven Amelia*. J.A. were the initials on one of the headstones," he said. "It means Young Amelia. *Almas Iguales*. A.I. was another set of initials. The sculpture is called *Equal Souls* in English. And then there is *Dos Rios*."

"D.R. I remember that one," Portia said. "I thought he was a doctor."

"There's a painting called *Dos Rios* that's missing," he said. "Portia, you said it yourself this afternoon, the secrets have been buried along with my family members.

But I don't think there are any family members buried in the cemetery."

"You think the artwork is buried there." Portia's voice was breathless and eager.

"It's a long shot, Princess. I think the cemetery is bogus. It was the family's way of protecting the art from Tanta-berra. We have to find out. Eduardo, get in touch with Luis. We'll need a bulldozer, but for now, round up shovels and some high-powered lights. I'm going tonight."

"Oh, Juan Carlos, do you really think you've found it?"

"*We* found it, Portia. You're as much a part of this as I am."

Portia nodded, an excited smile teasing her lips. "I'll go change my clothes."

"Portia," he said, "are you sure you want to go? If I'm wrong, it will be pretty gruesome."

"If you really want to see *gruesome* try and stop me, Your Highness."

He grinned. "That's right. You're not a wimpy princess."

He was glad. It wouldn't feel right going on this search without her by his side.

Whatever they found.

Seven

"I really know how to show a lady a good time, don't I?" With shovel in hand, Juan Carlos dug at the foot of a grave alongside Eduardo and Luis as the high beams of two cars cast the cemetery in an unearthly glow.

Dirt flew through the air and landed at the toes of her boots. If she weren't so excited, she'd be totally creeped out. "I can't think of anywhere else I'd rather be," she countered honestly.

Even her embarrassment with Luis had been forgotten.

"I can help out," she said, "when anyone wants to take a break."

Eduardo covered his laughter with a grunt.

Juan Carlos slanted her a be-serious look. "I'll keep that in mind, Princess."

Luis was too busy digging to look up.

She wrapped her arms around her sides as the night air became chillier. She'd refused Juan Carlos's suggestion to sit it out in the car and so she stood watching, waiting.

They were digging up the grave of J. A. Molina. The headstone dated the death to 1938.

After ten minutes of silent digging, she heard a thump. Eduardo's shovel smacked against something solid. Thump, thump. "I hit something, Your Highness," Eduardo said.

"Let's keep digging," Juan Carlos said. There was a

boyish tone to his excitement. "It shouldn't be long now before we know."

The men worked twice as fast now, focusing their efforts. The scraping sounds of shovels against wood filled the quiet night.

"Portia, will you get the flashlight and shine it down here."

The men were five feet below ground level now and working furiously.

She grabbed the biggest flashlight she could find and stood as close as possible over the grave site, sending beams of light down. Portia's heart sank. "It's a coffin, isn't it?"

"Maybe," Juan Carlos said. Under her flashlight, his eager eyes had lost some of their gleam. A layer of dirt remained on top of the box, and he used his gloved hands to swipe it off, searching for any hint of what lay inside. He found nothing written. "Let's bring it up."

It took some doing, but the three men hoisted the box up and set it on a patch of flat ground.

"Hand me the ax," Juan Carlos ordered. He made the sign of the cross over his chest. "And may God forgive us."

Luis handed Juan Carlos the tool and he carefully began to hack at the very edges of the coffin. Each blow of the ax brought the mystery closer and closer to an end. Eduardo used his shovel to help pry the lid of the box open.

It was time. Their work was nearly over. Juan Carlos hesitated a moment, drew breath into his lungs and then glanced at her. "Ready?"

She nodded.

"You might want to look away," he said.

"No, I will be fine with whatever we find." Her eye twitched, closing in a wink.

Juan Carlos stared at her. Perhaps he was equally as nervous as she was. With his gloved hands, he lifted the hacked lid. She beamed the flashlight on the contents, her heart thumping hard.

"There's no corpse." His voice elevated, he continued, "But there's something in here."

She held her breath, her pulse jumping in her veins. He unfolded a sheath, and found another box, no more than two by three feet, this one carved and quite ornate. He lifted it out and she shined the flashlight on it. *Joven Amelia* was etched in golden lettering on top.

Juan Carlos's hand shook. "It's here. Thank God," he said. Setting the box down on the ground, he kneeled, and she took a place beside him. He took great care to remove his filthy gloves and then opened the latch and lifted the lid.

Inside, surrounded by lush black velvet, there was a painting of a little girl, no more than ten years old, playing near the seashore with a much younger sister. The canvas was secured, not rolled up as one might expect, but mounted to a frame as if taken from the palace in a hurry. Portia would have to inspect it thoroughly and do some research, but she was almost certain that it was genuine, given the great pains the royal family had taken to hide the painting decades ago.

"It's beautiful," she said. "She is Young Amelia."

Tears welled in Juan Carlos's eyes. "We did it, Portia. We found the missing treasures."

"Yes," she breathed, her heart swelling. "Yes."

"Eduardo, Luis, come see."

Taking her hand, Juan Carlos rose and tugged her up with him. Once standing, he wrapped his arms around her waist and drew her close, so they were hip to hip. Joy beamed in her heart. It was a monumental occasion and she found no reason for pretense. As Juan Carlos had said, the way he looked at her left little room for doubt of his feelings, anyway. They were lovers. It was hard to disguise.

The bodyguards peered at the painting in its casing. Both seemed awed and a little surprised to be looking at a royal masterpiece lost for generations.

"Congratulations, Your Majesty," Eduardo said.

"Alma's precious treasures have been restored," Luis said.

The two men shook the king's hand. There was pride and resolve in all of their eyes.

Eduardo turned to her. "Princess Portia, congratulations to you, as well. It is a great find."

"Thank you, Eduardo. That's very kind of you to say." She stepped forward and placed a kiss on his cheek. "I'm thrilled to have helped in a small way."

Eduardo blushed, but gave no indication he was alarmed by her affectionate display. A smile tugged at his lips, bringing her a rush of friendly warmth inside.

Juan Carlos got right down to business again. "I would like you to secure the grounds tonight. When the bulldozers arrive, we will resume digging in the morning. Assemble a team. I would like to have all the art secured by the end of the day tomorrow, if possible."

"Yes, Your Highness," Luis said. "It will be done."

The men turned to do their tasks, and Juan Carlos took her hand and began dragging her away from the stream of lights. "Come with me, sweetheart," he said.

"Where are we going?"

"To bed, as soon as I can arrange it," he said. "But for now, this will have to do."

He pulled her behind the cars, out into the darkness under the stars. And the next thing she knew, Juan Carlos's hands were about her and she was flying, sailing through the air, spinning around and around. "We did it, Princess. We did it."

"Yes, yes, we did." Laughter spilled from her lips and a lightness of spirit filled her.

"This is an amazing moment. I'm glad to be sharing it with you," he said.

Her smile broadened. "I feel the same way, Juan Carlos. I'm bursting inside."

He brought her down to earth gently, her boots gracing the sacred grounds. And his lips sought hers instantly, kissing her mouth, chin, cheeks and forehead. His hands sifted through her hair and his dark, luscious eyes bored into her. "Do you have any idea how much I love you, Portia? I do. I love you, Princess. With all my heart."

"Oh, Juan Carlos, I love you, too." And there it was. Her truth. Her honest feelings poured out of her in this instant of happiness and joy. She could no longer hide away from the sensations rocking her from head to toe. The words she spoke were not damning, but blissful and joyous. She loved Juan Carlos Salazar II, King Montoro of Alma.

"You do? You love me?" His grin spoke to her heart in a language all its own. His was the sweetest of tones, as if he was in total awe of her love.

She nodded eagerly. "I love you."

He lifted her up and twirled her around once more before he set her down. His kiss this time made her dizzier than a dozen spins in his arms. His mouth claimed her, his lips demanding, his tongue penetrating through to sweep in and conquer. Her knees wobbled and she sought his sturdy shoulders for balance, her monumental declaration swaying both of them.

"Oh, Portia, my love. I cannot think of a life without you. Marry me. Be my wife. Be with me forever."

The words rang in her ears. It wasn't as if she hadn't expected them to come, but the surprise came only in her answer. "Yes, Juan Carlos. I will marry you."

The next morning, Portia woke in Juan Carlos's arms, opening her eyes to a face she had come to love. Handsome, breathtaking and dynamic. He was a man who got things done. He'd certainly pursued her to the point of her complete compliance. How could she not fall in love with this man?

"Good morning, fiancée," he said, kissing the tip of her nose.

"Hello, my love," she said.

They'd celebrated in this very bed well into the night. There was champagne and candles and bone-melting caresses.

As she plopped her head against the pillow, the sheets pulled away, exposing her bare shoulders. Her eyes lifted to the ceiling, focusing on tiles that were chipping away. The farmhouse, old and neglected as it was, had undeniable charm. She sighed. "Is this real?"

"So real," Juan Carlos said. "Here, feel my heart."

He grasped her hand and placed it on his chest. Under her fingertips, life-sustaining beats pulsed through his veins. "I am real. A man who loves a woman."

"But you are the king of Alma."

"And you are the princess of Samforstand…we are meant to be, sweetheart. Can you not see how perfect this is? Fate has stepped in and brought the two of us together. I can only marry a woman of royal blood. And that's you." He brought her hand to his lips and tenderly kissed one finger, then another and another. "When I became king, marrying was the last thing on my mind. But then I saw you at the coronation and all bets were off."

"And what if I weren't a princess? Then what would you have done?"

"I would have…" He hesitated and sighed, bringing her up and over his body so that she straddled his thighs. He nipped at her lips and wove his fingers through her hair, eyeing the locks as if they were made of gold. "Luckily, I don't have that burden."

"No, you don't," she said, taking his hand and placing it on her chest. The heat of his palm warmed her breast and she squeezed her hand over his. "Feel my heart."

His eyes filled with hunger and every cell in her body reacted to his sensual touch. "You are wicked, Princess."

She chuckled. "You bring it out in me."

"You see, we *are* a perfect match."

"Are we?" She nibbled on her lip. She'd disobeyed her hard and fast rule of not falling for a high-profile man. You couldn't get much higher than king. Was she destined to fame through association even though it's the last thing she wanted?

"Let me show you again, so that you will never doubt it."

His hands on her hips, he gently guided her over him and they welcomed the dawn with their bodies and hearts joined as one.

But her doubts remained, locked and hidden away, even as she agreed to marry him. Even as she claimed her love for him. Half an hour later, she was showered and dressed. She and Juan Carlos ate a quick breakfast of cereal and fruit, both anxious to get back to the cemetery site this morning. But Portia couldn't forget her six charges. She walked into the living area with bowls of water and cat food in her hands and set them down by the fireplace hearth, where Duchess had taken up residence. "Here you go, girl."

Duchess no longer looked at her with frightened eyes. She had at one time been domesticated, and she was beginning to remember her life before hunger and fear had changed her. Portia kneeled and watched the cat rise, stretch her neck and shake out her limbs, and then walk over to the water. She lapped furiously as five balls of fluff scrambled to be near her, one kitten losing his balance and plopping half his body into the bowl. He jumped back, as if hit by a jolt, and gave himself a few shakes. Tiny drops of water sprinkled Portia's clothes.

She giggled and pressed her hand to the top of the little one's head. Silky fur tickled her palm. "You are a feisty one."

Juan Carlos strode into the room. "Are you ready to go, sweetheart?"

She stood. "Yes. I can't wait to see what else we uncover."

According to Eduardo, two bulldozers and a full crew were working furiously this morning. In the middle of the night, he'd called upon and assembled a team of men he could trust with this secret. Soon, the entire country would know about the hidden artwork. What a story to tell.

Last night, Juan Carlos had shared his hopes of putting many of these treasures on display for Alma citizens as well as tourists who would come to view the find. It would be nothing short of a boon for the country. The restoration of the artwork would instill pride and honor in a country once diminished and downtrodden by a dictator. First, though, Portia, along with a Latin art specialist, would have to verify that the pieces were not fakes.

By the time they reached the site, half the graveyard was dug up. Dust swirled through the air from the many mounds of dirt dotting the cemetery. Ten men with shovels and axes were hoisting boxes up from the graves. Luis, with pen and pad in hand, was making an inventory list. As ordered, none of the boxes had been opened.

Juan Carlos helped her down from the Jeep. He took her hand and they walked to where Luis stood next to a gravestone marked with the initials P.P. Tasked with documenting and photographing each headstone before the box was brought up, Luis lifted his head to greet them.

"Your Highness, Princess," he said. "We have twelve boxes already accounted for. As you can see, we have more to do. We've placed them inside the tent over there," he said, pointing to a room-size tent set up outside the cemetery under guard by two men, "and they are ready for you to open."

"Thank you, Luis," Juan Carlos said. "Your men are working faster than I thought. Now, if you'll come with me, I'll need you to document what we find as I open the boxes."

"I'll take the photos," Portia said.

Luis handed over his digital camera and nodded. "Thank you, Your Highness."

Excitement stirred in her belly. To be a part of this find was a dream come true. How many dreams was one person allowed in a lifetime? All this joy in such a short span of time? She'd found adventure and love where she'd least expected it, in the arms of a king.

Inside the tent, Juan Carlos opened box after box, carefully removing the pieces for documentation. Oil paintings, sculptures, bronzed statues and the famed ancient Alma tiara had been locked away and hidden from the world for decades. Portia photographed everything, carefully making mental notes of the pieces she would research for authentication.

They worked alongside the men, until all the pieces were uncovered and the mock cemetery was emptied out. By late afternoon, they'd unearthed twenty-two boxes in all, the grave sites now nothing but pockmarks in the earth.

Juan Carlos climbed to the top of a pile of dirt in the center of the graveyard, his boots spread out, his voice booming to the loyal men who had labored here. As he spoke, shovels were held still, conversations died down. "The Montoro family cemetery has done its job to preserve what is sovereign to our country. You are all a part of Alma history now and I thank you for your hard work today. Until these items are authenticated, I would ask for your silence. Luis and Eduardo have assured me all of you can be trusted. The next step is to transport these pieces back to the palace in the trucks you arrived in. Again, thank you all for your diligence."

Juan Carlos jumped down from the dirt hill and once again, Portia was reminded of how well he fit the position of king. He was a true diplomat and leader. A man to be admired. Staunch in his beliefs and fair-minded…she was sure if the clocks were turned back in time to when Alma was last ruled by a king, he would have reigned over his people justly.

"What are you staring at?" he asked, approaching her.

She shook off her thoughts and smiled. "How handsome you are with dirt on your face."

He grinned. "I could say the same about you, Princess. The smudges on your face only make you more beautiful." He touched her nose, right cheek and forehead.

Goodness, she'd never considered what the hours of dust and grime had done to her fair complexion. "I must be a mess."

"Nothing a hot bubble bath wouldn't cure, and I'm volunteering to scrub your back," he whispered.

"I'll take you up on that, Your Highness."

And shortly after, they left the graveyard and returned to the farmhouse.

They had one night left to share here. And Portia was sure, Juan Carlos would make it memorable, bubble bath and all.

Portia was too much in love to think about her future and how marrying Juan Carlos would affect her life and her career. She had no details to cling to, only love, and it would have to see her through the tough decisions she would have to make. Now, as she sat at a long dressed table in the palace's elegant dining room, she gazed first at her secret fiancé seated at the helm. Dressed in a charcoal-black suit, he was beaming and full of determination. He appeared ready to make the announcement to his family. Rafe and Emily sat across from her with her friend Maria and Alex Ramon.

Gabriel and his wife, Serafia, sat to her left, along with Bella and James. James's little girl, Maisey, was holding tight to her chest a princess doll dressed in aqua-blue with hair the color of glistening snow.

"It's a lovely doll, Maisey," Portia commented, smiling at the child.

"She looks a lot like you, Portia," Bella commented. "I'm just noticing the likeness."

Maisey's curious eyes shifted to Portia and the girl giggled. It was true that she shared a resemblance with a famous cartoon character that all young girls seemed to love.

Juan Carlos covered Portia's hand, entwining their fingers. "Ah, but Portia is a one-of-a-kind princess."

All those close to Juan Carlos were here. He'd invited them for dinner tonight under the pretense of disclosing the facts around the graveyard find. Only he and Portia knew the truth.

"Before the meal is served, a toast is in order," he said. "We have much to celebrate tonight."

Waiters poured champagne into crystal flutes.

Once all the bubbles settled, Juan Carlos rose. "Thank you, cousins and friends, for joining me tonight. We all have much to be thankful for. As you know, with Portia's help, we have found the missing pieces of art at the Montoro family farm. Yes, it's true, we dug up mock graves to unearth the treasures. The finds are yet to be authenticated, but we are fairly certain our ancestors wouldn't have gone to such extreme measures to hide fake artwork. Portia will do the preliminary research on the items we've found and under her advisement we will also hire an expert to verify each piece.

"But that is not why I've called you here today. I have

something more personal to share with you." He turned to Portia, offering his hand. She took it and rose, warmth traveling up her cheeks. All eyes were on her and the king.

Juan Carlos went down on one knee, and gasps erupted from the diners at the table. She had no idea he would go traditional on her in front of his family. But how silly of her not to think it. Juan Carlos was a man of tradition and so as she gazed into his gleaming dark eyes, she began to tremble.

"Princess Portia, you know I love you with all of my heart. I have since the moment I laid eyes on you."

Tears wet her eyes.

"I have one precious thing left of my childhood and now, I am offering it to you." He reached into his jacket pocket and came up with a diamond ring, the stone so brilliant, it caught the chandelier light and virtually illuminated the room. "This was my mother's wedding ring," he said, his voice tight. "And here before our family and close friends, I ask you to wear it and become my wife. Portia, Princess of Samforstand, will you marry me?"

Not even a breath could be heard in the roomful of people.

Her cheeks were moist with tears as she nodded. "Yes, yes. Of course I'll marry you, Juan Carlos. I am honored to wear your mother's ring."

Her hand shook as he slid the ring that once belonged to his mother onto her finger. He stared at the ring, his eyes deeply reverent, and then grinned wide, looking foolishly happy. With the pads of his thumbs, he wiped at her tears and then took her in a kiss that nearly muffled the screams of delight and applause coming from behind her.

After the kiss, they were both swarmed with handshakes and hugs.

She was beside herself with happiness. The love and acceptance she experienced from his family and friends was more than she'd ever expected. There were no, *Are you sures?* or *This has happened so fasts*, but rather, "Congratulations" and "You two are perfect for each other."

After everyone returned to their seats, Juan Carlos lifted his glass of champagne. "Please join me in welcoming my fiancée, Portia, to our family. Today, she has made me the happiest man on earth."

Glasses clinked and sips were taken.

Portia's heart swelled. All doubts about her future were laid to rest. She and Juan Carlos would work things out. They would find a way to keep each other happy and not lose their own identity. She would be his wife in all ways. She would one day bear his child, an heir to the throne of Alma.

She locked the thought deep inside her heart and it filled her with joy.

"Jasmine, yes. It's true, it's true. I'm engaged to Juan Carlos. I wanted to tell you before news of our engagement reached the States. The king's assistant will be speaking to the media tomorrow to share our engagement news." Portia held the cell phone to her ear as she looked out the window of Juan Carlos's master suite in the palace. The king's room had a view of the gardens below, with its expertly groomed fall flowers.

"Congratulations, Portia. Wow. It's hard to believe. The king moves fast, doesn't he?" Jasmine asked, a little bit in awe.

"Yes, he does," she said softly, focusing on a row of red carnations growing in the garden. They were hardy this time of year. "He's quite persuasive when he wants something. That's why he'll be a great king and not just a figurehead. After news of our find comes out, the country will see how much Alma means to him. They'll rally behind him, and he'll be… Jas, forgive me, I'm rambling, aren't I?"

"Oh, my gosh, Portia. I hear it in your voice. You're really in love, aren't you?"

"He's amazing, Jas. And I resisted him as long as I could, but Juan Carlos…well, when you meet him, you'll see what I mean."

"I'm going to meet him?" She pictured her friend's eyes snapping to attention.

"Of course, silly. At the wedding. Jasmine, I want you by my side. I know it's a lot to ask, since the wedding will be held in Alma, but I'd be thrilled if you'd be my maid of honor."

"Portia…this is… Of course I'll be your maid of honor! I wish you could see me jumping up and down right now."

She chuckled. "I've got the image in my head. Just be careful. The last time you jumped for joy, you crashed into my dining table and nearly broke your leg."

"Okay, I've stopped jumping now," she said, out of breath. "This is all so very exciting."

"I can hardly believe it myself. Juan Carlos wants to be married, like, yesterday, so I think it's going to happen as soon as we can put all the pieces together."

"Count on me to help."

"Thank you. I was hoping you'd say that and I'm glad you're going to be in my wedding. Right now, I'm working on an art authentication project that will take me until the end of the week to finish. I should be home in three days. Then it'll be full steam ahead with wedding plans."

"I can't wait to see you. I have a million questions for you."

"And I don't have a million answers. But it'll work out," Portia said, taking a deep breath. "It has to. Have to run now. Love you, Jas."

"Love you, too," her assistant said, and then hung up.

"What don't you have a million answers to?" Juan Carlos was suddenly beside Portia at the window. His arms around her waist, he took the cell phone from her hand and turned her to face him. She looked into curious, warm dark eyes.

"All of this?" she said. She couldn't lie. The roller coaster was going fast and she was holding on for dear life. "I don't know how this will all work out. I have a career, a life and a job on both US coasts. As it is, I'm not home much."

He lifted her chin and tilted his head. She braced herself for the onslaught of his kiss. When he held her this way and gazed at her, she turned into a puddle of mush. The kiss was long and leisurely. He took his time with her and every bone in her body melted. Yes, her fiancé knew how to devastate.

"As long as we love each other," he said, "the obstacles won't be too great. I don't expect you to give up your work, Princess. I won't demand anything of you but your love."

When he spoke so sincerely, she believed him. She saw her future bright and clear. Nothing was more powerful than their shared love. "You have that, Your Highness."

His fingertips traced the outline of her lips. "I heard you say you'll be going in three days."

"Yes," she said. "When I'm through researching and authenticating what I can of the Montoro art collection, I'll head back to the States. I have appointments to keep."

"And you'll look into wedding protocols from your native Samforstand?"

"Yes, I know that's important to you. It is to me, too."

"Our union should reflect both of our heritages and royal traditions. The wedding must be a melding of both of our countries. The sooner, the better, my love. I can hardly stand the thought of you leaving." He sent her head swirling with another earth-shattering kiss.

"Well," she said, licking her lips. "We do have three

more days together. And nights." She arched her brows and slanted her head, playing coy.

Juan Carlos took the bait. With a growl, he lifted her up and carried her to the bed, unceremoniously dropping her so that she bounced on the mattress. A chuckle ripped from her lips. "Your Highness," she said, staring at the bulge growing in his pants. "It's half past eleven in the morning."

"Princess, I don't see a problem with that, do you?"

She shook her head, giggling. It didn't take much to tempt her new fiancé and she loved that about him.

He climbed onto the bed and Portia spent the next hour making up for the time she and Juan Carlos would be apart.

Eight

"Wow, Portia, you look beautiful in this dress. I think it's the one," Jasmine said, nodding her head in approval. Her friend was having a grand time getting her in and out of wedding dresses, much to the dismay of the shop owner who stood just outside the dressing room, hoping to be called in to aid and assist in the fitting.

Portia stood on a pedestal platform gazing at her reflection in the three-way mirror in the tiny wedding shop in Santa Monica. "You said that about the last three gowns I've tried on."

"I can't help it. They all look amazing on you. But this one with the ivory tulle and Swarovski crystals." Jasmine sighed. "It's heavenly."

"It is lovely," Portia said, admiring the lines of the dress. "It's such a big decision."

"I'll say. It's not every day a friend of mine marries a king. Princess or not."

Portia chuckled.

Once word of the new king of Alma's American fiancée had hit the Los Angeles newsstands, Portia had been inundated with offers of gown fittings, hair and makeup, photographers and wedding planners. She'd had requests for radio and television talk shows. She'd refused them all, trying to scale down the hoopla. She hadn't expected to be crowded at the airport by the paparazzi, or followed home for that matter. Once again, her personal life was under the spotlight.

None of it mattered, though. She was so deeply in love with Juan Carlos, the unwanted attention was manageable. On some level, she understood the public's desire for a fairy-tale love story. Ghastly news reports of wars, poverty and chilling murders needed some balance. The country craved something positive and lovely to grasp onto, and a newly crowned king marrying a princess, both of whom had lived in America, fit the bill.

Portia stepped out of the gown and redressed in her own clothes before letting Amelia of Amelia's Elegance into the dressing room. "Thank you for your time," Portia said to the shop owner. "I will keep this gown in mind. It's certainly beautiful."

Jasmine was careful handing the wedding dress over to Amelia. "This is my favorite, with the chapel length veil."

"I agree. It's certainly fitting for a princess," the shop owner said, nodding her head. "It's from a most talented designer. I shall put it on hold for you, if you'd like?"

Jasmine nodded. "Yes, the princess would like that."

Portia did a mental eye roll. Jasmine loved using the princess card for special favors.

"Your Highness, thank you for considering my shop for your wedding needs."

"You're welcome. I appreciate your time. You do have some stunning things here."

Amelia beamed with pride. "Thank you. We try to accommodate our clients with only the highest quality material and design."

"We have a few other stops to make, but I will personally call you when the princess makes up her mind," Jasmine said.

Amelia thanked them and walked them out the door.

"Did you love the dress?" Jasmine asked. "A bride has

to fall in love with her dress. They say as soon as she puts the right one on, she knows. Did you know?"

"Well, I did like it."

"But you didn't love it?"

Portia got into the front seat of Jasmine's car. "No, I didn't *love* it."

Luckily, no one had followed her to the dress shop. Jasmine got into the driver's seat and glanced around. "Did you hear? Rick Manning just got engaged to the daughter of a United States senator. It's all over the news. They claim to be crazy about each other."

Rick Manning, an A-list movie star, was dubbed the man least likely to ever marry. Handsome and charming and very much a ladies' man. "Yes, it was all over the news this morning. I've met Eliza Bennington. She's a nice person."

"Well, you can thank them both. Luckily, the tabloids have dropped you like a hot potato. At least, until more royal wedding news is announced. The dogs are on a different scent right now."

"I don't envy them. It's no fun having your every move analyzed."

"I hear you," Jasmine said, and pulled out of the parking spot. "Are you hungry?"

"Starving. Let's have lunch."

"Okay, but afterward, the great wedding dress search goes on."

Portia agreed to that plan and looked out the window. Jasmine was taking her maid of honor duties seriously. The truth was, Portia had a hundred loose ends to tie up before the wedding, and she missed Juan Carlos like crazy. They spoke at least twice a day since she'd left him at the airport in Alma.

"You are perfect for me, Princess. Always remember

that," were his last words to her as she boarded his private airplane.

It was after six in the evening when Jasmine dropped her off at home. She climbed the few steps of her one-level Brentwood condo, knowing she had another hunt on her hands. She'd promised Juan Carlos she'd look up royal wedding protocols from Samforstand. She'd been too busy with rescheduling her work appointments and dress shopping to dig into her old files until now.

She dropped her purse on the couch and then strode to the fridge and grabbed a Coke. Sipping from the can, she walked into her bedroom and pulled out the old cedar trunk from the back of her walk-in closet. The trunk held the few remaining things she had left of her parents.

Unlatching the lid, she found a massive amount of papers, deeds, bank account records and folders upon folders of news clippings about her parents when they were a young royal couple in exile. She lifted out an article written about them from the *New York Times*, just days before the tragic car accident that claimed their lives. Her eyes misted as she looked at a picture of the loving couple that accompanied the article. Her father was decked out in royal regalia with her mother by his side. They were young and happy and it hurt her heart still to look at them and think about all they had lost.

Her mother's wedding ring was in its original sapphire-blue velvet box, her father's tie clips and a gold wedding band were stored in a polished walnut case. She assumed most of their other possessions were sold to keep her comfortable and pay for her expenses. She'd been raised by her grandmother Joanna. But now all she had was her great-aunt, Margreta, who was a little senile. Portia paid for her care in a nursing home and visited her whenever she could.

As the evening wore on, she pored over every piece of paper in the trunk. She read every article and viewed every picture taken. Yet nowhere could she find any research that dated back to her great-grandparents' era of rule before they'd migrated to the United States after World War II. Surely, there had to be something? Having lost her parents early in life, she had only a fragmentary account of her heritage from her grandmother. Grandma Joanna hadn't liked to talk about the old days. It was too painful, a past wrought with the loss of her only son. Portia's questions about her parents were met with hushed tones and sadness and she'd never really learned much about them. She did remember her mother's bright smile and her father's light blue eyes. But even now, she wondered if those were true memories, or just recollections of the pictures she'd seen.

Her cell phone rang and a name popped up on the screen. She answered before the second ring. "Juan Carlos." She sighed.

His baritone voice drifted to her over thousands of miles. "Hello, Princess. I had to hear your voice once more before I started my day. I hope I didn't wake you."

She glanced at the clock. It was 8:00 a.m. in Alma. "No, not at all. I'm doing some research right now. I'm glad you called. How are you?"

"Besides missing you, I'm doing well. I'm scheduled to do a television interview later this morning. All of Alma is rejoicing over our art find, sweetheart. But I have a feeling the interviewer is more interested in our engagement. I'm sure I will be barraged with questions about our wedding."

"I'm sure you can handle it, Your Highness."

"What I can't handle is not being with my perfect princess. When will you be returning to me?"

"Give me a week, Juan Carlos," she said. "I need the time to get some things in order."

"Sounds like an eternity."

"For me, too, but I have a lot to accomplish. Jasmine

has been persistent. We are very close to choosing a wedding gown."

"I can't wait to see you in it. No matter which you choose you'll be beautiful. But what have you decided about your work?"

"I've managed to take a three months' leave of absence. I'm thinking of relocating to Europe. There are many American art collectors living abroad who might need my services. I...I don't have it all figured out yet."

"Take your time, sweetheart. I want you to be happy with whatever you choose."

"Okay. Thank you."

"I've been thinking. How does a Christmas wedding sound?"

"A Christmas wedding?" She pictured lush holly wreaths, bright red poinsettias and twinkling lights decorating the palace. "Sounds heavenly. But it's less than two months away."

Her fiancé was eager to make her his wife. She couldn't complain, yet her mind spun. She had so very much to do.

"We can make it work, Portia."

"Yes, yes. Okay," she said, smiling. The idea was too tempting to pass up. "Let's have a Christmas wedding."

There was a pause, and she pictured him smiling. "I love you, Portia."

"I love you, too, Juan Carlos."

The nursing home smelled of lye soap and disinfectant. Yet somehow the word *sterile* didn't come to mind as Portia walked the halls toward her great-aunt Margreta's room. Her aunt had once told her, "The odors of old age are too strong to conceal." Sharp old bird, Aunt Margreta was, back in the day. But Portia never knew what she'd find when she visited. Some days, her great-aunt was lucid, her wits about her. And some days, it was as if she'd fallen into a dark hole and didn't know how to get out.

This kind of aging was a slow, eternally sad process. Yet, as Portia popped her head into her aunt's room, she was greeted with cheery buttercup-colored walls and fresh flowers. Aunt Margreta sat in a chair, reading a crime thriller. A good sign.

"Hello, Auntie," Portia said. "It's me, Portia."

Her aunt looked over her thick eyeglasses and hesitated a moment. "Portia?"

Her voice was weak, her body frail and thin. "Yes, it's me."

The old woman smiled. "Come in, dear." She put the book down on her lap. "Nice of you to visit."

Thank heaven. Her aunt was having a good day. Maybe now, she could gather information about the Lindstrom monarchy that Portia hadn't been able to find anywhere else. She'd used up every one of her massive tools of research, including going through newspaper archives searching for an inkling about her family's rule and traditions carried out in Samforstand. She found nothing, which was very odd, and that lack of information brought her here today. Maybe Aunt Margreta could shed some light. She was her grandmother's sister and had lived in the homeland before the war.

Portia pulled up a chair and sat down beside her. "How are you, Auntie?"

"I can't complain. Well, I could, but it would do no good. I'm old, Portia. And you," she said, gazing over her glasses again. "You are as beautiful as I remember."

Portia took her hand and smiled. Aunt Margreta's hands were always soft, the skin loose and smooth over the aging bones. At ninety-three years old, she was as physically fit as one could expect, but for daily bouts of arthritis. But her mind wasn't holding up as well as her body and that worried Portia. "So are you, Aunt Margreta. You're a beautiful lady."

She'd always been a sweet woman, though as Portia remembered, she'd also been feisty in her day and not always in agreement with her sister, Joanna. The two would argue when they thought Portia couldn't hear. She never knew what they argued about, but as soon as Portia would step into the room, they'd shoot each other a glare and stop arguing, pretending things were all fine and dandy. Which they were, most of the time. Portia missed her parents, but she'd never discount the love Grandma Joanna and Great-Aunt Margreta bestowed upon her. It was the least she could do for her aunt to see to her care here at Somerset Village.

"Auntie, are they treating you well here?"

She nodded. "I'm fine, dear. The food's better now. We have a new chef and he doesn't cut corners. You'll see. You'll stay for lunch?"

"Of course I will. I'm looking forward to it."

"Then I'll get dressed up and we'll go to the dining room later."

"Okay. Auntie, I have good news." She lifted her left hand and wiggled her fingers. "I'm engaged."

Margreta squeezed her eyes closed. "Is it to Johnny Valente? That boy wouldn't leave you alone when you were younger. I never liked him. "

Johnny Valente? Portia used to play with him in grade school, two decades ago. He was a bully who'd called her Polar Bear Portia, because of her light hair and skin tone. "Gosh no, Auntie. I never liked him, either." She hoped her aunt wasn't digressing. "I'm engaged to…" How should she say this? "I met this wonderful man when I was visiting Alma."

"What's Alma?"

"It's this beautiful island country just off the coast of

Spain. I met him at his coronation. Auntie, he was just crowned king. His name is Juan Carlos Salazar, King Montoro of Alma."

Aunt Margreta put her head down. "I see."

Her aunt's odd reaction surprised her. "Do you like my ring?"

She gave Portia's left hand a glance. "It sparkles."

"Yes, it does."

"But it looks old."

"Yes, I suppose it's at least fifty years old. It was his mother's ring. He…lost his family at a young age also."

"In a car accident, just like your mother and father?"

"Yes, the same way. We have a lot in common."

Pain entered her aunt's eyes. "That's terribly sad, isn't it?" Her aunt made a move to get up from the chair. "Is it time for lunch yet, dear?"

Portia's eye twitched. "Not yet, Auntie."

Her aunt relaxed back into her seat.

"Auntie, I have a question to ask you. It's very important to me, so please try to concentrate. I will be marrying a king and, well, since I also have royal bloodlines, my fiancé wants very much for me to carry out the protocols of my homeland during our wedding. Do you know where I might find that information? I can't seem to find anything about our family's rule before World War II."

Aunt Margreta put her head down again.

"Auntie, please. Try to remember."

"There are no protocols from the family," she said stoically.

"But surely…there have to be. Have you forgotten?"

"No, my dear. I have not forgotten. Your grandmother and I never saw eye to eye about this."

"About what, Auntie?"

Margreta stilled. "Tell no one. Tell no one. Tell no one," she repeated.

"Not even me, Auntie? What is it you're not supposed to tell?"

Margreta looked straight ahead, as if Portia wasn't there. As if she was going back in time, remembering. "Don't tell Portia. She must never know the truth."

"What?" Portia absorbed her words, but they didn't make any sense. "What do you mean, I must never know the truth? What truth?" Portia grabbed her aunt's hand, gently squeezing. "Auntie, please. You have to tell me."

Her aunt turned to stare at her. "You are not a princess," she said. Her voice was sorrowful, etched in pain and Portia's heart sunk at her earnest tone. "Our family never ruled in Samforstand. Your mother wasn't royalty and neither was my sister, Joanna. It's all a lie."

Surely, the old woman was having a senile episode. "But, Auntie, of course Grandmother was queen. She raised me. I would know if she wasn't."

Silence.

"Aunt Margreta, please?"

"Yes, you're right, dear. You would know. Never mind."

Her aunt's quick compliance confused her even more. And she started thinking back about her life and how she'd never really seen any official documents regarding the Lindstrom monarchy. They'd been figureheads, holding no great power, yet she'd never known much about her homeland. It wasn't talked about. It seemed from her recent research the monarchy started to take shape in the United States, just after World War II.

"Oh, my God," she murmured. Her body began to tremble as tears stung her eyes. "You're telling the truth, aren't you? I'm not a princess."

Her aunt's eyes softened, dimmed by sorrow. "I'm sorry, Portia dear."

"But how can I believe that? How can that possibly be true?"

Could she take the word of an elderly senile woman who went in and out of coherency?

"There's a diary," her aunt said. "Joanna kept a secret diary."

"Where?" Now Portia would get to the truth. "Where's the diary?"

Aunt Margreta pointed to the bookshelf against the far wall overflowing with books. "Behind Agatha Christie."

Portia strode over to the bookshelf. Her hands were shaking as she parted half a dozen mystery novels. She lifted a weathered, navy blue soft-covered book from the shelf and brought it close to her chest. It had no title on the cover. Her heart racing, she took her seat next to Aunt Margreta and began reading the words that made a lie out of her entire life.

Portia lay quietly on her sofa, a cool towel on her forehead. She'd cried a river full of tears and every cell in her body was now drained. Princess Portia Lindstrom of Samforstand no longer existed. She never had. She was a fraud, a fake. An imposter. How could her family do this to her? How could they have perpetrated a lie that would affect her entire life?

How cruel.

How unjust.

Damn the circumstances behind their decisions right now. Their bold blatant betrayal was all that mattered to her. How dare they mislead her and let her believe in the fairy tale? She wasn't the snow queen. Hell, once the truth got out, she'd be deemed the black witch.

She'd been involved in one scandal already and it had taken years to live that down. But this? This was too much. The press would devour her. They'd make her out to be the villain, a lying deceiving bitch out to ensnare a wealthy king.

The humiliation alone would destroy all the positive good Juan Carlos had done for his country.

She muffled another sob. She didn't have it in her to shed more tears.

Feeling empty, she closed her swollen eyes, unable to rid herself of the thoughts plaguing her. The lies she'd been told, the deceptions perpetrated by her family. What of her career? Most importantly, what would she do about Juan Carlos? He was king, and as king he was pledged to only marry a woman of royal heritage. It was his destiny. It was what the citizens of Alma expected. Juan Carlos was the most dutiful man she'd ever known. This would destroy their relationship.

The towel was removed from her head. "Feeling better yet? Want to get up?" Jasmine asked.

"Nooooo. I don't want to ever get up."

Jas sat down on the floor beside the sofa. "Hey, that doesn't sound like the Portia I know. You've been wallowing for two hours."

"I'm not the Portia you know. I'm not… I don't know who I am. And I have a right to wallow."

"Yes, it sucks. But Portia, you are you, no matter if you have the title of princess or not."

"It's just…it's just so darn humiliating. I feel like a fool. I feel, well, I feel like everything's a lie. My childhood, my upbringing, my friends."

"Hey, watch it there."

"You know I don't mean you."

Jasmine reached for her hand and squeezed. "I know."

"All the doors that have opened for me because of my title, Jas… Those people will think the worst of me. They'll think I deliberately deceived them to get ahead in my career."

"When in truth, we know, they were using you. They

wanted to be associated with a princess. So it was a trade-off. You have nothing to be ashamed of."

"I'm ashamed of everything."

"And angry."

"Yes, of course. I'm spitting mad at my family."

"I'm not justifying what they've done, honey. But they came to the States after the war destitute, and like so many immigrant families, they didn't know how they'd survive here. And, well, pretending to be royalty from a tiny country…"

"It's far-fetched. Yet they got away with it."

"Yes, your grandmother speaks of it in the diary. How scared they were and how confused things were in Europe and Scandinavia after the war. There was a lot of rebuilding and restructuring and things just fell into place for them. Surprisingly, they weren't questioned. After all, we didn't have close ties to the monarchy of Samforstand the way we did England. Your grandmother speaks of Americans having much to deal with after the war. Hundreds of thousands of soldiers were coming home. Work and housing in our country was scarce. Things were chaotic."

"But others found a way to survive without deception. They worked hard and built honest, decent lives for themselves." Portia hinged her body up from her prone position and swiveled to plant her feet on the floor. Sitting upright, her head spun a little. "I don't know what I'd do without you, Jasmine. Honestly, you're the only person I can trust with this."

Jasmine rose from the floor and the sofa cushions dipped as she came to sit next to her. Her friend hung her arm around Portia's shoulder and they sat there like that for long minutes, quiet.

"I'm scared, Jas."

"I know."

"I don't know who I am. I can't expect you to understand fully how I'm feeling, but suddenly, I'm confused about everything. My heart is aching so badly right now."

"That's why I'm here, Portia. You're not alone."

She rested her head on Jasmine's shoulder. "Thank you."

The house telephone rang. "Want me to get it?"

"No," she said to Jasmine. "I can't talk to anyone right now."

Jas nodded.

Shortly after that, her cell phone began ringing and she knew both calls were from Juan Carlos.

They spoke every evening before she went to bed. Never fail.

Until tonight.

She couldn't speak to him and pretend everything was all right. She couldn't pretend that she was still a princess. She had a lot of thinking to do and she couldn't burden Jasmine any further in the decisions she'd have to make about her future.

Thoughts of Juan Carlos always squeezed her heart tight in a loving embrace.

This time, though, it was as if her heart was being strangled.

And the pain of losing Juan Carlos wouldn't go away anytime soon.

Portia sat in the throne room at the palace in Del Sol, her eyes closed, her heart pumping hard. Yesterday, she'd texted and emailed Juan Carlos one excuse after another as to why she wasn't answering his calls until she'd realized the only way to break it off with him was to face him in person. She'd flown half the night to get here. To see him one last time.

His family had been through a great deal to once and for all return the true and rightful heir to the Alma throne.

There'd been one debacle after another with his cousins, as they attempted to reinstate the monarchy, and the entire process had come under great scrutiny. All eyes were on Juan Carlos now and he'd made promises, staunch, determined promises to the citizenry that he would take his role seriously. By royal decree from decades ago, he was obligated to marry a woman of royal stature. The last thing he needed was to be made a fool of by marrying an imposter, a woman who hadn't a drop of royal blood flowing through her veins.

She wasn't his perfect princess any longer.

A tear dripped down her cheek. She wiped it away and steadied her shaky breathing. She glanced down at the engagement ring she wore. It was magnificent and maybe someday would belong to a woman worthy of wearing it and claiming a place beside Juan Carlos.

Her stomach ached at the notion of Juan Carlos living with and loving another woman. But it would happen one day. Rightfully so. She could only hope getting over him wouldn't destroy her.

She heard footsteps approaching along the corridor. She rose from her seat and mustered her courage. She'd never been much of an actress, but today she needed to provide an award-winning performance.

The door opened and there he stood, dressed in a crisp white shirt, sleeves rolled up—as if he'd been busy at work—and tucked into well-fitting black trousers. A lock of his neatly combed hair swept across his forehead and his tanned face showed a hint of stubble. Some days, when he wasn't going out in public, he didn't shave. She preferred him that way…a little rough around the edges. Tall, elegant, gorgeous.

Juan Carlos's gaze lit upon her and her heart tumbled. Oh, how she'd missed him.

"Portia, sweetheart. You're here." His warm winning

smile devastated her as he strode across the room. Genuine love entered his eyes. "I'm so glad to see you. You've come back to me early."

"Yes."

"I was worried when I couldn't reach you. But now I see, you wanted to surprise me."

He took her into his arms and heaven help her, she allowed him to kiss her.

His lips were warm, welcoming, filled with passion and beautifully familiar. She'd never been kissed the way Juan Carlos kissed her. She held her back stiff and didn't partake, but he was too caught up in the moment to notice her reluctance.

"We have much to talk about," he murmured, brushing his lips over hers again.

She stepped back and gazed into his dark gleaming eyes. "Yes, Juan Carlos. It's the reason I've come back to Del Sol so quickly."

He took her hand, covering it with his. "Come, let's sit then and catch up."

He began walking, tugging her along to the king and queen's thrones, two ornate tall chairs of plush red velvet and gilded carvings.

The irony of sitting upon that chair was too much. "I'd rather stand," she said.

"Okay." He looked at her oddly, but then nodded. "Would you like to take a walk? It might feel good to stretch your legs after the long plane ride. We can talk of the progress you've made with our wedding."

"No," she said. "No, Juan Carlos. I didn't come here early to discuss our wedding. I came to say that I can't go through with it."

"With what, sweetheart?" He blinked and appeared totally confused.

"The wedding. I can't marry you, Juan Carlos. I went home and really gave our situation some thought."

"Our situation?" He frowned. "You love me, I love you. That's our situation. We're engaged, Portia."

"No, as of today, we are not."

She inhaled and twisted the diamond ring off her finger. He was shaking his head, baffled. The gleam in his eyes dimmed. He almost appeared frightened. It killed her to wipe the joy from his face. "I'm terribly sorry."

"What is all this, Portia?"

She took his hand, spread open his palm and dropped his mother's wedding ring inside. "It's too much, Juan Carlos. We...we got caught up in the moment. Finding the art treasures put us both on a crazy romantic high and we took the little fling we had too far."

"Little fling?" he repeated, his voice hitching.

Oh, God, she'd hurt him. She knew she would, but she almost couldn't bear seeing that expression on his face. Better a small lie to save him, than the truth, which would make him look the fool in the eyes of his family and country. She loved him enough to suffer his anger and wrath. But the pain she'd inflicted would stay with her a long, long time.

"It happened so fast. You and I, we're different people. I love my job, Juan Carlos."

"You wouldn't have to give it up."

"Please understand," she said softly. "It isn't going to work out. I don't want to live here. I don't want to get married or have children right now."

His eyes snapped to hers. "I never rushed you about children, Portia."

"You'd expect it one day. And...and I'm afraid I'd disappoint you. I—I... It was a mistake to get engaged."

She backed up a step, putting distance between them. God should strike her dead for the lies she was telling. But it had to be done. Her sacrifice would make it easier on Juan Carlos in the long run. Yet her heart burned at the thought of leaving him forever.

"You're having cold feet. I hear it's common before a wedding."

"No, being away from here, from you, made it all clear to me, Juan Carlos. It's not cold feet, it's reality. I hope you'll understand and not make this harder on me than it already is."

He opened his palm to stare at the diamond ring. Then the sound of his deep wobbly sigh reached her ears. He was in pain. God, she hated this. "I love you, Portia," he said, searching her eyes.

Tears blurred her vision. Her throat constricted. She couldn't return his love. For his sake, she said nothing.

He gripped her forearms, gently shaking her. As if the impact would somehow clear her head of this nonsense. "Portia, you told me you loved me. You agreed to be my wife."

"I'm…I'm…" She took a swallow. Could she do this? Could she tell the biggest lie of all? She forced the words out. "I'm fond of you, Juan Carlos."

He dropped her arms. "Fond?"

She nodded.

"Then why are you crying, sweetheart?"

Her tears now were soaking her dress. She hated herself at the moment. "I don't like hurting you."

"Then don't. Stay and we'll talk this over. Give us time, Portia."

"I can't, Juan Carlos. It won't do any good. We're… over." She sobbed now, unable to hold back any longer. "I'm s-sorry."

He didn't reach for her. Thank goodness. If he touched her again, she'd melt into his arms. But he watched her carefully, as if trying to figure her out. Skepticism lingered in his eyes. He didn't believe her, but there was also resignation there and definite injury. She must have baffled him. He didn't know what to say to convince her she was wrong.

There wasn't anything he could say to her to change her mind. This was the hardest thing she'd ever had to do. She had to leave, to muster her strength and walk out the door. "I'll never forget the time I had with you... It was... *amazing*," she whispered.

He closed his eyes, shaking his head.

And that was her way out.

She turned her back on him and dashed away, leaving the palace and Juan Carlos and the love they'd shared behind.

Nine

"If you don't mind me saying so, Your Highness, you could use some sleep. Why not close your eyes while we travel," Eduardo said.

Juan Carlos sat facing his bodyguard in the reclining lounge chair on the palace's private plane. Under normal circumstances, Juan Carlos wouldn't travel so extravagantly; he wanted to be known as the king who flew coach. But it was imperative that this journey be kept secret and away from curious eyes. "Are you saying I look less than kingly, Eduardo?"

His bodyguard straightened in his seat. "No, I, uh, I know how hard this week has been on you, Your Highness."

"Eduardo, I'm in total agreement with you." Juan Carlos sighed. "I know I look like hell. I will fix that before we arrive in Los Angeles. The best I can, that is."

Eduardo's eyes softened. "Yes, Your Majesty."

Eduardo was quickly becoming his good friend and confidant. "Do you have a girl, Eduardo?"

"Yes, I do."

"Is it serious?"

Eduardo shook his head. "No, not really."

"Because of what you do for a living?"

"Yes. I cannot get serious with anyone while I'm away so much of the time. She understands."

"Ah, an understanding woman. It's lucky for me, not so fortunate for your girl."

"*Si*, that is true. But I am twenty-eight and not ready to settle down."

"I used to think that way. But sometimes fate steps in and knocks you over the head when a beautiful snow queen enters your path."

Eduardo chuckled. "Princess Portia."

"Yes, Princess Portia. And now I'm chasing her all over the globe."

"She is worth it, I would say, Your Majesty."

"*Si*, she is worth it."

He lifted the tumbler of bourbon he held in his hand and stared into the golden liquid. "I wish you could share a drink with me, Eduardo. We'll be in the air for five more hours. Surely the effects will have worn off by then."

"Thank you, Your Majesty, but no. I cannot drink while on duty."

Juan Carlos nodded. "Coffee then and a pastry?"

"I'd never refuse a pastry from Chef Andre, Your Highness. He showed me his creations before packing them up for this trip."

Juan Carlos pressed the button on the arm of his chair and ordered up coffee and pastries from his personal flight attendant. Then he rested back in his seat and sipped bourbon. Sleep was elusive lately and eating had become a chore. But he could tolerate a shot or two of bourbon when his mind wouldn't shut down. It helped blur the pain of losing Portia.

It had been one solid week since she'd left Alma and he hadn't heard from her since. What was she doing? Had she gone back to her work routine as if *they* hadn't happened? As if the time they'd shared together was nothing more than a passing fling?

He couldn't believe that. Something was up with her.

He felt it deep down in his soul that something had happened to Portia to make her deny their love and break off their engagement. Juan Carlos had waited patiently all week to hear from her, anticipating a call that had never come, and his patience was at an end. Now he was taking matters into his own hands. He knew enough about relationships to know women liked to be pursued. They liked to have men come after them. Maybe Portia was testing him? Maybe she'd expected him to come running and convince her she'd been wrong?

If only it would be that easy.

But he had to try.

Outside of his bodyguards, he hadn't told a soul of their breakup. He couldn't bring himself to share the news so soon after publicly announcing their happy engagement. He had hopes of winning Portia back, hopes of restoring their love. He'd vowed to bring honor and credibility back to the monarchy of Alma as well as to carry out his grandmother Isabella's dying wishes for the country. He wanted, needed Portia by his side. He and Portia belonged together. She was the love of his life.

Living without her would only be half a life.

Hours later, the plane touched down in Los Angeles, a place Juan Carlos had visited often. But this time, he had more than business to attend to—he had come to retrieve his woman. He'd managed to get a few winks of sleep, shaved and changed his crumpled clothes while they were in the air. Now he felt human again and more like himself, rather than the shell of the man he'd been this past week. Dressed in a slate-gray suit and neatly groomed, he planned on sweeping his princess off her feet again.

Returning home without her wasn't an option.

"Are you ready, Your Highness?" Eduardo asked, rising from his seat.

"Yes, and you have our little surprise all set?" he asked.

"I do. If it doesn't help your cause," Eduardo said, grinning, "nothing will."

Juan Carlos nodded. He couldn't disagree.

A frozen waffle popped up out of the toaster and Portia set it next to the scrambled eggs on her plate. She doused the waffle with maple syrup, grabbed a fork and took the plate over to the kitchen table. Breakfast for dinner was always an option when one didn't have the stomach to really cook. Or eat for that matter. Her belly squeezed tight as she looked at the food. She'd promised Jasmine she would eat something tonight.

Her friend had apologized profusely for breaking their dinner date. Jas had planned to cook a roast prime rib tonight, her specialty. They were going to do it up right with champagne and soufflé, and have a fun girls' night watching Turner Classic Movies on television. It was the only reason Portia had put on a dress, instead of wearing her usual comfy gray sweats. She didn't want to disappoint her friend.

"Poor Jas." She'd come down with a bug. Hopefully it wasn't the flu. Portia felt a little guilty about it, having dominated a lot of her time lately. Jasmine had been the best friend she could ever hope to have. Every day she'd come over to help Portia clean out her closets or rearrange furniture or cook a meal. Jasmine would bring in Mexican food on Taco Tuesdays and play card games with her until very late at night. She understood Portia needed to kill time so she didn't have to think too hard.

Now her friend was sick.

"For you, Jas, I'm going to eat this." She took a bite of her eggs and chewed and chewed. The eggs went down like rubber. She'd overcooked them again.

The waffle wasn't much better. It was still frozen in the center. Two bites later, she figured she'd fulfilled her promise and took her dish to the sink, dumping the contents down the garbage disposal.

Now what? She glanced around the condo. It was spotless. She'd been cleaning all week long. She had no official work to do. She hadn't been back to the office yet—they weren't expecting her anyway since she'd taken a three-month leave to deal with wedding plans and her new life as wife to a king.

She'd truly questioned whether to go back to her job. Could she continue with the pretense? How could she go back, when her friends and associates still believed her to be Princess Portia of Samforstand? Could she go about her life, living the lie? And what if she decided it was impossible to resume her life as usual? What if she revealed all the lies about herself and her family? What would that mean for Juan Carlos? His humiliation would be monumental. He would hate her. And appear a fool, a man easily duped.

She was at a crossroads in her life, and didn't know which way to proceed.

No one could possibly know how she felt right now. She was a phony, a fraud and an imposter. Jasmine kept telling her it wasn't her fault and no one would blame her if the truth got out. But Portia didn't know who she was anymore. Her life had been ripped out from under her. She felt at odds, lonely and bereft. Her emotions were all over the place. Anger took up residence, but sympathy crept in sometimes, as she imagined her family's plight after the war. Still, those emotions didn't come close to the emptiness she felt deep inside her heart. Because of something that had happened decades ago, she had had to give up the man she loved. The price was high, costing her her happiness.

The doorbell chimed and she jumped. "Who could that be?" she whispered. Surely, Jasmine wouldn't come out tonight. She was in bed with a fever.

Portia had a mind not to open the door, but the bell chimed once again and her curiosity had her heading to the front door.

She stuck her face up to the peephole and gazed out.

"Eduardo?" What on earth was he doing here?

"*Si*, Princess, it's me."

She cringed at his reverent greeting. She didn't deserve to be called Princess. The chain lock allowed her to open the door three inches. She peered out and he smiled wide. "Hello."

Eduardo had become her friend. Seeing this solid block of a man on her doorstep was a welcome sight.

"Hi."

"Will you open the door for me?"

"Oh…of course." She undid the chain and opened the door.

Eduardo stood rooted to the spot. "Are you alone, Princess?"

"Yes, I am alone. Why?"

"I had to ask as it is my duty to protect the king. It's good to see you, but I am here on official bus—"

Juan Carlos stepped into her line of vision from a place on the porch that had concealed him. "Thank you, Eduardo. I'll take it from here."

Portia's mouth dropped open. She blinked and started trembling. "Juan Carlos."

He held a cat carrier in his hand. "Before you say anything, I brought you a gift. Well, two gifts. May I come in?"

With a lump in her throat, she looked away from Juan Carlos's face to the two kittens from Duchess's litter she'd appropriately named Mischief and Mallow. The kittens—one black and gray and mostly all trouble and the other almost all white with spots of caramel color here and there looking like a toasted marshmallow—were sleeping, curled up into little balls of fluff. Mallow's head rested on Mischief's body. Their sweetness brought a tear to her eye.

"Juan Carlos, you...you brought them," she said, touched by the thoughtful gesture. Words she wanted to say tightened in her throat and wouldn't come out. Initially, her heart had lurched when she spotted Juan Carlos, though he looked worn out. His eyes were rimmed with red—from sleepless nights? His handsome face looked haggard, as if he'd been through a war and his hair, while combed, needed a cut. She should have known he wouldn't take no very easily. He wasn't a man easily dissuaded. It was one of the qualities she loved most about him. "You didn't need to do that," she said, finally realizing she wasn't up to caring for pets. She'd barely been able to care for herself lately.

"I figured you might like the company. They are yours as much as they are mine."

She gazed into his solemn eyes. "Come in," she said.

She'd been engaged to a man who had never stepped foot into her home. How telling was that? An impetuous engagement, even though love was involved, wasn't an ideal way to start a relationship. She understood that now. During the coronation and then while living at the farmhouse searching for hidden treasures, they'd lived in a fantasy world, untouched by outside influences. It wasn't reality.

Juan Carlos stepped inside and glanced around, taking in the details of her home. "It's as beautiful as you are, Portia. I wouldn't expect any less."

"Thank you," she said. Her heart thumped hard in her chest. Thankfully, Eduardo's presence helped defuse the situation at the moment. She peered over Juan Carlos's shoulder. "Eduardo, would you like to come inside?"

She'd spent enough time with Juan Carlos and his bodyguards to know what Eduardo's answer had to be. He would be securing the premises and standing watch outside. "I wish I could, Your Highness," he said. "Thank you, but I will be right out here."

It was just as she'd suspected. "Okay, I understand." She turned to Juan Carlos and pasted on a false smile. "Surely, you and I both know that bringing me the kittens wasn't the reason you've come."

"But you're glad I did?"

She glanced at the sleeping kittens. "I'm glad to see them. They are sweet and I did…miss them." She cleared her throat. She couldn't admit she'd missed Juan Carlos also. "They've been weaned from Duchess, I'm assuming?"

He nodded. "Early this week. Where shall I put them?"

"A good question. If you'd called and asked me I would've told you not to bring them, Juan Carlos," she said softly. "I'm not equipped to care for them."

"I'll take them back to Alma with me, if you prefer." His back stiffened a little.

"No, no. Now that they're here, I can't turn them away. I… They're special to me."

Juan Carlos set the cat carrier down on the floor of the foyer. When he returned his gaze to hers, his eyes bored into her. "I had hoped you would say the same of me, sweetheart."

Her eyes closed at his hopeful plea. "You shouldn't have come, Juan Carlos."

"I couldn't stay away. It's not finished between us."

She sighed. "It has to be. We're not right for each other."

He approached her and heaven save her, her pulse accelerated as he laid his palm on her cheek. She lifted her eyes to his. His heavy expression softened, as if touching her made all the difference. As if a light inside him was turned back on. "Not true. We're good together. We're meant for each other. I am here. Don't turn me away, Portia. I would hope I am special to you, as well."

His gaze dipped to her mouth. She swallowed. Oh, God, the pull, the magnetic force of his love surrounded her like a protective shield. She didn't know where she found the will to back up a step, and then another. She couldn't hide her emotions or the passion he instilled and as she moved, he moved with her, thrusting his body against hers until her backside met with the wall.

"I've come a long way for you, Portia." His hands braced the wall, trapping her, so that she could only stare into his face and see his truth. "I've waited my entire life."

His sweet, sincere words stymied any defenses she could muster. She put her hands on his chest but instead of shoving him away as she'd planned, her fingertips clung onto his shirt and her palms flattened against him. His breath hitched from her touch, and his immediate reaction to her nearly buckled her knees. How could she not love this man? How could she turn him away now?

"I came here to talk to you, sweetheart."

She whispered, "Is that what you're doing to me? Talking?"

He flashed a charming, inescapable smile. "Maybe showing is better than telling, after all."

Then his mouth swooped over hers and claimed her in a breath-stealing kiss. His lips were rough but not unkind, wild but not crazy, sexy but not demanding. Caught up in the kiss, she couldn't think beyond the pleasure he evoked. The love she'd tried to bury was resurrected and she fell deeper in love with this man, this honorable king who had come for her.

She'd missed him and didn't know how much until this very second.

His tongue played over her lips and she opened for him. Sweeping inside her mouth, he kissed her again and again. A fire was building in her belly. She was past the point of refusal.

She was putty. He could do with her what he liked.

And she would enjoy every second.

She was lifted, floating on air now, held by two strong arms. She wrapped herself around his body, nestling her head into his chest. "Where's your bed, Portia?"

She pointed to the doorway down the hall.

His strides were long and determined and steady.

He continued to kiss her without missing a step.

Juan Carlos set Portia down on a ruffled lavender bed-spread. Matching pillows, some big, some small, surrounded her head. He did a quick scan of her room decorated in soft whimsical colors. Wispy white curtains covered the windows and modern pieces of art, mostly pastels and some oils, adorned the walls. It was so Portia: soft, delicate, sweet.

God, he loved her.

And he wasn't going to leave here without her.

She was his prize, his love, the treasure he couldn't live without.

He unbuttoned his shirt, spread it wide across his chest and then gave it a toss. He kicked off his shoes and socks and gazed into her eyes as he unfastened his belt.

Her brows lifted, her lips parted slightly and a sharp breathy gasp escaped her lips. Her hungry expression softened his heart, but made every other part of his body hard. He had one night to change her mind. He wouldn't waste a minute. He took her hand and lifted her to her knees. "Come here, sweetheart," he demanded. "Touch me. Put your hands on my body."

Another gasp ripped from her lips and she moved to him. She wore a simple black dress with thin straps and short hemline. It adorned her breasts with just enough material to tempt him beyond belief. He ached to touch her, to shed her clothes and join their bodies, but first, he had to make her see how much she needed him, too. How perfect he was for her.

Her hands came to his torso and he gritted his teeth. She explored the breadth of him, tracing her fingertips over his chest, and then kissed everywhere her fingers had just touched. His body flamed; it was almost too much to bear. She was proving to him that they belonged together.

"Your touch is like no other, Portia. You know that. See what you do to me."

"We are good here, in bed, Juan Carlos," she whispered.

"We are good everywhere, sweetheart. Why do you fight me on this?"

She turned her face from him and disengaged, and he knew he'd pushed her too far. Something was eating at her. Something was making her hold back from him. "Don't retreat," he whispered. He couldn't let her think. Couldn't let whatever notions she had in her head continue to separate them.

He sank down on the bed beside her and unleashed his love for her, stripping down her defenses, loving her with everything he had inside. Holding her steady with one hand, he eased her dress off with the other, baring her upper body. He cupped her breasts, made love to them with his mouth and tongue and was rewarded with sighs of pleasure, little throaty moans of delight. Her throat, her chin, her lips. He devoured them all while covering her body with his. She arched her hips and they moved in the same unique rhythm, thrusting, aching, groaning until he couldn't take another second. He joined their bodies, pushing through her mental defenses and bringing them skin to skin.

Her eyes closed to the pleasure, her face beautifully masked in satisfaction. He thrust into her deep and long. It was hot and damp and sweaty and when he sensed her readiness, he called her name. "Portia." Her eyes snapped open. He stared into them and announced, "This is our place."

Connected by more than their bodies, she sighed and nodded her head.

Then he brought her home.

* * *

Early dawn broke through the curtains and Juan Carlos smiled in his drowsy state, his eyes still closed as images of making love to Portia flashed in his head. God, how he'd missed her. And now she was where she belonged. With him. After the night they'd shared, he hoped he'd convinced her that she loved him, he loved her and whatever was bothering her could be worked out and put to rest. It wasn't rocket science. Perhaps he'd pushed her too far early in their relationship. They'd only known each other for weeks. Not the months or years some take to cement their connection. She'd gotten cold feet. Any problems that arose could be dealt with. He couldn't see a reason why they shouldn't live their lives together. They'd made love twice during the night, and the second time had been even more thrilling and revelatory than the first. No one could tell him that Portia didn't love him. She'd displayed that in the way she'd taken the initiative, kissed him, touched him and made love to his body.

It was good, so good, between them. In all ways.

Juan Carlos rolled over to cradle her in his arms. They'd welcome the day together. But his hands hit upon cold sheets. He squeezed his eyes open. Portia was gone, her half of the bed empty. Was she always an early riser? He didn't know. They'd spent time together at the farmhouse in Alma on his schedule, not hers. There were still things they needed to learn about each other.

He hinged his body up, eager to see her. Eager to kiss her. Rising from the bed, he dressed in his trousers and shirt, ran a hand through his hair to comb down the spiky ends and then padded out of the room.

Halfway down the hallway of her modest three-bedroom condo, he halted, hearing mewling sounds coming from the living room. Of course, the kittens. Portia must have been anxious to see them this morning and tend to them the way she always had. Their carrier came equipped with kitty food, and water was their drink of choice. He grinned. He could almost picture her playing with them on the carpeted floor. Bringing them here had been a good plan to get his foot in the door and soften Portia's heart, but ultimately he'd done it to bring a smile to her face.

As he approached the sounds grew louder and no, they didn't appear to be coming from the kittens. It was a human sound, the heartbreaking echo of quiet crying. He stood on the threshold of the living room to find Portia, sitting up on the sofa, her arms around her legs, rocking back and forth with tears soaking her face.

The kittens were happily swatting at her feet, but it was as if they weren't there. Her sorrow was so deep she didn't hear him stride into the room. "Portia, sweetheart. What's wrong?"

She wiped her cheeks with the back of her hand, shaking her head. "You shouldn't have come, Juan Carlos," she whispered.

He narrowed his eyes. What on earth? Last night, they'd settled things. Maybe not verbally, but after the night they'd shared she had to recognize what they meant to each other. He'd come to retrieve her and bring her back to her rightful place, beside him on the throne of Alma. But now she was crying, looking so achingly sad. His gut clenched seeing her that way. "I don't understand."

He sat beside her and she unraveled her legs to face him, her eyes swollen from tears. "I can't be with you. I can't..."

"Sweetheart, my perfect princess, of course you belong with me. We don't have to rush into a wedding, if that's your concern. Whatever it is, we'll work it out. Just tell me. It kills me to see you in so much pain."

She rose then, yet her body slumped in defeat, her long hair falling onto her face. "That's just it, Juan Carlos," she said, shoving her hair aside. "I'm not your perfect princess.

I'm nobody's princess. I'm a fraud. I don't have an ounce of royal blood in my body. I cannot marry you. Ever."

Juan Carlos blinked several times, absorbing her words. He rose slowly, his heart pounding, his body shaking. "What you do mean you're not a princess?"

"I'm not. I never was. It's all a lie my family told after they migrated to the United States after World War II."

Portia spent the next few minutes explaining her family's duplicity to him. She gave him very little to hold on to as she presented the cold cruel facts that tore his life into shreds. Everything she told him made sense, yet nothing made sense. This couldn't be happening. Suddenly, he looked at Portia Lindstrom differently. She'd lied to him. Why? "How long have you known this?"

"I found out a little more than a week ago while researching our...my wedding rituals."

Juan Carlos stood ramrod stiff, his shoulders back and his heart breaking. "Yet you came to me and lied about the reasons for breaking it off between us. You told me you weren't ready to marry. You gave me excuses about your career and your love of the States. You knew, and yet you lied. How many other lies have you told me, Portia?"

"I didn't know what to do when I found out. Who to turn to. I'd just found out I'm...I'm an *imposter*." She spit the word out as if saying it stung her tongue. "I had trouble facing it, Juan Carlos."

His voice rose. "You should have trusted me with the truth. Or maybe you didn't want anyone to know the real truth? Maybe you wanted to keep on with the deception? Being of royal blood has its privileges. If I hadn't shown up here, what were you going to do? Live the lie forever?"

Her words from last week rang in his ears. *I'm fond of you. This isn't going to work. I don't want to get married. I don't want children.*

Had the woman he loved been nothing but a gold digger? Had her hard-to-get act been a ploy? All the warmth he had nestled inside evaporated. Last night had meant nothing to her. She'd deceived him over and over during the past few weeks. She'd broken off her engagement to him, but she hadn't revealed the truth to anyone. Of course, her precious career would suffer. She'd hidden the truth because she couldn't afford another scandal. She needed the art world to believe that she was a princess. So, of course, she had to come to him with lies about why she was breaking off their engagement in order to keep her secret.

"I took the bait and you reeled me in, didn't you, Portia? Then what happened? You ran scared when I offered marriage? Did you have a bout of conscience? Or did you finally realize you'd get caught if you didn't break it off with me? You couldn't marry me and risk being found out. Just think what would happen to your career if you were discovered to be a fraud. You'd never survive another scandal. Not professionally. No one in their right mind would hire you so you lied your way out of our engagement."

Her tears gone now, she squeezed her eyes closed for a second. As he waited, her breathing steadied and when she opened her eyes again, they were twin pinpoints of blue, focused on him. "You see things in black-and-white, Juan Carlos. There is no room for grays in your narrow line of vision. You only wanted me when I fit into your plans, but now you know the truth. I'm not royal. I'm flawed and can't be a part of your unblemished world."

His lips tightened. "You should've told me the truth, Portia."

"Another point against me. I'm human. I make mistakes." She folded her arms across her stomach. "Now that you have the truth, what are you going to do with it?"

He stared at her, wondering what had happened to the woman he'd fallen in love with. Thoughts clogged his head. She wasn't a princess. She had no royal blood flowing through her veins. She was an imposter. A fraud, as she put it. His shoulders dropped as he shook his head. He had no answer for her.

"You only loved the idea of me, Juan Carlos. You said it just a little while ago. You think of me as your perfect princess. But now you know I'm not perfect. Hardly that. And how can a man who demands perfection in everything and everyone want me? I was only good to you when I was Princess Portia of Samforstand."

He let that sink in. He loved her, wanted her as his wife. Now, nothing made sense, and blackness from deep in his soul overwhelmed him. His Portia, the woman he'd thought she was, was gone. She wasn't a princess, but a fraud. He couldn't marry Portia Lindstrom. According to royal decree he was obligated to marry royalty. She was once a part of everything good that had happened to him and now there was nothing left between them.

"We had a fling, and it's over," she whispered. "Let's let it go at that. I think you should leave. Go back to Del Sol, be the king you were meant to be. Give me some time, I'll make sure…no blame will come to you about this."

"Portia," he said. He couldn't bring himself to move.

"Go, please." Her quiet plea broke his heart. "You shouldn't have come back. Goodbye, Juan Carlos."

She picked up the kittens playing at her feet, hugged them to her chest and walked out of the room.

She was right. He should leave.

There wasn't anything left for him here.

"Mr. Tanaka, it was a pleasure seeing you again. I'll be in touch once I've found the right prints and antique paneled floor screens to separate your work spaces. You've given me a good idea what you are looking for. I promise you, you'll be happy with the collection I come up with for your magnificent new corporate offices."

"Thank you, Princess. I have faith in your abilities. Your recommendations for my home have worked out nicely. I'm grateful you would take time from your leave of absence to do this for me."

Portia shook hands with her client outside his private office, her belly squeezing tight every time he called her princess. The title she'd grown up with no longer rang true and his respectful use of it during their meeting reminded her constantly that she was a fraud. "Goodbye."

Mr. Tanaka, founder and president of a highly successful Japanese food chain, hadn't wanted to work with anyone else. He'd called her personally to request her expertise, offering a big bonus if she would consider advising him on the artwork for his new offices. She'd agreed without hesitation. Pining for Juan Carlos and what would never be had grown old. She couldn't cry herself to sleep any longer. Three days' worth of tears had exhausted her. But she was glad her secret was out. At least to him. Admitting the truth to Juan Carlos had been difficult, but it had also been liberating. There would be no more lies between them now.

He'd been angry with her when he'd left her condo the other day. She'd seen the pain in his eyes, too, and she'd shivered when he'd looked at her as if she were a stranger. It had been so very hard to hear him berate her. He hadn't believed her, and even thought so little of her that he'd accused her of putting her career above her love for him. His accusations had slashed through her body like a dagger. But ultimately, it was better to allow him to believe the worst about her. It was a clean break.

Still, the love she had for him would never die. It would be hard, if not impossible, to get over him. Even if he had believed her claims, he couldn't marry her. They would have no future. He lived by a stringent set of rules. He did everything by the book. It was a no-win situation. So she'd made the supreme sacrifice for his benefit. She'd dismissed him without defending herself. As if her life wouldn't be forever altered after knowing and loving him.

He would get over her. He had to. He had to go about his life as if they had never met. In the near future, she didn't know exactly when, she would quietly make an announcement that they'd broken off their engagement. Their whirlwind romance was over. And then at some later point, when it had all died down, she would admit to the world, or anyone who cared, that she wasn't of royal heritage.

She would not go on living a lie.

But for now her goal was to protect Juan Carlos from a scandal. She would not have him looked upon as a fool.

As she headed to the parking garage, her eyes clouded with tears. She was broken inside and there was no way to repair her. Taking on Mr. Tanaka's account would be a good distraction. She'd focus on work for the next few weeks and the terrible ache in the pit of her stomach would eventually go away.

She got in her car and glanced in the mirror. She looked a wreck. With the tips of her index fingers, she smoothed away moisture under her eyes. "No more," she whispered. She had to put on a happy face. It was Jasmine's birthday today and she was taking her to dinner to celebrate the big three-oh.

Ten

Juan Carlos ran a hand down his face. He stood at the bar in the study of his living quarters in the palace and poured himself a double whiskey, straight up. "It's impossible." He lifted the glass to his mouth and took a sip.

"What's impossible?"

He turned, a little shocked to find Maria standing beside him. He'd been so deep in thought, he'd almost forgotten about his dinner date with the Ramons tonight. Normally his senses were keen and no one could sneak up on him. Especially not a woman wearing a pretty dress and heels and smelling like something exotic. It served to show him how off he'd been lately.

"Sorry if I startled you. Your staff assured me I was expected."

"No, it's okay. You are." It was good to see a friendly face.

"Alex is running late. He's meeting me here."

Juan Carlos nodded. "That'll give us a chance to talk. Let me get you a drink. What would you like?"

"Just a soda, please."

He dropped two ice cubes into a tall glass and poured her a cola. "Here you go."

She took the offered glass and sipped. "So what were you mumbling about when I came in?"

The corner of his mouth crooked up. It was the best he could do. He didn't have a smile for anyone these days. "My life."

"Your life?" Maria's aqua eyes opened wider. "Your perfect, kingly, marrying-a-beautiful-princess life?"

He lifted his whiskey glass and pointed with his index finger to the bone leather sofa. "Have a seat. I have something to… I need some advice."

Maria arched an eyebrow. "Advice? About your wedding?"

He waited for her to sit and then planted himself on the other end of the sofa. "Maria, uh, there isn't going to be a wedding."

It was hard getting the words out, and seeing Maria's mouth drop open only added to his discomfort. "That's why I asked you here. I haven't told a soul yet. I can hardly believe it myself."

"But you and Portia seemed so perfect together. What happened?"

Perfect. He was beginning to really hate that word. Portia had accused him of demanding that everyone and everything around him be perfect. Was he guilty of that? Did he expect too much?

"We're not perfect. Far from it. We've broken up and I don't know what to think about it."

"Why? What happened, Your Majesty?"

"She came back to Del Sol almost two weeks ago to break it off. She claimed she didn't want to get married and move to Alma. She loved her career and didn't want it to end. She claimed all we had was a fling, and that she, we, were high on romance. Finding the hidden artwork and being on the adventure together made it all seem possible but when she got back home, she was hit with reality."

"Do you think she was running scared?"

He hung his head, staring at the ground. "Initially, that's what I thought. I believed I could convince her that we could work out logistics and that we belonged together."

He met with Maria's eyes. "I was fool enough to go after her. I was in love."

"Was?"

He shrugged. "From the day I met her, something inside me told me she was the one. I pursued her like crazy. She didn't make it easy and now that I'm home, putting the pieces together, I think I know why."

There was a beat of silence. Maria was waiting for him to continue. It was difficult to admit to anyone how wrong he'd been. "When I went to Los Angeles, we...connected again. And it was as it had always been—amazing. I thought I'd relieved her of her cold feet. But in the morning, I found her quietly crying. She said she wished that I hadn't come for her. I was confused and didn't know why she'd had a change of heart."

"Why did she?" Maria asked.

He shrugged and shook his head. "I think she was cornered and didn't see a way out, so she finally told me the truth. Portia is not who she says she is. She's not a princess. She never was. She claims she found out while trying to dig up protocols for our wedding. Her family fled to the United States right after World War II and assumed the role of royalty. They were impoverished and used their phony status to gain a leg up. Supposedly, Portia's great-aunt has a diary that confirms all this."

"Wow, this is...big. Poor Portia. She must've been devastated when she found out. I can only imagine how she feels right now."

He stared at her. "You mean you believe that she didn't know about this all along?"

"Why wouldn't I? More importantly, why wouldn't you?"

"I'll tell you why. When she came back to Del Sol a couple weeks ago she lied about her reasons for breaking it off. She made up one excuse after another and if I hadn't gone to LA, I would still believe those lies she'd told. Only when she couldn't get rid of me any other way, she was forced to reveal the truth."

"Oh, I don't know about that." Maria began shaking her head. "That doesn't sound like Portia. What did you say to her when you found out?"

"In the beginning I was shell-shocked. And then my methodical mind started working and I said some things out of anger. I practically accused her of being a gold digger. Now that I think back on it, she looked so...lost. She kept saying she was an imposter, and I couldn't sympathize with her. I wasn't in the frame of mind. I felt betrayed. She should have come to me with the truth from the beginning."

"It must've been a hard thing for her to admit. To herself, much less to the man she loved. Just think, everything she believed about herself and her life is a lie. If that were me, I wouldn't know what to do, who to turn to. I don't know if I'd have the courage to do what she did. It was a hard day for both of you."

He drew oxygen into his lungs. "I suppose. I still don't know what to think."

"What else did she say? How did you part?"

"She pretty much told me off. She said that I expected perfection in everything and that I only loved the idea of her." He stared into his tumbler at the last gulp of whiskey left. "That's not true."

"No?"

He gave Maria a glance. "No," he assured her. "I loved her."

"You still love her, Your Majesty. You can't shut down those emotions so quickly. And what if she still is that woman you fell in love with, without the title of princess in front of her name? What if Portia Lindstrom is the woman for you?"

"How can I believe that when she doesn't believe it? She

didn't try to defend herself against my accusations. She didn't try to convince me that I'd been wrong about her."

"Well, since you asked me for my advice, I'm going to give it to you. I know Portia a little bit, and I'm a pretty good judge of character. I have seen the way she looks at you. The eyes don't lie. She was deeply in love and happy."

A lump formed in his throat. In the short weeks that he and Portia had been together, they'd gotten to know each other pretty well. They'd shared an adventure or two, but it went deeper than that and he'd felt they were meant for each other from the very beginning. It was a sense he had, a feeling that clamped onto him and never let go. It wasn't an overreaction to her beauty or the fact that she was a princess. But that factored into the equation, at least a little bit, because her status meant he was free to seriously pursue her.

"I thought so, too," he said. "We were good together."

"Did you ever stop to think that she wasn't thinking about herself when she broke up with you? Maybe she loved you so much she didn't want you portrayed in a bad light. A hasty then broken engagement wouldn't instill much faith in the monarchy you are trying to reestablish. After the big splash announcing your engagement, how would King Juan Carlos appear to the country that trusted his honor? Wouldn't it make you seem frivolous? Or duped? Or worse yet, impetuous? Seems to me, if I was in that situation, I would do everything in my power to protect the man I loved from scorn and speculation."

He scrubbed his jaw and sighed. "The last thing she told me was that she would make sure no blame came to rest on my shoulders."

Maria smiled. "There, you see. Only a woman still in love would say that. She was shielding you from harm. I would bet on it."

"You would?"

"Yes, and you should, too, if you still love her."

"To what end? I can't change the future…"

"Who says you can't? You're the king."

"I'm not that kind of king. I don't want to break with tradition."

"No, you'd rather have your heart broken."

Juan Carlos sighed. She was right. He would never love another the way he loved Portia. Right now, he physically ached for her.

Maria continued, "Think of it this way. You'll rule with more clarity and fairness having Portia by your side. You won't be stung by bitterness and regret and live an empty life without her."

"But the people expect—"

"A ruler they can admire and look up to. If you make it clear to them that this is for the best, they will rally behind you, my friend. And as the newly reigning king of a lost monarchy you have the luxury of not needing a parliament to vote on changes you might want to make in your dynasty."

A slow smile spread across his face. "I hadn't thought of that." And just as the notion elevated his hope, another thought brought him down again. "No…it's too late after the way I walked out on Portia, without believing in her. She may not forgive me."

Maria scooted closer to him, the sparkle in her eyes grabbing his attention. "But she may. And I think she will. She sacrificed herself for you. Don't you think you owe your relationship one more chance? If you don't try, you'll always wonder and you'll live to regret it."

Did he still love Portia? Yes, very much, and the more he thought about Maria's argument, the more he began to believe she could be right. He couldn't throw away something so precious to him without giving it one more try.

A light flashed in his head as he began to formulate a

plan. Finally, after these past few days of living in a depressed stupor, he was waking up alert and seeing things much more clearly. He had the power of the throne behind him. He hoped it would be enough.

"Maria, I'm going to need your help."

"I'll give it gladly, Your Highness."

A knot formed in the pit of his stomach. "A lot will be riding on this," he warned.

"I know. But I have enough faith in love for both of us. Alex says I've taught him something about that."

Juan Carlos nodded. If only he had that same faith. He leaned forward to kiss Maria's cheek. "Thank you."

"What is it exactly that you've taught me, sweetheart?" Alex stood at the threshold of the study, catching Juan Carlos's lips leaving Maria's cheek.

"How important *trust* is, Alex," Maria said slowly, straightening her position on the sofa, "when it comes to matters of the heart."

Alex gave them a nod as he entered the room. "It's true…once upon a time my fist might've met with His Majesty's jaw seeing him kiss you. But now, I only see love shining in your eyes for me."

A chuckle rumbled from Juan Carlos's chest. It was a good sound. One he hoped to make more often, after Portia was back where she belonged.

The sound of her Nikes pounding against the treadmill echoed off the gym walls. Sweat beaded up on Portia's forehead as she gazed out the window of the high-rise. She was offered a view of distant mountains and below, a city waking just after dawn. It was a good time of day to work out, before the world came alive. She had about thirty minutes before the gym would crowd with businessmen and women coming for their daily fix. She'd be gone by then, away from any nosy members who'd try to talk to her, get to know her. Many people recognized her, but thankfully she was old news as the other royal couple—the Brits—were in town for a charity event and all eyes had turned to them.

It was a lucky break and she valued the bit of anonymity it afforded her.

"Oh…kay, Portia," Jasmine said, shutting down her machine. "I've had enough."

Portia continued running at a six-mile-per-hour pace. She had one more mile to go. "You've barely broken a sweat."

"You're insane this morning." Jas used her towel to wipe her face as droplets rained down from her eyebrows.

Portia slowed her pace, allowing her body to cool down. "I know. But this is the only time I have to work off my…"

"Sexual frustration."

Portia swiped at her friend's butt with her workout towel. "Shh…no. Stop that! Just frustration in general."

Jasmine reached over and pushed the Off button on Portia's machine. "You're done."

The treadmill's thrumming quieted as it shut down and Portia finally stood stationary facing Jas. "I know I am. So done." She sopped up her face and neck and allowed herself a moment of accomplishment. It had been a hearty workout.

"I meant on the machine, girl. You're being cryptic today. What's really bothering you?"

Aside from her broken heart? It was hard to put into words exactly but she tried to explain. "I'm almost finished with the Tanaka account, Jas. You've helped me so much this past week and we've been working at breakneck speed for long hours. When I'm through… I don't know how it will play out. I'm still officially on leave. I don't know what to do after this. I'm living a lie, but I can't do anything about it at the moment. I feel weird in my own skin right now."

"Wow, Portia, I'm sorry. Juan Carlos doesn't deserve you. You're hurting because of him."

"You got that backward. I don't deserve him."

"Oh, brother. Listen, I know it's going to take time getting over him, but you will, honey. I hate to stand by and see you beat yourself up over something out of your control."

"Thanks, Jas. It means a lot to know you have my back."

"I do."

They left the workout area and headed to the showers. After a quick rinse off, Portia dressed in her casual street clothes and combed her hair.

"Too bad we can't grab breakfast," Jas said, exchanging a look with Portia in the dressing room mirror as she slipped her long mane into a ponytail.

"Wish we could, but we've both got busy mornings. Sorry if I'm overworking you on this account."

"You're not at all. I was only looking for an excuse to have waffles and bacon this morning."

"And you wanted an accomplice, right?"

Jas nodded. "No fun eating alone."

"Another day, I promise."

"Okay, then I'll talk to you later. Oh, and thanks," she said, wrinkling her nose, "for dragging my butt in this morning." She pouted. "I ache all over and my legs feel like Jell-O."

"You'll thank me in twenty years when you're still hot and gorgeous."

"So I guess I'll have to be your friend forever now."

"BFFs. That's us."

"Yeah, that's us," Jas said, waving goodbye.

Portia rode the elevator down to the parking garage. Just as she was getting into her Volvo, her phone beeped. She glanced at the screen. Odd, she'd gotten a text from Maria Ramon.

I'm in town and would love to see you. Can you make time for me today?

"No," she whispered. Any reminder of Juan Carlos right now was hard to take. Seeing Maria would only bring back memories of her time in Alma. She did have a terribly busy day. Hadn't she just turned down a breakfast date with her best friend?

Another text came in. It's important that I see you.

Portia's breath caught in her throat. Her heart began to pound. She couldn't refuse Maria. She was a friend and more than that, Portia was curious as to what she wanted. But that didn't stop her hands from trembling as she typed her answer. Sure, would love to see you. Stop by this morning. She gave her the address and sighed, starting the car. She planned on working from home this morning, anyway.

As it turned out, Portia couldn't concentrate when she returned home. Those phone conversations could wait another day, she decided. She changed into a powder-blue silk blouse and white slacks, and brushed her hair back and clipped it on one side with a gemstone barrette à la Gwen Stefani. She finished with a few flips of mascara to her lashes and some pink lip gloss.

In the kitchen, she prepared coffee, arranged fresh pastries on a plate, and then brought it all to the dining table. Mischief and Mallow played at her feet, swatting none too gently at her toes. Before they destroyed her sandals, she scooped them both up and carried them to the sofa. "Here, let's cuddle," she said, laying them across her chest. They obeyed, burrowing into the warmth of her body. The sound of their purring brought a smile to her face. She stroked the top of their soft downy heads. She loved the two fur balls with all of her heart.

A few minutes later, the doorbell chimed and Portia jerked up straight. The quick move sent the kittens tumbling to the floor. The little guys landed on their feet. Oh, to be a cat.

Portia rose and glanced at herself in the foyer mirror, checking hair and makeup. She approached the door, but her hand shook on the knob. She paused, took a deep breath. *Stay calm, Portia. Maria is a friend.*

She opened the door to find Maria smiling warmly, her pretty aqua eyes bright. A sharp twinge tightened Portia's belly. "Hi, Maria."

"Portia, it's good to see you."

She stepped forward to give Maria a hug. "I'm happy to see you, too. Please come in," she said, retreating as Maria made her way into the foyer.

She glanced around, noting the high-vaulted ceilings and the living and dining rooms. "It's a lovely place, Portia."

She shrugged. "Thanks. It's a rental. I travel back and forth from coast to coast a lot, so I have a small apartment in New York City, too. I haven't really made this place my own yet." She'd never felt settled enough in either place to put too much of herself into them. Aside from her treasured artwork on the walls, the rest of her furniture was simply… there. She had no emotional attachment to it, which had never really dawned on her before now. "It's not a big place. Would you like a tour?"

"Sure." Portia walked her through the condo, showing her the home office, the guest bedroom, her master suite and the kitchen. They stopped in the dining room. "Would you like coffee and a pastry?"

Maria's eyes darted to the dish of fresh pastries. They were impressive. Portia knew the pastry chef at the Beverly Hills Hotel and she'd made a call this morning to have them delivered. "I'd love some. Thank you. It's good seeing you in your own element here. This is very nice."

"Let's have a seat," Portia said. "Everything's ready." Maria sat down across the table and Portia poured them each a cup of coffee. "I was surprised, in a good way, to hear from you this morning. What brings you to California?"

Maria cradled the cup in her hands. "I, uh, I had no real business here, Portia. I came specifically to see you."

"Me?" Portia halted before the cup touched her lips. "Why?"

"Maybe because I'm a hopeless romantic. Maybe because I found the love of my life in Alex and want my friends to find that same kind of happiness. Don't get me wrong, Portia, I'm not here to meddle, but I do think Juan Carlos made a mistake with you."

"He told you?" Portia wasn't sure how she felt about that.

"Yes, I know you've broken the engagement."

"Who else knows?"

"No one. I don't think he's told his cousins yet."

Portia nodded. Her belly began to ache. "Do you know everything?"

Maria's expression softened. "I know you're not a princess, Portia. Juan Carlos told me the entire story. I'm so sorry you were misled all those years. It must have been extremely difficult finding out the way that you did."

Portia's eyes squeezed shut at the truth of those words. "Yes." Oh, God. This was so hard. If only she could blink this entire ordeal away. Too bad life wasn't that easy. Soon everyone would know her dirty little secret and they probably wouldn't be as kind as Maria. "It's been an adjustment. My whole life is a lie."

"Not all of it, Portia."

She snapped her eyes open, just as Maria's hand came to touch hers. She welcomed the warmth of her friend's gentle touch. "I can't possibly know exactly how you feel, but I do know you. Portia Lindstrom is a wonderful, sweet, caring woman. She's smart and funny and she's terribly in love with a good man."

Portia shook her head. "No. Juan Carlos...there's nothing left between us."

"There's love, Portia. Don't discount it. It makes the world go round, you know."

"Well, I'm spinning fast, Maria. And I'm about to fall off."

"No, you don't have to fall off. I know Juan Carlos still loves you. He's made a terrible mistake. He was in shock, I think, hearing the news about your identity, and he regrets how you two left off. He's sorry for how he treated you, Portia."

"I accept his apology. If that's what you came for, you can tell him not to worry about me. I'm...fine."

"That's not why I came. You love him very much, don't you?"

Portia sat silent.

"I know you're protecting him, Portia. I know, because if I were in your shoes, I'd do the same thing."

"You would?"

"Yes. Isn't it why you initially lied about the reason you broke off your engagement?"

"Maybe."

"Maybe yes?"

"Okay, yes. That's why I lied. It was inevitable that we had to break up, so why should both of us go down with the ship? I was to blame. It was my family's illicit behavior that put us in this position. Juan Carlos didn't need to suffer, too."

"I thought so." Maria selected a pastry and eased it onto her plate. "Juan Carlos is very lucky."

Portia scoffed. "Hardly. I'm a fraud."

"No, you're not, Portia. You may not be a princess, but that's not all you are. Juan Carlos believes in your love."

"Then why isn't he here? Never mind. I'm glad he's not. It was hard enough breaking it off with him the first and second time."

Maria chewed her raspberry cheese tart with a thought-ful expression on her face. "The third time's the charm, they say. And he's not here, because well, he wants to see you again. In fact, it's urgent that he see you. But he wants you to come to Alma. What he has to say must be said in Del Sol."

"Me? Go back to Alma? I couldn't possibly."

"I was afraid you'd say that. I'm not to leave here with-out you, but…I think I have something that will change your mind."

"Nothing much could change my mind."

"Wait right here. I have something in my car. I'll only be thirty seconds," Maria said, rising. "Don't you think about putting those pastries away."

Portia smiled despite the mystery unfolding. What on earth was Maria up to?

Just seconds later, Maria walked back into the dining room holding a large package wrapped in brown paper. The box was the size of a small television or a microwave. Ridiculous.

"What do you have there?"

"Oh, no, I'm not telling. You have to open it. First read the note."

"I don't see a note?"

"It's inside."

Portia stared at Maria and shook her head. Nothing would get her to change her mind. But she had to admit, she was intrigued. Her eye began to twitch. *Damn. Stop it.* Okay, she was nervous.

"Go on," Maria said.

Portia dug her fingers into the wrapping and tore it away. Paper flew in all directions. An envelope with her name on it taped to the box popped into her line of vision. She lifted it off, pulled the note out and read it silently.

Portia, sweetheart,
Give me another chance to prove my love.
This was to be my wedding gift to you.
I hope you will accept it and me back into your life.
It speaks for itself.
Juan Carlos

Tears trickled down her face. The note was short, but held the words that could make all things possible. She loved Juan Carlos. Would always love him. And now, dare she take a chance? What could he have possibly sent that would impact her more than those loving words?

"Open the box, Portia."

"I'm afraid to," she said, eyeing the lid, her body shaking so badly she could hardly move. "What if it isn't…"

"It is. Trust me," Maria said.

Portia pulled open the lid and found yet another box. She lifted it out and set it on the table, staring at the ornate workmanship on the box, the beautiful wood carvings of intricate design.

She undid the latch and slowly eased the lid open. She eyed her gift and a soft gasp rose up from the depths of her throat. This was amazing. Sweet. The gesture meant more to her than anything else she could imagine. Her lips began to quiver, her heart pounded and her tears fell like heavy rain.

"It's the s-statue. My favorite p-piece of the artwork we…" She gulped and whispered, "It's from the hidden treasure we uncovered." A man reaching his hand out for the woman he loves. *"Almas Iguales. Equal Souls."*

A royal chauffeur met her at the Del Sol airport terminal, grabbing up her suitcases and guiding her toward the limousine parked just outside the entrance. She was taking a giant leap of faith coming here, offering up her heart once again. But Juan Carlos had done the one thing, given her the one gift that could change her mind. His generous gesture told her he understood her, believed in her and wanted her back in his life. She didn't see how it was possible. She didn't know what terms Juan Carlos would dictate to her when she arrived. Could she bank on his integrity? Could she trust in him enough to believe there was a solution to their dilemma?

His gift had jarred her into believing the best was yet to come. But as the hours had worn on, she'd started to doubt again. It had taken Maria and Jasmine both to convince her that if she didn't travel to Del Sol and give it one last try, she would live to regret it.

"He's been solely devoted to you since the minute he set eyes on you," Maria had said.

"Think of your time at the farmhouse," Jasmine had prodded. "How many other men would rescue feral cats and give them a good home, much less a royal palace, to make you happy? And don't forget how he battled a snake to keep you safe. He's been there for you, Portia. And he'll be there for you again."

"Go, give your love another chance," they'd both chorused.

So here she was back in Del Sol where in less than an hour, Juan Carlos would address the citizens of his country in a speech that would set the tone for his rule.

The driver opened the limo door. "Thank you." She slid inside and immediately turned, startled to find Juan Carlos in the seat beside her.

"Hello, sweetheart."

The richness in his voice seeped into her soul. She faced the most handsome man she'd ever known. His eyes were deep dark shades of coffee and cocoa, flecked with hints of gold, and he was gazing at her in that intense way that made her heart soar. His smile was warm, welcoming and filled with the confidence she lacked at the moment. Oh, how she'd missed him. A whisper broke from her lips. "Juan Carlos."

"I am glad you came."

He didn't reach for her, didn't try to touch her, and she was glad. She had to catch her breath just from seeing him. Anything more would send her into a tailspin. "I, uh, I don't know why I'm here."

He sighed. "It's because you love me."

She couldn't deny it. "Yes."

"And I love you, above all else. I have misjudged you and I am truly sorry, my love. I hope your being here means you have forgiven me."

A lump formed in her throat. How could she explain the complexities of her feelings? "I do forgive you. Though it hurt, I realized you reacted as anyone might."

"But I am not just anyone, Portia. I am the man who loves you unconditionally. And I should have recognized that sooner. I should have believed in you."

"Yes. But that wouldn't have changed the outcome. Our situation is impossible, Juan Carlos."

He only smiled. "Did you like my gift?"

Tears welled in her eyes. "It's magnificent. I was truly surprised by the gesture."

"Not a gesture, sweetheart. It's a gift from my heart to yours. And I have another gift for you. One that will make all things possible. I am only asking for your trust. Do I have it?"

She hesitated for only a moment. And in that moment, she realized that yes, she trusted him with her life. She trusted him to make the right decision. She trusted him. With. Her. Heart. She nodded.

"Good."

He took her hand and lifted it to his lips, pressing the

softest, most reverent kiss there. The sweetness of the gesture left her floating on air. "I have missed you."

Their eyes met then. His were unflappable, determined, loving. She saw everything she needed in their brown depths. Then his hands were on her, cupping her face, his thumbs stroking her cheeks as his gaze flowed over her face. She was out of her depths now, living in the moment, heat crawling up from her belly to lick at her. When his lips rained down on hers, devouring her mouth in a kiss to beat all kisses, tremendous hunger swept her up and carried her away.

His groans matched her unbridled sighs. "I cannot live without you in my life," he murmured between kisses.

"I feel the same," she whispered, as he dragged her farther into his embrace. She was nearly atop him now. His hands were in her hair, his tongue sweeping through her mouth, their bodies trembling, aching.

"We have arrived, Your Highness," the driver announced through the speaker. They'd arrived? She didn't remember them taking off.

Juan Carlos stilled. "All right," he said to the chauffeur.

They had indeed arrived at a secluded private entrance in the west wing of the palace.

Juan Carlos sighed heavily and pulled away from her. "One day, we will finish this in the limo."

"I'll look forward to that." Her eyelid fluttered. Heavens, another unintended wink? She was hopeless.

Intense heat entered his eyes and a savage groan rumbled from his chest. "You are a temptation, Portia," he said. He took a second to smooth the hair he'd just mussed. The care with which he touched her and gently pulled tendrils away from her face sent shivers down her spine. Then he smiled wide and destroyed her for good. "You will attend my speech?"

"Yes." That was why she had come. His only request

was that she be in attendance when he spoke to the press and his fellow countrymen. Her flight had been delayed and there was a moment when she'd thought it an omen. A moment when she almost turned back. But Portia wasn't going to run from the truth any longer. No matter how bad. No matter that her life would be forever altered. She had gotten on the plane ready to hear what Juan Carlos seemed eager to say. He would be giving the speech very shortly. "I will be there."

He nodded, satisfied, and the door on his side of the car opened. The driver stood at attention waiting. "You'll be driven to the palace lawn now," he said to her. "I will see you very soon."

Then he climbed out of the car and was gone.

Juan Carlos stood tall and erect at the podium looking out at the crowd that had gathered on the palace lawn. Dressed regally in a dark suit and tie, he scanned his audience. Luis and Eduardo flanked him on either side, on the lookout for signs of danger. News crews from Del Sol's three television stations were in attendance, as well as reporters and journalists from far and wide. Portia saw Juan Carlos now, as the king surrounded by people who banked on his every word. He was a model citizen, handsome, refined, a man to be admired. He was the king of his people. The press loved him. Even more, they loved the idea of him *with Portia*. Who didn't love a good fairy tale?

Her stomach ached. She had no idea what he was going to say, but it was important to him that she hear him say it. There was no doubt she loved him. And she was fairly certain of his love for her. So she stood in the front row, but off to the side somewhat with Maria and Alex Ramon. Maria slid her hand over hers and squeezed gently. God, how Portia needed that show of support right now. Her legs were two rubber posts, holding her up only by sheer stubborn will. She swallowed as Juan Carlos tapped the mike, ready to begin his speech.

And when he spoke, his voice came across clear, strong and confident. Tears of pride pooled in her eyes. He addressed the crowd, garnering cheers as he began his speech. Then he graciously spoke of the future, of how he planned to work alongside the parliament to better the country. He spoke of helping the needy, working with charities and letting the people of Alma have a voice.

He seemed to seek her out of the crowd and as those gorgeous dark eyes landed on her, her breath caught in her throat. He trained that killer smile on her once again. How unfair of him to have such power over her, to stop her breathing with a look, a smile.

All eyes in the crowd seemed to turn her way. She was no stranger to the press, to having people recognize her, but today, she wanted no such attention. She'd rather be invisible.

Maria squeezed her hand again, giving her silent support. Portia inhaled and began breathing again.

"I have one more announcement to make," he continued to his audience. "Actually it is the reason I have called you here. I have made a decision that will change the ways of the monarchy for the better, I hope. For decades past, those in power, the honorable men and women who held the highest rule of the land, often did so out of duty. But with their duty often came great sacrifice." Juan Carlos glanced at Portia again briefly and then went on. "Many true loves went unheeded. Many of those loves were lost to baseless marriages, unions that held no great affection. The sacrifice was thought to keep the bloodlines pure. I have called you here today to say that my rule, this monarchy, is one that looks forward to the future, not backward at the past. It is time to bring the monarchy into the twenty-first century.

"As you know, Portia Lindstrom and I are to be married. Our engagement was swift, yes, but when it's right, you know it deep in your heart." His fist covered his heart and he awarded the crowd his beautiful smile. "And I am here to tell you it is right."

His eyes sparkled and he sent her a look filled with so much love, Portia's heart did somersaults. "Recently, it's come to light that Portia is not the true princess of Samforstand. In fact, she has no royal bloodlines at all. She came to me when she learned this news from an elder in her family. It seems there was much confusion about the legal heirs to the throne after the chaos and hardships of World War II.

"My family went through great hardships at that time, as well. Many of you here today know all about the recent trials and tribulations my family went through to find the true heir to the throne. Our great-grandmother's recently discovered letters proved to all of us the high price that was paid to keep to the letter of law when it came to royal protocol. In those letters we learned that her son, king Raphael Montoro II, and his direct descendants were not the rightful heirs to the throne, and thus am I standing before you today, a Salazar, as your king.

"Similarly, Portia has discovered the truth of her family's past and now needs to move forward with her life. But I will not allow mere decorum to once again steer the Montoros' destiny toward a tragic outcome. We will not let history repeat itself. We will not sacrifice our love in the name of an outdated custom. Portia Lindstrom is here today, as my fiancée, and princess or not, she is the love of my life and will become my wife."

Juan Carlos put out his hand. "Portia? Will you join me here? Be by my side."

The crowd was stunned into silence. Cameras angled her way, shots were snapped off by the dozens.

"Go," Maria whispered. "He is changing a centuries-old tradition for you. Don't leave him waiting."

She blinked, coming to grips with what had just happened. The depth of his commitment astonished her, delighted her and sent her hormones into a tizzy. She caught Eduardo giving her a smile and an encouraging nod from behind Juan Carlos. She smiled back.

Maria was right; she couldn't leave the king waiting. Not for another second. If he could do this for her, then she wouldn't hesitate to show him her love. With him by her side, she could conquer anything. She wasn't a wimpy princess. Well, she *wasn't* a princess at all, but she wasn't wimpy, either.

Her head held high, she stepped forward and made her way to the podium. As she reached it, she took Juan Carlos's outstretched hand and gazed into his eyes. In them, she saw her life, her future. The details were negotiable, but the love, that never wavered. She loved him. She would always love him. Thank God, King Montoro of Alma was a determined man.

Juan Carlos pulled her close and there before the world, bruised her lips in a kiss that left no one doubting their king's commitment. "Juan Carlos," she murmured. "Everyone's watching."

"Are they?"

Cameras clicked like crazy and she had no doubt this epic scene would go viral.

When Juan Carlos broke off the kiss, he nudged her tight to his side to present a united front and turned to the crowd. "Portia is a wonderful, bright, talented woman and in the days and years to come, you will all see in her what I see. I ask only that you welcome her today. Give her the same chance you gave me."

The crowd was silent and Portia's heart plummeted. And then a sole cheer rang out from a man shouting his support. And then another cheer went up and another, in a show of loyalty. And soon, the entire gathering displayed their acceptance as boisterous cheers and booming applause echoed against the palace walls, the citizens of Alma giving the king their allegiance.

They had accepted her.

Portia couldn't keep a wide, teary-eyed smile from spreading across her face. She was grateful for their support, but she was certain that even if the crowd had turned hostile, nothing would have deterred Juan Carlos. He had her back, and that was the best feeling in the world.

The speech over, Portia walked off with Juan Carlos. "I love you, you know," she said, winding her arm around his waist and leaning her head on his shoulder.

"I do know, but I think I'll need to hear you say it about a thousand times. Tonight?"

She nodded. "Tonight." She lifted her lips to his. "Do you think you can make me say it a thousand times?"

He laughed. "Oh, I know I can. Just let me alert the chauffeur we'll be needing the limo soon."

Her eyes went wide. "Juan Carlos, you don't play fair!"

"Sweetheart, I play for keeps. Princess or not, you're a royal temptation that I can't live without."

"So you're keeping me?"

"For as long as you'll have me."

"Forever, then. It's settled."

"Settled," he said, grinning as he picked her up and twirled her around and around.

She floated on air.

And her feet never did touch the ground again.

Epilogue

One month later

Juan Carlos couldn't stop grinning as he held Portia in his arms and danced to the royal orchestra's rendition of "Unforgettable" under hundreds of strung lights and a moonlit sky on the grounds of the newly restored farmhouse. This place that Bella and James would someday call home was where Juan Carlos and Portia had found love, too, and it seemed fitting to have a small intimate exchange of promised vows here in front of their close friends and family. His new bride dressed in satin and ivory lace, with his mother's diamond wedding ring sparkling on her finger, was the most beautiful woman on the planet.

"Are you happy?" he asked, fairly certain his answer was found in the sky-blue gleam in her eyes.

"I don't think I've ever been happier."

"That's how I want to keep it, sweetheart." He pressed her close and kissed her forehead, brushing his lips over her cheeks and nose and finally landing on her sweet mouth.

"I loved our sunset wedding," Portia said. "This is a special place."

Their first dance ended and Juan Carlos swung Portia to a stop in the center of the circle of their guests, who applauded them, their dance and their marriage. Portia's elegant grace, her help in discovering the hidden artworks and her work with local charities had endeared her to the country. Even the doubters had begun to come around as she constantly proved to them that she belonged at his side. It was a good thing, too, because Juan Carlos would rather give up the throne than live without Portia.

His cousins approached. "Welcome to the family, Portia," Rafe said, his very pregnant wife on his arm. "We couldn't be happier for you both."

"It was a lovely ceremony," Emily said.

"Thank you. I've heard all about your special ceremony, as well," Portia offered, glancing at Emily, Rafe, Gabe and Serafia. "I've never attended a double wedding before."

"We wish we would've known you then," Serafia added.

"Might've been a triple wedding, who knows?" Gabe said with a teasing smile.

Juan Carlos found it all amusing. His cousins had met their wives in uncanny ways and now every one of them was married. Rafe had resumed his position as head of Montoro Enterprises and the company was thriving. Good thing, too, because Rafe's father had decided to retire in Alma. After the ceremony he'd been the first to offer his congratulations, giving Portia a kiss on the cheek and wrapping Juan Carlos in a tight embrace. Juan Carlos owed a great deal to the man who had raised him from early childhood.

Gabe, the younger of his male cousins, had finally shed his bad boy ways and settled down with his lifelong friend and love, Serafia.

"I think I just felt something," Bella announced. She took James's hand and placed it on her small rounded belly. "Here, see if you can feel the baby."

James kept his hand there several seconds. "I'm not sure," he said softly, diplomatically. "It's early yet, isn't it, honey?"

"Maybe for you, but I think I felt it." Bella's eyes were two bright beams of light. She was carrying James's child.

James kissed her lips. "I can't wait to feel our baby, too."

Portia slipped her hand in Juan Carlos's and they watched the scene play out. James had one child already and Bella was proving to be a fantastic stepmother to one-year-old Maisey. And now, their family was expanding. Juan Carlos was glad that Bella and James had settled in Alma and James was back playing professional soccer—football as they called it here—and winning games for the home team. Things had been rough there for a while between James and his father, oil tycoon Patrick Rowling. Patrick had picked James's twin brother, Will, to marry Bella. The arranged marriage was an antiquated notion to say the least, and Bella was having none of it. James was the man for her. And then Will had also found love with Catalina Ibarra, his father's maid. The whole thing had sent Patrick into a nosedive but he was finally coming around and softening to the idea that perhaps his sons could make up their own minds about their love life and beyond.

"Now that we're all here together, I have good news to share with all of you," Juan Carlos said. He couldn't help his ever-present smile from intensifying. He had his family's attention now. "I'm told by Alex and the prime minister that Alma has never seen a better year. The country is well on its way to being financially solvent again. Thanks in part to our efforts here, I might add. With the discovery of the lost art treasure, tourism will climb, especially once we put those pieces on public display. We are working to that end. Since the state of Alma is now finally secure once again, a sizable portion of the Montoro fortune has been repatriated. It has been decided that the money will fund a new public school system named for my grandmother Isabella Salazar."

"That's wonderful," Bella said.

Rafe and Gabe slapped him on the back with congratulations.

"If it wasn't for Tia Isabella's determination to see the Montoros return to Alma in her lifetime—and those letters I discovered—none of this would even be possible," Bella said.

It was true. Juan Carlos wouldn't be king, he would never have met Portia and who knew what would have happened among his other family members. "We owe my grandmother quite a bit."

They took a solemn moment to give thanks to Isabella.

And then the orchestra music started up again.

Couples paired off and moved onto the dance floor.

Little Maisey Rowling had woken up from her nap. Wearing pink from head to toe, she was sitting on the front porch playing with the palace kittens alongside Portia's maids in attendance, Jasmine and Maria Ramon.

"I owe those two women a dance," Juan Carlos said to Portia. "If not for them, you may never have come back to Alma. Actually, I owe them much more than that."

"Yes, but first, my love, I have a wedding gift for you. I hope it will match the one you gave me. I cannot wait another second to give it to you."

"Okay," he said, eager to please her. "I'm yours."

She tugged him to the back of the house, to the garden area that was in full bloom, despite the late fall climate. Oh, the miracle of royalty that made all things possible. She sat him down on the white iron bench and then took a seat beside him.

"Juan Carlos," she began, taking his hands and holding them in her lap. "You have given me your love, a new family and a beautiful palace to live in."

"You deserve all those things, sweetheart."

"But there's one thing missing. One thing I want and hope you want, too."

He had no clue where she was going with this. He had everything he wanted. "Have you found another brood of cats to adopt?"

She shook her head and grinned, her eyes beaming with the same glow he'd seen in Bella's. His heart stopped beating. He gathered his thoughts and came to the only conclusion he could.

"You're not?"

She nodded now, bobbing her head up and down rapidly. "I am."

"We're going to have a baby?"

"Yes!"

A glance at her belly gave him no indication. "When?"

"Seven months from now."

Carefully, he pulled her onto his lap. "I'm…I'm…going to be a father."

"Yes, you are."

He curved his hand around her nape and brought his lips close to hers. "You're going to be a mother."

"Yes."

The idea filled him with pride. His Portia would give him a child. It was the best gift in the world. His mouth touched hers reverently and he tasted the sweetness of her lips. "I couldn't be happier, sweetheart."

"I'm glad. Our baby will grow up in a home filled with love. Neither one of us knew our parents for very long. But now, we will have a family of our own. It's quite unexpected…"

"It's all I've ever wanted, Portia. For us to be a family."

"Really?"

He nodded. His throat constricted. His emotions had finally caught up to him today. His life had come full circle—the orphaned boy who would be king, married to his heart's desire, was to have a family all his own now.

There was no better kingdom on earth than for a man to share his life with the woman he loved.

He and Portia were two of a kind.

Almas Iguales.

Equal souls.

* * * * *

LET'S TALK
Romance

For exclusive extracts, competitions
and special offers, find us online:

f facebook.com/millsandboon

⊙ @millsandboonuk

🐦 @millsandboon

Or get in touch on 0844 844 1351*

For all the latest titles coming soon, visit
millsandboon.co.uk/nextmonth